Sins Of The Orchid

EVA WINNERS

Playlist

IF YOU'D LIKE to hear a soundtrack with songs that are featured in
this book, as well as songs

that inspired me, here's the link:

https://open.spotify.com/playlist/1e2xO55XFfZKAd8MqYi6On?si=
QxceRcd-TIe2NyuqfDrfpg

In no particular order...

"Panic Room" - Au/Ra
"All my friends are fake" - Tate McRae
"Hurts So Good" - Astrid S
"You broke me first" - Tate McRae
"Does She Know" - Astrid S
"Champagne & SunShine" - PLVTINUM
"@ my worst" - Blackbear
"Monsters" - All Time Low
"Fucked Up" - Bahari

"Let Me Down Slowly" - Alec Benjamin
"Swim" - Chase Atlantic
"Good 4 U" - Olivia Rodrigo
"Into It" - Chase Atlantic

Prologue

"Fire one bullet, and I'm throwing a grenade into the bunker." My chest constricted at hearing the familiar voice. "And throw your weapons onto the ground."

My eyes searched frantically. This was like my worst nightmare.

"I'm waiting," he taunted. "Tick, tock. Tick, tock."

My brother threw his gun to the ground.

Holding my breath, I watched as a man descended the stairs with five men behind him and two at each side, protecting him. It hardly seemed like a fair fight. So many of them against just the two of us, weaponless.

"Hello, Orchid," he drawled, his voice toneless. His cold, unflinching dark stare met mine and images from the last time I saw him flashed in my mind. Blood, screams, betrayal, death.

I never knew this man, I realized. His thin lips curved into a grimace, a taunting smile. He despised me, his hate gleaming in his eyes. It couldn't be more evident.

This was like my worst nightmare. He was supposed to love me, cherish me. Protect me. Yet, he lurked in the shadows of my life for years hunting me, waiting to kill me.

He betrayed *us*. Hurt *us*. Left *us* to die.

1

"You've given me a run for my money," he said with menace in his voice, then flicked his gaze behind him. "Hasn't she? Come here so she can see you."

I watched as a pair of black combat boots descended the stairs, revealing more and more of a man's body. My mind revolted against recognition, and my stomach churned.

No, no, no, no.

My heart shattered and a piercing pain followed deep in my chest.

The worst betrayal.

Were the men in my life always destined to betray me?

CHAPTER 1

Amore

THIRTEEN-YEARS-OLD

New York.
Concrete jungle.
Home of La Cosa Nostra.

New York was unlike any other city I had ever been to. Sensory overload. The smells of exhaust fumes. The frantic energy. Constant ear-splitting sounds of police cars, ambulances, and car horns.

The streets were *always* crowded. Some places smelled, while others looked pretty on the outside and hid the ugly truths lurking within. It had only been two weeks since I'd arrived, and already, I hated being here. I had no friends, nobody to talk to, and the family I didn't know existed were complete strangers to me.

My biological father, who I just met two weeks ago, was some kind of mobster. A don. The head of the Bennetti family. At least that was what I'd been told.

In the span of two weeks, I learned that my whole life was a sham. I had no idea who I was anymore. I was no longer Amore Anderson or Amore Regalè, the fashion heiress to the Regalè family. Instead, I was

Amore Bennetti, daughter to the notorious head of the Bennetti crime family, Savio Bennetti. One of the five families of Cosa Nostra.

On the surface, Cosa Nostra etiquette very much resembled the world I grew up in. Impeccable manners out in the open. A white-picket-fenced home surrounded by guards. But behind closed doors, men in this world carried guns like an everyday accessory and women viciously gossiped and attacked if they despised you.

Like my stepmother despised me.

My heart constricted at the thought of spending another day under my father's roof. I wanted to run away, go back to three weeks ago when everything was fine. When my mother was alive. When we were happy.

Up until a month ago, I traveled the world with Mom and the man I believed to be my father, George Anderson. Mom worked for my grand-mother Regina, who was the owner of one of the greatest fashion empires. George was a textile biologist, trying to find new organisms that had the potential to be turned into bio-fabric, like some spider silks. They were out not only to engineer the next best material in the fashion world but to help minimize the damage being caused to the environment thanks to some of the ways textiles were currently being manu-factured.

At thirteen-years-old, I knew more about the fashion world than any girl my age should or would care to admit. But Regalè Fashion was my legacy, one that I would one day be responsible for. That's what Grand-mother Regina kept telling me.

I thought I had years, decades, before that would all fall to me, but it seemed that decades wouldn't be an option since my parents were dead. Correction, since my mother was dead. George... he wasn't my real father. He was never meant to be part of the empire.

For thirteen years of my life, I called that man my father. He taught me everything I knew. What should I call him now?

My stepfather? No, it sounded too cold for someone that gave me so much.

I wished everything was the way it was before everything happened. Before I saw my mother tortured and killed in front of my eyes. Before I heard my father's... George's screams. The buzz of this city reminded me of the dangers in the jungle, and frankly, I wasn't sure which was more terrifying.

This city would chew me up and spit me out. Just like the jungle did.

The sudden blare of a car horn had me jumping and glancing over my shoulder as people shoved past me. I'd been released from school an hour ago, but the man that usually picked me up, an uncle I never knew I had, Uncle Vincent, wasn't there. So, I started out my trek to find my way home.

This school would end up breaking me. They already think I'm a freak. An Italian girl with an Irish face. I started at the high school last week after a series of tests confirmed I was much further ahead in my studies than my fellow middle schoolers.

The counselor thought he did me a favor by placing me in a higher grade, but those high school kids were brutal. Lunch breaks and waiting for my ride after school were particularly painful. I just wanted my old life back, to feel normal again.

I glanced around and noted I was lost. Again. Today, the bullies decided to linger around while I waited for my uncle, and taking advantage of him not showing, they decided to dance around me, taunting me before taking my phone. So, I headed home on foot. They kept following me until about two blocks ago.

So here I was! Lost, no phone, and no way to get home. The overwhelming sounds of the city had me turning in circles, looking for any clues as to where I was, or where I needed to go to get home. I sighed, long and hard, my chest constricting in that familiar way. The panic attacks that started since my mom and George's murder threatened to swell, making it hard to concentrate.

Don't panic now, I silently whispered to myself. There were men in suits walking in and out of the building next to me, but it barely registered. I was in my school uniform with a backpack on my shoulder.

Leaning back against the glass window, I slid down onto my butt, dropping the bag onto the ground next to me. I pulled my knees to my chest and buried my head into my lap, breathing in and out.

I felt alone, missing Mom and George. The loss was still raw, dreams too vivid and memories too fresh. Until their death, there wasn't a day that passed by without me talking to Mom. And now... I was so alone.

Dad's wife hated me. My brothers didn't know what to make of me. Not even my father knew what to do with me. He didn't know of my existence until three weeks ago when he got called into the jungles of South America to come and collect me. The Carrera Cartel found me in the jungle. Another day and I wouldn't have survived. It was a miracle they found me. My mother was saving me even in her death. She reached out to a contact, the head of the Carrera Cartel, and to my father, asking for help before she went in search of George and me. If only she would have waited for them before she went looking for us.

She could have been...

The pain in my chest threatened to explode. It was too hard to live with the knowledge that I caused my mother's death. If only I would have listened to her. I just wanted her back in my life, my mom and... George.

Grandma Regina lived around here somewhere too, but when Dad came to collect me, those two got into an argument and Dad forbade her to come around me. It didn't deter her. She kept coming, but each time, their arguments grew worse and worse.

I could do twelfth grade math, but I couldn't understand what their argument was about. Nobody talked to me; nobody understood me. I didn't understand them either. I shouldn't cry; I was too old for tears Grandma would say. She was strong; I wasn't. A queen in her own right. She was the strongest woman I had ever known. I wanted to cry until everything was back to normal.

"Hey, kiddo."

The voice was close. A pair of luxurious, black Oxfords entered my line of vision, draped in tailored black slacks.

One heartbeat passed, and I lifted my head, my grip around my legs tightening. My line of sight kept traveling up the custom three-piece suit until reaching his face. Dark eyes stared at me, studying me. That was another thing about this place. Everyone around my dad's family had the same coloring. Different shades of brown eyes, olive skin, dark brown hair. These men were no different.

They looked like the men that kept visiting Dad, like my brothers.

I looked nothing like any of them. My hair was curly and bright red, and my eyes green. The Irish came from my grandmother. I had my mother's eyes, but red hair hadn't been seen in Grandma's family for a long while. It didn't sound like an insult when Mom used to say it, but when Elena, Dad's wife said it, it sounded like the worst insult. She screamed at Dad to have a paternity test done because there wasn't a single trait I possessed that was Bennetti. It wasn't like I wanted to be here either... Grandma wanted me. They should have just sent me to live with her.

The younger of the two stepped forward, though he was still much older than me. His dark suit fit him perfectly, making him look dominant and was the epitome of good, expensive style as my grandmother would say. As a granddaughter, and now heiress, to her fashion empire, I always wore the latest and greatest trends and designer clothes. Even as we trekked through the forests and mud of the jungle. George always laughed and thought it ridiculous, but we had a reputation to uphold.

"Stai bene?" I recognized the Italian words but didn't understand the meaning. The guy offered a smile and kept his voice even and soft when he spoke up, I guess to reassure me I wasn't in danger. "Are you okay?"

My eyes darted behind him where an expensive black car was parked. Like the one we used to have when we lived in Europe. I didn't hear the car pull up, maybe it was already here. Lorenzo, my new-found brother, warned me to pay attention to my surroundings. He said it was a consequence of being a Bennetti. I was failing at that too. He was good to me, but he kept his distance. Not that I could blame him. His mother glared at him when he passed me a basket of bread, never mind speaking to me.

I exhaled, my heart heavy in my chest, as I watched both men eye me curiously. I nodded hesitantly, eyeing the man warily.

"Bad day at school?" he asked, lowering down to my eye level as he pulled up the pant leg of his suit.

I tracked the movement of his hand, noting a tattoo snaking down his forearm. He wore a white, crisp shirt, his sleeves rolled up. While it was still warm here for late September, it was nothing compared to the heat and humidity of the jungles in South America.

I swallowed hard, staring into his eyes. They were the darkest brown I had ever seen. I nodded again, unable to utter a single word. It was so much more than just a bad day at school. My face was wet, my nose runny, but the worst pain was in my heart.

An older man that resembled the younger man stepped forward. "What's your name?"

The city was a bad place. Dad told me never to trust anyone, but he didn't say anything about being rude. If I refused to answer, they would think I was rude.

"Amore," I whispered in a small voice.

The young guy that spoke to me first chuckled. "No, that's a feeling. I am Santino. What's your first name?"

Swallowing hard, I watched both men warily. "It's Amore. Amore Bennetti."

I had never seen a simple name have such an impact. The expression on both men's faces turned to shock, then disbelief.

"Who's your father?" Santino asked, his voice careful.

The question was simple, but tears pooled in my eyes again, threatening to spill, and to my horror, a hiccup escaped me. I worried if I started crying again, it would flow like a broken dam.

"Savio Bennetti," I breathed out, tears finally winning again and rolling down my cheeks. It was the first time I'd referred to him as my father out loud, and it felt like a betrayal to Mom and George.

"Savio Bennetti doesn't have a daughter," the older man responded.

Unceremoniously, the way I knew my mom would scold me if she was still alive, I wiped my eyes and nose with the back of my hand.

"Mom and Dad—" I stopped because George wasn't Dad. "He just found out."

The old man now lowered down to his knees too, his eyes in line with mine, as if he was searching for the truth in them.

"You are Margaret Regalè's little girl." I wasn't sure if he meant it as a question or a statement, but I nodded, nonetheless. My lower lip trembled, just as it did every time I'd think of my mom and George. "Same eyes. You have your mother's eyes." My throat choked from all the emotions. "How is Margaret?"

Tears escaped again. My mom always said I was a happy baby, happy kid, and barely ever cried. But I'd made up for it over the last few weeks.

"She is dead," I whispered, the pain still too raw. The images I didn't want to remember flashed in front of my eyes, and I shut them tightly, as if that would shut them out. But they were all in my brain, ingrained in my memories. They were igniting something within me that I was scared to evaluate.

"It's okay, kiddo." Santino brushed his big hand against my cheek, the touch oddly comforting. His thumb wiped the tears, and my heart ached because it was the first comforting touch since Mom and George died. I craved it like the air I breathed. I missed their hugs and kisses; the love they offered me. Mom was always affectionate.

It was different with Dad's family. Most of them didn't know what to do with a girl in their house. Dad's wife glared at me and hurt me when nobody looked.

My brothers seemed to speak in riddles around me, and if it wasn't riddles, they spoke more in Italian than English. I didn't speak any Italian, although I was beginning to pick up on some of the basic phrases. But at least they were nice to me.

"Amore, didn't your dad tell you not to go into Russo's territory?" The older man questioned as my eyes shifted to him. I didn't know what he meant. Scrunching my eyebrows, I tried to remember if I ever heard of Russo's territory.

I shook my head. "He said not to roam the city," I rasped.

A small smile appeared on both men's faces. "He is right about that. Why are you roaming the city?"

I squared my shoulders, meeting both their eyes.

"I was waiting for Vincent to pick me up. I promise," I said softly. "But the boys saw me waiting and wouldn't leave me alone."

"Boys?" Santino asked.

"The boys in school," I murmured.

The old man smiled, the creases in his eyes making him look less imposing. I've met enough men to know these two could be dangerous, but also protective. My instincts told me to trust them.

"They probably don't know what to do with you." The old man told me with a smile. "Your mother was quite a looker too."

My eyes snapped to him, Santino completely forgotten.

"You knew Mom?" My voice was barely a whisper.

He nodded. "She liked to eat at my restaurant," he explained. I wanted to hear more, ask so much more. "Did she show you where she went to school?"

I shook my head. "You must have seen it. It is in the middle of the city."

"I never lived here before," I explained, my fingers fidgeting.

"Where did you live then?" Santino asked.

I shrugged. "Everywhere," I told them. "First we were in Europe, then in Africa, Asia, and last year in South America. I've never been to the States before. Until now."

Both looked at me pensively. It probably sounded weird to them, but somehow we never made it back to the U.S.

"Should you call your dad or Vincent?" The older man asked. "He probably won't be happy to hear you are in Russo territory."

I glanced around me. "What's Russo territory? How do you know?"

Both of them shook their heads. "We are the Russo family," the old man explained. "I'm Riccardo Russo, this is my eldest son Santino Russo —" A shout came from across the street, and I followed the old Russo's gaze down the street. There was a boy there, maybe a few years older than me, waving wildly. "Ah, and there is my youngest son, Adriano Russo."

The boy that joined us looked vaguely familiar, a wide smile on his face.

"Are we having a party on the sidewalk?" he greeted us all, his eyes curiously on me. "Hey, I know you. You're the chick from my school. Super smart chick. Youngest girl in high school. You just joined last week or so, right?"

"You go to Townsend Harris too?" I asked him. It must be why he looked vaguely familiar.

"Yeah, I'm in the eleventh grade."

"Some boys gave Amore a hard time," Santino explained.

Adriano frowned. "Probably those assholes from the East Side." His eyes were like his brother's, but not as dark. There was a striking resemblance between the two but somehow they seemed very different. One was dark, while the latter seemed easygoing. "Don't worry, I'll talk to them tomorrow."

"But won't that make them even madder?" I questioned. I'd prefer to remain invisible. Though so far, I've failed miserably at keeping myself invisible. I blamed it on my horribly bright hair.

"Adriano will make sure you are safe in school," Mr. Russo chimed in. "Won't you, Adriano?"

"Of course, Pà." Adriano's eyes turned my way. "What grade are you? I thought I saw you in my Algebra class."

"I'm in ninth grade."

"And you are in eleventh grade math?" Adriano's voice was full of awe. "How many grades did you skip?"

I cleared my throat. I hated when people looked at me like I was a freak.

"My mom and da... ummm, George homeschooled me while we were in Africa and South America," I tried to explain. "They covered a lot more than my grade level. It's the only reason I skipped a grade."

"Ummm, okay." Adriano rolled his eyes and despite myself, I smiled. "If that makes you feel better, we can go with that. I'd say you are probably super smart. How about you help me with math? Otherwise, I might flunk it."

"Sure, math for you taking care of the bullying boys." I smiled, and suddenly the day seemed brighter. "Seems like a fair trade."

Adriano extended his hand to seal the agreement. I put my palm against his warm hand, and we shook on it, both of us smiling.

"Okay, kiddo," Santino interrupted our agreement. "How about you call your Uncle Vincent or your dad, so there is no trouble."

"Vincent?" Adriano asked, confusion on his face.

"Amore is Savio Bennetti's daughter," his dad explained, and my heart fell at Adriano's expression.

The glances they shared told of unspoken exchanges. I didn't think they were good either.

"Does that mean you don't want to trade math lessons for the bullies?" I needed friends, and I liked Adriano right off the bat.

He shoved his hands into his jean pockets. "I don't know if your dad will be okay with it," he explained uncomfortably. "He probably won't like it."

"Why not?"

"Geez, didn't your dad explain anything to you?" Adriano blurted out, and the next second, Santino shoved his shoulder against him in warning.

On an exhale, I rose to my feet. "No, he didn't. I think Father and my brothers are still in shock and don't know what to do with me," I admitted. I forced a smile on my lips. "It's okay. I can give you some pointers on math, regardless, so you don't flunk."

"I'll talk to Bennetti," his dad interrupted. "You two kids don't worry about that. Let's just call him so he knows you are safe."

I lowered my eyes. "Ummm, I can't. Those boys took my phone."

Anger flashed in Santino's eyes, and I shrunk back. "Adriano will ensure you get it back," he announced. "Otherwise, those boys will get a visit from me."

"Oh, shit." Adriano grinned. "Someone will be pissing their pants."

I glanced curiously at Santino. There was a predator lurking underneath his expensive clothes. I didn't know it at that moment, but his tattoo marked him as a feared man among New Yorkers.

"Let's go inside, kiddo." Santino stood up and extended his hand to help me. Reluctantly, I put my small hand in his, and he pulled me up. "You'll be okay, I promise."

I nodded. I trusted him, my instincts assuring me he'd never hurt me.

CHAPTER 2

Amore

We entered the restaurant, my hand in his, and he squeezed gently in reassurance. "Don't worry, my aunt likes to talk everyone's ear off. Just nod."

I smiled, with a soft tilt to my head. The moment we entered the restaurant, a commotion started. A woman with silver gray hair and a big smile hugged Santino and Adriano, then pressed a kiss on Mr. Russo's cheek. Something tugged at my heart seeing the affection. Each time I got back home, everyone stiffened and gave me awkward smiles. Lorenzo and Luigi were better this week than last. For the last two days, they teased me when I got back home. At least I think it was teasing.

"Chi è questo?" *Who is this?* I recognized the words.

She watched me through her dark eyes. They were warm, though slightly guarded.

I extended my hand. "Hi, I'm Amore," I introduced myself. "Ummm, I am just learning Italian. But I understand a little bit."

A smile tugged on her lips. "Ah, bella ragazza!" She pulled my hand and took me to the window seat. "Sit here."

She sat herself next to me, cornering me in my seat. My eyes widened, darting between Santino and Adriano. Those two just chuckled. Adriano slid into the booth seat across from me.

"Amore, this is Mrs. Rossi," Santino's father introduced, and my eyebrows scrunched. "My sister-in-law."

"Ah."

I gave a little nod. "Nice to meet you." I liked the woman, but she was too close to me. I tried to scoot unnoticeably, but it seemed each time I moved, she followed.

"Hai fame?"

I shook my head. The woman pinched my collar bone and I flinched. "Ouch."

She stood up, and I exhaled a sigh of relief. "Too skinny," she murmured. "Eat. You eat."

Adriano shook his head. "Let her be, Zia."

"Beautiful girl has to eat."

My cheeks flushed at the compliment. Nobody ever thought of me as beautiful except for Mom and Grandma.

"So, Amore Bennetti, tell me something about yourself," Adriano drawled, a little mischievous gleam in his eyes.

Just like with the others, the woman jumped at my name.

"Che?" Her eyes searched out Santino and Mr. Russo. "Che?" she asked again in a higher pitched voice, and my eyes darted to Santino in worry. He offered a smile, reassurance in his dark eyes and instantly my pulse eased a bit.

Rushed words in Italian slipped through her lips as she glanced my way every so often. I couldn't catch a single word.

Santino responded in a similar fashion. Whatever he said, it got the woman into another stream of long, fast Italian.

Santino slid next to me, taking the spot his aunt previously took. Thankfully, he let me have my space.

I cleared my throat. "M-maybe we shouldn't tell anyone else about my last name?" I suggested in a small voice, eyeing their aunt's vivid conversation with their father. I didn't understand why my last name sent everyone into panic. Was it maybe because Father was head of a crime family? I should explain I had nothing to do with it, but I didn't even know how to explain it.

"Too late." Adriano kicked back. "Now that Zia knows, the entire Cosa Nostra will know."

14

My head snapped to him. "Cosa Nostra?" I whispered.

"Please tell me you know about that," Adriano groaned.

I swallowed hard. "Y-yes. Five families. Criminals." I nibbled on my lower lip. I didn't want to be in more trouble. My heart raced at the admission. "I-I don't know much more than that," I replied in a quiet voice.

Adriano chuckled. "Man, you'll be fun to educate. And one day, your dad will probably marry you to one of the other families to strengthen his position."

"Adriano!" Santino warned his brother. My eyes shot to Santino, then to Adriano and frantically back to his older brother.

"W-why would he do that?" I rasped.

Before either one of them could answer, their aunt came back shaking her head. "Bennetti in my kitchen. My kitchen! How?"

I shrunk even further. "Let her be," Santino warned.

"It's not the child's fault," Mr. Russo said. She shook her head and went back to speaking Italian with him.

"Don't worry." Santino pulled his phone out and read through his messages. "They are just mad they didn't know you existed."

"If it helps, neither did Father," I said, staring out the window. The sun heated the pavement, and I knew how hot it could be against my bare feet; the chaos of people rushing somewhere, nowhere, with a purpose I couldn't quite grasp myself. It was a jungle out there. Different from the one I escaped, but a jungle all the same.

He will save us. My mother's voice rang in my ears.

Nobody came to save us. The heat in the jungle felt worse than the burnt soles of my feet against the blacktop pavement.

The scent of blood and dead bodies under the scalding sun. Dead eyes.

Drip. Drip. Drip.

Blood soaking into the brown earth, turning it red.

The plate hitting the marble surface shattered through the death images, causing me to jump and bringing me back to life. A wounded whimper escaped me.

"Mangia, mangia." It was Mrs. Rossi that startled me.

I swallowed hard and shook my head. "No, thank you."

Panic. Death. Destruction. Payback. The need to make them all pay was so strong, it terrified me. Vengeance and hate was never part of me. But something cracked seeing my mother tortured, seeing her die.

And the entire time, I couldn't do a damned thing. I was helpless. I closed my eyes, my heart drumming against my chest hard.

Do. Not. Panic. Do. Not. Panic.

I swallowed hard, bile rising in my throat.

Do. Not. Panic.

"Kiddo, stay with us." Santino's voice pulled me back from the screams that echoed in my head. My eyes found his dark gaze, finding comfort in them. Safety. "That's right, kiddo. Stay with me."

My hand came to my chest, the intense pain squeezing air out of my lungs. Like someone sat on my chest, the oxygen felt in short supply. Inhaling deeply, I exhaled slowly. The buzzing in my ears grew by the second, making me disoriented. I focused on his dark depths and took another lungful of air into my lungs. Then I slowly exhaled through my constricted chest.

"Again," he instructed in a low voice.

I followed his command and repeated the motion. My lungs slowly loosened, making it easier to breathe. He nodded his head and offered barely a hint of a smile.

"Good girl," he murmured.

His praise warmed me on the inside, and the pain that had been my constant since we went through the horror in the jungles of South America dulled just a tiny bit. I wanted to keep Santino Russo with me forever so I could forget the pain. His strength seemed to be able to erase it with ease.

"Her father is on his way. Give a heads up to the men and have them on alert. Nobody is to hurt him." Mr. Russo's voice sounded in the distance. I heard him, but the words barely registered. I felt safe in Santino's dark gaze. "Amore, your dad is on his way."

I peeled my eyes away from Santino and looked at Mr. Russo. "Thank you," I answered in a small voice.

"Hey, Amore," Adriano's cheerful voice chimed in. "How about you help me with math now? As a down payment for getting your phone back tonight." My head slowly turned his way. There was a wide,

16

happy grin on his face. "If I don't do well, I'll have to get weekend tutoring and that will be fucking hell."

"Language, boy," Mr. Russo scolded, but Adriano's grin didn't evaporate. I liked seeing him grinning, his mischievousness easing the air around us.

"Okay," I answered. Math was my order in chaos. And fashion was my passion. "You have your books?"

"I'm going to get my homework. Mr. Salvatore is a pain in the ass with his paper homework."

I nodded and watched him go to the back of the place, then come back with his books. For the next twenty minutes, the world and past were forgotten as I worked through advanced Algebra problems with Adriano.

Santino left our table to stand with his dad, the two speaking in Italian and looking at the map while Adriano and I finished all his homework.

"Just follow these steps and you can solve any problem," I told him. The door chimed but I didn't pay any attention, all my focus on the problem in front of me. Adriano didn't look like he believed my explanation about the methods of resolving math problems.

Suddenly, tension spiked and awareness shot through me. I raised my head from the homework to find Adriano's gaze on the door. I followed his gaze and saw my father standing there. Along with Lorenzo and Luigi, my two brothers, and Uncle Vincent. Vincent never married and was Dad's twin brother, though they looked nothing alike. Though right now all the men had something in common. They looked furious.

"What is my daughter doing here?" he barked, his sharp tone making me jump in my seat.

My pulse leapt into my throat. So far, Father had kept his temper and anger hidden, but his wife kept telling me he'd kill me if I stepped out of line. The terror of those words drilled into me.

"I didn't mean to—" My voice shook with fear. I didn't want him to kill me. Elena told me he killed many men for less. My eyes darted around looking for all the possible exits. I had to run.

"Calm down. She got lost." Mr. Russo kept his calm, though his jaw ticked with irritation. "She was upset, some boys took her phone, and we took her in until you got here."

The two men kept their eyes locked, communicating without words. I noticed all the men kept their hands on their guns, including Santino. Sweat broke through me and my pulse spiked.

They are like those men in the jungle.

My father's gaze traveled to me as if seeking my confirmation. Fear gripped me, settling into my bones. I hated that I felt so weak, so vulnerable. These men instilled fear into this city, and I was no exception to fearing them. This world was different from the one I was surrounded by until recently.

I should be stronger though. Like Mom. Like Grandma.

"Amore?" Dad's voice penetrated through my fear. There wasn't a threat in his voice, just concern.

Inhaling deeply, I finally nodded. "Y-yes. Vincent... Uncle Vincent wasn't there at my dismissal."

"Yes, I was," he protested, his eyes flashing with annoyance. He has been late picking me up from the first day I started the new school, but I kept the words to myself. "Your dismissal was at three, and I was there five minutes before."

"Wednesdays are two o'clock dismissal," Adriano chimed in.

"But Elena—" He cut himself off. Somehow it didn't surprise me. Elena hated me. I didn't know why, but she hated me so much that I feared I wouldn't survive long in Dad's household.

"Mama has been giving Uncle Vincent the wrong times since she started school," Lorenzo growled.

Displeasure flashed in my father's eyes, then his eyes returned to me. Instinctively, I wrapped my arms around myself.

"Amore, is that true?"

I wanted to shake my head in denial, but I couldn't. Mom always taught me not to lie. If I couldn't tell the truth, it was better not to say anything at all. Except in this case, if I tell the truth, I risked my father's wrath too. He wouldn't believe me. If I lied, Elena would continue her torture. I was doomed either way. The eyes of seven men lingered on me, waiting.

"Our bella Amore is scared," Adriano's zia chimed in. "Davvero?"

"Amore?" My father ignored her, his eyes on me.

"It's not a big deal," I muttered softly, my eyes darting to the exit in the back. Ever since the jungle, I always looked for any possible exit strategies.

Father pushed his hand through his hair, making it disheveled.

"Jesus," he muttered.

"Show us your forearm, Amore," Lorenzo urged. My head whipped in his direction, and at this moment, I hated this family. I wanted out. I wanted my grandmother Regina. She would never hurt me or put me on the spot like this.

"No," I blurted, surprising myself with the defiance in my voice.

Father's eyes looked between Lorenzo and I, all the while I shook my head. When I refused to move, Father came over.

"Show me, Amore." His voice was soft, but the command was clear. The head of the Bennetti crime family wouldn't tolerate disobedience.

I didn't understand why Lorenzo was doing this now. He caught his mother burning me with the cigarette, but he didn't stop her. He stood, eyes wide. Whether in shock or concurrence that I deserved it, I wasn't sure. I took advantage of his shock and his mother's hesitancy when she was caught. I ran out of the room like the devil himself was chasing me. I locked myself in my room and didn't come out until the next morning when I had to go to school. Lorenzo never brought it up, but now I wasn't sure what he'd tell his dad.

"Please don't," I begged. My voice croaked, pleading, and in my mind I already despaired. I wondered if there would be some way I could find Grandma Regina in this city.

Suddenly, it was as if the entire scene unfolded in slow motion. Father took my hand into his and rolled up my sleeve.

"What the fuck—" Adriano's voice shattered the silence.

Burn marks and bruises covered my upper forearm. Elena had been extinguishing her cigarettes on my forearms whenever nobody was around, and I wasn't fast enough to escape. It took me a few days to realize I had to stay focused and alert at all times.

The silence was so thick, I could hear someone's heartbeat. Or maybe it was my own. Would I bleed out like my mother if he sliced my throat? Or would he simply shoot me and death would come instantly?

Drip, drip, drip.

Was it blood or water?

"Who did this to you?" Father's voice was colder than the Arctic and fear shot through me.

"P-please." I tugged on my hand but couldn't free it. Our gazes locked in a battle of wills; he demanded to know, and I refused to cave. Since the moment I learned this man was my father, my world shattered and became something unknown. I wanted to go back to my world, to the familiarity of Regalè Enterprise and the people I knew from a young age. Mom and Grandma had been grooming me to take over before I learned to walk, and fashion had been a part of me before I even spoke my first words.

Elena was more than happy to educate me on the ways of my father. Don of the Upper East Side. Brutal, cruel, ruthless. She instilled fear of him into me before I even got to know him. Now, I was scared to get to know him. I didn't trust him. My stepmother said Father would always take his true family's side over a bastard daughter.

"It was Ma," Lorenzo said, interrupting our battle of wills. The room stilled, and you could hear a pin drop. Fear tasted sour on my tongue. "I am sorry, Amore. I should have stopped it, said something. I was just so shocked."

I bit into my lower lip nervously. Elena's words from the day before echoed in my head. *Dad will never take your side.*

"I-I'm sorry," I choked out, my eyes burning. Another hiccup escaped me; my nose was stuffy with the tears that threatened to start pouring again. "You can send me to Grandma Regina. I can stay with her."

"No." No explanation but there was so much fury in that one little word, and I stiffened.

"Mom pressed cigarette butts on her skin," Lorenzo continued to explain. I wished he'd stop talking.

Dad's eyes flashed, anger burning in them, and a loud growl echoed through the room.

"When?" he roared, and my tears won. His head turned to Lorenzo and Luigi. "When did this fucking happen?"

Trembling with terror, my breathing accelerated, and adrenaline shot through me. I jerked my hand away and scooted away from him, as far as I could go.

"I won't let you kill me," I whimpered, and he whipped his head back to me, shock in his dark gaze.

His eyes drilled into me like he was trying to understand me. He hadn't been able to get a read on me from the moment we met.

The dead, lifeless eyes of my mother flashed in my mind. Would the same fate meet me? I refused. I couldn't die until I was old enough and strong enough to make those men pay for hurting my mom. For breaking my family. I had to keep my last promise to my mom.

Both Dad's hands came to grip my face. Though his hands were rough, the gesture wasn't.

"What are you saying?" His voice was hoarse, full of angst, like he hadn't spoken in days. "You are my daughter. I will never let anything happen to you." I blinked my eyes in confusion. I heard the sincerity in his voice, but I was scared to trust him. Trust sometimes gets you killed. "Jesus, Amore." He sounded disturbed. "Why in the hell would you think I'd kill you? You are family. My family."

I swallowed hard. He called me his *family*.

"Ma probably told her that," Luigi mumbled begrudgingly. "She is getting out of hand, Pà."

My eyes darted around these men. Even though the Russo family and the Bennetti family didn't seem to get along, they had a lot more in common than I did with my brothers and my father.

"I want to go home," I said in a small voice. "Grandma will keep me safe."

"Never!" The ruthless man underneath the surface was evident in his answer. "You are my daughter."

He got to his feet and advanced to his sons. "Why didn't you tell me?" he shouted. I had a feeling he was even more furious because of my request. "That is your sister," he yelled. "A fucking kid."

"P-please." I rocked back and forth, wrapping my arms around me. "P-please."

My face was a mess, tears and snot running down my face. "I-it's okay. It's better if I g-go with Grandma." I didn't belong here.

Father turned around to me, his face full of fury, and instinctively, my body flinched backwards again, to make myself invisible, pushing myself further into the corner of the seat.

Santino stepped in between me and Dad, blocking my view of him.

"Cool off," Santino told him. "The kid is about to pass out from fear."

"Bennetti, you got to calm down." Mr. Russo stepped in. "You are scaring her."

I could hear a deep inhale and then exhale.

"When did it happen?" Father repeated his earlier question.

"I think she's been hurting her since she came." Lorenzo's voice was full of anguish. "I kept seeing bruises, but I only caught it yesterday."

A string of curses, in Italian and English, left my father's lips. I couldn't see him and, strangely, having Santino in front of me made me feel safe. I couldn't explain it, which made me doubt my reason. But when you'd seen what I'd seen, reason might have fled already.

Father spoke up again. "Lorenzo, stay here and watch your sister," he ordered. "I'll be back when it's safe for Amore."

"Savio, you stay with your daughter," Uncle Vincent chimed in. "I can take care of everything for you. Your daughter needs you."

"No!" Dad's answer was instant. "I've got this. Lorenzo will stay and keep Amore safe."

"Sure, Pà. I won't let her out of my sight." Lorenzo moved over and sat next to Adriano. The latter muttered something about fraternizing with the enemy, but Lorenzo ignored him, his eyes locked on me.

"I really am sorry, Amore," my brother apologized again. I nodded, hesitant to fully trust him. I knew it wasn't his fault. He was older than me, but Elena was his mother. I was a mere stranger to him and Luigi.

"Get out of my way, Russo," Father demanded. "I'm calm, and I want to see my daughter."

Santino stepped aside but remained close, his strong presence providing protection. Part of me wanted to keep him close to me forever. His protection could have saved us in the jungle.

Father sat next to me and took my face in between his hands, and this time his touch was tender, fatherly. Like George's used to be.

"I'll fix this, Amore," he vowed in a low voice. His thumbs wiped my tears away, the same way Santino did earlier today. His dark eyes softened, and he shook his head. "We'll start over. I'll do a better job, I promise. I'm your father, and you'll stay with me. We'll keep you safe." He pressed a kiss on my forehead. "Your brothers and me. She won't be there to hurt you again. Okay?" Today was the first time he had shown tenderness, and my throat hurt from the emotions I tried to swallow.

My eyes flickered to my brothers. "That's right, Amore. We'll handle it," Luigi concurred. "You are our baby sister. We protect our own."

Elena was their mother though. She was their own too.

Dad wrapped his big arms around me. "It didn't start well, but we'll end it great. Yeah?" I nodded silently, and my heart squeezed in my chest with memories of hearing those words before. "Your mom's favorite saying. I borrowed it."

He remembers Mom.

He pressed another kiss on my forehead, then stood up and walked over to Mr. Russo. Santino strode over to stand by his father's side, as Luigi stood by Dad's side.

Lorenzo's eyes returned to me. "Pà will take care of it. Trust him."

My eyes flashed to the group of men. I couldn't see how, not unless Dad moved us somewhere else. "Is he going to get a divorce?" I asked.

Lorenzo and Adriano chuckled, though I failed to see what was funny.

"Don't worry about that," Lorenzo assured me. Dad and Mr. Russo spoke in rushed Italian, while Santino looked pensive. I couldn't even guess what they were all so vividly talking about, but they all seemed tense. Then they nodded and Dad's eyes returned to me.

"Amore, you stay here with your brother and the Russos," he said. "I'll come back when it's safe."

He shared a glance with Mr. Russo and headed out with Luigi, Uncle Vincent, and Santino.

CHAPTER 3

Amore

THREE YEARS LATER

"Get off of your high horse, Bennetti." Grandmother's voice carried through the foyer. "Amore is my heiress. She'll inherit the entire Regalè Enterprise and needs to know how to run it. Your goddamn criminal underworld is too small for her. She will head the business, not serve some little man that will never measure up."

"You have a big goddamn mouth," Dad hissed back, trying to rein in his anger. Those two bickered like cats and dogs.

"And you are blind if you think you can hold her back."

Santino and Mr. Russo stood next to me, all of us in the large living room. I shifted back and forth between my feet, fidgeting with my hands while tension built in the room. I threw a silent apologetic glance at both of the powerful Russos.

Dad was in the middle of speaking with the Russo heads when Grandma and I interrupted their meeting. Grandma brought me home late, and it went south from there. I begged her to remain in the car or just leave. Grandma never listened to anyone. She followed me into the house with her bodyguards rather than just dropping me off. She said it was for my own safety, but sometimes I truly believed she just liked to agitate Dad.

You'd think at sixteen I would have at least some freedom. But the older I got, the more protection Dad and Grandma assigned to me. And since I was under both my father's and the Russo's protection, it didn't matter where I went in New York, the eyes of the Cosa Nostra watched. It was almost suffocating.

"Goddamn it, Regina. If you can't follow my rules—"

"Oh crap," I muttered under my breath. Grandma was notorious for doing what she wanted and not following anyone's rules. "Here we go."

Santino raised his eyebrow as the cackle of laughter happened. Grandma loved doing everything that upset others—namely Dad.

"You measly, little man. She'll be running a billion-dollar empire someday, and you want her to learn it sitting in your living room." I could hear Dad's grumble even from here. "Or would you prefer to marry her off and hand over her inheritance to one of your despicable, worthless associates?"

To say my grandmother was disapproving of Dad's title as the boss of the Bennetti crime family was the understatement of the century. But it was how Dad met my mother. She went to his restaurant, the one he co-owned with Mr. Russo, on Madison Avenue, before the Russos and Bennettis had their fallout. She was significantly younger than him, fifteen years, but he said they fell in love. Unfortunately, he was married. Then Mom got pregnant with me and never told him. My mother lived in a penthouse tower on 5th Avenue, and Dad ran the underworld. Well, part of it anyhow. The Russo family ran the rest of New York, the bigger part, and several other territories.

I smiled awkwardly at the highest members of Cosa Nostra. "She doesn't mean it," I grumbled in a low voice to Mr. Russo. "She just likes to agitate him."

"You don't say," he answered goodheartedly. The crinkle around his eyes softened his features. Despite the knowledge that Mr. Russo was one of the most feared men in the mafia, right along with his son Santino, I liked them. I liked all three Russo men. Their kindness three years ago changed my life in this city.

"Good to know you don't find us despicable and worthless like your grandmother," Santino commented dryly.

My eyes flickered to him, and I knew my cheeks had turned deep red with blotches on my chest. I hated how easily my skin depicted my embarrassment. I didn't find either one of them despicable or worthless, but I knew they were dangerous.

At twenty-four, Santi was already the don of the Russo family for all intents and purposes. His father couldn't be prouder and trusted his son to run all the affairs of his underworld empire. He had become well-known in the underworld for his ruthlessness. His hands were drenched in blood.

There was a feud going on between the Russos and the Venezuelan Cartel that kept causing trouble in his and Dad's territory. Santino had been killing them off, one by one, for a year now. Every morning, the newscaster spoke of another cartel member found dead.

Dad was of course on his side. So was I. The Venezuelan Cartel killed my mother, and I wanted them all extinguished. Besides, Santino would always be the savior who extended his hand when I needed it most.

I looked at him under my lashes and noticed his eyes hardened as his gaze flicked back in the direction of my grandmother's voice. He didn't like her either.

It bothered me that nobody from this world seemed to care for Grandma. I loved her very much, and I knew she loved me. She was my only connection left to Mom. She often told me stories about her when she was a kid, roaming this city just like I was. Except I had guards and the eyes of Cosa Nostra on me. Thankfully, I really liked my main guard, DeAngelo. It was the first topic my grandma and dad agreed on.

This distaste they all had for each other would eventually grow a wedge between my father's family and Grandma. I'd inherit Regalè Enterprise, and she was right that I needed to understand the business. But somehow, I felt shifting to the princess tower and her business would pull me away from everyone else I loved.

I came to love my father and brothers, Adriano, and the rest of the Russo family. Adriano and I have become close, despite our age difference. If someone made fun of him for being nineteen and being best friends with a sixteen-year-old, he'd beat them up and move on. Not the most mature approach, but it was effective.

Either way, I didn't want to give up any of my family once I took over Regalè Fashion. I wanted it all, a happy family with my grand-mother in it and the empire she had built. Grandma had poured her soul into it, and I loved everything about it too. So did my mother. I owed it to all of them to follow their path.

"She doesn't mean that," I muttered in a low voice. "She's just mad that Dad is putting restrictions on her time with me."

Neither one of the men seemed surprised. I wished Adriano was here, but he was out of town taking care of some business for Santino. Usually, he was my listener. Despite our age difference, we always lent each other our strength. I did it for him and he for me, that's how it worked between us.

"And what do you want, Amore?" Santino asked, surprising me.

Nobody had ever bothered asking me that. Not even Adriano. Santino's tall frame towered over me like a dark, brooding cloud. I wasn't done going through my growth spurt, but I knew I'd be much shorter than him. Adriano was shorter than his brother, too, by at least two inches.

I turned my head back in the direction of my grandmother and father, though I couldn't see them. I could only hear muffled voices.

I finally shrugged. "I want it all."

"Meaning what, kiddo?" I felt mild irritation crawl up my spine at being called kiddo. Nobody called me kiddo except for him. Of course, I was almost nine years younger than him, but the kiddo term wasn't right for teenage girls and boys.

Santino always seemed to challenge me, whether knowingly or unknowingly. Frustration clawed at my chest because for some stupid reason he fascinated me too. *It isn't a crush*, I told myself.

"I want to run Regalè Enterprise and stay around Dad, my brothers, and Adriano."

"Ah, princess. Not us too?" Mr. Russo teased, though there was no venom in his voice.

"Of course, you too," I muttered, keeping my eyes on Mr. Russo and blushing excessively. Truth was that I wanted to stay around Santino too. I really liked him, but it agitated me that he only saw me as a kid.

The door to Dad's office flew open and he came out along with my grandmother. I rushed to both of them.

"I'm sorry, Dad," I apologized quickly. "We were working on a new design, and I lost track of time."

Dad patted my arm. "That's okay, Amore. Your grandmother should be watching the time, not you." A frustrated breath left her, but she kept her mouth pressed in a thin line. Grandma might have been in her late seventies, but she was still a beautiful woman. Her silver white hair was always done in the latest fashion, and she dressed better than most twenty-year-olds. "You can go to Grandma's next weekend. She's taking you on a weekend trip to Italy."

I squealed my delight and threw myself into Dad's arms. "Thanks, Dad. I promise I'll check in all day long and send you pictures."

He squeezed me tight. "DeAngelo will go with you and a few other guards. I want you safe."

Eagerly, I nodded my agreement. I knew it was hard for him to let me go, and I wasn't about to make it harder.

Jumping up and down, I clapped my hands with enthusiasm. "Oh my gosh, Italy!" I couldn't contain my grin.

"Bring your designs, Amore," Grandma chimed in, heading towards the door. I noticed she never acknowledged Mr. Russo nor Santino. "Now I'm leaving before your dreadful father changes his mind."

I shook my head. Why did she always have to go poking a bear with the stick?

"Be nice to Dad, Grandma," I warned her, she never even acknowledged my words as she strode out the door like the queen that she was. She really had the best last name, Regalè.

She slammed the door behind her, and a dozen curses left Dad's lips.

"I hope I don't regret this," Dad grumbled under his breath. "DeAngelo is to be with you at all times." Dad pressed a kiss on my cheek.

"You won't regret it," I vowed, smiling. "I'll make sure Grandma doesn't do anything silly and DeAngelo will be with me. Promise."

The Russos and Dad chuckled. "Then all will be well," Mr. Russo announced softly. "Your mother would be proud of you."

My smile faltered a bit. It had been over three years but the loss still hurt. Profoundly so. There were times when I imagined talking to her and listening for her advice. Of course, it never came but it helped to talk.

"Now go do your homework, Amore," Dad said, the knowing look in his eyes. He knew Mom's death still hurt. It was a sore subject and a wound that didn't seem to heal as fast. I worried him a lot those first few months with my nightmares. But as I got older, I learned to rein them in a bit better.

"Okay, Dad."

He pressed another kiss onto my forehead. "Don't stay up. I'll be late."

"Be careful," I said softly. He might have been the head of the Bennetti crime family, but he wasn't untouchable. He was a good father, and I wanted to keep him in my life.

He strode to Santino and Mr. Russo.

"Don't do anything I wouldn't," I added teasingly, drawing a smile out of all three.

They left through the front door without a backward glance as I watched their backs. Taking a deep breath, I went to search for DeAngelo.

Maybe we could squeeze in an hour of self-defense training before I started on my homework.

CHAPTER 4

Amore

Packing my bag for the weekend with Grandma, I couldn't be more excited. Our first weekend together away from New York. She told me she had a bag for me already, but I wanted to make sure I had everything I needed, my phone, favorite sweater, which Adriano had gifted me, yoga pants, and, most importantly, a drawing pad for new design ideas.

The horn blasted from the driveway. Adriano's impatience would be the death of me one day. I picked up my cell phone and typed a message.

Don't sit on the horn, dude! Coming. I smiled as I pressed the send button.

I shoved a few more things into my bag, then glanced at myself in the mirror. I wore a light blue dress that came down to my knees. The back plunged into a V cut, leaving my skin exposed, but I'd pulled a little white cardigan over so Dad wouldn't see it. Combining it with a pair of white Chanel flats, I thought I looked good. I'd look better without a cardigan, but I could easily take it off later. Regardless, I didn't look much older, but I thought I'd pass for an eighteen-year-old at least. Adriano told me not to worry about that part, but I couldn't help it.

I hurried out of my bedroom with the pink weekend bag hooked on my shoulder. I loved pink accessories. Unfortunately, with my hair color,

I couldn't pull off wearing pink clothes. Otherwise, I'd be in pink all the time.

"Whoa, whoa," Lorenzo shouted after me. "Where are you rushing to?" My step faltered, and I turned around just as he caught up with me. "You look dressed up for a date."

I smiled. Seeing Lorenzo always brought a smile on my face.

"I'm spending a long weekend with Grandma. She's taking me to Italy," I told him. He frowned, just as every Bennetti man did every time Grandma Regina was mentioned. "Adriano is driving me to her place."

He took the bag off my shoulders and flipped it over on his own. "I would have driven you."

When I expressed I wanted to learn self-defense, Lorenzo made it happen. He always took time to take me to Grandma's or for some ice cream if he sensed I felt down. It didn't matter to him that I was sixteen and he was twenty-one; he spoke to me like we were equals.

I guess with Luigi being the oldest son, at twenty-three, Dad always kept him included in his business and by his side. Lorezno had the luxury of more freedom. Kind of like Adriano, being nineteen, had more freedom than Santino. Though the latter gave the impression of being even older than his twenty-four years.

"I know." I leaned closer to him and whispered, "Adriano and I are stopping at his college frat party first."

Lorenzo's eyes darted around to ensure nobody was close by. While he understood my need to live up my teenage years, Luigi and Dad didn't. Those two were overbearing and protective. I knew it was difficult for Dad to agree to raise me somewhat normally. But his kind of normal didn't extend to going dancing or to any kind of parties without him.

The daughters of men in the mafia were raised under a tight leash. Arranged marriages in Cosa Nostra happened to strengthen the position of men in the underworld. I had yet to meet a woman that married for love in this world. They used women as pawns, keeping them in a controlled environment. Driven by their bodyguards, never left alone with a member of the opposite sex.

A five-year-old outside of this world had more freedom than an eighteen-year-old locked in the gilded cage of the Cosa Nostra. While I wasn't a part of it, many other daughters were. They were pawns in large-scale drug or arms trafficking agreements.

Thankfully, that wouldn't be my fate. I grew up differently than most girls in the mafia world and had tasted a limited amount of freedom. I had experienced more in my life than some of the married women in this world.

Of course, it wasn't easy on my dad. Grandma and he bickered about my future all the time.

Dad, while overly protective, understood he'd alienate me by enforcing a completely different lifestyle. And my grandmother fought to raise me the way my mother would have wanted.

Grandma could be just as overbearing as my father, but with our common love for designing and fashion, we spent a lot of time together. I found freedom in expressing my creative side, so it felt like she granted me more liberties and freedom. But I knew it wasn't so. Still, I couldn't fault either one of them for their overzealous need to protect me. Especially considering that the Venezuelan Cartel was present even in New York.

"Where is the party?" Lorenzo questioned.

I groaned out loud. "You aren't going to crash it, I hope," I hissed low under my breath.

He tilted his head, watching me with a mild reprimand in his eyes. "I just want to be sure you are safe."

"I will be," I told him. "Adriano will be there. He won't leave me." *Not unless he is getting laid.* But I'd never tell my brother that.

"He better not," he retorted. "Not if he wants to live. Tell me where?"

"NYU," I finally admitted.

"Ah, your dream university," he uttered softly. "You just can't wait to get there."

I rolled my eyes, though a smile played around my face. "I'll text you if I need you."

He looped his arm around my shoulders as we resumed walking. "So, after that, he'll take you to your grandma's?" I nodded. "Maybe I should come along? After all, you are underage."

"Don't be a party pooper," I complained, narrowing my eyes at him annoyed.

"You better call me at any hint of trouble," he deadpanned, and my expression instantly softened. I couldn't blame him for worrying.

Ever since he caught his mother hurting me and his delayed reaction, he has blamed himself. We had a conversation about it. He wasn't to blame. He admitted that Elena hadn't been much of a mother to them, loved scheming and turning Lorenzo and Luigi against each other as well as their father. Dad put up with it, knowing that his sons were strong enough to ignore their mother. But her hurting me physically took it too far. Both of my brothers had become my protectors in every sense of the word since that day. They assured me they didn't hold any resentment against me for what happened to their mother. Their exact words were, *"She made her own bed and ultimately she had to lie in it."*

She was still their mother. So, in a sense, all three of us mourned the loss of our mothers. It made us even closer.

"I promise." I hugged him tightly, then stepped back, taking my bag back. He nodded and went down the hallway, probably into the library. He loved to hang out there. It was our most favorite room in the house.

I made my way down the stairs and through the large marble foyer, turning a corner in the hallway near my father's office when I collided with a solid chest.

"Ouch," I murmured, rubbing my forehead. "Watch where—" The words trailed off as I stepped back and met dark eyes.

Santino!

"Kiddo, you have to watch where you are going." A flicker of impatience in his dark brown eyes had taken me aback. He had a cell phone in one hand and must have been reading a message when we bumped into each other. So, he wasn't paying attention either.

"Well, you should too," I told him, annoyance flashing in my eyes. I hated the *kiddo* endearment. By anyone, but most of all him. I tilted my head towards the phone in his hand. "Shouldn't text and walk. Nor text and drive."

A tiny bit of amusement sparked in his eyes.

"You have gotten brave, Amore," he drawled.

This man of the Cosa Nostra has killed numerous men; stronger people than me have cowered before him, but I knew he wouldn't hurt me. I'd stake my life on it. I didn't know why, but I felt it deep down in my bones and my heart. He was my safety, my protector. Always had been.

And it wasn't because of my father. He wasn't scared of my father; this Russo was a lot tougher and harder than my father. I wore no rose-colored glasses when it came to my dad. So, I gathered that the reason he'd never hurt me was probably because Adriano and I were so close.

"Maybe I have been brave all along," I told him, tilting my chin up in defiance. I probably looked like a spoiled brat to him. "You just happened to catch me on a bad day. Once." I referred to how we met.

His hand came up and he ran his thumb across his jaw, like he was seriously thinking about that. Maybe he'd finally stop thinking about me as a kid. Then he shook his head, as if he dismissed a thought that was ridiculous, and slipped his hands into his pockets.

His gaze dropped down to my outfit, eyeing it clinically like a doctor studied his patient.

"You and Adriano going out? To that college party?"

My eyes darted instinctively around us, and a triumphant smile played on his lips.

"Shhh," I scolded him, scrunching my eyebrows. I understood the irony of shushing a killer, but he let me get away with it. He probably let me get away with a lot.

"You are going to get yourself in trouble," he warned. I loved my big brothers, but I wished Santino wouldn't behave like them. The only one that didn't treat me like a big brother was Adriano. Maybe it was the reason we always got into trouble together. I was just another friend to him, and I loved that about my best friend.

I rolled my eyes, annoyance flaring in my tone. "I wish everyone would stop saying that," I muttered. "It is just a little hang out."

"Don't get in trouble, kiddo."

"Damn it, Santi," I hissed, anger clear in my voice. "Would you stop calling me kiddo?"

The dark gaze that usually remained unmovable shone with amusement. "I don't think so, kiddo."

Why couldn't he see me as something more than just a kid? I was sixteen, a lot older than a kid! But if there was one thing I knew about Santi, it was that he'd always do what he thought best. After all, it was the reason he was already seen as the don.

I shrugged my shoulders and blew out an exasperated sigh. "Whatever."

His lip tugged upwards. I hated that I seemed to amuse him, like an entertainment show.

"Give me your phone." His request threw me off, and I narrowed my eyes on him.

"Why?"

"Don't you trust me?" he mused.

Another sigh left me. I trusted this man more than was probably wise. I couldn't fight it. He offered me the first comforting touch when he wiped my tears away three years ago. He even stood up to my own father to keep me shielded from Dad's temper. And he was my best friend's brother. So, on an exhale, I dug through my bag. Once I had my phone, I took it out, unlocked it and handed it to him.

I could tell I pleased him by giving him my phone without an argument, and for some reason, my chest warmed. It was probably a stupid feeling. I cared about the Russo men, they were my second (or maybe third) family, and it felt good to know that Santino cared about me too.

"I'm putting my phone number in it," he said, never raising his eyes as he typed in his contact info. "If something happens, call me. I sent myself a message from your number, so I'll know it's you."

Santino Russo, the don, gave me his number. Internally screaming. My cheeks flushed and giddiness overwhelmed me, but I hid it. He would not appreciate me jumping up and down at the idea of him giving me his number. In his mind, he gave a number to a kid. In mine, a drop-dead gorgeous boy gave me his phone number.

"Thanks. But like I just told Lorenzo, "I commented nonchalantly, "... everything will be fine."

He nodded then left me standing there as I watched his strong, good looking back disappear down the hallway. He always wore three-piece suits and looked impeccable. Sometimes I wondered how the ruthless don killed other men wearing such expensive suits. Shaking my head at my stupid thoughts, I entered Dad's office and found him looking over some documents, never hearing me enter.

"Hey, Dad," I announced my presence.

His head snapped up, and instantly, his tensed posture relaxed. He stood up and came around the desk.

He opened his arms and I stepped into his embrace, finding comfort in them. It was funny how life turned out. When Dad first came and got me in Colombia, I was certain I could never care about this man. Yet, he had done so much for me, and sacrificed so much that I knew there was no other father that could compete with him. I was incredibly lucky to have two fathers that cared deeply for me and an amazing mother.

"I just wanted to let you know Adriano was taking me to Grandma's." He frowned but didn't say anything. I knew his frown was for Grandma not Adriano. "Thank you for letting me go on this trip with her."

He pressed a kiss onto my forehead. "Just stay close and never leave without one of her buffoon bodyguards. I guess they are better than nothing, although I'd rather send one of your brothers with you. DeAngelo is the best, so stick to him."

I nodded. "I will be safe, promise."

"Where is DeAngelo?" he questioned.

"He's already at Grandma's," I told him. I might have given DeAngelo a little white lie, leading him to believe that Dad was bringing me. I couldn't very well have him trailing us to the college party.

Guilt rushed through me, and for a second, I debated if I should tell Dad about the short detour that Adriano and I had planned but then decided against it. There was no need to worry him, he already had a lot on his plate.

"I better go." I smiled and pressed a kiss on his cheek. "Love you. See you on Tuesday."

"Call me every day and text me every hour."

A choked laugh escaped me. "I'll try to remember to text you every hour. But not when I'm sleeping."

He grinned. "If you happen to wake up, then text me."

I shook my head, smiling. "Okay, I will," I promised.

"Love you, Amore."

"Love you too, Dad."

One more hug and I hurried out of his office and out of the foyer into the fresh air. Adriano was waiting for me, leaned against his Mustang, flicking his lighter. He was constantly playing with that damn thing.

"About time," he complained, taking my bag from me and throwing it into the trunk. Giving me a quick peck on my cheek, he opened the door for me, and I slid into the seat. Once he was behind the wheel, I started talking.

"Sorry, I ran into Lorenzo. Then your brother."

"Santi is here?" His eyes briefly glanced in my direction.

"Yes. He knew you were taking me to this party. Did you tell him?"

"No, but I assume he knows now."

Ah, damn. Santino suspected Adriano was taking me to a college party, and I had confirmed it. Sneaky gorgeous bastard.

"So how was the trip?" I inquired, changing subjects.

"It was good. Just business stuff." Adriano might tell me a lot of stuff, but he has never told me anything about the underworld business. I didn't know whether it was to protect me or the Russo empire. "You look pretty."

I chuckled at his compliment. They came easily from Adriano's lips, too easily. He dished them out like candy.

"Thanks. I couldn't pull off looking much older. I'd need a lot of make-up and a different kind of dress, but then I'd never succeed in leaving the house."

"You look perfect," he drawled. He sounded sincere and my cheeks colored. I eyed him, observing his jeans that hugged his legs just right and the plain white t-shirt that showed off his biceps. White looked good on him, just as it did on Santi, highlighting their tanned skin tone.

"You look good too," I replied. "Like the perfect college boy."

He threw his head back and laughed, carefree. It was why I liked Adriano so much. He was so carefree, and I wanted to soak up his happiness. He was the polar opposite in character to his older brother. Santino was tense and dark; Adriano was happy, relaxed, and mischievous. Albeit both brothers were ruthless and dangerous when dealing with the enemy.

Adriano took my hand and pressed a fleeting kiss on my knuckles.

"As long as you think I look good," he murmured against my skin.

"I do," I said with a chuckle. "You know you look good. Otherwise, you wouldn't have girls fawning all over you all the time."

He waved his hand, still holding mine, as if dismissing all those other girls. But it flattered him, I knew it did. I have seen firsthand what a smooth operator Adriano was. He'd drop a schmoozing comment with a hint of a compliment, make a girl blush, then greet her in the hallway by her name and boom. They ran after him, proclaiming their undying love and welcoming him into their beds. Then when he wanted to get rid of them, he'd act like we were an item.

I loved him, but he acted a bit like a manwhore. Still, I'd never rat him out. He had my back; I had his.

Twenty minutes later, we were at the party. It didn't take long at all for Adriano to bask in female attention. They were attracted to him like bees to honey. I was actually impressed that Adriano stuck with me for longer than usual. He had to be worried some boys would get too close to me.

He roamed the room with me, introducing me to everyone. To my delight, everyone thought I was a freshman. Girls kept asking in round-about ways whether I was Adriano's girlfriend. I'd just smile and avoid answering. We had an odd friendship, but it worked for us.

With spiked fruit punches and other drinks floating around, Adriano became more relaxed. I stuck to ginger ale. Grandma would crucify me alive if she smelled alcohol on me, and I wasn't willing to jeopardize our Italy trip.

"Hey, babe." Adriano kissed my cheek. "I'm going to step away for a second. Dance with geeks only, and if something happens, you scream for me."

I rolled my eyes. It didn't take him long to find a girl. Probably record time, and I suspected his last name probably had something to do with it.

"You saying 'scream for me' sounds so suggestive," I muttered under my breath. Adriano threw his head back and laughed.

"Maybe I'm trying to corrupt you," he said, his eyes twinkling.

I rolled my eyes. "Please don't." Besides, fantasizing about one Russo was more than enough.

With a blonde girl that pretty much entangled herself around him, he walked away. He threw me a glance over his shoulder and winked before disappearing up the stairs. The dorms were on the second floor.

"Care to dance?" A light, male voice had me forgetting Adriano. I met blue eyes and a warm smile.

"Brad, right?"

He grinned. "You remember," he said, pleased he left an impression.

Truth was I always remembered names. My grandmother insisted on it, saying it was key in running a business to always remember facts and names.

I smiled. "I'd love to dance," I told him.

As we danced to Tate McRae's "That Way," Brad pretty much gave me his life story while I smiled and nodded. I had to admire a nineteen-year-old boy that had a detailed life plan.

CHAPTER 5

Santino

New York University held the wildest campus parties. I should know, I frequently attended them while I was a student here.

I pretended to listen to the chick next to me, all the while seeking out Amore with my gaze. She kept yapping about her father that worked for the FBI, hinting she knew who I was. I didn't give a shit. I got a read on her within the first sixty seconds of opening her mouth. She fancied herself a rebel against her father if she got herself involved with one of the notorious Russo men.

"... Dad's specialty is the mafia underworld of New York." This girl talked too damn much. "Do you know that red haired girl is the daughter of Don Savio Bennetti?"

My muscles tensed and my fist closed around the beer bottle in my hand. My eyes latched on Amore's form gliding across the dance floor, a polite smile on her face as she listened to her dance partner talk her ear off.

A pulse ticked in my jaw, annoyed that anyone dared to look Amore's way. She shouldn't be here, especially not alone. I was pissed off that Adriano had disappeared. *Damn fool!* Didn't he see every boy in this room staring after her, salivating for her. She was too young to be left unattended. If DeAngelo was here, he'd have her back. His attention never wavered from her while on the job.

But like this, it left Amore open and vulnerable. When I added my number to her phone, I also shared her location with my phone. Good thing too! I had a bad feeling about the two of them tonight, so I followed my intuition.

Adriano would get her killed with his carelessness. He thought with his dick too much, and Amore, the good friend she was, indulged him and covered for him all the time. I'd admire her loyalty if only it wasn't that it was putting her at risk over and over again.

Just a month ago, Adriano let her drive his brand-new Dodge Viper. She had no license, no experience driving for fuck's sake, and he put her behind a 624 horsepower sports car. She barely made it five miles down the road before she crashed into a tree. Thankfully, the airbags and seat-belts saved the two idiots.

My eyes drifted back to Amore. She was still dancing with the same guy. They both swayed to the music. His hands rested on her hips, but thankfully, he maintained some distance between the two. Otherwise, I'd have to break his fingers. Nobody would be taking advantage of the girl under my watch. Though this guy looked harmless enough.

Her bright smile lit up her whole face. That happy smile hadn't left her face since I arrived. She was on her third consecutive dance with the blonde guy. He still hadn't shut up, and I caught her stifling a yawn a few times. But she still looked deliriously happy and relaxed.

The blonde next to me kept rubbing herself all over me, though I didn't give her any indication I was interested. It was how it usually worked. You showed them no interest, they ran harder after you.

Except Amore. She refused to run after anyone. Even my brother. I didn't understand their dynamic, but it seemed to work for them. She even played his girlfriend when an overly obsessive girl he fucked wouldn't get the picture that she had been dumped.

My eyes went back to the kid I found crying three years ago in front of our restaurant. She had come a long way. My lip twitched at her complaint earlier. I had a sense that for a while now she hated when I called her kiddo. She might not have been a kiddo anymore, but she was a girl, still too young to be a woman.

Though dressed as she was now, she could easily fool these boys into thinking she was of age. She looked beautiful in her blue skater dress with the back cut in a V shape. There was no way to overlook her with her long, wild red hair and her radiant smile. Over the last few years, she had matured a lot, but her emotions were an open book to me. I thought they were clear as day for anyone with two eyes, though sometimes Adriano seemed oblivious to it.

"Do you want to go somewhere quieter?" The blonde next to me purred.

With one last look at Amore's way, I turned my attention to the blonde next to me. She told me her name, but I didn't retain it. All I knew was that she was twenty-two, flunked two college years, and her father worked at the FBI. I didn't give a fuck what her name was anyhow. I'd never see her again.

"No, I don't." I removed her hand off my arm. For a moment, shock stunned her face. It couldn't possibly be the first time she experienced rejection.

Then she quickly got herself together. "No strings attached."

"I'm still not interested." My smile lacked any hint of warmth as I locked my eyes on her. "Now, I suggest you get lost. Otherwise, you'll understand why my reputation for being ruthless precedes me. And your FBI blue collar father won't be able to save you."

The conversation was over. I left her shocked and speechless behind me and walked away, irritated that she'd think she could possibly change my first refusal.

I'd give it to blondie, she was determined, and by the time I got rid of her without actually killing her, I lost sight of Amore. One minute she was there; the next, she was gone.

I rushed to the last guy she danced with.

"Where is the red-haired girl?" I gritted out.

I thought for sure the blonde would piss his pants.

"Sh-she went to the bathroom," he stuttered.

I grabbed him by his neck. "Which one?" I hissed. There were twenty fucking bathrooms in here.

"End of the hallway." He tilted his head. It was the one with multiple stalls. My phone dinged at that same exact moment, signaling a text message.

It was from Amore. "Help."

I froze, my blood icing through my veins. Unbuckling my holster, my strides ate up the distance toward the bathrooms. I heard a mocking voice as I approached it.

"Come out, come out. Wherever you are." Whoever it was, the man was soon-to-be-dead. "We'll finish the fun we started with your mother."

Rage filled my vision, and I flung the door open just in time to see the prick banging on the closed stalled door. Before he could react, I was behind him and closed my fist around the back of his shirt, then yanked him back.

"Here I am," I growled, hauling him up by his collar. "Finish the fun with me." My lip curled at the sight of his eyes widening. I punched him in the gut with my gun, his breath coming out on a shattered gasp. The next blow hit him in the jaw. Another blow to his nose. A howl ripped out of his throat. Instinctively, he tried to stumble backwards, but I clutched him harder.

"No, no," I growled. "You aren't going anywhere."

I continued my blows, fire washing over me, igniting the fury in my veins. My hand grabbed a fistful of his hair and shoved him hard against the stall door. Then again and again, his forehead hitting repeatedly against the door, leaving a red mark on his skin and the door.

He slid to the floor, lifting his head. Blood trickled down his temple.

"Amore?" I called out.

Silence. My heart clenched. If this motherfucker hurt her, I'd slice him piece by fucking piece.

"Santi?" Amore's voice came out in a whisper, tentative, unsure if it was a trap.

"Yes. Stay there and don't open the door until I tell you," I ordered.

"I-I'm scared, Santi." Amore's whimper scorched fire through my veins. This man scared her, unlike anything I have heard or seen from her before.

The scumbag tried to crawl away. Fucking coward! At the sight of his watering eyes and blood gushing out of his nose, I couldn't help but feel satisfaction. I wasn't done; not even close to it.

"Chill, *chamo*." He called me *dude* in Venezuelan slang. I narrowed my eyes on him. He didn't look Venezuelan with his blonde hair. But that didn't mean anything. There were German Venezuelans, and they have been playing in the cartel business too. This couldn't be a coincidence. "I was just going to talk to her. We go way back. Don't we, niña?"

A haze of red tinted my vision and my anger erupted anew. I wrapped my hand around his throat, my enraged energy filling the bathroom. Stupid, taunting bastard. I lifted him off the tiled bathroom floor.

"Your road ends here," I gritted through my teeth as I squeezed harder. His body twitched, his hands clawing at me. But I felt none of it as I watched the light extinguish in his eyes.

Once he stopped breathing, I went into the furthest stall, shoved his dead body in it, propped it up on the toilet, and locked the door.

Goddamnit! I let my emotions and anger overcome all my senses. I should have kept him alive to question him. I never lost my cool, but I had gone fucking bananas. The bastard was nothing but a pile of bloodied and beaten flesh with a few broken bones.

I dialed Renzo, ignoring my bloodied knuckles. "Need clean up." I recited the address. "Body is in the last stall."

Ending the call, I went to Amore's stall. "You can open it now."

I heard her shuffle with the lock and then the door opened. The sight of her stark pale face and her green eyes full of terror shattered my heart. She was trembling, shaken up over the incident. Not that I could blame her. Her family and guards kept her sheltered, keeping the ruthlessness of our world at bay around her.

My arm snaked around her waist, pulling her into a hug.

"It's okay, kiddo," I murmured into her hair. Her small body trembled in my arms. She just buried her head deeper into my chest, and I felt more than heard her inhale and exhale, keeping her panic attack at bay. I witnessed only one of those when she first moved to New York, but speaking to Adriano and her father, I knew she hadn't had one in a while. "I got you. Just keep breathing and keep it together."

Her arms wrapped around me, her shuddering breaths hitting me right in the chest. Her father refused to say what happened to Amore before he found out he had a daughter. All anyone knew was that her mother was killed and Amore witnessed it. Something like that was traumatic enough to scar anyone, never mind a child.

I recalled her last panic attack. It happened right after Elena's funeral. That bitch deserved to die, hurting a fucking kid and burning her with cigarettes. I was fairly certain that fear triggered Amore's panic attacks. That one full blown panic attack I witnessed was hard to forget.

Amore's face was pale, her big moss color eyes full of fear dominating her face as she stared at her grandmother and her father arguing. They fought tooth and nail over who should be her legal guardian. Their hate for each other ran deep.

Her grandmother moved towards Amore to pull her closer, and the sound of guns being drawn echoed in the room.

"P-please." Amore's voice shook as much as her body. "P-please. D-don't."

"Go ahead and shoot, Bennetti." Her grandmother was stupid to challenge her father. "Scar your daughter even more. Because seeing her mother die and your wife torturing her wasn't enough."

Gasps sounded all around the room, and Amore paled even more. That girl would pass out any moment, her breathing erratic. Those two idiots should stop bickering for her sake.

"I'll protect her," he gritted out.

"Amore, come with me," her grandmother instructed. "You don't belong here."

She took a tentative step towards her grandmother, the woman she had known since birth. It didn't take a genius to realize the kid was scared out of her mind. The underworld scared her.

Amore's eyes ping-ponged between her father and grandmother, both with guards at their back and guns pointed at the other. DeAngelo was the only one that took position next to Amore, his only concern for her.

Everyone watched the thirteen-year-old whose clammy skin paled with each passing second.

"Amore," I spoke softly. "Breathe, kiddo."

Her pupils were dilated, the color of her eyes almost extinguished as she frantically watched her family with guns pointed at each other. It was a first for a funeral, even in the Cosa Nostra.

"Let's go, sweetie." Her grandmother pulled her. "You are too good for these people."

Her father stepped forward, ignoring the guns pointed at his chest.

"She is my daughter. She stays with me. You kept her away from me for thirteen years. Hid her from me. Now she is mine, and you'll have to kill me to get her."

"That can be arranged," her grandmother told him frigidly.

Amore swallowed, her breathing shallow, her hands trembling. I felt sorry for her. She was thrown to the wolves, losing her mother and a man she believed to be her father, only to be pushed and pulled between the Bennetti and Regalè family.

Bennetti stood his ground, ready to start a war against the Regalè empire to keep his daughter.

"I'll stay." Amore's small voice sliced through the tense silence. Everyone held their breaths, unwilling to miss a single moment. Like some damn soap opera.

"Amore, these people are criminals. You are—" Regina didn't get to finish her statement.

"I-I'll stay," Amore repeated, her eyes on her father. She feared him, only knowing him for several weeks, and yet, still she'd stay. Regina would have a fierce, strong heiress in her granddaughter one day.

A gun went off. One of Regina's buffoons accidently fired and suddenly the whole foyer burst with shouting voices and screaming. I pulled Amore from the middle and out of the crossfire before she got killed. DeAngelo had the same idea and protected her with his body.

"Take her somewhere safe," I ordered him and my brother.

Adriano tugged on her, but if I thought she was pale before, it was nothing compared to now. She was deathly white now, perspiration glistening on her skin as she gasped for breath.

The terror in her eyes. "I-I..." Her hand reached out to me, gripping my shirt weakly.

She tried to say something, and I grabbed her shoulder, shaking her slightly. "What's the matter?"

She struggled to breathe, grabbing at her chest with one hand.

"Don't let me die," she whispered, the words barely leaving her lips.

"Everyone stooooop!" My brother shouted at the top of his lungs. "She's dying."

It worked. Everyone stilled and suddenly, Bennetti and her grandmother were next to me, kneeling beside her limp body as she gasped desperately for air. Amore's small hands tugged on my shirt, holding on to it for dear life.

"Did you hurt her?" Bennetti growled.

"It's a panic attack," her grandmother said, her hands on her face. "Amore, breathe! You are safe. Breathe!"

Blood seeped out of her nose, a stark crimson red against her pale skin. Her startling green gaze hazed over, and her dark lashes fluttered, struggling to remain open. She was losing her battle because her grip on my shirt loosened.

"Baby, breathe!" Bennetti's voice broke, his hand shaking her.

"The monsters are gone, Amore. Nobody is here. You have to breathe," her grandmother begged. "Breathe, Amore. Please, love. Breathe. You have to breathe. Remember the promise." My head snapped to her grandmother. "Fight, Amore. You can do it."

My gaze went back to the small body in my arms. Her eyes shut, and the depths of the green lakes blocked from my view. Without thinking, I leaned over her small body, pressing my mouth on her cold lips and breathed air into her.

She wasn't dead yet, but fuck if I'd let her die in my arms. Breathe, Amore. My order was silent, hoping she'd hear it. Another breath into her mouth. Breathe, Amore.

This kid mattered, and I'd always save her.

CHAPTER 6

Amore

S anti's arms around me held me tight as I kept my ear pressed against his chest. I listened to his steady heartbeat. *Thump. Thump. Thump.* And I found my focus. My panicked breathing eased and slowly evened out. The buzzing in my ears slowly ceased, and I found safety in his arms.

I never expected to see that blonde Venezuelan again. When I spotted him, I acted on instinct and went to hide as I typed up one word and sent it to Santi. I have no idea why I sent him the alert. He was the first one I thought to scream for, and he was at the top of my text messages. It seemed like a no brainer, except it wasn't rational. He was supposed to be across town.

A wrong decision could have cost me everything.

The images of my mother's tortured body played on repeat in my mind, and my heart ached. It was a dull ache, but it still hurt whenever I thought about it. More often than not, I tried to not think about it. It triggered my panic attacks and nightmares.

The rancid smell of musty body odor, blood, moisture, and the decaying vegetation of the jungle caused my fear to flare up and were triggers for my panic attacks. From all my experiences in South America, that was the only one that remained.

DeAngelo had been training me to become stronger, to learn how to protect myself. Today, I failed miserably at it. The fear I felt at seeing the Venezuelan almost paralyzed me before I finally woke up from my stupor and ran. I'd have to work harder. I could have been killed by this guy too easily. There was no way I'd be another victim to the Venezuelan Cartel. I'd pave the way to my own future and find a way to avenge my mother, eliminate all those men that hunted us only because our blood-line traced back to the old cartel. I wouldn't be a scared little girl anymore who needed saving.

Perèz Rothschild, my great-grandfather, started his own drug traf-ficking business, teaming up with other cartel heads. Perèz became one of the biggest drug distributors to the Cosa Nostra and other criminals, courtesy of my grandfather. That cartel caused more deaths than several Cosa Nostra crime families combined. But then Grandpa was killed while Mom was pregnant with me. It broke Grandma's heart. She blamed it all on his criminal life and wanted nothing to do with it. All ties to the Perèz Cartel were cut. Or so everyone thought.

Raising my head, I met Santi's eyes. He came to my rescue. *Again.* I have no idea how he got here so fast, and I wasn't going to question it. I pressed my forehead against his chest, and Santi's strong, steady heart-beat overwhelmed all my other senses and peace washed over me. It didn't matter to me that he was one of the most feared men in the Cosa Nostra; to me he'd always be my savior.

The door flung open, and Santi acted on instinct, shoving me behind him, barricading me with his strong body.

Adriano rushed in and both of us exhaled in relief.

"What happened? The guys said you ran off into the bathroom and some scary dude was looking for you." His eyes darted to Santi. "I guess that scary dude is Santi," he muttered.

Santi wasn't scary. He was my savior. I was grateful he came when he did.

"What are you doing here?" Adriano questioned his brother, his posture tense.

In a split second, Santi was in his brother's face. "Don't ever fucking leave her alone and vulnerable again. She could have been taken or killed.

"What? How?" Adriano paled a bit, and guilt that the brothers were quarreling spread through me. It bothered me to see them arguing about me.

"A Venezuelan attacked her." Santi's fury pulsed in the air. His one hand was clenched so tight, his knuckles turned white while his other flexed and unflexed like he was practicing strangling someone.

The two brothers glared at each other, animosity brewing in the air. But the truth was that it was my fault as much as Adriano's. I sent DeAngelo ahead of me, knowing I'd be left alone for a bit since Adriano tended to hook up with girls all the time.

"He's from the Venezuelan Cartel," I rasped in a low voice, and both their eyes snapped to me.

"How do you know?" Adriano questioned.

"You're sure?" Santi asked at the same time.

I swallowed hard, then nodded. "Yes," I answered in a small voice, fidgeting with the hem of Santi's Brioni suit jacket. It kept me from freaking out. "I'm positive."

"Fuck!" Adriano pulled me into his arms. I let go of Santi's hem, which I was gripping, or risked pulling him over. "I'm sorry. He was probably watching me."

"It's okay. He wasn't watching you," I whispered. Adriano's familiar cologne invaded my lungs, but it was all wrong, mixed with the hint of a woman's perfume. Pulling away, I put distance between us and found myself closer to Santi, his scent cool and expensive, like fine Italian leather, replacing Adriano's.

"If I knew the Venezuelans were here, I would have never left her alone," Adriano justified himself to Santi.

"Yes, Adriano. Enemies will come and announce themselves. Just so you can keep your dick in your pants and do the right thing!" Santi's words sliced through the air, accusation clear in his voice.

Goosebumps blossomed on my skin, sending shivers throughout my body. Just the thought of the Venezuelan Cartel getting their hands on me sent icy terror through my veins.

"Please don't argue," I begged as I came to stand between the two of them. "It isn't Adriano's fault, Santi."

Santi's jaw ticked and annoyance flared in his eyes. I didn't like to see him pissed off, especially not at me. I waited for him to reprimand me or call me stupid for discounting what had just happened, but the words never came. He would have been right to chastise me, but I wouldn't let him put all the blame on Adriano.

"I am at fault here too, Santi. You cannot blame Adriano without blaming me." I exhaled shakily and our eyes locked. Santi's gaze hardened, and I knew he didn't like me defending Adriano. "We've snuck into a lot of parties before. Neither of us could have anticipated this time would be different."

Who would have ever thought a member of the Venezuelan Cartel would be here, on a college campus? I was terrified at the possibility of the men that killed my mother being in this country, not to mention this city.

"Where have you seen that guy before, kiddo?" Santi asked instead, switching to his killer mode.

My eyes locked on Santi's bloody knuckles. More often than not, they were bruised and red. I took his hand and walked us over to the sink. Once I turned on the water, I cleaned off his knuckles. He didn't even flinch. Like he had bloodied his knuckles so many times, they were numb.

Once they were cleaned up, I turned off the tap and handed him a paper towel. He took it and dried his hands, then spoke as he threw it into the trash. "You know that guy, Amore, from where?"

I winced at his cold tone. Santi could be scary sometimes, though he always made me feel safe. Even now, as pissed off as he was. Adriano misread my hesitance to answer and took my hand into his.

"It's okay, Amore," Adriano murmured, consoling me. "You can tell Santi."

A slight flicker of anger flashed in Santi's dark gaze, but he didn't say anything. I didn't understand why it bothered me that Adriano and I angered him. While Santi held me, it felt like the entire universe ceased to exist. I couldn't explain it, and it didn't make sense. Santino was the most feared man in the city, heck probably in the country. He had eliminated more than one rival family, methodically and ruthlessly. But none of it scared me. It made me feel even safer with him. Without even trying, Santi became my knight in shining armor. There wasn't an ounce of doubt that he'd keep me safe. Always and forever.

Santi Russo was my hero. My rescuer.

I sucked in a shaky breath and wiped my eyes. "I saw him with the men that killed my mom and George."

Santi looked at me in surprise. "The Venezuelan Cartel killed your mother?"

My heart pounded hard against my chest. Santi looked crazed, in a furious kind of way. Not at me but at the world. His dark eyes promised retribution, the muscle in his jaw ticking. I had never seen him so pissed off. Like he wanted to burn the world down. For *me*.

Okay, I was probably reading too much into it. I couldn't help but see him as my knight.

"Amore, did the Venezuelan Cartel kill your mother?" Santi repeated the question.

I swallowed a lump in my throat. "Yes."

I took a deep breath. I haven't done a good job dealing with my demons. It has been years since Mom's death, but I still couldn't garner strength to face those memories. The torture she endured. Each time I thought about it, my chest squeezed tightly, gripping my heart painfully and limiting my oxygen intake.

Santi relaxed his shoulders and though his face remained tight, his voice was gentle. "I'll run his history, and we'll see what we find out. Coincidences like this don't happen. You know that, kiddo. Right?"

There he went again, calling me kiddo. Why couldn't I be more than a kiddo?

I just nodded my agreement. He was right, it wasn't a coincidence.

"Now, let's go," Santi ordered his brother and me.

"Hold on, I'm not ready to—" Adriano tried to take over, but it didn't take a genius to realize Santi would shut him down.

"Then stay," Santi growled. "Amore is going to her grandmother's, and I'll drive her."

Adriano didn't want to leave. It was written all over his face. He probably hadn't gotten into that pretty girl's pants yet.

"Where is Savannah?" I asked him.

"She's waiting upstairs." I guess he made her wait while he came to check on me.

I cleared my throat, uncomfortable with the meaning of it.

"Should you go say goodbye to her?" He pressed his mouth into a thin line, and I knew the answer. He wouldn't leave her yet. On an exhale, I suggested what I knew he wanted to hear. "Why don't you stay and ummm.... talk to her. I think Santi is right. I should go to Grandma's now. Besides, we are leaving for Italy early in the morning."

Adriano's eyes, similar to his brothers, flashed with hope. "Are you sure?"

My heart sank a tad bit that my best friend would so easily be persuaded, but I tried not to take it personally. I've seen firsthand with my brothers that men were horny douchebags. Except Santi. I had yet to see him with a woman, although I heard plenty of stories of his heartbreaker ways.

I nodded. He hugged me and pecked me on the cheek, just as Renzo came into the bathroom. He must have not expected me here, his eyes roaming over the three of us.

"What happened, Boss?" he questioned Santi.

"Venezuelan in the last stall. He tried to get Amore. We'll need to get more info."

He nodded.

Renzo's gaze shifted to me.

"Where were you, Adriano?" Renzo asked, his eyes on me. "You two are always joined at the hip."

"He was busy showing off his dick," Santi gritted out, and Adriano flinched at the accusation.

"There is too much testosterone here," I murmured, my mood swinging from scared to annoyed and agitated.

"You okay, kiddo?" Renzo asked and suddenly I'd had enough. Anger, fear, and annoyance flared within me at everything.

"Would you all stop calling me kiddo!" I exclaimed, my chest heaving, and I knew angry blotches probably marked my neck. Being a fair skinned, red haired girl was a bitch. "Y'all are driving me fucking nuts! We should get going before the police come."

The three of them looked at me weird, almost as if expecting me to burst into tears. Maybe I would later, but now... I wouldn't. I needed to get my mind off everything, get to Italy and focus on things I could control and change.

Disbelief lurked in Santi's dark eyes, and his soft chuckle followed. "Calm down, kiddo. Renzo will handle the situation here, Adriano will go chasing pussy, and I'll take you to your princess tower at Regina's."

Regret hit me immediately. It was a terrible time to dwell on endearment titles. He just saved my life, and I sounded like a spoiled brat complaining about the *kiddo* title. It wasn't as if I acted like an adult, sneaking into the college party.

None of this was anyone's fault but mine, and maybe Adriano's, for the way tonight ended. "You won't tell Dad and my brothers I was here." I held Santi's dark gaze. I didn't need to beg Renzo because whatever Santino decided, he'd go with it. "Please, Santi."

A few heartbeats passed before Santi finally caved. "I'm too old for this shit," he grumbled. He nudged me forward. "I won't say anything." He paused, then added. "Now, let's go, Amore, before I change my mind."

Relief washed over me. Dad would put a stop to my trip with Grandma if he heard about this. I was safe with her. She kept a team of bodyguards, and DeAngelo was the best.

I gave Adriano another hug, relief washing over me. Santino was known for keeping his promises. I'd heard Father and my brothers comment on it on more than one occasion.

"When are you back?" Adriano asked me in a low voice, but we were still within Renzo and Santi's earshot, and although those two were talking in hushed Italian, I knew they could hear us.

"Tuesday."

"I'll text you tomorrow," he promised. I nodded and upon another gentle nudge by Santi, I scurried along.

The second we exited the bathroom, loud music assaulted my ears. The hallway was crowded, college kids everywhere.

Something warm enveloped me and I realized Santi had draped his jacket over my shoulders. I shot him a questioning look, and he murmured softly, "It's a chilly night."

I nodded, accepting his explanation. His scent from it immediately cocooned me, and I inhaled deeply. I should've been terrified by the violence he unleashed in the bathroom. He killed that Venezuelan, but I felt safe. I always felt safest around him.

Placing a steady hand on the small of my back, he urged me forward.

"Here" by Alessia Cara played while a group of boys were playing beer pong and riling each other up. Girls either hung all over the boys or stood together, whispering to each other and eyeing the guys.

I knew the moment the girls spotted Santi. The chatter got just a notch quieter. My eyes traveled over the group of girls as they all gawked and giggled at him, hoping for his attention or a glance. Anything. It was much worse than how they reacted to Adriano. I looked over my shoulder and met his eyes. He was focused on me.

"You good?" he questioned.

"Yes."

Unlike Adriano, Santi's eyes remained on me and never wavered to acknowledge anyone else. A gorgeous blonde girl waved his way, but he didn't so much as flick his gaze her way. Why did I like that so much? Too much.

Returning my attention to where I was going, I told myself not to debate too much about my reaction to Santi. I knew he would never see me as anything more than a kid. I was sixteen; he was twenty-four. We probably had nothing in common and this puppy love would eventually die out. I just had to get through it - it was like a rite of passage.

Every girl goes through it. Right?

The crowded room proved to be a challenge to shuffle through. Santi shoved a few boys around to allow me space to get through. It was kind of mind numbing. A wild, drunken party here, and a dead body in the bathroom right down the hallway. It became so startlingly obvious that there was a defining line between a normal life and the mafia life.

Where do I belong? I pondered.

Five minutes later we were outside. The fresh air hit me, and I inhaled deeply, letting the smell of alcohol and mixed fragrances wash out of my lungs. September was my least favorite month. Mom and George were killed the first week of September.

"My bag is in Adriano's trunk," I told Santi who stood next to me, probably waiting for me to get a move on.

"Let's go get it."

We walked through the parking lot, and though Santi was relaxed next to me, I sensed he was alert to his surroundings. Spotting Adriano's Mustang, he went straight to the back of the car, pulled out a swiss knife and flipped it open.

"What are you doing?" I asked in a whisper, my eyes skimming the parking lot. I didn't want to get in trouble. And breaking into a car was sure to land us in trouble. Not that Don Russo would care.

"I'm getting your bag."

"You can't break into Adriano's car," I scolded, the irony of reprimanding one of the most ruthless men in the Cosa Nostra didn't escape me.

He just chuckled.

"It's either a knife or I shoot the trunk open. Take your pick, kiddo."

I narrowed my eyes on him. He could be such a jackass sometimes. I pressed my lips together and tapped my foot impatiently. I liked Santino Russo, but it didn't mean I saw him under the illusion that he was perfect. The man liked to push people's buttons.

The trunk popped open, and he grabbed my bag.

"Here we go. The pink travel Gucci bag is in our possession." Was he making fun of me? "Now, let's get out of here."

He grabbed my wrist and started walking. My eyes flickered to his big hand wrapped around it. I knew his entire arm was tattooed, down to his fingers. My heart fluttered seeing his tattooed hand against my pale skin and excitement rushed through me.

"Why were you here anyhow?" I asked him curiously. "Aren't you too old for college parties?"

"I sure am." He ignored my question, and I shook my head. Santi would only tell me what he wanted to.

He opened the door for me, and I slid into the car. "Put your seatbelt on," he warned, and I rolled my eyes. He sounded like my dad, treating me like a damn kid.

Unlike his brother, Santi drove extremely expensive cars. I knew nothing about vehicles, but I knew enough to recognize it was one of the rare cars.

"What kind of car is this?" I asked him as he got into his seat.

"1963 Ferrari 250 GTO."

"Huh, nice." I had no idea what it meant. The only part I understood was Ferrari. "Can I drive it when I get my license?"

He threw his head back and laughed like he'd just heard the funniest joke ever.

"No, kiddo. You can't."

"Why not?" I challenged.

"Because barely a month ago, you crashed a Dodge Viper. Isn't that enough reason?"

Of course, he wouldn't forget that. Dad and Santi had to bribe quite a few people to ensure the accident wasn't recorded. My brothers swore I'd lose my license even before I got it. Not much support on that front!

"Well, Adriano said he'll let me drive his Mustang," I said, glancing at Santi. He had the most gorgeous profile. Strong and beautiful. I was in full swoon mode.

"Then you can drive his Mustang. You won't be driving my Ferrari." I blew a piece of unruly hair out of my face. "If you value your life, you won't even attempt to drive it." He paused and flicked a glance my way. "Ever."

Well, that was one way to shut me down.

I couldn't help myself and I snickered. "It is just stupid to drive a car like this to a college party." His hand reached out my way, and he tugged on a piece of my hair.

"Ouch. Stop it." I slapped his hand away.

"Better watch your mouth, Amore," he warned, but there wasn't a threat in his voice. "I love my cars, and nobody is allowed to drive them. Least of all a kid that doesn't even have a license."

Begrudgingly, I had to admit it made sense. I shifted my weight, and the car was forgotten as I stared out the window, the blur of the city streets passing us by.

"Amore?"

"Hmmm."

"Tell me what happened to you and your mother." His voice was gentle, but the soft command was still clear in it. After all, he was an acting don, so it was part of his DNA.

I wrapped my arms around myself. I hadn't told a single soul what I'd seen, though now I had a strange urge to spill it all.

"I didn't even thank you," I muttered softly instead.

"But you did call me stupid."

I exhaled a heavy sigh. "That was rude of me. Thank you for being there and saving me." He nodded but didn't say another word. "You are most definitely not stupid."

The corner of his lip curved up, but he didn't reply.

I swallowed hard before I continued. "The Venezuelan Cartel got us while we were in the Colombian jungle." I bit hard on my bottom lip, the stinging somehow grounding me. "They...the men captured George and I. Mom tried to save us."

Santi patiently waited, giving me time to gather my emotions. His eyes were the only thing that flickered dangerously. I gulped, the familiar ache gripping my chest. "T-they tortured her for days. I-in front of me." I squeezed my hands together, the knuckles turning white. My voice shook, and I couldn't say another word about it. Not without risking tears. It was too hard, the pain still too raw.

We drove in silence for the next few minutes. It was almost worse since it was too easy to get lost in the bloody images and painful memories.

"Can I put music on?" I asked him, my voice slightly raw with emotions. "I'm not sure if touching your radio is allowed, since driving your cars isn't."

Santi gently tugged on my hair again. "You can, but only if you behave."

The admission made me feel somewhat lighter. Maybe Dad was right all these years, saying that talking about demons would help. Yet, the words never left my mouth until now, and the little information I shared with Santi hadn't destroyed me. Yes, my heart ached but it didn't leave me feeling raw and torn apart. I still had a long way to go, but tonight, for the first time, I felt hope that I could handle it. All of it.

I leaned over and started playing with the radio. Sia's "Cheap Thrills" came on and I smiled.

"Ah, look at this," I murmured teasingly. "It is a Friday night. The only thing I didn't do was put makeup on."

"You're too young for makeup."

"I'm sixteen," I retorted dryly.

"Exactly my point. A kid."

I decided not to answer. Nothing I said would convince him otherwise. He'd come back with another smartass comment.

The tunes played and we both got lost in our thoughts, until I realized I didn't recognize the neighborhood. "My grandmother's place is on the Upper East side," I told him.

"I know. I'm taking a backway."

It looked to me like he was taking the long way home, but I didn't want to point it out. The idea of spending more time alone with him appealed to me.

I wasn't surprised he knew where Grandma lived. Santino Russo knew everything about everyone. At least that was what Luigi always said. Unlike Lorenzo, Luigi was hot-tempered, and unfortunately his motto, shoot first, ask questions later, didn't help his case. I loved him, and he would do anything for me, but my eldest brother was a disaster waiting to happen.

He told me once that despite his reputation as a badass, the people he killed left a mark on his soul. I asked him why he didn't think before killing someone. His answer was better to kill than be killed. He just said he'd have to live with a black soul. His reasoning was slightly disturbing, but it seemed to be how men in the underworld lived.

Lorenzo, on the other hand, was calm and level-headed. He was liked by all, but his lack of intensity made people feel at ease around him. It definitely played in his favor with the ladies. So, it was no wonder I was much closer to Lorenzo. Sometimes the intensity of my other brother was a bit too much. I guess it would make him a good don one day.

"I'm sorry you had to kill another person," I blurted out, my voice small. "I'm sure you didn't need this tonight."

He threw me a side glance and then returned his eyes to the road. "I'm not sorry. Better him than you."

Maybe the people he killed didn't leave a mark on his soul.

"You know, I heard that talking about it helps," Santi said softly.

"Does it help you?" I asked him curiously.

"To be honest, Amore, I never felt the need to talk." Somehow his admittance didn't surprise me. "But you are different. A better person than I ever was. So, I think talking would help you. So that you can put it behind you."

Underneath the killer suit, Santi was a good man. I never talked to anyone about what had happened, not even Adriano. I just couldn't speak the words. Yet, somehow, this evening, Santi had me saying more about it than I'd said in the last three years.

"I try not to think about it," I admitted in a hushed tone, my eyes focused on the road in front of us but not really seeing it. The images of Mom's brutal murder haunted me, but I still tried to shove the memories into a deep, dark corner. Except, every so often, they revolted and slammed into my brain. "Th- the images... they give me nightmares. I know it's stupid."

Santi's hand curled around my own hand, that had been resting on my thigh and scrunching the material of my dress, threatening to shred it. The moment his hand covered mine, calm washed over me.

"Nah, not stupid," he replied. "You were a kid. Seeing something like that scars you."

I nodded, though it didn't seem like it scarred Santi, and I knew men in the Cosa Nostra were young when they were pulled into the underworld. Truthfully, men in the Cosa Nostra were molded into ruthless men. Some were just more ruthless than others. I overheard Luigi once say that Santi was a ruthless, deadly combination of flame and gunpowder. His impending wealth and position as the future don had everyone bowing to him before he could speak his first words. Of course, the same was true for Luigi.

"Did it scar you?" I asked, turning my face to look at him.

"Can't say that it did. It's different with you though." He released my hand, and I already missed his warmth. "You grew up away from all this, the Cosa Nostra and this way of life. Probably a good thing. You kept your innocence, your light."

I tilted my head.

He thought me innocent. Hardly!

The hunger to avenge my mother and kill every single member of the Venezuelan Cartel burned with such acid within my chest, I was scared it would swallow me whole sometimes. My eyes traveled over his hand on the wheel and the other on his gear shift. His knuckles on both hands were always bruised. Today it was because of me.

"I want to find them all and kill them," I whispered my shameful admission. It was the first time I had spoken the words out loud. "I don't think I'm that innocent."

Santi's nostrils flared. "They deserve to die."

His expression was so intense, my heart rattled in my chest in the most painful way.

"But can we be the judge and the jury?" I whispered.

He arched an eyebrow and then shrugged. "The first man I killed deserved to die," he said, surprising me with his admission. "He trafficked women and tried to force them to work as prostitutes in Russo territory."

"Oh." It wasn't what I expected him to say. I always assumed they killed people that didn't want to pay them some kind of protection fee. Dad and my brothers kept me out of all their business, so I resorted to Al Pàcino and Robert De Niro movies to figure out the whole mafia business. "I guess he deserved it then."

I remained quiet thinking over his words while the soft words of an unknown country song filled the car. I wasn't sure what kind of station played country songs right after Sia. It didn't seem to mix well together. He pulled over in front of my grandmother's Fifth Avenue penthouse.

Neither one of us moved, waiting.

"My mom loved country music," I muttered, not really sure where I was going with it. "The really old country songs. I don't know why. It didn't fit with her style, you know." I turned my head to find Santi's eyes on me. "She wore the latest trends, stunning designer clothes and shoes. And then she'd turn on her CD player and an old Willie Nelson song would come on. Or Alan Jackson and George Strait. I wanted to ask her why she loved it so much. I felt like there was a reason, but I figured I'd ask her one day when I was older. Or getting married." My lip trembled and I bit into it, to hide how upset I was. My chest aches so damn much right now. "I didn't know time would run out." I glanced up at the skyrise. The entire building belonged to my grandmother. "I asked Grandma, but she didn't even know Mom liked country music."

Returning my eyes to Santi, I drowned in his gaze, sadness filling me down to the marrow of my bones. I forced a smile. "I'm just being stupid. It has been three years since they…" I swallowed hard, unable to say the words. "Anyhow, in the grand scheme of things, worse things happen to people. At least with the man you killed, you saved many women. I'm just not sure what Mom and George's deaths accomplished. And it makes me scared because I'm blind to what the cartel wanted exactly."

It didn't seem that a blood relation to the old cartel was reason enough to go through the trouble of kidnapping, torture, and murder.

Santi's hand came to my face, pulling my head close to him, then he pressed his lips to my forehead. It was an older brother gesture, but I soaked it in.

"Don't ever be scared, Amore." I felt his hot breath against my skin on my forehead. "Your father and brothers would tear down this world to keep you safe, so would your grandmother. And I… the Russo family, would burn it all down for you."

I nodded and knew right then and there that I had lost my heart. My sixteen-year-old heart crushed on Santino Russo hard.

"Thanks," I rasped, my voice full of thick emotion.

"Let's take you to your tower, kiddo," he added teasingly, trying to ease the tension. "I'll get your bag."

We both exited the car, and he threw wrapped bills of money to the valet. "Keep it here and safe. I'm coming right back."

"Hi, Derek," I greeted the valet guy. He has worked for Grandma for as long as I have visited her. I guess that would be four years now. "How are your wife and baby?"

"Miss Bennetti, nice to see you again." He smiled wide and waved his hand. "Wife and baby are doing well. Thank you for the gift. My wife loved it."

I grinned. "Excellent. I'm so glad."

Santi nudged me forward, his hand wrapped around my elbow.

We passed the doorman and I waved to him. Santi wasn't the chitchat type, so we continued without stopping. We strode to the elevator where he pressed the button and the door slid open. We entered and I leaned over to push the button for the penthouse.

"It's triggered by my fingerprint," I explained. He handed me my bag, and I unzipped it to grab my phone when I dropped my drawing pad, my drawings falling all over the floor.

"Damn it," I muttered, and we both knelt at the same time to pick them up. I saw from the corner of my eye that he looked at each one of them. Embarrassment shot through me. I wasn't bad but I had a long way to go before I was good.

"These are very good," he commended. He studied the drawing that I hoped Grandma would allow me to turn into a real dress. It was a deep blue strapless dress that cascaded down to the floor with a small train in the back. "Great, actually."

I smiled and my cheeks warmed up. "Thanks. I'm just playing around with it. I want to ask Grandma if she'd let me turn one of them into a product."

"She is stupid if she doesn't."

"Ummm, I still have a lot to learn."

The elevator dinged, signaling we were at the top floor, and the door slid open.

"There you are!" The elevator opened directly into Grandma's elaborate living room, and she was there waiting for me in front of it.

"Hi, Grandma," I greeted. "Remember Santi?"

She raised her eyebrows, and her gaze narrowed on him. She was a petite woman, but everything about her was so regal that you couldn't help but act with reverence. Though it didn't seem to have the same impact on Santi. He eyed her with cold eyes, and I almost swore there was a challenge in his gaze.

"Vaguely," she retorted. "You are Santiago Russo's son, right?"

"Yes."

"Well, I hope you are less trouble than your father was at your age."

"Grandma!"

Santi's lips curved into an almost cruel smile. "I can guarantee you I am more trouble than my father ever was."

I chuckled, amused at his answer, but immediately stifled it when Grandmother's gaze snapped to me.

"I knew your father and Amore's father when they were both your age. They were enemies and here they are today, miracle of all miracles, working together."

I wasn't sure what she was hinting at, but I didn't like it. She has always been against Dad, even when he tried to work with her. There was no need to keep egging him on, and she certainly shouldn't be insulting the Russos.

"Don't be rude, Nonna."

Her eyebrows scrunched in distaste at the title, which I rarely ever used because she hated it. Her eyes, so similar to mine, locked on me, and I held her gaze. Then she smiled, like nothing had happened.

"Excellent," she said and strode away.

I turned to Santi, who was looking after my grandmother, his brows furrowed in annoyance.

"Sorry about that," I apologized on her behalf.

His eyes came back to me. "Don't worry about it." He didn't seem worried but the crease between his brows remained. "What was that about?"

I shrugged. "She is like a major diva and sometimes just walks away. Or she was mad because I called her *Nonna*. She hates that."

"Huh?"

"I know, weird."

"Kind of like you hate it when I call you *kiddo*?" A grin flashed on his face, and I couldn't help but smile.

"Yeah, kind of like that. You don't have to be a pain in the ass, Santi, and rub it in."

He winked, his beautiful lips curved into a half-smile, and then tucked his hands into his pockets. "You are safe now. Have fun on your trip, kiddo. I have to get going."

I groaned out loud as his eyes danced mischievously. He knew exactly how to get to me.

"I won't bring you a present back from Italy," I retorted dryly as he entered the elevator.

Before he was blocked from my view, he flashed me another smile, and I realized that I had seen Santi smile more today than in the last three years.

CHAPTER 7

Amore

TWO YEARS LATER

I t was always the same when I went to the Russo's.

It didn't matter that I was just shy of eighteen and was way too old to be crushing on my best friend's brother. But despite all my efforts, my fascination with Santi refused to ease. My heart fluttered each time I thought of him, he was the hero of all my dreams. I hadn't seen him in months and could barely contain my excitement at a chance to have a glimpse of him.

I'll turn eighteen this weekend, but I still wouldn't be old enough for him, yet my heart couldn't care less. It was fixated on him and only him. There was no rhyme or reason to my infatuation over him. I have seen plenty of other handsome boys, but none of them mattered to me.

Maybe I needed to meet more boys in order to forget Santino. I didn't hang out with anyone except my brothers and the Russo boys. Scratch that, the Russo boy, namely Adriano. Santi I barely saw, but I was always painfully aware of his presence around the city. Though I suspected he was busy dealing with the same issues as my father and brothers.

Uncle Vincent dropped me off at the front door of the Russo residence and promptly my heart jittered.

"Want me to walk you in?" he offered.

After Elena had purposely given him the wrong times to get me from school and left a window open for anyone to hurt me, he took it upon himself to be extra diligent about my drop-offs and pick-ups. He even went on my extra-curricular trips with me. The latter wasn't really welcome, but thankfully, the high school years were coming to an end in just a few weeks.

"No, that's okay," I told him, smiling.

"One of these days, these Russo boys will break your heart," he muttered. He didn't like me hanging out with them. He marveled at the fact that Dad allowed it. Of course, any other boy would have been dead, but he allowed me freedom to hang out with Adriano. "And then I'll have to break their knee caps."

I chuckled at the image that generated in my mind. He could never succeed in winning against Santi. He was ruthless and strong, and nobody could touch him. Adriano was strong too, and even if he succeeded with Adriano, Santi would go after Vincent.

"I won't let them break my heart," I promised with a grin. I pressed a kiss to his cheek, then reached for my door handle. "And I like you alive better than dead. So please don't even try to break their knee caps, then I don't have to worry about Santi coming for your poor knees."

He grinned and pressed his hand over his heart. "Ahhh, she likes me."

I pulled on the door handle. "I have always liked you," I said. "Don't wait for my text. Adriano will bring me home."

"I figured, but if something changes, you call me."

"You have a hot date tonight," I teased him. "Enjoy it."

Uncle Vincent was a famous bachelor. He looked good, at least ten years younger than his fifty-six, with streaks of silver through his black hair. Women in their mid-twenties chased him. He was always put together, wearing a wrinkle-free suit and behaved like a gentleman, but he never hesitated to carry out Dad's orders. All the men in this world were brutal, some more than others. Considering what I witnessed when I was thirteen, you'd think knowledge of their brutality would terrify me. But it made me feel safer. I was certain the more brutality these men had, the safer I would be. As long as I didn't see them pull out guns on each other.

Did it make sense? No, it absolutely didn't.

I shut the car door and waved him off, then turned around to face the narrow building in front of me. While we lived in a quiet, spacious community on Long Island, the Russo family lived in the middle of Brooklyn. When I first met them, they lived in the Bronx. Well, Adriano and Mr. Russo did. Santi lived in Brooklyn. He bought himself a house his last year of college, and a few years ago, he bought his papà a place in Brooklyn too. I guess it was too much driving back and forth between neighborhoods when they worked so closely together. I heard while Mrs. Russo was alive, they lived on Long Island too, but I didn't know where. Adriano told me she was killed on the street by a rival family. Santi and his father eliminated that family from existence. He didn't elaborate further, and I didn't want to ask, the wounds of a dead mother still fresh for me.

Though it made me want to be like Santi and hunt down all those men that killed Mom and George.

One day. Very soon.

DeAngelo said I was ready. The years of training had paid off. We had started to gather information about Venezuela, working off my memories.

The door opened even before I rang the bell, and Maria, Mr. Russo's housekeeper, held the door for me.

"Amore." She beamed. "So good to see you. Where were you last week? I needed our womanly interaction."

I laughed at her calling me a woman. Santi certainly didn't see me as one. He didn't even see me as a girl. I was convinced he thought of me as his younger sibling, or something close to it.

"I was at Grandma's." She rolled her eyes as she nudged me inside. "Ah, Amore. You'll be a wonderful heiress one day. A perfect Regalè."

"Don't let Grandma hear you," I retorted. "It will make her head even bigger."

We both laughed as we walked into the living room. Mr. Russo and Adriano were both there, the former reading the paper and the latter on his iPhone. Mr. Russo and my father were similar in so many ways that I couldn't understand why they didn't get along before. I often wondered what made them quarrel, rather than be best friends. They were the same age, went to the same school, had the same interests, and their fathers were members of the Cosa Nostra and ran the mafia of New York together. Together they were stronger.

"Hello, Mr. Russo." He sat in his rocking chair. He was the only human besides my own father that still read the actual paper.

"Ahhh, Amore." His dark eyes lit up. "I was wondering when you'd come around again. It's been a few days. A week to be exact."

I grinned. "I had to work my free time at Regalè Corp, but I'm back now."

Adriano came up to me and lifted me off the ground. "And we missed you."

A giggle escaped me. "Really? You weren't too busy?"

"I'm never too busy for my girl," he drawled.

"Well, I'm glad you said that, Russo, because I'm here to collect. Time to pay up and with interest!"

Mr. Russo and Adriano both threw their heads back and laughed.

"Collect what?" I whipped around and my cheeks instantly blushed at seeing Santi. He appeared at my back, wearing a three piece with a gun holster clearly visible. My heartbeat sped up like a rollercoaster. Crushing on boys was such an inconvenience, but I couldn't stop it with Santi any more than I could stop breathing.

Of course, he was nowhere to be seen when I dressed up cute, but today, when Uncle Vincent brought me straight from school, Santi would be here. I wore my school uniform with my skirt that came to mid-thigh, leaving my legs bare. I tied my white blouse into a knot, leaving a glimpse of my belly exposed. It was May and another one of those warm spring days.

His gaze studied me, clinically, like a big brother, disapproval in his eyes. Yes, my school uniform skirt was shorter than it should be, but I looked cute. At least I thought so until right now. Now I felt like a kid that attempted to dress up and failed miserably.

God, I was dying for him to see me like a woman.

It had been a while since I had seen Santi. Somehow we kept passing each other, though usually each time I visited the Russo residence, I was stupidly dressing nice in the hopes that I'd see him. I loved nice clothes and most of it I designed myself, but I never had self-doubt until I dressed in hopes of impressing Santi. Then I doubted every piece of clothing.

I collected myself and forced a calming breath.

"He owes me a driving lesson," I announced, hiding my crush behind a wide smile. "I need another two weeks' worth of hours."

I was late in getting a driver's license. Initially, I wasn't overly pressed. Plus, I had a slight phobia of driving. After all, I had crashed and dinged a good number of vehicles. Just thinking about getting behind the wheel had me breaking into a sweat, but I had to bite the bullet. I was dealing with a lot of things head-on lately.

Working out a plan with DeAngelo's help to find my mother's killers.

Finishing high school.

College.

Learning to drive.

The latter one, I did begrudgingly.

Adriano groaned. "Jesus, I was hoping you'd forget."

Spending this last school year without Adriano, I realized how much I was lacking in my independence. It sucked to depend on others for a ride. So, I finally bit the bullet and started the process of getting a license. Hopefully, without destroying any more vehicles.

"Not this time, Russo," I teased him.

"Let me go get my helmet," Adriano half-joked, and I smacked him playfully. "I want to survive to graduate college. It was the whole purpose of getting you to help me with my assignments," he grumbled.

He was at NYU and in his last year. I hoped to go to NYU too, but a better opportunity came up. I'd study in Italy and work in one of Grandma's offices in Milan. The plan was to leave for Italy after the summer. Grandma and Dad agreed on one more thing, miracles of all miracles. I would live in Milan, and I honestly couldn't wait. Vincent and Lorenzo were coming with me. DeAngelo too.

"You didn't really need my help," I told him. "Now stop stalling, go get your stupid helmet, and let's go. I'm not getting any younger, and my driver's license is within my grasp."

Mr. Russo chuckled. "You heard the girl, Adriano."

"You should wait another year before you start driving," Adriano recommended with a smirk on his face. "You shouldn't drive in Italy, and you'll be out of practice when you get back home."

"Italy, huh?" Santi asked, crossing his strong arms and leaning against the doorframe.

Ah, he was the perfect Italian.

"Yep. End of the summer." I grinned happily. "I can't wait."

I could see the outline of his muscles under his fine clothing and my pulse skyrocketed. I wanted to see Santi in a bathing suit so desperately. I could only imagine how strong his body was underneath that three-piece suit, that olive skin covering his ripped abs. He was every girls' wet dream.

I groaned silently, mentally scolding myself. These hormones were killing me slowly and sweetly. My imagination fed my poisonous dreams.

At twenty-six, Santi had the world and women at his feet. I was nothing but a kid with a snotty nose to him.

Santi's eyes observed me. "You'll burn like a tomato," he remarked, referring to my fair skin tone. Unlike my father, my brothers, and the Russo men, I was fair skinned. There wasn't a hint of olive skin on me, but thankfully, I tanned to a light golden.

"Well, there is this thing called sunscreen," I retorted dryly.

His lips twitched into a smile. It was weird because Adriano told me Santi barely ever smiled and though he was always serious, he'd always smiled when I challenged him.

"Amore is probably looking forward to some freedom," Mr. Russo chimed in, with a knowing look in his eyes. "It will be good for you and Adriano to get some space from each other."

I frowned at the odd comment. "I'll miss him. He'll come and visit." Turning my eyes to my best friend, I asked, "Right, Adriano? We said October."

"Yes, we did. I'll chase all those Italians away."

I shook my head. "Aren't you Italian too?" I mocked him lightly. He just shrugged. "Now go get your helmet. Or don't, I don't care. I want to drive, and I'm not depending on you or any other man for the rest of my life."

"Ahhh, Amore. Now you sound like your grandmother." Mr. Russo sounded amused.

I shook my head. "Somehow I have a feeling that is not a compliment," I joked.

"Your grandmother might be a stubborn woman, but she is incredibly strong and smart." It was the first nice thing any man of the Cosa Nostra uttered out loud about the great Regina Regalè. Mr. Russo chuckled at my widened eyes. "We might not like her, but it would be foolish to discredit her."

"Hmmmm."

"You know, Amore, most women in our world don't drive," Adriano muttered, pushing his hand through his hair. He was trying desperately to get out of his debt.

"Well, I'm not most women," I reprimanded him. "And I won't marry into this world, so I have to drive. Now pay up, Adriano."

"How do you know you won't marry anyone in this world?" Santino asked curiously.

I smiled. "Because my grandma would never allow her fortune into this world. I didn't grow up in this world, and I won't die in it either."

Santi raised his eyebrow. "You seem sure."

I shrugged. The only man that I'd stay in the world of the Cosa Nostra for was Santi. "I am."

Adriano put his hand on his heart. "Oh my heart! You wouldn't marry me?"

I chuckled at his goofball ways. "If you teach me how to drive, I might."

"Ah, sneaky, sneaky."

"And take me to have some ice cream," I quickly added.

"Well, now you are getting greedy."

"Kind of a downgrade from sneaking into parties," Santi retorted sarcastically, and I glared at him. Adriano and I still attended parties but usually with DeAngelo's attendance to ensure I was safe.

"We could do that too, you know," I challenged, tilting my chin up. "After all, we are older and wiser now."

Amusement flickered in his eyes; his stare slightly condescending.

"You are playing with fire, kiddo."

He fucking insisted on calling me kiddo, and I hated it. He knew I disliked it. My chest and face warmed, anger itching my skin.

Santi is a jackass and didn't deserve my girl crush.

Turning my eyes away from Santi, because staring at the man for too long wasn't good for my health, I focused on my best friend and Mr. Russo.

"You better make the girl happy, Adriano," Mr. Russo chimed in, probably sensing the silent battle between his eldest son and me. "Go get your helmet and teach Amore how to drive. Then take her to have some ice cream."

Adriano grumbled. "You wouldn't say that if you saw her drive. New York City is a safer place without Amore Bennetti behind the wheel." I glared at him in fake disdain but couldn't keep my lips from twitching. He continued complaining, "Why do you need a license? Vincent drives you everywhere. Learn to drive in Italy."

I leaned against the wall, still in my school uniform. "No."

"I don't want you to kill another beautiful machine," Adriano whined. "You totaled my Viper, scratched my Mustang. We won't even list your father's cars you damaged."

I glared at him. "Just stop being a baby and go get your helmet or body shield. You owe me. I might even buy *you* ice cream."

My voice sounded more agitated than I felt towards my best friend, and it was all his brother's fault.

"You are richer than the Kardashians and Steve Jobs combined," Adriano grumbled as he went off, and I rolled my eyes at his back. "You should buy me ice cream."

"Technically, my grandmother is," I yelled after him.

Both Santi and Mr. Russo shook their heads as I remained behind waiting for Adriano to get ready.

"Business went well?" Mr. Russo asked Santi, the two shared a fleeting glance, and after Santi's short nod, Mr. Russo went back to reading his paper.

Everyone in the Bennetti and Russo families always spoke in codes. I learned not to pay attention to it, though sometimes I couldn't help but be curious.

"So, Amore, I gather driving is not going well?" Santi's voice shattered through my thoughts. "Still, huh?"

I eyed him suspiciously. Was he making fun of me?

"I'm doing okay with it," I answered him hesitantly. I wouldn't give him ammunition to continue looking at me as a kid.

"What's the problem?"

"I said I'm doing okay," I muttered, slightly agitated.

He took off his jacket, then rolled up his sleeves, and I stared at his forearms. My gulp sounded too loud in the room. The gun holster was completely overlooked as I studied his physique. That right tattooed hand of his alone was attractive. Put it together with the entire Santino Russo package and you were doomed. Because his appeal was magnetic. There was something so unhinged in his controlled nature, so different from Adriano's energy. My heartbeat raced and my ears buzzed with adrenaline. I liked Santi's hints of his psychotic and unhinged ways.

Restless heat snaked through my veins. I didn't completely understand this response to him, but I knew this crush on Santi Russo had to go. I should leave for Italy pronto. Pronto! Maybe Dad could allow me to go a few weeks earlier so I could get settled.

Yet, even as I thought about leaving, I regretted a future without Santi in it.

"Don't worry, Amore." Mr. Russo put his paper down, watching me. "I remember when your mother learned to drive. She was smart as a whip, but it took her a bit to get comfortable behind the wheel."

A swish of air got stuck in my lungs.

"Really?" My voice sounded strange to my own ears, like someone else was speaking. "How do you know?" I swallowed hard. "Grandma said her driver taught Mom how to drive."

It was true. When I told Grandma I was struggling with driving, she offered her driver, Anthony. I was tempted to take the offer when she said he taught Mom how to drive but then decided against it.

Mr. Russo chuckled. "No. Your father and I taught Margaret how to drive."

"You?"

He nodded and went back to reading his paper. I glanced at Santi, but I couldn't tell by his expression whether he knew this or not.

"Why would you both teach her to drive?" I questioned him, unwilling to let it go. "How did she get to know you both? I thought she met Dad in his restaurant?"

"She did," he replied, lowering his paper. "Bennetti and I opened that restaurant together to clean money." I frowned at that admission. "Of course, we are no longer cleaning money there." I shook my head. It was the most I was ever told directly about this world. "She came and we both noticed her. Of course, she picked him."

Was he telling me what I thought he was telling me? I wasn't sure. I peeked around the corner to make sure Adriano couldn't hear me. I wasn't sure whether he should hear this or not.

"Ummm, Mr. Russo, are you saying..."—I searched for a word that wouldn't sound too vulgar.--"... that you and Dad... hmmm... had a crush on my mom?"

He chuckled. "That is one way of putting it. It was what caused the wedge in our families."

I frowned. This was getting more bizarre by the minute. Santi didn't seem surprised by his father's admission.

"But weren't you married?"

"Ah, Amore. You have a lot to learn about this world. Your mother was forbidden to both of us, but with unparalleled beauty and connections that we wanted to capitalize on, it made us both act reckless." Why did his words hit me wrong? It was the first thing that made me not like him, and by the look on his face, I could tell he knew it. I blew an unruly curl out of my face. "I didn't say it was right. Maybe one day you'll understand."

Suddenly, I didn't want to talk about it anymore. I'd much rather be scrutinized by Santi for my driving and argue with him about my kiddo title than discuss my mother and two men that seemed to have an infatuation with her all those years ago.

I turned my head and locked eyes with Santi. In his dark gaze, I found my calm and safety.

"My reflexes are not good, and it makes my driving bad," I said. I swallowed hard, hoping both men would allow me this subject change. I wasn't ready to hear more about Mr. Russo and my mother. A blush colored my cheeks, whether it was due to my admission at my poor driving, or that I wasn't ready to hear more, I wasn't sure.

"What's wrong with your reflexes?" Santi asked, his soft tone washing over me like the comfort of the warm southern sun. I wanted to soak up his warmth and keep it with me forever.

There were so many secrets around me. They started unraveling the day Mom and I set foot in South America, and they questioned her about who Grandpa left in charge of the Perèz Cartel. Something about a broken vow. I didn't even know he was head of the Perèz Cartel. Jesus Christ! We ran a fashion empire, not a criminal empire. Everyone kept me in the dark, sheltering me from the past. Instead of helping, it left me blind and vulnerable. It left me to make a fatal decision. Now Mom was dead, and I was the only one left. I wasn't only heiress to the Regalè fashion empire but also to the Venezuelan Perèz Cartel. Except, I wanted nothing to do with it.

Mr. Russo's comment about Mom's connections confirmed that Dad knew my heritage. Both dons did. Yet, nobody bothered to explain it to me. My bodyguard, DeAngelo, was the only one that believed leaving me clueless made me vulnerable. I agreed. DeAngelo's family was part of the Colombian Cartel that rescued me from the jungle five years ago.

I wanted to talk about it with Santi so bad. He lived and breathed this stuff. He could help me do it safely and successfully. After all, he had cleaned out New York City of his enemies. But I didn't dare to ask him for help with this. I knew he was ruthless when it came to hunting his enemies, but he also had certain notions about responsibilities of women versus men. And I couldn't be certain that he wouldn't try to use me for my connections to the cartel.

I refused to be used. I had a promise to keep, and it was important to me that I succeed. No, I couldn't risk telling Santi. While he didn't mind keeping my outings from my father, he wouldn't keep something like that from him.

"Amore, what's wrong with your reflexes?" he repeated.

I shrugged, acting nonchalant while every fiber of me screamed against the silence and the secrets. "The instructor said I keep getting sidetracked."

"Maybe you should hold off driving and let your Uncle Vincent drive you? After all, he'll be with you in Italy." Santino's suggestion made sense, but it pissed me off, and he read it in my eyes. He just chuckled, unperturbed. "You wouldn't want to cause an accident, would you?"

I flinched with an old memory that flashed in my mind.

"You'll get in trouble and cause an international incident. Stay put and no jungle trotting in a hunt for the orchids." My mother's voice was a clear command. There wasn't much she forbade me, but this one she was adamant about. I should have listened. Curiosity was my downfall. And George's too. He came up to me and assured me it would be fine. So, we snuck out and went trekking through the jungle.

The most beautiful, delicate, and exotic orchids grew in that area of Colombia. I wanted to see them firsthand so I could use them for a new dress I was drawing. The flower grew on trees, and a local told me there were many orchids of different colors growing there. It was the only spot in the world that they grew. They were almost extinct, but she told me close to the Venezuelian border, only ten miles from our current location, you could find an abundance of them.

I quickly pushed the memory away and caught Santi's eyes on me. He noticed too much, everything. His dark eyes drilled into me, as if he could see into my mind.

"I'm back, baby." Adriano came back at that moment grinning widely, and I tore my gaze away from his hot, older brother.

He wore his standard jeans, hugging his legs, and a white t-shirt that accentuated his build, a helmet in his hands. He was good looking and there were plenty of girls fawning over him. I was quite content being his best friend. Crushing after one Russo was bad enough.

"Got the helmet, I see." I narrowed my eyes on him. "Jerk."

He brought his other hand forward. "I brought one for you too," he joked, and my cheeks flushed.

"Double jerk," I spat. "For that, I'll be sure to scrape your side of the car."

"We'll see you at your birthday party, Amore," Mr. Russo said, interrupting our dispute. Since I moved to New York, Dad always threw a birthday party for me, and the Russos were always invited. So was my grandmother, very reluctantly.

"See you, Mr. Russo," I said as Adriano pulled me along. "Santino." I tilted my head and headed out the door into the warm spring day.

More than likely, I wouldn't see Santi for another few months. He hadn't been to my birthday party in several years.

CHAPTER 8

Santino

Considering Adriano and Amore were joined at the hip, I didn't see Amore often. I had my own place, and somehow we kept hitting up Pà's house at different times. But each time we crossed paths she had grown another few inches.

It made me feel like a perv seeing her dressed in that school uniform. Did her father let her walk out of the house like that? It was clear her uniform was a lot shorter than school code. I had plenty of girls in my high school years to know how they pushed the dress code limits.

Amore was no exception.

Her long slender legs left a lot to the imagination. I wasn't into girls, and she'd forever be that little girl crying that needed saving to me. But I'd be a blind man not to see Amore had grown. She was still a kid to me, but there was no mistake she'd be a gorgeous woman one day. A knockout.

You'd drown in a sea of green staring into those eyes. Like sparkling emeralds. They were the most striking green I had ever seen. With her red curls, you'd think she was Irish. Her father was don of the East Side, and her mother came from one of the most prestigious and well-known Manhattan families. The Regalè family owned a multi-billion-dollar fashion company, and Amore Bennetti was its sole heiress.

She had come a long way from that kid who sat in front of our restaurant crying on the sidewalk. Every once in a while, I'd still see that shattered look in her eyes, like today for a fleeting second. But most of the time, she was a happy kid.

The way she tilted her head was like a queen greeting her subjects. There might be vulnerability in her but also some incredible strength and a regal manner. After all, she was Regina's heiress. One day, she'd be one of the wealthiest women in the world. I was by no means broke, but the millions I owned didn't scratch the surface of the Regalè fortune.

She and Adriano had always been close. Even with Adriano being in college, there wasn't a day that went by where they didn't speak.

Amore Bennetti didn't know it, but the day she stepped onto Russo territory, she brought peace to two ruling families of the Cosa Nostra. Her old man and my old man came to terms and stopped sparring. Instead, we joined forces and started eliminating the Venezuelan Cartel from the city. The problem was that they kept coming back. It had something to do with her heritage, I was certain of it.

It was the main reason her old man agreed to send her to Italy. It was safer for her there than here.

I knew my father and Bennetti had a fallout over a woman. They both wanted her, but she chose Bennetti. But pride was a hard thing to swallow, and Bennetti ended up losing her too, just in a different manner.

Seeing his daughter off to Italy would be hard for Savio. Hell, it would be a hard one for my father too. He liked her being around. In another few weeks, she'd graduate high school, and at the end of the summer, she'd move to Italy. Adriano already planned weeks to visit her as much as possible over the next four years.

Like I said, joined at the hip.

My eyes darkened, and so did my mood as I stood in the midst of the container of dead bodies. There wasn't much that churned my stomach, but this sight did. There were girls as young as twelve and as old as fifty, all dressed in white nightgowns. It made me want to rage, to fly to Venezuela and burn the motherfuckers to ashes. Leave nobody alive.

Rivalry was one thing, but butchering women was something entirely different. And the Perèz Cartel wasn't even trying to hide it. A "P" logo was branded into the back of each woman's hand.

The Perèz Cartel was causing too much trouble. No matter how many of them I killed off, more sprouted. It was like a damn hydra, each time you cut off one head, two more emerged.

Things escalated the night that Venezuelan scumbag attacked Amore, which was almost two years ago. On the surface, it looked like there was no connection between the dead guy and the Perèz Cartel. Amore insisted he was cartel and I believed her. After all, you don't just forget your mother's killer. So, we dug deeper and found the connection.

The Venezuelans were back to selling heroin on Cosa Nostra territory. And were fixated on the Bennetti girl. Suddenly, it looked like Amore and her mother weren't targeted randomly. There was a lot more to this story than a random kidnapping by the cartel. The question was why they would target them considering neither Amore nor her mother participated in the underworld activities—before or after the old Perèz's death.

Papà agreed. In an effort to somewhat preserve Amore's perception of her freedom and independence and not send her into a panic, we set up men all around New York to keep an eye out. Everyone knew her and wouldn't dare look the other way if someone attempted something. Besides, DeAngelo was one of the best, and he kept his sights firmly on her, like she was the apple of his eye. Bennetti had increased the number of men watching his territories too.

There was one thing I disagreed on with Pà and Bennetti.

They both refused to believe the Venezuelans would dare cross the territory. Bennetti said they had too much to lose. From where I stood, it looked like they had too much to gain. They'd expand their territory over the Costra Nostra and try to overtake New York. I wouldn't let that happen. So, crossing into the Cosa Nostra territory resulted in their death. For any member of the Perèz Cartel that dared to step foot into our city.

I ran his information by my contact at the DEA. Imagine my surprise when I found out that the prick was the kid of George Anderson, the man that Amore believed to be her father for her first thirteen years. Of course, I couldn't keep that piece of information from Bennetti. He was just as surprised when I told him. His only concern was Amore's safety. I cared about her safety too, but I also cared about keeping the Cosa Nostra on top and all my territory. Because I knew if we fell to the Perèz Cartel, then none of us would be able to keep her safe.

The question was how did George Anderson's son become connected to the Venezuelan cartel and Perèz Rothschild?

Even more intriguing was that there wasn't a counterattack, unless they didn't know who killed him.

My phone rang. I glanced at the caller ID. It was Amore. She rarely called. Scratch that, she never called, but to answer her call now, it felt wrong. She wasn't part of this world. I didn't particularly like her grandmother, but I agreed with her on that point. Amore Bennetti didn't belong among the Cosa Nostra. Even less among the cartel.

The men of our world would eat her alive. Heck, sometimes I thought Adriano would eat her alive. She let him get away with way too much. She was rather self-sufficient but letting a made man get away with so much was a recipe for disaster.

I declined the call then silenced the phone. Adriano was with her. He'd call if there was trouble. He hasn't repeated the incident from that night when the Venezuelan scumbag almost got his hands on Amore. It sickened me to think she could have been one of these girls. No woman should ever find herself in this position; at the mercy of monsters that were willing to trade them like stock.

We did plenty of shit, smuggled drugs, guns, sold them with high profits, but we didn't sell women. The ruling families of the Cosa Nostra had a standing agreement. Hell, it was one of the rare things all five ruling families agreed on.

This dock location was owned by my shell company. It had a prime spot due to its isolation. The Colombian Cartel was our prime drug supplier.

We had waited for our shipment of crates with the product we intended to distribute throughout the East Coast. Instead, we had death delivered to our door.

I unlocked my phone and shot a message to Carrera. Gabriel Carrera ran the Colombian cartel. Out in the normal world, his name was whispered in fear and his presence avoided at all cost. In our world, he was another ruthless bastard, just like the rest of us.

But he proved to be a worthy and useful ally. Much like my own father, his was still around but had handed the reins of the business over to his son.

The food didn't arrive. Restaurant is poisoned.

The message was coded but he'd understand. He sent me a vomiting emoji back, and that guy hated fucking emojis. Someone was pissed, and together, we'd tear the motherfuckers down. He hated the Venezuelans; a personal, family vendetta that had been going on for quite a few years.

CHAPTER 9

Santino

"Thanks for meeting me so soon." Luigi strode toward us. Renzo and I just arrived.

It was only yesterday that I saw Amore when Adriano took her out for a driving lesson.

An hour ago, a call came in from Bennetti's brother. Vincent barely ever called me, but whatever this was, it was bad because the old Bennetti and his son were so shaken up, they couldn't make the call. It was the only reason I agreed to meet. Renzo and I were dealing with plenty of our own shit after that container of dead bodies was dropped on our doorstep.

I watched Luigi, his face ashen white. I have never seen him like that. "What's going on?"

We were at the docks in New Jersey. It was where Benentti usually got his shipments since all the docks in New York were owned by the Russo family. Every once in a while, he would have to re-route it, and we'd come to a mutual agreement allowing him to use ours. But I liked to keep my business mine, and he obviously liked to keep his business private too. After all, you never knew when you'd become rivals again.

"We got a shipment," he started but visibly gulped, his eyes were wide, and a slight line of perspiration glistened across his forehead. "Our product didn't arrive but in its place..."

My gaze flickered to the warehouse where the shipment was more than likely stored. Bennetti was lighting up a cigarette, his hands shaking. The last time I saw Bennetti light a cigarette was when he found out his wife was torturing his daughter.

"Yes?" I encouraged him.

Luigi pushed his hand through his hair. "You better come and see it for yourself."

Renzo and I shared a look. I couldn't fathom what got them all worked up so bad. We followed him in silence towards the open warehouse.

"Bennetti," I greeted him.

"Russo," Amore's old man acknowledged me.

My eyes darted around the shipping container. "What the fuck?"

The image was almost like deja vu, except every single dead woman in this container had red hair.

Like Amore.

Almost the same shade, but not quite. I counted twenty girls around Amore's age, of a similar build and all dead. Some with their eyes closed while others, with their dead gaze, stared into a void. The last thing they saw was terror, and you could see hints of dirt and traces of tears smeared on their deathly pale skin.

No wonder old Bennetti was so shaken up. At first glance, every single one of these women could pass as Amore.

I took another step and lowered onto my one knee. I took a strand of one dead woman's hair into my hand.

Colored. Her hair was colored.

This was a message. It was a coordinated attack. First my shipment yesterday and now this. I'd bet my dick and my life on it. This wasn't a coincidence.

Dropping the strand of the dead girl's hair, I looked up at Luigi. "Any message?"

His eyes traveled to the wall behind me where there was a note pinned. I stood up, careful not to step on any bodies. These women deserve at least that much respect.

Fuck! So much unnecessary death!

I read the pinned paper.

Sins of the father are the daughter's to pay.

You crumbled my empire.

Now I'll crumble yours.

Blood for blood.

It's her turn to scream.

Rage as cold as ice shot through my veins, and my teeth clenched with fury, making my jaw hurt. Death surrounded us, women that could be Amore but weren't.... a warning. They didn't have her, but they were coming for her. The question was why?

Regardless of the reason, one thing was for sure. They had signed their death warrant. I would kill every one of those fuckers. There would be no mercy from me. My ears buzzed and blood pumped through my veins feeding the inferno, making me see red.

Fiery rage.

Crimson blood.

Scarlet hair.

I inhaled a deep breath, the smell of death and blood mixing in my lungs. Then my eyes locked on a woman, her eyes a pale blue, staring into nothingness. Wrong eyes. I needed to focus my mind on the green gaze, the colors of cool moss that soothed me from within. I needed a clear head. If I was to protect Amore, I needed a clear mind and lethal aim.

I re-read the message. The message was clearly for Savio. *Blood for blood.* The question was were they coming for Savio's blood or Amore's? If this container was any indication, my bet would be they were coming for Amore. In order to make her father pay.

Turning back to Luigi, I hardened my gaze and my tone.

"Amore can't stay in New York."

CHAPTER 10

Santino

I threw the bloody clothes into the fireplace of my office and lit the match. The fireplace came in handy, more than once, for burning evidence. We came back from our raid in Harlem barely an hour ago. It was rather bloody and deadly, for them. I had to clean up in my private bathroom before getting to my office work.

I was still annoyed that the most important one got away. He was the one we needed. That fucker was after Amore.

Carrera got a tip. The men that dumped those dead women on my dock were hiding in Harlem. We didn't hesitate.

I had a weapons room in most of my establishments that I used for business. I tucked one gun in the back of my pants and one in my holster.

"Help yourself," I offered Carrera. He had his own weapons, but I'd rather go straight to the location and deal with this than take a detour.

With a nod, he stepped forward and armored himself with knives and a couple of guns.

"This next thing might take the relations with Venezuelans to a whole new level," Gabriel said. "Are you ready for it?"

He studied me, expression grim.

"They took it to a whole new level when they dropped a container full of dead women on my dock," I gritted out, my eyes cold and my jaw ticking. "When they attacked Amore."

He stilled. "They attacked her again?"

Gabriel waited, his whole posture tense. Carrera had never met Amore, but for some reason, his interest in her rubbed me the wrong way. Call it me being an overprotective big brother... no, not brother. Maybe a cousin. Whatever!

"No." I didn't elaborate further. The truth was that this war started a long time ago with Amore's grandfather. And when they came into my city and dared to attack a girl under my protection... they took shit to a whole new level.

Carrera stood back as I took one more weapon and left. We swept out of the room, down the hallway, and out the back door from my downtown strip club.

It took us no time to get to Harlem. This specific area has been the center for many gangs and crimes. It was the worst neighborhood to find yourself in alone and at night.

Renzo, Luigi, and Lorenzo were with us. If Adriano wasn't with Amore, I would have had him here too. If I called him, he wouldn't hesitate, but I didn't want to do that to Amore. She tolerated it, but I didn't want her to be upset. Besides, her birthday was coming up.

Carrera had two men doing a lookout on the street while the rest of us followed down the dark alley.

"This is it," Carrera uttered in a low voice, pointing to a black back door. He knocked once and the door immediately opened.

The person who gave the tip stepped out into the night and closer to us. I narrowed my eyes on him. There was nothing remarkable about him. He was in his thirties, blonde hair and blue eyes, a little shorter than six feet. Definitely shorter than my six foot four. Something about him struck me familiar, though I couldn't quite place it. And it was too dark to see him clearly.

"Estos estan dentro." They are inside. His eyes flickered my way, and something flashed in them but before I could call him out on it, he nodded at Carrera and took off.

"Who's that?" I asked Gabriel in a low voice. "Do we trust him?"

"He's their run boy. Though last time I saw him, I swore he was shorter."

My sixth sense revolted, but before I could question him further, Luigi stormed inside the house. Damn idiot! He always acted first, then asked questions later. I understood his need to kill the men that delivered all those dead bodies, but we'd be no good to anyone dead.

"Fucker," I muttered under my breath. Lorenzo shook his head, acknowledging his brother's recklessness. The Bennetti family would be much better off if Lorenzo took over as the head of the family. At least he wouldn't charge headfirst into a war.

Gabriel and I stepped through the door and around the corner. In sync, both of us fired off bullets at the same time into their foreheads.

I scanned the room, but Luigi was nowhere to be seen. I really didn't need this right now.

Kicking down the first room's door, there were another two men. I took them both out, putting bullets straight into their hearts.

Lorenzo yanked me backward, at the same time the sound of the cock of guns readying sounded off on the left side of us. As we took cover, someone blasted five holes through the drywall but luckily nobody was hit.

The next sound didn't bode well for us. I heard the clip of an assault rifle, and I lunged to the right, shooting the man behind us that was ready to offload lead into all of us.

"This is a fucking trap," I hissed.

I met Gabriel's gaze, and I read the same conclusion in his eyes. "I'm going to fucking kill him."

Not if I get him first, I thought silently. I'd fucking torture him until he begged for death.

Another round of gunfire echoed from a room down the hall. Luigi flew through the door and a man stepped out, the barrel of his gun facing his forehead. Fucking idiot!

I sprinted towards him and shot him in the back of his skull before he could pull the trigger.

Luigi slapped a hand on the ground, all revved up and a stupid grin on his face.

Grabbing him by his arm, I pulled him onto his feet. "Stop being reckless," I ordered him. "Or I'll shoot you myself."

I hated fucking men that acted like imbeciles. And Luigi Bennetti was one of them. He was lucky I liked his brother and his sister.

Lorenzo grabbed my arm and held me back. He gestured to the next room. "Let me clear that room with my idiot brother, you and Gabriel clear the others."

The gunfire echoed through every floor of the building until eerie silence fell. And that was when I remembered.

The tip guy looked like the attacker on Amore from two years ago.

"Fuck," I muttered and dialed up Bennetti.

Just as I sat down behind my desk, my office door swung open.

"Russo, you got to come. Now!" Renzo's voice was persistent. I raised my head annoyed, meeting his slightly worried look.

What the fuck now?

I just needed one night for everything to go smoothly, so I could get home before two in the morning and chill for a while. It has been two days since Bennetti's fucked-up shipment of dead bodies. I wasn't in the mood for shit today after days of one fucked up thing after another. Carrera and I had hunted down the Venezuelans that fucked with our shipment, as well as Bennetti's, so I had my share of killings for a few days. Even by my standards.

"Can't it wait?" I grumbled.

It wasn't as if there was an active invasion going on. I'd hear shots being fired if someone was attacking.

"If Bennetti finds out about this, we're all dead. So hurry your ass up and come over here. Santi, you have to take care of her before her father sees her! He'll blow this club to pieces."

There could only be one *her.*

I rose from my spot behind the desk and left the comfort of my office to deal with a teenager that should be home right now. Goddamn it, wasn't she supposed to be home? Her birthday party was tomorrow.

I followed him through the dark hallway from the back of the club, where the offices were, to the front, where customers hung out and the stage was. That was putting it eloquently - it was the stripper's podium.

The second I entered the room, I froze.

Is that...? No, it couldn't be. The girl twirled on the pole, sliding down like she had done it a million times, and the moment the spotlight hit her red hair, it was my confirmation. Amore Bennetti danced on the stripper pole. Thank fuck she had clothes on, but that little school uniform was almost worse than being naked.

No wonder Renzo was all frazzled.

Twice in a fucking week. I knew Adriano took her driving after school and should have dropped her off at her father's house, not my goddamn nightclub. Tomorrow was her birthday, and if her father caught her on the stripper pole, she'd never live long enough to celebrate being eighteen.

A loud roar and whistle broke through the room and fire raged through my veins. "Go, girl. Take some of it off!" some soon-to-be-dead idiot shouted.

"Who let her up there?" I gritted out.

Her father would blow a gasket if he found out Amore was in my strip club. There was a lot he tolerated, but this he wouldn't. He'd go to war for it, right after he killed Adriano for allowing her to be in that position.

"Shut off the fucking music!" I roared through the room. Men were eye-fucking the seventeen-year-old girl... *Eighteen tomorrow*, I corrected myself as if that made it any better. I was about to kill every single one of these men. The music halted, but Amore didn't. I glared at the men. "Get the fuck out. And if one word of this slips, I know who to come for." I shifted my eyes over every single one of them, so they knew I was serious, and I'd hunt them down.

They scurried along and that was when I saw Adriano. "What the fuck, Adriano?" I shouted. "Amore, get the fuck down!"

"She can't hear you," he drawled, swaying on his feet. Was my brother drunk? I balled my fists, resisting the urge to punch him in the face. He was still young and trying to live up his college years. I was reckless at his age too, except that I was already working every free minute for Pà and the underworld.

I needed Adriano to step up and do better than this. I'd been slowly involving him in the Cosa Nostra business and our family business, but he was too easily distracted. I kept waiting for him to prove to me he could be trusted to do what needed to be done; that he had balls to do what was necessary. He wasn't giving me much to go off right now.

I stepped up onto the stage and grabbed Amore by her waist. She startled, a little squeal escaping her mouth. She had damn earbuds in.

"What the hell?" she asked, her hand pressed against her chest. She swayed on her feet, and I narrowed my eyes on her. She better not be drunk, or *I* would blow a gasket, not her father.

Her eyes lit up when she recognized me.

"Heeeey." She smiled lazily. She was fucking drunk. She smelled like tequila and strawberries. Her small hand came up to my chest and patted. "Hey," she repeated, her full lips curved in a wide smile.

Damn fucking kid!

I took her hands by the wrist, removed them off my chest and pulled her off the stage. I couldn't have her close to a stripper pole. I'd lose my goddamn license. The kid wasn't even legal, yet she was in my nightclub and drunk as a damn sailor.

Glaring at my brother, who was equally drunk, I snapped, "Explain yourself!"

I warned him not to repeat that shit from a few years ago. He had to keep his head straight and watch his and Amore's back.

"We had a competition," he slurred his words. "I think Amore won."

"I like winning." She grinned. They both laughed stupidly though there was nothing funny, their eyes unfocused.

"You two were supposed to be back at her place. Not getting drunk and coming to my club."

If the roaming Venezuelans would have caught them...

I couldn't think about that shit. It would send me off the edge.

"Amore, where is DeAngelo?"

Amore giggled, unbuttoning her white blouse and fanning herself. I grabbed her slim fingers to stop her from opening any more buttons. Her fucking bra already peeked through the top. Fucking Bennetti was going to kill everyone, and then I'd have to kill him. All because of these two damn idiots.

"We lost him." She chuckled drunkenly.

"Lost him?"

She waved her hand away, swaying on her feet. Her hands fidgeted and she resumed unbuttoning her blouse before I stopped her again.

"Tell me what happened," I ordered her.

"We drove," she slurred. Then her smile turned to a frown, and she turned her big, emerald eyes to me. Like I was her savior, though I wasn't sure from what. "I scratched Dad's car," she sniffled. *Ahhh, there it was!* "It's the last time." She wiped her nose with the back of her hand, and I recalled the similar gesture from our first meeting. "Dad said three strikes, you're out. Except this is like the twentieth or so. I don't even like baseball."

I bit the inside of my cheek. Damn, she was wasted.

"Why didn't you go get ice cream? That always makes you feel better." They would have fared better if they got ice cream rather than alcohol.

"Ice cream can't console me, Santi," she muttered, swaying on her feet. "I'm never going to learn how to drive. Maybe I need two men to teach me." She sniffed again. "Like Mom." Then she shook her head. "I just don't get it."

I still remembered the shock on her face upon hearing my father's admission. I didn't necessarily agree that it was wise to tell Amore, but in his old age, Papà wanted to right all the wrongs he had done. I guess it was his way of coming to terms with death. He had another twenty years to go at least, but just like the old Bennetti, he had grown softer in his old age.

"What was the competition about?" I asked instead of commenting on her mother. It was better she forgot about that.

Adriano shrugged. "If she can get to the top of the pole, we'd sneak into your garage and fix the dent."

"I thought it was a scratch?" I questioned them. I didn't know why I bothered. They were both drunk as shit, and the only thing they would be doing was damaging the car even more. Or worse, my garage.

"There is a scratch and a dent," she murmured, tears glistening in the cool moss of her gaze.

"And when did you come up with that idea?" I asked them both. "After a bottle of tequila?"

Adriano wrinkled his nose. "I drank bourbon. Amore had tequila. We only had a bottle."

I should beat my little brother for being so damn stupid. I'd bet money he drove drunk too, and with Amore Bennetti in the front seat of his car. He would get her killed one of these days, if her father or I didn't shoot him first.

"I really like your garage, Santi," she announced, smiling. The way her brain worked was a mystery to me.

She started fanning herself again and attempted to open another button. I gently smacked her fingers.

"Ouch, fucker," she muttered, and I raised my eyebrow at her foul language. I have never heard her curse before. She was too drunk to realize what she had called me. "It is so hot in here, Santino," she complained. "You have to pay the electric bill and put some air in here. The ladies will sue you when they die of heat stroke." She bent over, putting her hands on her knees. She was too drunk to reason with, but the strippers preferred it warmer since they danced with little to no clothes on. Swaying on her legs, she came forward and rested her forehead against my chest. "I'm getting heat stroke. Jesus, it is way too hot."

Renzo smirked and choked out a laugh but quickly covered it with his hand when my darkened gaze glared at him. His hand came up to his face, pretending to be scratching his chin and clearing his throat.

"Who gave you alcohol?" I questioned.

Never changing her position, Amore lifted her head from my chest, watching me like I was a God. There were stars in her eyes. She thought she hid it, but she was bad at hiding her emotions, her misplaced flirtation with me.

It was the reason I kept my distance. I wasn't about to encourage the kid's fantasies. Okay, maybe she wasn't a kid anymore, but she sure as hell wasn't a woman. Then she surprised me, grinning wide with trouble written all over her face.

"Daddy had it in the back of his car. We had to check they didn't crack, you know."

This time Renzo threw his head back and laughed while I glared at him. This was the last thing I needed tonight. I still had a shit ton of work to get done.

She swayed forward again, her head bumping into my stomach. My hands came to her shoulders to steady her, and she raised her hands to my hips, clutching my Brioni suit. Freaking girl was ready to fall over. It was like watching a baby roll over because they were still too young to support themselves while sitting.

"Whoa," I warned, when her hands came to my ass. I peeled them off, giving a pissed off look to my brother.

"Santino, you are so hot," she murmured. "You really need air conditioning. You are going to melt. Or I'm gonna melt." She took my hand and pressed it against her cheek. "I don't want to melt. I saw them burning her flesh. It wasn't pretty." What the fuck was the kid talking about?

Then her whole body retched, and she puked all over my Salvatore Ferragamo Oxfords.

Fuck me!

CHAPTER 11

Adriano

"Rise and shine, party boy." My brother's voice came from a distance. I wished it would go away. My head was throbbing. "Last night wasn't such a great idea after all, was it? The rays of sunshine bring a whole new perspective."

I groaned out loud. Last night? What happened last night? Sometimes my big brother was a pain in my ass. He did everything right; I did everything half-assed.

"Get up," he ordered in a stern voice. I swore that fucker was born with the attitude of a don. Well, fuck him and his semi-don status.

"Fuck off, Santi," I muttered, my mouth dry. He just had to stop talking and let me get back to sleep. "I'm going back to sleep."

"No, you are not," he responded. "You are going to get cleaned up and go with Pà to Amore's birthday party."

"Fuck you." I hated when he thought he could boss me around. "I'll go to Amore's place tonight or tomorrow."

"Her birthday party starts in two hours. You will be there on time," he growled in warning. I didn't know what was up his ass, but I wasn't in the mood for my older brother's preaching. Not today. Not ever!

"She won't mind."

"Adriano, I swear to God—"

"You go then," I told him. "What the fuck do you care anyhow? She's not your friend. She's mine."

"Then be a fucking friend and go to her party."

"She doesn't mind if I don't show." Santi was pissing me off. "I'll see her later."

The silence lingered, and I didn't bother opening my eyes. I rolled over and pulled a pillow over the top of my head.

"In case you are wondering what happened last night," he said in a low tone, which sometimes scared the shit out of me and everyone else. Not that I would ever admit that to him. Sometimes Santi acted like a psychopath. "You and Amore got drunk and snuck into my strip club. She spent the night hunched over the toilet, with me holding her head up."

The events of last night slowly started pouring in. Amore damaging her father's car, being upset. Opening the bottle of tequila and bourbon. *Fuck*! Amore on the stripper pole. Her father would kill me if he found out. He might be on his way to kill me now.

I jolted out of the bed. "Where is Amore?"

"Luigi came and got her," Santino answered, a clear scowl on his face. "What in the fucking hell were you thinking? She is underage, fucking seventeen."

"Eighteen today."

"Underage," he gritted out in a low voice. "Her father would have killed you if something happened to her."

"Is he coming here?"

"You are fucking lucky Luigi owed me a favor," he growled, getting into my face. "I am still tempted to smash your face into the nearest wall and knock some sense into you."

Like I said. My brother was a psychopath.

I pushed my hands through my hair. My head was pounding. I couldn't even imagine how badly Amore's head hurt. She had never gotten drunk before. I might have been the one to come up with the idea of opening the alcohol. Usually, Amore wasn't for breaking certain rules. I, on the other hand, was into breaking every goddamn rule under the sun. It made life more exciting. Truthfully, she could be boring sometimes, but somehow our chemistry complemented each other.

After all, there was only enough room for one adrenaline junkie in our relationship.

Besides, she had a hard enough time learning how to drive, never mind how to be cool and exciting. And yesterday, she drove even worse than her usual self. She banged up her father's car pretty bad, and it went south from there.

I recalled her throwing up on Santino's shoes. Then she apologized in her unique way.

"I'll make you better shoes, Santi." She looked like shit. I swore there was a hint of green under her pale skin. "They might be real leather but animals are killed for them." She swayed over to him, raising her head to meet his eyes, and Santi scrunched his nose. She probably smelled like vomit but was too drunk to realize it. "My product will be environmentally friendly, and animals won't suffer for it."

Despite his fury, Santi actually offered her a semblance of a smile. The bastard never smiled.

Through the haze in my brain, I recalled Santi driving us both to his place, where Amore finally passed out on his couch.

"How pissed off was Luigi?" I asked my brother. Amore's brothers were protective of her. They might not have known they had a sister for the first thirteen years of her life, but now they'd kill anyone that harmed a single piece of red hair on her pretty head.

Santino folded his arms in front of him. "He wasn't pleased, that's for sure. But he was reasonable. He took her back in his car. You will take her father's car back."

"Ah, fuck," I muttered. "Bennetti won't like the dent in it."

I cursed myself for getting drunk. That fucking bourbon her old man had in the back seat was some serious shit. I was going to fix that dent regardless of if Amore got to the top of that pole. It was a stupid damn challenge anyhow, and one I came up with after half a bottle of bourbon.

"I got it taken care of," Santino retorted dryly.

"How?" He would have had to stay up all night to fix it by himself.

"Don't worry about that. Though next time you two come up with a bright idea like this, I'll beat the living shit out of you. Are. We. Fucking. Clear?"

97

Santino would be a don in name soon, but he wasn't quite there yet. So, for now, he couldn't order me around and punish me for disobeying. He was only my brother. So, his threats didn't scare me, though he'd follow through on beating the crap out of me. No matter brother or don.

"Are you going to her birthday party?" I asked him.

"No, I have business to attend to."

"What is going on?" I asked. In recent weeks, Pà has kept me out of most business dealings. I wasn't sure what the fucking deal was, but it agitated the crap out of me.

"The Venezuelans. Now, get ready and don't be fucking late for her party."

"Fine," I muttered, rolling my lethargic carcass off the bed.

Half an hour later, I was at the Bennetti residence. The white villa, right at the edge of the city, was impressive. White marble columns at the front of the house gave the home a Mediterranean feel. If only the white fucking glare didn't hurt my eyes. It was brighter here than in heaven, for fuck's sake.

The first person I spotted when I pulled up to the house was Amore, throwing up. My car windows were rolled down and the sounds that traveled through the air were not pleasant. The palm of her hand pressed against the oak tree, supporting herself. Her dress hugged her body as the breeze swept through it. My father and hers stood by her side, one rubbing her back and the other holding her hair away from her face.

Guilt swelled in my chest. It was her eighteenth birthday, and I fucked it up for her. She was looking forward to it all week, and now she was miserable.

At my tender age of twenty-one, Santi said I should have known better than to let her drink. *Water under the bridge*, I told him. I couldn't fix what happened in the past. It was a waste of time and energy to dwell on it.

Unlike me, when Santi was my age, he was already running the show in our family business. Now at twenty-six, he was the youngest and richest member of the Cosa Nostra. We couldn't all be overachievers. Even Amore superseded me in everything. She was super rich, super smart, and super pretty. Not exactly my type, but she held charms that no other girl compared to. Except she never even batted a lash at any of my compliments. She was completely immune to my charms.

Hmmm, a challenge maybe? I thought to myself. It wasn't such a far-fetched idea. Amore grounded me. She just saw *me*. Not my brother. Not a Russo. Just me, and she accepted me just the way I was. She never compared me to Santi, nor to our father or anyone else.

I parked the car, put my shades on to hide my eyes, and exited the car. Amore's father heard me first and raised his head to meet my gaze.

"What the fuck happened yesterday?" he growled. "Luigi said food poisoning. Where did you eat?"

Food poisoning? Was Luigi trying to have Bennetti burn down a restaurant?

"It was some food truck."

He opened his mouth to say something else, but Amore retched again, and another round of vomiting began. Both the old dons fussed over her, like two Nonnas. She had a unique way with people; everyone wanted to please her.

I strode over to the nearby oak tree and leaned against the bark, pushing my hands into the pockets of my jeans. The sun shone, the weather was perfect, but she looked miserable. I guess alcohol and Amore Bennetti didn't mesh well at all. There was no way she'd survive the entire day at this party in her state.

"How about I take Amore inside so she can take it easy?" I suggested. "I'll stay with the birthday girl and tend to her."

Amore's eyes met mine, pure misery reflecting in them. Her gaze looked a much darker shade of green right now with the shadows under her eyes. She was exhausted, and it was barely one in the afternoon.

"We have guests," Bennetti muttered. "It's her birthday party."

"She won't make it through this party," I told him. "She looks like she is ready to fall off her feet."

"Savio, I think Adriano is right," my father reasoned with him. "The only way she'll start feeling better is if she gets rest."

"I'm sorry, Dad." Amore raised her head to meet her father's gaze as she wiped her mouth with the sleeve of her white dress. The spring dress that came up to her knees was some light material, probably environmentally friendly, which she always talked about. She looked pretty and innocent. It would seem I corrupted her a step too far last night. "I can ask Grandma to go home. So you two don't kill each other."

My girl. Always the peacemaker.

"Just let them," I said, striding to take her arm.

She shook her head. "Not funny."

I thought it was.

"I'm taking you inside. Maybe we'll have some ginger ale to settle your stomach."

"Just help me to my room please," she muttered, all her coloring dangerously pale. "I'm sure you have work to do for your papà and Santi."

Right, I thought sarcastically. She didn't know my papà had reverted to babying me within the last few weeks and kept insisting on keeping me out of our family business. It was pissing me the fuck off.

"Not to worry," I assured her bitterly. "It seems both my big brother and my father have put a pause on my work in the Cosa Nostra."

"Adriano." My father's voice warned behind me. Of course, he would hear that. He didn't hear any of my complaints for weeks, but he would hear this.

"I'm sorry." Even sick as a dog, Amore found compassion. She patted my hand, though she seemed to have barely enough strength for that small physical activity too.

She was better than I was. I had tried not to let it get to me, but today I failed. The truth was that I resented that decision. At my age, Santi was fully integrated into our family business and pretty much running the show.

"Don't worry about it," I told her. After all, today was her day. "Let's get you that ginger ale."

An anguished groan left her lips. "I just want to sleep," she murmured.

Santi said she barely got any sleep last night. "You have to stop puking your guts up first."

"If she gets worse, you come and get me," her father instructed. Amore was the apple of his eye. If he knew she was so sick because of me, I'd be bleeding on this lawn. He'd be sure to shove my face into her vomit as I took my last breath.

"Want me to carry you?" I offered to Amore.

She shook her head but held on to my arm as we walked towards the house. The smell of puke and her own strawberry scent mixed in my nostrils. The soft tunes of Pavarotti drifted along the May breeze, guests played soccer, laughed together, and mingled while some pretended not to look our way. The day wouldn't remain a fond memory to either one of us.

"What's wrong with my granddaughter?" The voice came from behind us. Of course, it would be Regina fucking Regalè.

"What the fuck does it look like?" I growled, as she stepped in front of us. "She is sick. I'm taking her inside. Enjoy the party."

"Watch yourself," Regina growled. The woman was a damn tigress, regardless of her fragile stature.

"Adriano didn't mean it," Amore chimed in, sidestepping her. She couldn't wait to get to her room. "I-I'm so sorry, Grandma," she continued in a weak tone. "I'm not feeling well. I just have to get some ginger ale and some rest."

Her grandmother's eyes traveled to her father. "Does she need a doctor?"

"No!" Both Amore and I spoke at the same time.

"N-no, thank you," Amore murmured, sharing a quick glance with me. "I just need some rest. Go and enjoy the party."

Her grandma scoffed. "There are criminals of the Cosa Nostra here. There is nothing to enjoy. If you are going to bed, I'm going home."

"Good riddance," Bennetti muttered behind us.

She leaned over and pressed a kiss on Amore's cheek, ignoring Savio. "I had DeAngelo put your gift in your room earlier. Happy birthday, my love."

"Thanks, Grandma."

She strode off like a queen, and our fathers left us to go join the guests. Savio glanced over his shoulder one more time to ensure his daughter was good, and she offered a weak wave.

Once out of earshot, I shuffled her slowly into the house and up the stairs.

"I hate tequila," she whined.

"Oh, crap. And I got you a bottle of it for your birthday," I teased her. She turned slightly greener. "Don't you dare throw up in here. I don't want to clean that shit up."

"Jerk," she muttered.

I opened the door to her room. With light golden walls, white crown molding, and white accents everywhere, Amore's room still looked like a perfect, principessa bedroom. Meticulous except for the corner she had dedicated to designing her clothes, full of drawings and a mannequin with fabric over it.

She kicked off her pink designer heels, not even bothering to put them away and crawled under her blankets.

"Want to open your gift?"

"If you want," she muttered, her voice barely audible.

"You sound so enthusiastic about it," I countered.

"I feel so sick, Santi," she murmured, her eyes drooping, like she couldn't keep them up. And like a light, she was out.

Santi!

She called me *Santi*. Something in my chest squeezed, and if I was honest, I didn't like it. She had never bothered with my brother or even brought him up to me. She was my friend, not Santi's. Why did she call out to him?

She was mine.

CHAPTER 12

Amore

THREE MONTHS LATER

"Are you sure this is wise?" I asked Adriano for the hundredth time. I was leaving for Italy tomorrow, and it would be bad to get into trouble on my last night home. That drunken night before my eighteenth birthday was enough adventure to last me a long while. I spent the night throwing up into Santi's toilet while he held my hair. I cried, actually cried from misery, begging him to give me something to make it better. There was no chance he'd ever see me as a woman after that incident.

I was sick as a dog for the next three days. Just the thought of tequila made me queasy. I never wanted to get a whiff of it again. *That drink is poison!* I hadn't vomited that much in my entire life. The first night I was sure I'd die. Even when my stomach was empty, I couldn't stop retching. I was pissed off at Adriano for coming up with such a stupid idea, but I was furious at myself even more because I let it happen.

Adriano and I had a tiny fallout afterwards. I was childishly mad that he wasn't feeling any symptoms while it felt like I was dying. We didn't speak for a week. Then just as I was about to leave the house with Lorenzo to go find my best friend, Adriano pulled up at our front door in his Mustang.

A heartbeat of silence before we both muttered at the same time, *I'm sorry*.

And all was forgiven and forgotten. One week without talking to him was hard. We might not have seen each other every day, but we talked *every* single day. About everything and nothing, and I never realized how much I relied on our little talks.

'I missed talking to you'. Those were Adriano's exact words, and it was exactly how I felt. So, I hugged him and made us both promise that we would always talk. Even when we were mad at each other.

So, we moved on from that whole event and agreed I'd never have tequila again. We spent our summer hanging by the pool when he wasn't working for his big brother, and I wasn't working for Grandma. I hadn't seen Santi since that night he kept my hair out of my face as I puked into his fancy Kohler toilet.

I wasn't sure how I'd ever be able to look Santi in his eyes. Those whiskey brown eyes that made me weak at my knees and had my heart rattling in my chest.

Maybe the next few years in Italy would cure me of my crush on Santino Russo. I convinced Dad to let me go earlier than anticipated so I could get settled in. So, this was Adriano's goodbye date with me until he came to visit. We had dinner at Per Se, a fancy restaurant at Columbus Circle. He reserved us a window table, so we had a spectacular view of Central Park and Columbus Circle. People knew him there; he was a frequent customer, but it was a first for me.

So far, the evening was going very well. We laughed as we dined and sampled every dessert. Then at the end, he surprised me with gelato. A lemon poppy seed ice cream. He said it was all the rave in Europe, and he'd had it shipped over. It wasn't my favorite flavor, but we still ate it all.

"Ready for some dancing?" Adriano asked with a wolfish grin. He parked his Mustang in the employee's spot behind his brother's nightclub, The Orchid.

Usually, we crashed college parties, but he had graduated, and summer break was still on-going. So, this was a major upgrade. Attending The Orchid nightclub was considered *being in*. I never felt the urge for it. One, because I was still under the age required to enter the club, two because Santi owned it, and the last reason was the main reason. Mom and George had a nickname for me, *Orchid,* because I loved the flower so much. Now, it was just a reminder of their death.

"I'm still under twenty-one," I reasoned with Adriano. He loved parties and good times. Even more, he loved the life of the Cosa Nostra. Both Russo brothers were molds of the same life, but somehow Santi had turned out harder, darker, hotter. Adriano had some of the darkness too, yet he hid it behind his charm and smiles while Santi didn't bother.

"We won't be drinking. Just dancing," Adriano tried to reassure me. "Santi is meeting some of his associates, so he won't be around. And the guys here know me." I tilted my head, eyeing him suspiciously. "Trust me," he drawled.

Should have been my first clue, but our evening so far had been wonderful. I really didn't want to ruin it. He must have read uncertainty on my face. "You look so beautiful today. I'm not ready to end the night. I won't see you for three months."

Warmth spread through me. I saw firsthand how charming he could be when he wanted something. While I didn't fall to my knees for him like most women, he had the ability to convince me to do what he wanted when he really wanted something. It was his specialty, after all.

His brother probably threatened people to get them to do what he wanted; Adriano sweet talked them into doing it.

So, I caved. I wanted to spend a few more hours with him before calling it a night. The next three months, until he came to visit, would be long without seeing him.

"Okay," I relented with a sigh. We both exited the car. He came around and took my hand, pressing a soft kiss onto it.

"You look really beautiful," he complimented me. He looked me over, grinning widely. "Really, really gorgeous."

I grinned at his comment. He was going all out with compliments today. "Thank you."

My eyes traveled down my body. It was a dress I designed on my own and had sewn it with Maria's guidance. It was off white, embellished with glittering rhinestone straps across the low neckline and shoulders. It was by far the most feminine dress I had ever worn. The material was a mix of silk and satin, which hugged my curves. I paired it with a pair of pink heels and a matching pink clutch. I had left my red curls cascading down my back, and I even put a light lipstick on and applied mascara. It made me feel slightly mature, maybe even twenty-one.

Adriano had been calling me beautiful and gorgeous all summer. It wasn't usually what he did, so it kept throwing me off. Besides, I'd seen the girls he usually went for, and I certainly wasn't his type. My eyes sized him up. He looked good too in his dark jeans and black silky button-down shirt. He truly looked like a suave, Italian guy.

As we approached the entrance, the bouncer recognized Adriano instantly and opened the chain link fence for us without question or ID. His eyes darted to me, his gaze roaming down my body. I tensed for a second but then flushed, realizing he was checking me out, not scrutinizing my age.

Maybe this will be exciting after all, just like Adriano said.

We strode into the nightclub and a familiar beat sounded all around us.

"This will be fun," Adriano announced.

I grinned, easily swayed by my best friend and the excitement rushing through me.

Striding to the dance floor, he cleared a path for me. It was already crowded, people enjoying themselves. I saw the bar and suddenly the nightclub's name made sense. The whole bar was set up in the shape of an orchid and colors flashed around, throwing off different glows, changing the color of the orchid.

I loved the setup, though bitter memories lurked in the back of my mind.

"Shall we dance?" Adriano inquired all gallantly and interrupted my thoughts. He was acting like he was my real boyfriend and that this was a real date.

I smiled happily. "Why not."

CHAPTER 13

Santino

Carrera and I sat in the private booth of my nightclub, along with Renzo, and Carrera's right-hand man seated with us. The lighting was dark and though loud music played out in the open, in the private booth the volume was slightly muted to allow for conversations. The lights had been flashing over the dance floor, but nobody could see into the private booths.

It wasn't unusual for me to hold meetings in my nightclub. It was easier to keep them off the radar. Both Carrera and I even brought dates but dismissed them the minute we sat down at the private booth. One of the bouncers would ensure they got home safely.

"We raided another place in Harlem last night," Renzo grumbled. "It's like they are everywhere."

The Venezuelans were causing a lot of trouble. They kept coming into the city despite the fact that all their efforts to take over the Cosa Nostra territory failed. Even when they succeeded in bringing their product into the city, the cartel never got a chance to distribute it. It was true for the Venezuelan Cartel, and it would be true for the Colombian Cartel. This was not their territory and never would be. The Carrera Cartel understood that, hence our mutually beneficial business relationship.

There was only one man that nearly succeeded in penetrating the Cosa Nostra. It was Amore's grandfather. But before he succeeded, he was killed. The word on the street was one of his own took him out.

"They are searching for something," I said. We kept one of the men from two raids ago alive and he spilled that much. Though he knew barely anything. Their job was to establish their presence in the city, take over the streets with their product and—this last bit was the most disturbing—take pictures of random red-haired girls. With the focus on NYU.

"Or someone," Carrera added, his eyes skimming the dance floor. Gabriel Carrera might have had a right-hand man and a bodyguard, but truthfully, he didn't need one. He was more than capable of taking care of himself, assuming anyone dared to even fuck with him. With tattoos on pretty much every inch of his skin, excluding his face, people usually steered clear of him.

When I didn't respond, he cocked his eyebrow. "Otherwise, why take pictures of girls at NYU? Obviously, he is looking for a girl."

My gaze darkened and the image of Amore cornered into the bathroom at the college party two years ago flashed in my mind. Could it be that they are tying up loose ends?

"Let's focus on the next shipment so we don't end up empty," I told him. I wasn't willing to share with him anything about Amore Bennetti. Yes, she had her father and brothers, even my own brother to protect her, but somehow the kid found her way into my chest.

Focusing on the task at hand, we'd come up with new routes for our product to arrive safely from Colombia. Going on a killing spree each time a shipment was coming in wasn't feasible nor sustainable. For either one of us. So, we devised a plan. Only four of us would know it. The captain of the boat wouldn't know his route nor the final destination until his last day at sea.

Carrera's eyes roamed back to the dance floor. I assumed he was probably looking for his date, though he didn't even give her a second glance once we stepped into the club. I checked my phone for a quick status update when his words had me raising my head.

"I might be out of practice," Carrera said, a smirk on his face. "But

I'd bet money that the wild red-haired little thing over there is underage."

I followed his eyes and met the red-haired wild child. Though she didn't look like a child. In fact, far from it. Her body... fucking Christ. What was she wearing?

The dress she wore was provocative. Too provocative for an eighteen-year-old. Sparkling dress. Sparkling eyes. Her bright coppery hair. How in the fuck did her father and brothers let her leave the house like that?

She looked like a woman. The dress, if it could even be called that, played peekaboo, exposing her skin each time she moved. It was sleeveless with a low V-back exposing her sun-kissed skin. She swayed around and I saw her front with the plunging neckline, and my ears buzzed with anger.

Suddenly her presence sucked all the oxygen from the air. Everybody and everything around me faded.

Temptation. She looked like an innocent and sweet temptation.

Her dance partner whispered something to her, and she threw her head back laughing, her wide smile lighting up her face. Frustration clawed at my chest, irrational, and the blood in my veins burned a little hotter seeing her wrap her hands around her partner's neck.

Where in the fuck was her bodyguard? Or my damn brother? Because I knew he was the only reason she'd be here.

"Want me to go get her?" Renzo asked in a low voice, and I clenched my teeth so hard, my jaw hurt. No, I didn't want him to fucking go get her. I didn't want any man close to her.

Carrera cocked his eyebrow. "A friend of yours?"

Definitely not a friend. Not a kid either. Not anymore. *Jesus fucking Christ.*

I didn't need this shit now. I had enough on my plate without worrying about some prick dancing with a woman under my protection.

Not. A. Woman.

She wasn't a woman. Not yet. I hadn't seen her since the night that I had held her head as she threw up all night. It was only three months ago that it happened, but she looked... I couldn't even think about it.

I had to calm down, otherwise I'd punch my way through the nightclub. Amore raised her arms over her head and rolled her hips to the music. Every single pair of male eyes were on her. All her attention was on her dance partner, a wide smile spread across her face, and his hands resting on her hips. For a moment, I regretted not hearing her silvery laugh due to the loud music and distance between us. Her face was bright, and she seemed happy.

Something dark slithered through my veins at seeing someone with her, his hands on her hips. Their bodies inched closer to each other with each passing second.

Then realization struck at the lyrics they were dancing to. "*Can you come fuck me right now...*" was playing and she was lip-syncing it like her life dependent on it. For fuck's sake. She looked like she was auditioning for a role in *Striptease*.

How in the fuck does she even know those lyrics?

By the looks of it, she was having a great time.

"Shit, she really knows those lyrics well," Renzo muttered, and Carrera chuckled with amusement.

"From the look on your face, I gather you know her," the latter stated matter-of-factly.

Fuck, yeah I knew her! At least the kiddo that didn't lip-sync '*come fuck me right now*'. But this woman, girl.... I wasn't sure that I knew her.

The guy she danced with moved along with her body and followed her lead. His hands moved to Amore's ass and everything faded away.

I stood up and stalked away from the private booth, more furious with each step that took me closer to the dancing couple. I became a predator focused on his prey... on her. If glares could kill, everyone on that dance floor would be dead. The last thing I ever wanted was to witness Amore Bennetti dancing to "FMRN" by Lilyisthatyou.

Today might be the day I killed my little brother for leaving Amore Bennetti alone, yet again!

CHAPTER 14

Amore

I was having a great time. Adriano left me with a friend of his, Marco. He was funny, easygoing, and a great dancer. He was also gay, so it made my time with him even more fun. I didn't have to worry about him having ulterior motives or flirting with me. We spent the next six songs dancing together and lip synching.

About two songs ago, Adriano spotted a blonde bombshell and disappeared. A slight disappointment washed over me since it was my last night in the States before I left for Italy, but I couldn't say I was surprised. Adriano was a notorious skirt chaser. There were too many temptations here, and he couldn't resist. Besides, Marco's dancing was a thousand times better than Adriano's, not that I would say that to my best friend. Either way, it worked out.

The song by Lilyisthatyou came on and I let it all out. I shouted the lyrics, twirled, and moved, uncaring of everything. I knew Marco wasn't attracted to me, so I took advantage of practicing my sensual moves. It was probably an epic failure, but it didn't bother me.

'You only get better with practice', my grandma always said. And I intended to practice and be good at it.

Okay, so maybe she was talking about drawing and designing, but I applied it to this as well. It was liberating to dance like nobody was watching. Marco was, but he didn't care if I swayed my hips or ground clumsily against him.

"If you want to keep your hands, get them off of her." A growl sounded behind me, the icy tone of it sending a chill down my spine. I could hear the threat in it even through the loud music, startling me to a stop. "Or I'll cut them off."

I whipped around and saw Santi's furious face glaring at me and Marco. Just like that, the good time evaporated, and my stomach dropped. He wasn't supposed to be here.

"S-Santi, what..." My voice trailed off at the thunderous glare he shot my way. I was underage, yes, but I hadn't done anything wrong. Just dancing.

Santi's angry eyes came to me. "Your dance is over!"

Where in the fuck was Adriano? Every single time DeAngelo wasn't with me, some shit happened.

I scoffed with fake bravado. "You don't get to dictate that."

He wore a suit with his jacket unbuttoned, showing his black vest that hugged his big, strong body. Light scruff covered his jaw, and his thick, dark hair matched his dark expression. He was just as intimidating and breathtakingly handsome. His presence demanded attention, and we had plenty of it now. Everything about him screamed power, wealth, and sex appeal.

My hand shook as I raised it and tucked my hair behind my ear. Warmth curled low in my stomach, but I ignored it.

"My club," he said darkly. "My rules."

Okay, he had a point there. But I wouldn't go down that easily. "I was just dancing with a friend. You don't need to be a dick." Instantly heat warmed my cheeks because an image of his dick flashed in my mind. Or at least, the way I pictured it would look. My hands grew clammy, feeling self-conscious.

Surprise flashed in Santi's dark gaze at my bravado and his jaw tightened. Maybe I was pushing my luck a tad bit too far.

"The girl is not dancing with anyone but me," Marco chimed in, attempting to push Santi away. I would commend him if it was anyone else. Santi didn't even budge from his spot. Marco was nuts if he thought he could beat Santi Russo. The look Santi gave him—pure murder.

"Nobody touches her," Santi snarled. "And if you want to get out of this alive, I suggest you get your hands off her. Now!" Marco didn't move and Santi continued in a hard tone. "I am seconds away from cutting them off your body. Now get fucking lost."

I shoved my body in between the two of them. "Are you nuts?" I snapped at Santi. "This is Marco. He is Adriano's friend from college."

"I don't give a shit." Santi's hands came to my shoulders, and he literally lifted me off the ground and moved me over. Like he was moving a piece of annoying furniture out of his way.

Before I could blink or say another word, Santi's fist flew through the air, punching Marco right into his face.

My mouth dropped, watching Marco's body in slow motion drop to the ground. When Santi went to make another move, I grabbed his hand.

"Stop, Santi," I shouted, my eyes frantically searching for Adriano. "Marco is a friend."

He shook off my hand and readied to punch Marco again. This time, I jumped on his back, wrapping my arms around his neck.

"Get off of me, Amore," he hissed, fury fuming off his body. He easily peeled my hands off him and moved me out of the way, ready to land another punch at Marco.

"Jesus, fucker." Marco spat blood onto the floor and guilt swelled in me. "You'd be eye candy if you weren't such a jerk."

Santi glanced to the side, and I followed his gaze. Renzo and another guy were there.

"Take her," he ordered.

I glowered at them. "You fucking dare touch me, either one of you, and my brothers will have you killed."

Renzo raised his hands in surrender, though a small smile played on his lips. "Not touching you." *Jackass!*

The other guy was scary. He seemed completely unperturbed with my threat. He probably didn't know who I was, and I had never seen him before, though that didn't mean much. Tattoos marked his neck and hands. I couldn't exactly tell the color of his eyes in the darkness of the club, but I saw he had an eyebrow piercing.

I scowled at him as he took a step towards me. "Inkman, don't you dare!"

"His name is Gabriel Carrera," Santi hissed.

"I. Don't. Care." He had no right to tell me who I should dance with. He wasn't even my friend, and I barely saw him anymore.

"Where is Adriano?" Santi's eyes flickered around. Even though we stood to the side, we already had a small audience.

I shrugged my shoulders. It was better not to say anything than lie to him. Yes, he was being a dick, but when he glared at me like that, he acted like a true don ready to make everyone pay who didn't bend to his will.

"He's probably chasing a piece of ass," Renzo snickered. I glared his way, narrowing my eyes on him. It wasn't like he was better.

Marco stood up off the floor, wiping the blood off his mouth with the back of his hand.

"Didn't I fucking tell you both to stick together?" Santi raged. We were getting a bigger audience by the second. "He was all over you. He could have drugged you and fucked you in the first corner. You want that for your first time, huh?"

I swore, right now, I felt like I was steaming. I was so hot and embarrassed. Every inch of my skin burned hot from anger.

"My sex life is none of your business," I hissed. "And you don't know when my first time was or will be. Jackass."

"Fucking wrong," he snarled, his eyes piercing me. "Everything in my club is my business."

I rolled my eyes, though it was fake as shit. On the inside, I shook; though whether it was from excitement or worry, I wasn't sure. Santi would never hurt me, but I wasn't stupid enough to think he wouldn't teach me a lesson.

"Where the fuck is Adriano?" he bellowed. "Or should I just kill this fucker for touching you and get it over with? I don't have all goddamn night!"

My heart drummed against my chest. I had never seen Santi so furious before. A muscle ticked in his jaw, and my heart rate ticked up another notch.

"I-I, you can't hurt Marco," I begged, getting myself in front of my dance partner.

Santi scoffed. "Watch me. Nobody is allowed to put their hands on you."

His anger made no sense, nor did his reasoning.

"He's gay. I'm not his type," I stuttered my explanation, confused at Santi's anger. "He is safe, and I like him."

I took Marco's hand and squeezed my assurance, sharing a quick glance with him. He snatched his hand out of mine.

"Probably better you don't touch me, or this psychopath might start using me as his personal punching bag again."

"I am so sorry," I apologized. Even under the dimmed lights, I could see the swelling on his cheek. I turned my head to find Santi looking even more pissed. His jaw was pressed so tight, I was sure he was grinding his teeth. It seemed to me he was making a big deal out of nothing.

"Get out of my club," he growled at Marco. He didn't have to tell him twice because bouncers were already behind him, and he just shook his head when I opened my mouth to protest.

"Have fun in Italy," he said in the way of a goodbye.

I watched his stiff back as he walked away from us escorted by the bouncers. Once he disappeared out of my sight, I whirled around.

"That was unnecessary," I hissed. "I'm out of here. Your club sucks anyhow."

I took a step to go around him, and in search of Adriano, when he grabbed my wrist. His hand felt rough, calloused on my skin, and suddenly a cool breath of fear shot through my bloodstream. Maybe I pushed him too far.

"You aren't going anywhere alone," he ordered.

I blew out a frustrated breath. "You know, I was having a great time. My last night before leaving. But of course, you'd show up and ruin it."

The reasonable part of me knew that if Adriano and I remained together, this scene wouldn't be happening. Yet, I couldn't help but be furious with Santi.

"We are going to find Adriano." He ignored my comment, fury like a fire in his eyes.

"No." I was half-tempted to stamp my heel down.

"Amore," he warned.

I pressed my lips together and stared at him, unwilling to say anything. Instead, my fist clenched the material of my dress into a ball, making it even shorter.

Santi stood there in a dark three-piece-suit and a black tie. The contrast between us stark. He seemed to be towering over me, larger than life. His gaze fell down my body, and I felt it, as if he actually grazed my skin. My breathing stilled, his eyes lingering on my scrunched material, showing off more of my thigh than appropriate. I immediately released it, and he continued tracing my legs with his eyes until it reached my shoes.

Why was my body so in tune with him? His gaze alone made me feel breathless, itchy, and heated. It was killing me.

His heavy gaze returned to mine, burning with something I had never seen in his eyes before. And for some inexplicable reason, the way he looked at me sent every fiber of me into over-excited mode.

My stomach made a few somersaults, making me feel strangely breathless. Itchy. Hungry for *him*. I couldn't tear my eyes away from him, his darkness hypnotizing me. Then he gave his head a slow shake, as if clearing his thoughts.

He turned to Renzo and the tattooed guy. "We are done here."

That was one way to dismiss people.

"I'd rather hear the night was just getting started," I mumbled under my breath without thinking, and instantly, heat ignited within me.

Renzo stifled his laugh, hiding it behind his hand while the tattooed guy smirked in amusement.

I went to sidestep him but his calloused hand around my wrist tightened. His grip was firm but not painful. But his touch... It felt like fire licking my skin, igniting an inferno through my bloodstream. He was branding me with his touch, and he'd only placed his hand on my wrist. Christ! I could only imagine how good it would feel to have his hands all over me.

Does he know what his touch is doing to me?

He pulled me along, almost like I was a bratty child, which pissed me off. We walked through a dark hallway, running into couples making out. He never even hesitated, moving like they weren't even there until we entered a room that looked like an office. He shut the door behind us, and instantly the loud music dulled, like we were far away from it.

"Now what?" I spat, mad at myself for feeling this damn attraction towards him while he talked to me and treated me like I was a child.

"What the fuck are you wearing?" he snapped back at me.

I blinked at the sudden change of his mood and glanced down at myself. "A dress."

"That is not a dress," he hissed. "It can barely be called decent material. You look like a kid playing dress up."

The words hit the mark and shook up my confidence.

I blinked my eyes, hurt swelling in my chest. "I-I designed it myself."

A string of Italian curses left his lips as he strode back and forth in front of me.

I watched him pace and realized he was trying to calm down before continuing our conversation. Frustration rolled off his body along with the whiff of his cologne - masculinity mixed with leather and whiskey. So good, like a man.

I narrowed my eyes. He wasn't the only one pissed off; I was too. He couldn't look at me one second with fire in his eyes and call me a kid the next. I wasn't a kid anymore. Yes, I was younger, but nobody should call me a kid. Something boiling hot itched under my skin. An agitation that he refused to see me as a woman. Young woman, yes; but still a woman. Not a fucking kid.

Santi finally stopped; his piercing, dark eyes locked on me.

"Amore, you can't wear stuff like that." His eyes traveled down my body, and for the first time, it felt like his gaze wasn't clinical. "You are underage," he rasped. "Drinking and hanging out at clubs will get you in trouble."

I frowned at his reasoning. That was the dumbest thing I had ever heard.

"First, I haven't had a drop of alcohol," I told him angrily. "And second, I'm eighteen. Most girls my age dress more provocatively than this. I'm not a kid nor a little girl." I glanced down at my dress. I loved it

117

and didn't care what fucking Santi said. "You don't get to tell me what to do, Santi. You are nobody to me."

Something flared in his eyes, and I realized in the far corner of my mind that I was playing with fire, but I'd gone too far to stop now.

"And that man was somebody to you?"

"Like I told you, we were just dancing. Not that it is any of your business." I took a calming breath before I continued. "If I want to dance with a guy, I will. If I want to kiss a guy, I will. What I do is my business."

The room temperature dropped, and the air stilled. His whole body tensed, and I held my breath, watching him warily. It was hard to get a read on a man like Santi. The one thing I knew for sure was that he was well-known and feared in the underworld. Rightly so. When Santi put his mind to something, he always made it happen. I heard whispered words between my brothers and father about the Venezuelan Cartel he had been eliminating out of the city.

"Is it now?" he drawled in a dangerously lazy tone.

My brows knitted. "What?" I asked, confused. What the hell was he asking?

"You think who you kiss is only your business?" His eyes darkened around the edges, and his shoulders tensed further. Something dark flared in his whiskey gaze, hot and bright. The intensity of his stare was strong. Time seemed to slow.

Another long second stretched by before I could muster a response.

"Yes, of course," I barely choked out. I couldn't breathe, every fiber of my being on high alert. I felt like prey that had already been caught and didn't even know it.

He strode over, slowly, his eyes narrowed on me, like he'd hunted me all night and finally had me exactly where he wanted. I had never seen him look at me like this. But somewhere deep inside me, I liked it. Very much.

My heart thundered against my ribs and adrenaline rushed through my veins. I should be questioning my reaction to this man, instead I focused on his heat that burned right through me.

He leaned over slowly, both palms resting above my head, and I was trapped under the darkness of his eyes.

"So, you want a kiss?" he purred. His voice turned dark. Smoky. It kindled a heat through every inch of my body. My stomach instantly erupted with butterflies and my cheeks flushed.

Yes! My mind screamed, my breathing erratic as I desperately tried to calm my heart. I had wanted his kiss for so long, but this felt like a trap. Santi only saw me as a kid.

"I-I didn't say that," I breathed out instead. I held his stare as a bead of sweat rolled down my spine, leaving a trail of heat in its wake. A hum of electricity surged through my blood, sending tiny shudders down my spine. God, I just wanted to feel him a bit closer to me.

The side of his lip curved into a knowing smile, and I wanted to wipe it off his face. But even more, I wanted my first kiss to be with Santi Russo. To taste his mouth. Feel his hands on me. I'd had plenty of boys ask me out or attempt to flirt with me, but none of them could ever measure up to someone like Santi Russo. He had set my standards high without even trying.

I held my breath in anticipation. He was so close to me right now that I could feel his heat and smell his cologne. Clean and woodsy. All I had to do was shift forwards and his lips would be on mine. But I had a feeling that would break the moment. So, I remained still, waiting. Leaning in, he ran his nose up the side of mine, his lips brushed delicately against mine.

A sharp inhale echoed between us. My heart raced so hard, I worried it would explode in my chest. He stilled for a fraction of a second before his mouth pressed to mine, this time firm and demanding. He tasted amazing, like whiskey mixed with chocolate.

His body was so close to me, it burned mine everywhere he brushed against me. The frantic beat of my heart drummed in my ears. His mouth clashed with mine, and I exhaled into his mouth, our breaths becoming one. His tongue pushed through my lips and tangled with mine. I moaned into his mouth, starved for more. I wanted him to keep kissing me, touching me.

I wanted *more* of whatever this was. It was so much better than I had ever imagined it. The pull was strong, magnetic, and the intensity shattered me completely, then put me back together.

The world as I knew it changed forever.

My hands came around his neck, rubbing myself against him, his body warm and hard against my soft one. His heat melted me into a puddle. I should have better self-control, but with Santi, I had none. His mouth left me panting, consuming every breath.

If there was a perfect *first kiss*, this was it.

Santi Russo was everything and so much more. I'd give anything to touch his bare skin and feel it under my fingertips.

His one hand came down to my bare thigh, his calloused palm rough against my skin. The heat erupted into a full-blown volcano, every nerve within my body blazing with sensation. I rubbed myself against his body, loving his hands on me, his mouth devouring me. This was what I had been waiting for.

And I knew nobody else could deliver but Santi.

In a move so sudden, he ripped his mouth from mine. Breathing hard, I stumbled back against the wall and watched him, holding my breath, wishing he'd kiss me again. I wanted him to do more. He felt good; he felt right. Like a piece of me that only he could put together.

"Jesus," he muttered under his breath, running a hand through his hair.

Next, a string of curses followed. Each beat of my heart increased the ache in my chest. He took another step backwards, and the sense of loss hit me so hard, it was staggering.

I had him for a second and lost him the next.

But the feel and taste of him would remain seared into my flesh forever. His touch felt like soaking on a hot day in the azure waters of the Mediterranean Sea as the waves carried you back and forth, lulling you into a sense of safety, only to drown you in it.

Would the storm that came along with Santi's kiss drown me?

CHAPTER 15

Santino

A more's moan resonated through me and brought me back to earth. Fucking shit! I was ready to tear into another man for touching her, and I just devoured her lips like it was the last taste I'd ever get and made a hypocrite out of myself.

I had crossed the line that couldn't be set straight again.

Those lips were the softest thing I had ever felt. The way her body melted against mine, and I hadn't even touched her. The palms of my hands were pressed against the wall as I kissed her like tomorrow would never come. I had no fucking idea when my one hand inched up her dress. She made the entire world fade, and the only thing that was left was the taste of Amore Bennetti.

Strawberries.

She tasted like strawberries with dew and spring water.

Jesus fucking Christ! She was still a kid.

Her slightly hitched breathing and hazed shimmers of emerald eyes told me otherwise, but I knew better. Goddamn it!

"This was a mistake," I finally said.

The shattered look she gave me felt like a punch in my chest. What the hell was the kid thinking? Scratch kid. Girl. *Fuck!*

We stood there, watching each other, and I waited for something, anything to come out of those lips. Or maybe a tantrum. I'd let her even get away with slapping me. Nothing.

Then the door flung open, Adriano came through it looking disheveled, his shirt half tucked and belt on wrong. He must have gotten the news before he had a chance to clean himself up after fucking a random girl. Whoever it was, I'd find out, and she'd be banned from my nightclub. If he would have kept his pants on and by Amore's side, none of this would have happened. I wouldn't have tasted Amore Bennetti.

Fuck! Now I even laid blame.

I was fucking burning up. Heat crawled beneath my skin, the want clawing at my chest to take what was mine.

Not. Mine.

A simple kiss with Amore Bennetti was a clear breach of the trust that her brothers and father had in me. Fuck, why did it feel so right! I had never been more worked up about a woman than her. In all my twenty-seven years, I thought I had it all. Apparently not.

Lust, I told myself. Nothing more. Nothing less. Yet, in the most unsettling way, Amore's lips on mine branded me in the most fucked up way. Her soft lips on mine, her shallow breaths brushing against my mouth, her slightly clumsy way of brushing her tongue against mine. Her taste. *Fuck. Me.*

"What happened?" Adriano questioned, his eyes ping-ponged between Amore and me.

Amore answered before I could, her eyes darting to Adriano.

"Your brother was being a dick to Marco," Amore deadpanned, shrugging her slim, bare shoulders. "Then thought he could preach to me about what I should or shouldn't do or wear. Typical, male dickhead." She smoothed her hair and pushed an unruly copper strand behind her ear while plastering a smile on her face for Adriano. "Are you ready to take me home, Adriano?"

She wouldn't look at me, and it hit me all wrong. But what did she expect? I was nine years older than her.

I fought the urge to grab her nape, pull her back into the kiss and slide my tongue against hers and invade her mouth. I wanted to savor her strawberry taste. It almost felt like a *need*.

"Santi, what did you do?" Adriano tried to sound righteous, and it rubbed me the wrong way. He had no rights to her, always left her vulnerable while he chased other women.

With the cold and imperious stare I was known for, I snarled, "Don't you fucking dare."

My brother's eyes narrowed on me, as if assessing whether he should start arguing with me now or later.

"Let's go, Adriano." She took his hand and gently tugged him along, never sparing me a glance.

I watched her slim, open back as she walked out of my office and never looked back.

CHAPTER 16
Adriano

Amore shut the car door on her side a bit too forcefully, which was unlike her. There wasn't much that pissed her off. She had an easy personality, though slightly stubborn when she set her mind on something.

The parking lot was buzzing with life, people going in and out, but Amore was lost in her own world, and I suspected she was steaming. Whatever happened while I was gone, it had pissed her off.

"I'm sorry." It was her last night before she went to study in Italy. I meant for it to be memorable. "How about ice cream before I drop you off?"

She turned her head sideways, her big green eyes on me. "At this hour? Nothing is open."

It was only five past eleven.

"Adriano, most ice cream places close at ten. Just take me home."

I took her hand in mine. "You are upset." There was no sense beating around the bush. She pressed her lips tightly, unwilling to dwell more on it, but I was just as stubborn as she was. "I shouldn't have left you alone."

"No, you shouldn't have," she snapped, surprising me. "It would have been nice just for once if you would have pressed pause on skirt chasing. My last night before Italy where I'll spend the next four years," she grumbled accusingly, "And you couldn't just spend it with me uninterrupted."

Her complaint surprised me. She never seemed bothered about it before.

"I thought you'd have a good time dancing with Marco."

"I did," she hissed. "Until Santi came and smashed his face."

"So why are you mad at me?"

"Are you really that daft?" she hissed. "If you would have just stayed with us, we could have ended this night on a perfect note. Instead of this clusterfuck."

I narrowed my eyes on her. She was flushed and breathless when I burst into Santi's office. Almost as if... they were fooling around. I shook my head. No fucking way! Amore wasn't even Santi's type. He usually went for blondes and mature women that only did as he commanded.

Amore was neither.

Even if her life depended on it, she was determined to follow through with her plans once she set them in motion. Her grandmother wanted her to study business; Amore took fashion and business. Her father wanted her to have guards with her at all times; instead, Amore convinced DeAngelo to teach her how to fight, so she could defend herself and retain some space.

No, I misread the situation. Santi would never even bother to look at Amore as anything other than our adopted sister.

Shifting the car into drive, I left The Orchid behind us and headed for the grocery store. We'd have ice cream whether she liked it or not.

An hour later, we sat in her father's courtyard, eating Ben & Jerry's directly out of the container while seated on the hood of my car.

"Sorry I snapped earlier," Amore broke the silence.

"And I'm sorry for being a dick and ruining the night by leaving you alone."

She nodded and that was how it usually went with us. Amore was a forgiving person, maybe a bit too forgiving. She didn't hold grudges, but she had a tipping point. It was a little thing I had noticed about

Amore over the years. She never forgave people that hurt the ones she loved.

It wasn't surprising. She was loyal to a fault at times. Santi, Lorenzo, nor Luigi believed the two of us would stick together and remain best friends. But for some reason, she cared about me and always stuck up for me; always covered for me. Even when she was attacked two years ago, she didn't blame me, and she was scared out of her mind.

But today, something had shifted. I just wasn't sure what.

"I don't want to lose you, Amore," I rasped. Something in my chest squeezed at the mere thought of it.

There were four years between us, but I never felt them. I wasn't sure if it meant I was not acting my age or Amore was acting more mature than hers. Probably the latter, though everyone seemed to treat her like a kid. Overprotecting her.

Her small hand came to my thigh and squeezed gently. "You're not," she assured me in a soft voice. "After all, who would buy me ice cream?" she teased, her green eyes glimmering. "We'll be friends forever. You are family, Adriano."

I covered her hand with mine. "Forever. We stick together forever."

She smiled. "And don't you forget it, Adriano Russo."

Slipping off the hood, she put her ice cream into the bag. "I better get some sleep," she murmured, stepping into my arms once I was on my feet too. "I'm going to miss you."

Hugging her tightly, I pressed a kiss to the crown of her head. "I'll be there to visit in a few months," I murmured against her hair. She always smelled like strawberries. It suited her with that hair of hers. "We'll talk every day, all day."

"All day?" she choked out, laughing. "That's a bit too much. We'll both be busy all day. But we can touch base every day. Even if it's a short message."

I nodded my agreement. "Every day," I uttered. "I promise."

I was leaving the Bennetti residence when my cell chimed. I pulled out my phone and slid open the message.

NYU.
Got V.C.

The message was from my brother. It was cryptic but plenty clear to me. He had captured the Venezuelan Cartel at NYU. For some odd reason, they kept scouting the university as if searching for someone.

CHAPTER 17

Amore

TWO YEARS LATER

Death.

It shattered you from the inside. It tore at your heart and left you bleeding slowly, crimson red soaking up your soul. Untimely death added a layer to it. It ate at you from the inside, a range of feelings from terror, fear, anger, all the way to sorrow, then repeating the cycle all over again. When I saw my mom die, the terror and fear became a permanent part of me. I'd often thought of Mom and George but never for too long. It hurt too much and led to a dark place.

But this death, Mr. Russo's, hit me differently. For three reasons. He was murdered, but Santi had hunted those men down and killed them all. It felt good to know that. I was doing the same with my mother's killers, and it gave me hope I'd feel even better when I made them pay.

Secondly, the grief on his sons' faces made me hurt right along with them. I wished there was something I could do to ease their pain. Seven years ago, they changed my life in New York for the better. Mr. Russo and his sons, whether they admitted to it or not, helped me gain a father and brothers, a family, when I needed it the most.

Adriano was the added bonus, the cherry on top. I still wasn't sure what Santi was.

My obsession. Or maybe my doom.

Thirdly, the burial felt like a definite closure. The gloomy weather of April and wet mist all around us was appropriate. It reflected the loss, allowed you to grieve so you could let the person you loved go. To a better place. I never had that with Mom and George. Their bodies were lost somewhere in the South American jungle. Their tombstones were just shells.

Shoving the dark thoughts aside, my eyes drifted over the flowers covering the casket that was about to be lowered into the ground. Mr. Russo's final resting place.

Uncle Vincent and I stood to the side since we arrived late. The storm over the Atlantic delayed our flight, leaving us barely enough time to shower and change before Uncle Vincent drove us over to the cemetery for the burial. Lorenzo stayed behind in Italy.

It had been two years since I'd seen Santi and almost six months since I'd seen Adriano.

My best friend stood with his brother, and my heart ached for them. As the casket was slowly lowered into the ground, I saw Adriano discreetly wipe the corner of his eyes. Santi's face, on the other hand, was an unmoving mask. He remained still as a statue, his dark hair glistening with the mist, his eyebrows scrunched together, his lips pressed in a thin line, and his jaw tight.

He was just as beautiful as I remembered, except harder somehow. And he wasn't a soft man to start with.

My father stood behind them along with Luigi. Everyone wore black. I'd never seen so many people in one spot. A wide range of influential families of the Cosa Nostra gathered to see this man off. Everyone that was somehow connected to the Cosa Nostra in some way was here. Mr. Russo was a ruthless man during his lifetime, there was no mistaking that. He wouldn't have been a made man if he wasn't. But they respected him. I knew the same was true for his eldest son.

Me, on the other hand... I was one of those peculiar cases stuck between this world and the elite families of New York that didn't get their hands dirty but were just as scrupulous as these men. They just hid behind fake smiles and bodyguards that did their dirty work for them.

Right now, I have one foot stuck in both worlds, but my activities over the last two years have been tipping the scales in favor of my father's world. Of course, nobody knew it except for DeAngelo and the men that worked for us, hunting down my mother's killers. The men that tortured her for days. That broke her.

I wrapped my arms around myself, the chill seeping into my bones. I wasn't sure whether it was the mist and cool April temperatures or this whole scene. Or maybe it was both.

Adriano called me to tell me what happened. Mr. Russo was strolling to get his daily paper when the drive-by shooting happened. He had twenty bullets in him, and they killed five innocent bystanders.

My eyes traveled to my best friend. It was a shock to the system to hear him break down. I spent hours on the phone with him as he cried, and I cried with him. But I must have been a horrible friend because the whole time I worried about Santi too. I hadn't heard from, nor spoken to Santi since that night at The Orchid. His words still hurt, but in the grand scheme of things, that pain didn't compare to this. Who was comforting Santi? Or did he take it all out by hunting the men that killed his father?

I didn't know how many men of the Venezuelan Cartel Santi had killed. They all deserved it. But it made me wonder whether he would bestow the same fate on me if he knew my blood relation to Perèz Roth-schild. No matter how reluctant. Would it matter to him that those same people killed my own mother, regardless that she was his grandchild?

As if sensing my thoughts, Santi lifted his head and our eyes locked. The air stilled, the time seemed to slow, and the world faded, leaving me alone with the man that was drowning. He didn't move a muscle, not a single change to his expression. But his gaze hit me right through to my soul. There was rage, sorrow, and loss in those dark depths. I wanted to make it better for him. Except I knew he would never accept help from me. He didn't consider me old enough, even for that.

People started moving, approaching the Russo brothers and offering their condolences, but Santi's eyes never strayed from me. He shook hands, acknowledged words spoken, but all the while, his piercing gaze pulled me into his darkness. Challenged me to come forward.

What was it about him that always tugged on my soul? Two years away should have cured this pull. I'd had plenty of dates with men since that kiss, plenty of kisses too... but none of them moved me. My heart remained unmoved, as if it was only beating for Santi.

Unhealthy obsession. It was the only logical explanation.

My father and Luigi showed up at our side, and I turned my attention to them, all the while aware of Santi's eyes on me. It was like an itch, a burn on my neck that wouldn't fade away.

"Amore, I didn't think you'd make it." Dad wrapped me in his embrace, and I returned the comfort.

"Sorry it took so long to get here. There was a storm and the pilots had to land the plane and wait it out."

"You are here now. Safe. That is all that matters."

I shifted to Luigi as Dad turned his attention to Uncle Vincent. They discussed some threats, but they kept switching between Italian and English too quickly. I couldn't follow their conversation with Luigi's attention on me.

"My baby sister." He grinned.

"Hey, brother," I greeted him. I hadn't seen him since Christmas when he, Dad, and Adriano came to spend time with me in Italy.

He pulled me into a hug. "Look at you, sis. I hardly recognize you."

I smiled. "You just saw me."

He tenderly brushed his finger over my cheek. "That was four months ago. Every time I see you, it's like you've grown more."

"I'm still the same size," I told him begrudgingly. To my dismay, my growth ended once I reached five foot five. "We get older every day," I added.

Truth was that some days I felt even older than my twenty years. Maybe leading a double life wasn't for me, though I refused to give up until I saw the man that killed my mother dead. It was my promise to keep. Santi killed one all those years ago at that NYU party and though I was scared, it also felt gratifying to know he was dead. He hurt my mother; Santi hurt him. It was only fair. And I would kill his accomplices.

"I hear your grandmother is happy with all your work and wants to transfer the reins to you," Luigi commented.

"It's too soon. I'm not ready," I admitted reluctantly. The truth was I feared taking the reins of Regalè enterprise would pull me away from my father and brothers. The Russos too. Not that Santi cared too much about me.

Luigi watched me soberly and then nodded. "You are ready, but if you feel it is too soon, then it's too soon. She needs to let you finish college in peace at least."

A pair of hands came around me from behind and wrapped around my waist.

"I was sure you wouldn't make it," Adriano whispered into my ear, his voice slightly choked.

Turning around, I met his eyes. He was alone. Santi was still in the same spot as more people offered condolences. He was officially the don now. At twenty-nine, he was the youngest one in the history of the Italian mafia. At least that's what Adraino said.

"I promised I'd be here. No storm would keep me away." I took his hand into mine and squeezed it in silent comfort. I wished there was something I could do for him. For Santino too.

My eyes darted to his older brother again, like a magnetic pull I had no control over. The two brothers were so similar, yet so different. Santino was probably more alone now than ever. His jaw was pressed so tight, I'd thought he'd break it.

Adriano's face was tense too, but it looked more grief stricken than furious.

"Amore, will you ride with Vincent to the Russo residence?" Dad asked. When I looked at him in confusion, he explained. "Or do you want to join your brother and me? The tradition is to hold a reception after the funeral."

It was hard to picture the Russo family anywhere but in their city home. Maybe because that was a period before I had known them.

"Come with us," Adriano pleaded as I went to break away to go with Dad and my brother. "It's at our Long Island house."

My step faltered and I glanced between Adriano and my family. I didn't think Santi would be happy about that.

"Ah, I'm not sure." I wasn't sure what to say. I didn't want to overwhelm the two brothers. They needed their own space and time to deal with their grief. "You and Santi should have some alone time," I muttered. "And I just got back."

"No, we don't. Right now, I need *you*. Please."

A rush of awareness ran from my nape down to my bloodstream.

"What's going on?" Santi's voice came behind me and washed through me, sending shivers down my spine. I sensed him before he even uttered a word. His voice was deep and indifferent while my stomach clenched with nerves.

How much was he hiding behind that voice? I turned around to meet his gaze. It felt like I needed to mentally prepare for being so close to him. Except I didn't have enough time.

"Adriano wants Amore to ride with you two," Luigi answered. "She doesn't want to impose."

Up close, the impact he had on me was even more intense. My heart drummed hard; my hands wanted to fidget. Instead, I just clenched the material of my dress. I forgot how much taller than me he was, forcing me to crane my neck to meet his gaze. When our eyes met again, it was like all the air was whooshed from my lungs.

"I'm sorry for your loss, Santi," I breathed out, my voice soft and slightly quavering.

He nodded, the unspoken words lingering in the air. I just wished I knew what they were.

"Come with us," Adriano begged as he squeezed my hand, oblivious to the tension between his older brother and me. Then his eyes sought my father's permission.

"Go ahead, Amore," Dad urged me softly. "Luigi, Vincent, and I will meet you there."

I didn't know how Santi felt about it, so I searched for his permission. He gave me a silent nod.

"Okay," I agreed reluctantly. It wasn't smart; I knew it deep down. I should keep my distance from Santi Russo but like a moth to a flame I went.

I got in the back of Santi's 1968 black Ford Mustang Bullitt. It was kind of appropriate for today's mood. Santi always had rare and expensive cars. I had heard a lot about this one since Adriano often talked about it. Santi collected a variety of expensive cars. Adriano only collected Mustangs.

The drive to their home was silent. I sat in the back seat behind

Adriano while he stared out the window, and I focused on Santi's hands and leg movements as he shifted his car. It wasn't rhythmic, but something about the smoothness of it settled me.

My hands were folded together in my lap, my black dress, something I designed myself, had a crew neck with long sleeves and came down to my knees. It was conservative but also hugged the curves rather than hung on me.

I thought back to the last funeral I attended. It was my stepmother's funeral. God, that seemed like a lifetime ago.

Different life.

Different me.

A single stupid decision by a naive child in the midst of a jungle had set so many things in motion, altered so many lives. My mother died, so did George, and I found out George wasn't my father, but an Italian Don was. Elena lost her life because of me.

Nobody spoke of it, but my father did it. Because of those bruises and burns. In order to protect me. How many people died protecting me? So much had changed. That little girl disappeared and in her place came me. I wasn't sure who I was. Amore Regalè. Amore Bennetti. Or someone entirely different.

We just came back from Elena Bennetti's funeral. The woman, my stepmother, who I had known for two weeks, had managed to inflict so many scars, visible and invisible ones, to my body. On top of the ones that I had already gotten in the jungles of South America.

The funeral was a small gathering. Dad limited it only to certain people that were approved by him. I wore black. Lorenzo helped me pick out the dress. When I questioned him whether it would seem fake that I was wearing black for someone that I didn't know, he just murmured, "That's the way of the mafia and their families. Welcome to the world of the Cosa Nostra."

Then he hugged me. He promised to always watch over me and not to think about Elena. But guilt wasn't easy to wash away.

Shouting behind the closed door of Dad's office was clearly heard by everyone. The moment we got back from the funeral, Grandma and Dad went into his office, fury and anger dominating both their faces.

At this point they were screaming at each other. Everyone's eyes remained glued to the office door, nobody willing to move, pretending they didn't hear it. Most of the people hung around in the living room since it had rained outside.

The door of the office opened, and my grandmother Regina stormed out, my father right behind her.

"Amore, you are coming home with me," she ordered me.

I held my breath, my eyes fixated on my newfound father. Time stood still, everyone watching the scene unfold. My grandmother's men stood by ready to defend her. Two of her men came behind me, and I suspected it was to grab me and run if the situation worsened. My father's family and my brothers put their hands on their handguns, ready to pull them at any second.

"She is my fucking daughter! She isn't going anywhere." Dad's roaring and possessive tone surprised me. Yes, he made his wife pay for burning me and torturing me, but he hadn't known about my existence for the first thirteen years of my life. He even admitted himself that he didn't know what to do with me.

"Only by genetics." Grandma Regina, despite her small form, was a force to be reckoned with. She bowed to no man; she listened to nobody. She was the queen. "You know nothing about her. Two weeks under your roof and your own wife tortures her. What's next? She is scared of you, otherwise she would have confided in you. She doesn't belong here, Bennetti!"

My heart thundered so hard, my ears buzzed, and I found it hard to breathe. The air was heavy, too thick.

"And whose goddamn fault is that?" he shouted, pointing his finger at her. "You kept her away from me. You and Margaret!"

"You were a married man!" she screamed back at him. "We had her reputation to think about. She deserved better than to become the whore to a criminal."

"Grandma," my voice was a shaky whisper that nobody heard.

"You fucking hypocritical bitch," Dad yelled. "Get the fuck out of my house! And never come back."

"She is my granddaughter. I have a right to be in her life."

"Not if I say you don't! I'm her father, and I trump you. I don't give a shit who or what you are. Stay the fuck away from my family and my daughter."

My whole body trembled, and my hands shook as I brought them to my lips, trying to keep the sobs from coming out. I bit hard into my lip, the pain grounding me. My dad's face was red with rage, the vein on his neck throbbing, evidence of him trying to control his temper and failing.

"She is my flesh and blood. My only grandchild." My grandmother's voice shook. "I can give her so much more than you could ever dream of. She is the only heiress to the Regalè Empire."

"She is a Bennetti. Always has been and always will be. You know it. It is you that kept her away from me. Get out now before I have you killed."

My grandmother's arm reached for me. On reflex, my hand went for her fingers when everyone pulled out their guns.

Hell rose, and I readied for the worst. My skin crawled with images of my mother's dead eyes, the scent of the burning flesh, and my stepdad's tortured screams echoing somewhere in the distance.

"Go to your room, Amore." Dad's voice was an order that wouldn't tolerate disobedience, but I couldn't move.

I stood frozen, staring at the scene unfold. The silence was too loud, the thundering in my brain increasing with each heartbeat.

Shoving the unpleasant memories into yet another dark corner, I focused on the two brothers.

"Trying to figure out how to shift?" Santi's voice startled me, and I lifted my head, our gazes meeting in the rearview mirror.

"Maybe," I shrugged. "I might want to take your car for a test drive."

Santino Russo loved his cars. Anyone that valued their life would never touch any of them.

His lips barely curled upward but his eyes remained unmoved. "Only if you have a death wish, girl."

I rolled my eyes at him. From kiddo to girl. I wasn't sure if this was a step up or step down.

"Amore's driving has gotten better," Adriano glanced behind at me. "Though she hasn't tried a stick yet."

My cheeks flamed at his terminology. "Manual shift," I corrected him. "Manual shift, Adriano. That's the proper terminology."

Adriano chuckled. "Same thing. Don't have a dirty mind, Amore."

I narrowed my eyes on Adriano but remained silent, avoiding his brother's gaze because all my dirty thoughts revolved around Santi Russo, and the day he buried his father was not the time to think about it.

My eyes scanned the crowd, looking for Adriano. He had been slipping in and out of my vision all afternoon. I kept out of the way, quietly watching everyone. The other three families of the Cosa Nostra hung around, every so often throwing their glances my way. I didn't usually frequent gatherings of the underworld, so I was a novelty to them. The only families of the mafia I socialized with were my own and the Russos. My gaze drifted through the room, and I spotted Gabriel Carrera at the same time he spotted me.

Inkman, I thought dryly of the nickname I assigned to him.

He started walking towards me, his stride confident. Was he part of the Colombian Carrera Cartel? Or was his last name just a coincidence? It was a fairly common last name, though I had to admit, he looked fierce and scary.

"Miss Bennetti," he greeted me. I had only met him once at The Orchid. The same night I got my first kiss and my first rejection.

"Mr. Carrera."

"Please call me Gabriel."

It wasn't like I would see him around a lot to call him by his first name.

"Amore."

"How is Italy?" I cocked my eyebrow. Maybe he knew a bit too much. He must have read my thoughts. "Adriano said you are studying in Italy."

Ah.

"I love Italy," I answered. "So, you work with Adriano and Santi?"

"When necessary. Yes." My brows knitted at his cryptic answer. "Santi and I have common goals."

Sensing he wouldn't elaborate, I glanced away from him and spotted Santi's zia rushing towards the kitchen.

"It was nice seeing you," I said, glancing at Gabriel. "Excuse me."

Pushing off the wall, I strode after her.

"Can I help you?" I offered. She whirled around and I spotted tears glistening in her eyes.

She swallowed and nodded. I followed after her and helped her in the kitchen for the rest of the afternoon. Renzo hung around the kitchen too, though I wasn't sure if it was because he wasn't in the mood for company or just wanted food.

"Thank you for your help, Amore." Santi's Aunt Giulia smiled, though it was a slightly sad smile. I've seen her only once before, the day I met the Russo men. She was Mr. Russo's sister-in-law, but I rarely went around the Russo extended family.

Her silver white hair fell down her back in cascades. She was still very beautiful but unlike most Italian families, she had beautiful, shattering blue eyes.

"No problem," I told her, tucking my hands into my dress. "Do you need anything else?"

She shook her head, and I offered a smile. "I'll go find a corner and hide then."

She chuckled. "That's a good idea. I will do the same in a few minutes."

I nodded and went through the house. The place was huge, very beautiful, but too big for a bachelor. I wondered why Mr. Russo moved to the city after his wife died. The words he told me when he admitted that it was my mother that caused the wedge between the Russo and Bennetti family made me think that maybe he didn't love his wife. Or maybe made men were just unfaithful by default. Would Santi be unfaithful to his wife?

A sharp pain pierced through my chest thinking about Santi with another woman. I didn't like to think of him marrying. I was stupid to even think any thoughts about it. With his looks, Santi had a trail of heartbroken women behind him. Santi Russo was none of my business and the best self-preservation was to stay clear of him, so I pushed all the thoughts about Santi and his women away.

Besides, I knew marrying a made man wasn't in my cards. Not if I wanted to keep the Regalè Empire going, and I promised Grandma that

I would. Like my grandmother always said, I wasn't born in the world of the mafia, and I wouldn't die in it. She always said that she never had the intention of having Mom nor me involved in the underworld side of her business.

Most people had left by now and the house had quieted down. Dad, Uncle Vincent, and my brother left after speaking to Adriano. He promised them either he or Santi would bring me home. It better be Adriano, and I told him as much. Nobody knew about that kiss Santi and I shared but being alone with him was out of the question.

Curiosity and the need to be alone had me climbing the luxury marble steps up to the second floor. Once there, my footsteps were silenced by the plush carpeting as I roamed down the corridor. The house seemed cold, which I guess made sense since nobody lived here on a regular basis.

A door at the end of the corridor was wide open and I strode to it, peeking inside.

A beautiful, large library with warm tones and a marble fireplace stretched in front of me. Dusk had darkened the room, the rising moon throwing off the only light coming through the windows and casting shadows throughout it. Slowly walking through the room, I let my fingers sweep over the wooden furniture. Everything was clean and pristine.

Even in the dark, I could see the beautiful books stacked from top to bottom in the bookcases. The bookcases spanned every inch of the room except for the window at the back of the room where a leather lounge chair sat.

It smelled like leather and old books here, kind of like George's old library. I used to spend so many hours in his library, playing by the fireplace while he worked on his research papers or planned our next adventure.

Flicking on the desk lamp, the ghosts of the past faded away and an amber glow cast soft shadows through the room.

I fell in love with this place in one, single breath. The place was heaven. It kind of reminded me of Mr. Russo and Santi. Definitely not Adriano. He hated to read with a passion. The place even smelled like Santi.

I curled up in the chair, tucking my legs beneath the linen of my dress, and pulled the book off the little coffee table. It was like someone was here and left it there to come back to. Was it Mr. Russo? Or Santi?

Flipping it over, I read the description of it. Cartel and drug smuggling of South America. Frowning, I almost set it back down, but something nudged me forward to open the book and start reading it. The dangers, cruelty, murders, massacres, greed... it was all laid out with one of the most dangerous cartels of South America. It was kind of ironic that someone from the Russo family was reading this book when they probably worked with similar kinds of men.

The Perèz Cartel. The Carrera Cartel.

My heart hammered as my eyes skimmed the pages, seeing the names I recognized. My grandfather's, great-grandfather's.

The book was so engrossing, I didn't hear the door open, nor click shut, nor did I hear the footsteps that followed. The tingling sensation of being watched had me glancing up from my book to find Santi's eyes staring at me.

"Santi." I jumped up, my feet tangling against the hem of my dress, and I would have nosedived straight into the carpet if he hadn't caught me.

His strong arms shot out and wrapped around my waist, pulling me back up as I fumbled against him. We both froze at the same time. The smell of his cologne was familiar, and adrenaline shot through my system, pushing my heart rate into overdrive.

"Last time I caught you like this, you got sick all over me," he said, his tone a mixture of deep timbre and smooth liquor washed over me. The suffocating heat from his touch threatened to combust.

I looked up, willing my breaths to come out steady, and caught the corner of his mouth tugging upward.

"Ah, you had to go and ruin the moment," I teased him in a slightly breathless tone. My pulse drummed in my ears, and my heart tripped up at his closeness. I laid my hand on his forearm to steady myself. I was painfully aware of his strength, his touch sending a hum of electricity through every fiber of my body. And his heat! It was making me lightheaded. Correction. *He* was making me lightheaded.

It was wrong. My body's unwilling reaction to his closeness.

If I was smart, I would excuse myself and leave, but my body refused to listen. This crushing after Santi would be the death of me. "I'm really sorry for your loss, Santi."

His eyes locked on my hand, and I feared that maybe I shouldn't be that familiar. After all, last time we parted on not-so-great terms. I quickly pulled my hand back while his words rang in my ears. *Mistake.* He called kissing me a mistake.

His dark eyes locked with mine, the gravity of his gaze trapping me in its depths. I always felt safe around Santi but never comfortable. Something about him always unnerved me. Maybe it was the fact that he was so handsome with his broad shoulders and tattooed hand that had killed who knew how many people. Or maybe it was the darkness I sensed around him, the dominant energy all around him.

"Thank you." His voice was rough. "I think I need a drink."

He went to turn around, but I quickly stopped him, my hand reaching for his sleeve.

"Here, sit down," I told him, nudging him towards my chair. "I'll get it for you. Just tell me what you're drinking."

A small smile played on his lips again. "Okay. I'll have whiskey" He tilted his head to the corner on the opposite side of the room. "The mini bar is there."

I hurried across the floor, my feet still bare and footsteps silent on the rug.

"This house is beautiful," I told him, glancing over my shoulder. He sat in my chair... no, his chair that I occupied earlier.

"You've grown up, Amore."

I almost dropped the glass I had picked up. It was best not to comment on that.

"What kind of whiskey?" I asked, lowering down on my knee and scouting through the assortment.

"Michter's," he answered. I focused on the task of selecting the right bottle. "Two fingers."

"Ice?"

"Please."

I added two cubes of ice from the bucket to his drink and poured two fingers of whiskey into it. As I walked back to him, his eyes darkened, locked on me. The way he looked at me made me feel *hot* inside. His deep brown eyes were the same color of the whiskey that swirled in the glass, and when the light hit them just right, with thick, dark lashes that gave him a sharp expression, it was hard not to feel unnerved as he watched you. *All* his focus on you. Combine that with an unhealthy crush, it was deadly.

Gently sloshing in the glass, the clinking ice woke me from my stupor. I handed him the drink, our fingers brushing against each other, sending an electric buzz straight through me.

I took a step back and leaned against the windowsill, watching him take a sip of whiskey and suddenly I felt thirsty for a stiff drink. Though I hadn't had a sip of alcohol since that tequila night with Adriano.

"Where is Adriano?" I asked, breaking the silence.

"He drove back into the city." His answer surprised me; I didn't expect Adriano to leave without me.

"Why?" I frowned slightly annoyed but then immediately scolded myself. He buried his father today; he didn't deserve my nagging.

"He is following a trail for me."

With an erratic beat of my heart, I realized this left me alone with Santi Russo. I wasn't sure how many guests still lingered downstairs, but it was probably better I called Dad or Uncle Vincent to come and get me.

Santi extended his hand with the glass.

"Want a sip?" My eyebrows tugged together, trying to figure out whether it was a trick question. I was still underage, at least in the States. "It's been a rough day."

I eyed his tattooed hand, wrapped around the glass then finally accepted the offered glass. He watched as I brought it to my lips and took a small sip. The coughing was instant.

"Crap," I muttered through my itchy throat, and watery eyes. "This is just as bad as tequila."

Dark amusement ghosted in his eyes. "No way. Everything is better than tequila."

Clearing my throat, I rolled my eyes. "True," I said softly. "I haven't been able to smell tequila since that day."

"Anymore wild, drunken nights?" he asked.

I shrugged, handing him back his drink. "No drunken nights."

His fingers brushed mine and my pulse fluttered. This thing with Santi was just a schoolgirl crush, nothing more. But it would eventually be the death of me. It had to be smothered and eliminated.

"But, yes to wild nights?" he asked, his expression hooded.

"I'm not telling you," I blurted out. "You'd tell my father, and my return trip would go down the toilet."

A smile tilted his lips. "I'm not exactly the kiss and tell type of guy."

My mind went blank at all the possible meanings of that statement. I was all for kissing Santi, always had been. Maybe it would be a way to get over my dying crush for him. Though the last time, it didn't take him long to pronounce it a mistake.

I should go before I did something stupid. If Adriano was gone, there was no sense in staying here.

"Hmmm, I'm going to go." I shifted off the windowsill. Santi stood up from his chair at the same time, and we found each other standing too close, his body brushing against mine. He towered above me, his heat drawing me in.

I watched him take another sip of his drink and place it down onto the side table where the book about the cartel sat.

"You grew up," he drawled in a soft voice.

I swallowed and not a single word came to mind. His attention made butterflies dance in my stomach. How pathetic was that!

His gaze slid down the length of my body, his voice smooth, making my pulse race. Unwanted heat sparked inside me, and it was hard to keep my face stoic. Santi was every woman's dream. At twenty-nine, he had half of New York's women drooling after him and the other half pretended not to fantasize about him.

His mouth twisted into a devastating smirk, one I imagined him using on other women. Instinctively, I took a step backwards and pressed myself further into the window, trying desperately to put some distance between us. I needed it to keep my head. To keep myself from reaching out.

He leaned closer, taking a deep breath and his broad chest filling the space between us.

"Strawberries."

My brows knitted in confusion. What is he talking about?

"You smell like strawberries."

The warmth in my stomach spread like fire through every inch of my body and spilled into my chest. I swore it felt like my heart glowed, though I wasn't sure why. Maybe at the way he spoke those words, insinuating.

"What are you doing, Santi?" I asked, my voice strangely breathless and raspy under his gaze. After what had happened last time he kissed me, I should be offended every time he was near me. Yet the opposite was true.

A hot, hungry desire flashed in his eyes, setting off the flames I wanted to contain.

"I like your perfume, Amore." Jesus, when he purred my name like that, I was ready to melt into a puddle of mush.

A voice whispered inside me, warning me to push him away and leave this room, but my body refused to listen. A war waged between my body and mind, and it didn't bode well for me.

"I-I'm not wearing perfume, Santi," I whispered, my voice wavering.

My body pressed against his, winning the internal battle. His expression simmered into something dark and hot, and a shiver ran down my spine as his fingertips came to my neck, his thumb gently brushing against my raging pulse.

"I want you, Amore Bennetti." So direct, yet it didn't surprise me. There was so much sex laced in his voice, I thought I would combust into pleasure just from his words. "Spend the night with me."

I hesitated for a second. It had been what I had wanted for so long. Santi was the first boy that brushed my tears away, the first boy to hold my head as I puked my guts out after getting drunk, my first crush, and my first kiss. The question was whether he would be my first heartbreak because I had a feeling getting over Santi would be devastating.

Except I wanted him. I had always wanted him.

Determination settled within me. He felt right to me, and I had never been the one to give up when I wanted something.

"Okay," I whispered.

Santino Russo would be my first everything.

CHAPTER 18

Santino

The moon glow over Amore's features made her appear surreal, like an angel with flames of fire for hair. I came into the library seeking solitude. Ever since Pà was gunned down, I have felt only rage and sorrow, hunger for revenge. The anger and guilt swelled inside me, threatening to burst like a dam under the pressure.

Then I saw her there. Amore Bennetti in my library. For my taking. If there was anything to ease this pain, it was her.

She is still a kid, I told myself. I had no business standing here with a twenty-year-old girl that watched me with eyes of green and innocent infatuation in her stare. Yet, the kid and girl faded away. All I saw in its place was a woman.

A woman with curves and a soft body that called to me. I wanted to know every inch of her body and soul; break her, only to put her together again and ruin her for any other man.

Amore Bennetti was mine.

Adriano said there were plenty of times boys chased after her in Italy. I wasn't a boy, and I certainly didn't fuck like one.

I waited for her to push me away. But instead, her small hand came to my chest, her fingertips wrapping around my tie, then gently tugged on it. She was nervous. I didn't blame her, not after what had happened two years ago. We haven't spoken nor seen each other since.

But the moment she accepted my invitation, I knew she was mine, and now I would take her. Somehow over the last two years, since that first innocent kiss, she had become my obsession. My craving. I told myself it was fucked up. All wrong. It didn't matter.

Her whole body pressed against me, her skirt softly crushed between our bodies, and I closed the distance between us as I lifted her into my arms.

Her hands wrapped around my neck, and I strode out of the library and into my bedroom. The one I hadn't stepped into since we left this place behind. Our housemaid had cleaned the entire house in anticipation that either my brother or I would decide to move back, but the chances were slim to none.

She tilted her head up, her eyes watching me with so much trust, it hurt my heart. I lowered my head and licked the seam of her mouth until she parted those lush lips for me. God, I fucking missed her. Her strawberry smell, her smiles, her green eyes. I didn't understand this reaction I had, but I knew I'd never share her.

Once inside my bedroom, I pushed the door with the sole of my shoe and it clicked behind me, locking Amore inside the room with me. Never breaking the kiss, her tongue danced in perfect harmony with mine. She had grown more confident in her kiss, making me wonder how many boys she'd had. It didn't matter because she would have none going forward.

I would take her everything - her body, heart, and soul. Nothing less would do.

I slid the dress off her body. Her undergarments followed, then I gently lowered her onto the bed, her red hair sprawled across the pillows. The soft light of the moon filtered through the large window and illuminated her face and those stunning eyes locked on me.

Her golden skin was in full view. Her hands reached out and loosened my tie. Then her graceful fingers fumbled, working on the buttons of my shirt. Impatient to feel her skin against mine, I helped her and discarded it onto the floor. The rest of my clothes and shoes quickly followed.

Her hands came up to my chest, the touch soft and tender. I didn't do gentle, but for her... fuck, I'd try. Her wide eyes watched me with awe and curiosity, no shyness or reservation in them.

"You are beautiful." Her voice washed over me like honey. Leaning upward from the pillows, she brushed her mouth against my skin, right above my heart. My chest swelled, filing a dull void with the scent and touch of this woman. I wrapped my hand around the nape of her head and crushed my mouth on hers. I swallowed her soft moans, her lips soft against mine.

Sliding my hand behind her back, the smoothness of her skin like silk under my palms. A soft moan sounded against my lips. I broke our kiss, lifting slightly away from her and let my eyes travel down the length of her body. She was fucking gorgeous. She had an hourglass figure, her body soft, ready to melt under my rough palms.

Taking one of her breasts in my hand, I rubbed my thumb over her nipple. Her sharp inhale had me pausing, my eyes searching out her emerald gaze. The desire and hunger hazy in her stare matched my own.

"Santi." My name on her lips was the most beautiful melody.

She arched herself into my hand, and I resumed tormenting her nipple with my fingers. I moved over her, settling my weight between her thighs. Our mouths found each other again, hungry and demanding. Like a thief, I demanded it all.

My free hand crawled between her thighs, touching her soft skin there and spreading her legs wider for me. My fingers found her soaking wet folds, and the moment I brushed against her core, she arched into my touch.

So damn responsive. It was sexy as fuck.

The girl was forever gone. The only thing in front of me was a woman. She was my perfection in an unexplained way. My blood boiled, needing her like the air I breathed.

I have had my share of women. They were a passing blur, but Amore was different. My instinct warned me that she could inch her way deep into my black soul and permanently find a home there.

CHAPTER 19

Amore

Desperation for more clawed at my insides and desire pulsed between my legs. His touch and mouth burned me in the sweetest way possible. His kisses were making me delirious. I ran my hands up his chest, over his neck, and into his thick, dark hair.

His finger slid inside me, and I thought I'd shatter into a million pieces. He kept kissing me, lazy and sweet, but he held back. I felt it like my own emotions.

"Santi, please," I begged against his lips. "Harder."

A groan resounded in his chest, and then he thrust his finger into me harder and pulled my bottom lip between his teeth. Kissing Santi Russo was wet, messy, and hot. The most delicious sin I had ever committed, and I intended to sin for the rest of my life. With him.

His mouth traveled down my neck to my breast until he captured a nipple in his mouth and white lights sparked behind my eyelids.

"Fuck," I breathed out. His mouth on my skin was marking me with each touch as his forever.

His thumb teased at my clit at the same time, and my eyes rolled back into my head, my pulse throbbing between my legs. I kept arching into his hand, rubbing myself against him, desperate for release.

"Not so fast," he ordered in a hoarse voice, removing his fingers and halting my hips. I whimpered my complaint. I had waited too long for this, my impatience clawing and demanding that I satisfy this need.

He lowered his head again and drew my nipple into his mouth, tugging on it, sucking. My hands tangled through his hair, pulling him closer as sensation exploded through me. My core burned, the pulsing ache like flames igniting every fiber of me. He shifted his attention to my other nipple, the cool air tingling over the abandoned flesh.

His hands slid down my body. He released my nipple and his lips trailed lower, leaving in its wake a searing trail. With his wide shoulders, he nudged my legs even wider. I lay spread open for him, and I didn't feel an ounce of shame.

The only sensations brewing in my blood were gratification and greed for this man. The moment his tongue connected with my clit, my hips bucked underneath him, and I weaved my fingers through his hair as a loud moan caught in my throat.

His hands held my hips still while he continued feasting on me, lapping, sucking, and nipping. I attempted to arch my back, but his hand kept me pressed against the mattress. His teeth grazed my clit, and I raised my ass to rock against his mouth. I forced my hands off his hair, fearing I'd pull his hair out with how hard I gripped the strands.

"Oh, oh, oh." My moans echoed through the room. My hands fisted the sheets, and his tongue lit my body on fire. It was so good. "Santi... fuck!"

His hands eased their pressure and my hips lifted up into his face, needing more of this sensation. His tongue was working me mercilessly. As he pressed his thumb harder against my clit, my legs tightened around him, and my climax shattered through me. My back arched off the bed, and I lost all control of my body.

White pleasure exploded through me, my hips writhing underneath him, and my fingers gripping his hair. Flames shot through my veins and lights exploded behind my eyelids. A shudder fluttered through me, and a languid heat spread through every fiber of my body. I felt like I was spiraling out of control, my cries filling the room.

He kept lapping at my juices, like he wanted to savor every single drop, while my body shuddered under him. As he rose to his knees, his body came up blanketing mine and he settled his cock between my thighs.

His eyes were dark, intoxicating. He raised his finger, bringing it up to my lips. He traced his thumb over my lower lip, leaving a coat of wetness across my mouth and a shiver ran down my spine. I swept my tongue across my bottom lip, tasting myself. His eyes flashed with something hot and hard.

My eyes lowered, seeing his thick length straining for my entrance, and instantly I was aroused again. The throb between my legs returning. But he was big... so big. I worried he'd split me in two. I didn't even realize I shifted away from him.

"Santi," I whispered, my voice hoarse like I hadn't talked in weeks. "You are too big."

Our gazes met, his darkness commanding my body. I realized I have always relished in Santi's darkness. Maybe because in it, I also found safety. I wasn't sure, all I knew was that I wanted him and felt safe with him.

"It will fit," he assured me with a tortured groan. "You can take it. Trust me, baby."

A shuddering breath left me, and my eyes locked on his large cock. I trusted him; I really did.

I swallowed. "I haven't... I haven't done this before."

If he decided to stop now, I'd kill him, but it was only fair I warned him. Anticipation hummed between my thighs, an aching need for him consuming me.

If I thought he'd stop, I was dead wrong because something feral and possessive crossed his expression, and he pressed his lips against mine.

"I'll be gentle," he rasped.

"Not too gentle," I choked, attempting to tease, but his eyes darkened, and passion burned in them, setting me aflame.

"The second time nothing will save you," he croaked. "But for your first time, I'll be gentle. Trust me."

My heart fluttered in my chest and drifted off to him.

"I trust you," I whispered. I trusted him with all my heart.

I could feel his hard shaft poised at my entrance. He felt hot against it, my pussy clenching for more of him and my breathing erratic. I watched in fascination where our bodies connected. Two becoming one.

"Fuck!" he cursed, and my eyes snapped to him.

"What's the matter?"

"Condom," he gritted out.

"I'm on the pill," I moaned, raising my hips, feeling his shaft slide deeper. My eyes lowered again, something so erotic about seeing his length pressed against my entrance, the tip of it barely inside me. It ignited a heat at my core. "I'm clean."

He breathed out. "I'm clean too." He lowered his forehead against mine. "I always use a condom."

I lifted my hips further to encourage him forward. "Please," I panted. "Don't make me wait."

"You are an eager woman," he choked out in an anguished chuckle.

"At least you called me a woman," I muttered. "Now, fuck me, Santi."

I barely registered as he moved, and his hand curved at my nape as he brought my head up. His eyes grew dark, and every nerve flared within my body with excitement. With life. For Santi.

"I say when I fuck you." There was a tightness in his voice, laced with sex and tension that I was dying to break.

"Fine," I said. "When will you fuck me?"

He shook his head, though a flicker of amusement danced in his eyes, mixing with his strained desire.

Holding my gaze, he nudged deeper into my entrance with the tip of his hot, hard cock. There was a slight sting, and I frowned at the pain. He was trying to be gentle, but I almost wanted him to thrust in hard, ripping my barriers in one move. This... this was too painful.

He pushed his hips forward, the shallow thrust causing me to whimper. He pressed his lips against my mouth, and my lips parted, welcoming him in. A noise unlike any other trembled from my lips as he pushed in further. My skin was hot, burning through me.

"It's okay," he murmured against me, our breathing as one. His kiss turned harder, biting and sucking. I hungered so much for him, I needed more. Yet the pain had me hesitating. "You feel so good, baby."

His words sank into my heart and filled me with warmth. I wanted to please him, make him feel good.

I lifted my ass, needing more of him inside me. This fucking ache was killing me.

He nudged further, entering me slowly, his big size stretching me. Breaking our kiss, I watched in fascination at our joined bodies, and the sense of completeness overwhelmed every single cell of me.

"So fucking tight," he breathed out in a raspy voice. "Fuck, I can feel your pussy clenching around my cock. So fucking good." His dirty words made my insides shudder with need.

Santi was the man for me. He was the only one I wanted. It had always been him and warmth blossomed in my heart, searing his name on my soul. He continued to move slowly, deeper. I didn't want slow. I wanted hard and fast. I needed him to send me over the edge.

As if he heard my thoughts, he pushed further, breaking my barrier, and I hissed out a breath. He stilled and my nails dug into his shoulders, urging him on. My heart pounded against my ribs and blood rushed through my veins.

"P-please," I panted. "I need you."

He slipped in even deeper, pushing in every inch of him, filling me to the hilt. The stinging pain burst, and a whimper slipped through my lips. He instantly stilled, letting me get used to his size.

"Fuck. You're so tight," he muttered with a grunt. "The perfect pussy."

His hips tentatively moved; his eyes locked on mine. Shuddering breaths mixed with his groans, a mix of all the emotions swelling in my chest. His grunts. His eyes. Everything about him was thrilling, tempting, so exhilarating.

Shifting my hips upward, grinding against him, I relished in the friction our bodies made. It felt amazing. As I stared at his face, his eyelids lowered. There was burning hunger in his dark gaze.

"More, Santi," I begged. He needed more. I needed more.

He started to move faster, pumping in and out of me, and the sense of being overwhelmed in the best possible way flooded me. I gave in to it, my back arching off the bed to meet his thrusts despite the pain. The pleasure outweighed it by a million.

"You take it so good," he rasped, as he thrust even deeper, moving faster and harder.

His one hand moved between our bodies and the moment his finger touched my clit, circling it hard and fast, pleasure shot through every fiber of me, spiraling me higher and higher.

Crying out his name, I gave in to the surge of pleasure and the languid heat that drowned out every other sensation. I let myself go to it with the knowledge he'd catch me. His hips worked like pistons, thrusting into me, through my orgasm and my clenching pussy, as grunting noises left his lips. He went even deeper, and I could feel him everywhere.

"Amore," he growled out my name, and his head tilted back. His mouth parted as his muscles seized and he spilled himself inside of me. He buried his head in the crook of my neck, his breathing matching my own. Two hearts beating as one.

His cock twitched inside me, his cum or my blood leaking out of my pussy, and I already decided, I would have more of him. More of this.

Still inside me, his eyes searched out mine, and I looked up at him. I *loved* Santi Russo. The crush was long gone and love for this man was ignited. If I was honest with myself, I had loved him for years.

His mouth lowered to kiss me, the gentle brush of his lips against mine. I wanted to stay like this forever, joined as one, belonging to him and only him. And I wanted him to belong to me.

When he pulled out, I winced at the sharp pain. Maybe him staying inside me forever wasn't the brightest idea. He kissed my lips again.

"You okay?"

I nodded. I glanced down to find the evidence of my virginity on the white sheets. I wrinkled my nose and he chuckled.

"It's normal," he smiled, then pressed another kiss onto my nose. God, this Santi, the gentle one, would kill me. "Let's get cleaned up. A warm bath will ease your sore muscles."

He rose and scooped me up from the bed. It was on the top of my tongue to tell him I loved him, but the fear of rejection swallowed my words.

CHAPTER 20

Santino

A more slept soundly in my arms; her naked body sheltered by my own. I stared at her fair skin with little freckles on the tip of her nose that I had never noticed before. I couldn't resist, leaning over to press a light kiss on the tip of her nose and then trail my mouth down her neck. She responded immediately, her fingers pushing through my hair, fingernails scraping against my scalp.

"So fucking beautiful," I murmured against her neck, inhaling deeply. The scent of strawberries comforting. She tasted like fresh picked strawberries. I had to get some self-control around her; otherwise, I'd pounce on her again and she was exhausted. She had to recover before I buried myself into her again.

A virgin.

Mine.

Her old man would shoot me if he knew what we had done. In our world, virginity was sacred. Yet, she gave it to me so freely, willingly. Though honestly, she wasn't part of the Cosa Nostra. Not really. Her grandmother's influence and immense wealth succeeded in keeping her out of it. Her only connection to the underworld was her father and brothers.

The words she uttered so many years ago to me and my father rang in my ears. '*I didn't grow up in this world, and I won't die in it either*'. Things changed. She was mine now. She'd be part of my world, but I could protect her and limit her exposure to the underworld.

I'd have to talk to her old man before he got wind of the situation. I already knew what I planned on doing. I would make an arrangement to marry her. I didn't care what Bennetti's conditions would be, I'd give it to him. She would be my wife, but only after she finished college. She had another year. Until then, I'd play her boyfriend. Whatever she needed. I could wait. I could be patient when I needed to.

"I should go home before my father or brothers notice I'm not there," she murmured sleepily. It was almost eleven at night, and I was determined to keep her in my bed.

"They think you are with Adriano," I told her. Luigi texted me, asking if Amore was staying over. It wasn't anything unusual since Adriano and Amore have been joined at the hip since she was thirteen. I told him yes, keeping it short. "I told your brother you'd spend the night."

She wasn't the typical girl in the Cosa Nostra. The old Bennetti had to learn that early on or risk losing her. Amore liked her freedom, coming and going to her grandmother's, and if he would have shackled her to the same rules of the Cosa Nostra women, he would have lost her. He knew full well that with one word from his daughter to her grandmother, the damn dragon woman would bring fury to his door. He'd fight but he'd lose.

Because Regina Regalè had her own power and superseded the whole of the Cosa Nostra and five families combined.

"I like the sound of that," she said softly, her hands exploring my body, her eyes inspecting the ink on my arm curiously. She wasn't shy about her body nor her desire. She owned it better than most mature women.

The need within clawed through me to take her again, fuck her and hear her moans, my name on her lips. *Jesus!* Just a few hours and she has already become my vice. Her smooth skin felt right under my rough palms, and she tasted better than anything. Her moans seared through my veins and into my brain. She'd remain part of me. I knew it as well as I knew my name.

"I like your tattoo," she whispered, her hands skimming over my right forearm and all the way down to my fingers. "Does it mean anything?"

I pointed to the handgun wrapped in the tree vine, orchids, and the cross. "Cosa Nostra, God, and family."

She studied it curiously.

"In that order, huh?" she teased.

Seven years living under the umbrella of the Cosa Nostra and somehow Amore avoided most of the brutality of our world. Though from what little she told me, she witnessed it when she saw her mother die. Maybe God granted her a reprieve after what she had been through. Or maybe it was her grandmother who insisted she be kept out of the Cosa Nostra and keep the Regalè fortune out of this world. "And the other tattoos?"

She sat up and pulled her knees to her chest, still holding up the blanket to cover her body. Her copper hair was stark against the light of the moon, white sheets, and her sun-kissed skin. She had blossomed into a beautiful woman. Italy suited her.

"When do you go back to Italy?" I asked her, avoiding her question. I didn't want to tell her the skull represented the death I brought to men that dared cross me.

She sighed. "Day after tomorrow. I could only get a reprieve for three days' worth of missed classes from the dean."

I nodded in understanding. "How about I come and visit you?"

"In Italy?" I nodded and her eyes narrowed suspiciously. "Seriously?"

"Yes, in June, after school ends. Adriano said your classes end in the middle of June, and I'm guessing you are not coming home for summer again."

I'd never admit it, but I was kind of disappointed when she hadn't returned home, not a single time over the last two years. That damn kiss was something I thought about more often than I should have.

She shrugged her slim shoulders. "Probably not. I'm working in the Milan office in July and the London office in August. Then my classes start again."

No wonder her family was so proud of her. Amore was just as ambitious and capable as her grandmother. Except Amore had a soft heart, unlike her dragon of a grandmother.

"That's settled then." I pulled her into my arms. It will be torture to survive two months without her.

"Santi?"

"Hmmm?"

"Are you alright?" she whispered.

Slightly shifting off the pillow, so I could see her face, I furrowed my brows and a noise of amusement escaped me. "Tonight was one of the best nights I've had in a while. A long while."

Her cheeks flushed a pale pink, almost matching the shade of her hair. "I meant with your dad gone and everything." Her fingers fidgeted with the hem of the sheet.

Pain vibrated through my chest; except this time, it didn't make me want to go on a killing spree. Or into a rage pushing me to hunt down every member of the Venezuelan Cartel in the city. This time, it was more of a dull pain of a loss, and I suspected it had something to do with her.

"He was a good man," she whispered.

"Yeah, he was." I pulled her closer to me, and she put her head onto my chest.

She didn't need to know that I had the streets swarming with men hunting for the Venezuelans responsible for shooting my father. I had more men on the streets than all the other four families combined. My reputation stretched far, and word got around of my extra-curricular activities in hunting these men. Nobody wanted to cross paths with me, so information was pouring in. I wouldn't rest until the very last member of the Venezuelan Cartel was dead or gone from my city.

"Santi?"

"Hmmm."

"You-you're not going to tell me this was a mistake tomorrow, right?" Her body tensed just slightly, but enough for me to notice.

"You were never a mistake," I told her. "And that kiss two years ago" —her breathing hitched—"it wasn't a mistake either."

Her eyes sought out mine, hesitant trust in her emeralds. "Really?" she asked softly.

"I'm dead serious." I pressed a kiss to her forehead. "Go to sleep, Amore. I have a busy day tomorrow."

A soft scoff left her lips. "What?" I questioned her.

She raised her head, an undignified expression on her face. "I don't want to sleep. I want more sex."

And just like that, my good mood returned, and I couldn't hold back my chuckle. I had lost my father this week and felt nothing but anguish and rage until tonight when she gave me all of her. She was the best medicine, but I feared I might have created a sex addict.

I leaned down to kiss her, angling her face.

"What have I done?" I murmured against her lips. "I've created a monster."

"It is a long time to wait until June for sex, Santi." She pouted. "Unless I find myself a substitute."

I growled, possessiveness flaring inside me. Her mouth was swollen, her skin flushed, and the thought of anyone seeing her like this made me want to go on a murder spree.

"If I catch you kissing or touching anyone else, I'll hunt them down and kill the motherfuckers." My glare intensified, so she knew I meant business. "And if they touch you, I'll burn the flesh off their hands so that the pain is the last thing they remember before I slice their throats."

A soft gasp escaped her, her eyes widening. "That's a bit much, don't you think?"

"No, I don't," I told her, my voice growling. "I swear to God, Amore, if I find out another man touched you, I'll hunt them down and chop them into pieces. Their hands will be delivered to you in a box. As a reminder that only I touch you."

"You are bluffing." She swallowed, gasping.

My jaw ticked, my teeth clenched, and my gaze froze to ice.

"I. Do. Not. Fucking. Bluff."

Suddenly, she smiled and her whole face lit up. "Okay, then lots of FaceTime sex."

I shook my head in disbelief. Jesus, she was riling me up too easily. Her hands snaked behind my neck, and she pulled me closer. "Don't worry, Santi," she murmured against my ear. Her lips skimmed my throat before she slowly kissed her way up, across my jawline, settling on my lips. "I only want you. But I'm not ready to sleep yet."

She deepened the kiss and heat erupted in my groin. She was a quick learner, I'd give her that. She slid her tongue into my mouth, and my cock went rock-hard.

I sat back in my chair and cracked my knuckles in the conference room of my underground casino. There were no windows here. So, unless you kept track of time, you'd never know whether it was the middle of the day or middle of the night. It was barely noon, twenty-four hours after I buried my father. Somehow, I didn't expect to be in this frame of mind. Craving for Amore eased the unleashed hunger for revenge.

Gabriel Carrera, Renzo, and Adriano had our two *guests*, Venezuelans, tied up in a chair while being tortured and bleeding onto my fucking hardwood. I couldn't stand the mess on my floor. That shit irked me to a motherfucking rage. For some idiotic reason, Renzo and Adriano thought to bring them here.

The restlessness clawed up my spine. I had dropped off Amore barely two hours ago at her father's house and an edginess already itched under my skin. I wanted her with me, underneath me, on top of me... any fucking way, as long as she was with me.

I didn't know how I was going to get through the day, let alone two months before her school was out. *Fuck!* I was too old for this shit.

Adriano and Renzo rocked in their chairs, both of them sensing my agitation. Neither one of them wanted the short end of that stick. I couldn't blame them, though I knew how irrational this burn for her was. I was officially Don of our family, and all I could think about was the woman with smooth, soft skin, red hair, a tight pussy, and enveloped in a strawberry scent.

"Now, tell me, gentlemen," I said, my voice impassive and cold. "The name of the man that put a target on my father."

Both men started shaking their heads frantically. "W-we don't know who you are."

"Then why are you pissing yourself?"

I wanted to pop a bullet in both of their heads. I was so fucking done with the games. All these fuckers worked for the cartel but didn't know the name of their boss.

"P-please—"

He didn't get to finish. I hit him on the side of his face with the handle of my gun. The skin on his face cracked and blood poured down his cheek. Maybe I'd torture one while the other was watching. It could be a fairly good incentive. I hit him again at the images of my father's frail body shot up with multiple bullets bleeding out on the concrete.

These bastards were scared to get out of the fucking car and pick a fight with a sixty-year-old man. I hit him again, and the rage that Amore calmed down now simmering back to the surface. I hit him again and more blood spilled out of his mouth.

"Santi, he won't talk if he's dead," Adriano stated the fucking obvious.

"Luckily, we have two of them. We'll kill one."

I grabbed his face and held his jaw tight. I wouldn't flinch if I cracked his jaw with my hand. It was everyday fucking business to me. He wanted pain; I'd be more than happy to oblige.

"The name," I gritted out.

"I don't have one," he whimpered, while the other captive was literally shitting himself.

Landing another punch to his face, I felt his bones crack under my knuckles and a loud yelp fell from his lips.

"Give. Me. The. Name," I gritted out again, too frustrated to deal with fucking morons. I grabbed him by his throat and squeezed hard, choking the life out of him. His face turned purple. "Address."

"Bronx, zip 10456," he wheezed out. I eased up, just barely, so he could finish the address. "East 167th St."

I resumed squeezing his throat, his eyes rolling into the back of his head.

"Stop!" It would seem the other captive couldn't stand the idea of torture, and I hadn't even started on him. "We weren't even in town when they ordered the hit on your father." He added frantically.

Anger crept beneath my skin, searing and clawing to make them pay.

I swallowed down the burning rage while a red haze swam in my vision. Rage rushed through me, drumming in my ears.

I grabbed the chin again of the same guy who denied knowing me and tightened my grip. "I thought you didn't know me."

"It was meant for Bennetti," he rattled out. "His bastard kid is next."

A deathly stillness fell over me. They meant to hurt Amore.

"Bennetti doesn't hang in the same neighborhood." Adriano came forward, his eyes burning. He was protective of Amore. I allowed Pà to keep Adriano out of the family business, but I would need him now. More than ever. Besides, he wouldn't keep to the sidelines when Amore's safety was in question.

"He and the old Russo were going to meet. They were both supposed to be there." The Venezuelan with the bloodied face frantically looked around, searching for help. There would be nobody to help him here.

With a lazy, autocratic stare, I pulled out my gun and put a bullet into their skulls. Two seconds apart.

They had fucked with the wrong family.

CHAPTER 21

Amore

I sat cross-legged on the couch with Adriano next to me.

He played Warcraft on his iPhone while at the same time watching *Avengers*. It was our go to movie, and we'd seen it at least a hundred times since we'd been friends. Dad was in his office, and Luigi was somewhere with Santi, probably hunting the cartel. It was the reason Adriano was pissed off. He felt he should be out there with the boys.

"Are you okay?" I asked Adriano. He seemed a bit off. But then, so did I. I was still high from tumbling between the sheets with the man of my dreams. Santi Russo. Just his name and I was swooning and sighing. Last night was so much better than I could have ever imagined. Amazeballs. Pinnacle. But it wasn't just physical for me. My chest swelled with so many feelings for him. I loved him. Always have and I suspected I always would.

"No, I'm not okay," Adriano gritted out his response, bringing me back to earth. "I should be out there going after those men. Not sitting here, twiddling my thumbs with you."

I winced at his harsh tone and my eyes snapped to him. Before I could tell him to take his attitude home, he must have realized his mistake and immediately wrapped his arms around me, regret on his face.

"I'm sorry. It just pisses me off to feel helpless." I could understand that feeling. I have felt helpless against the dreams and nightmares that plagued me since my mother's death. It was only once I started training with DeAngelo and working towards a goal—revenge—that I started to heal. I imagined Adriano probably felt the same. He wanted to avenge his father's death, just as much as Santi. "It makes me feel incompetent," he admitted begrudgingly.

I took his hand in mine. "Trust me, I know," I rasped.

Sometimes I wanted to admit to him or Lorenzo about what I was doing. The only thing that held me back was the worry of them putting a stop to it. Despite Adriano being my best friend and laid back, just as Lorenzo was, they were still made men. The concept of protecting women and not letting them get close to danger was ingrained into them. They couldn't grasp that women could be just as strong as men and fight their own battles. I couldn't risk them pulling me away from the purpose that had been pushing me forward.

Revenge of my own. A promise to keep.

"I know. And I'm sorry for snapping like that." Adriano pressed a kiss on my cheek, his way of telling me he really meant it. He looked tired, and I felt a twinge of guilt at not being there for him last night. But he left and never said anything.

"Santi said you followed a lead yesterday," I stated. "He probably doesn't want you to overexert yourself," I added, trying to comfort him.

Adriano cocked his head, eyeing me suspiciously, and my cheeks flushed. Just thinking about last night sent me into a heatwave. Besides, I felt I might have said too much.

The silence was killing me, the nervous energy brimming through me. I wasn't prepared to share what happened yesterday between his big brother and me.

"Santi said you spent the night?" Adriano questioned me, with a wary look on his face. Or maybe I was being paranoid and reading too much into his expression.

"Yeah, I was waiting for you," I muttered. *Sort of.* Well, initially I was. Then I got sidetracked with his big brother. *Ugh.* "I asked him to bring me home this morning."

I kept my expression guarded, resisting the urge to fidget. Though I couldn't help my blushing.

"What room did you sleep in?"

There wasn't much sleeping going on, I thought wryly.

"A small one," I answered vaguely.

"Santi slept in the master bedroom." I wasn't quite sure if he meant it as a statement or a question, so I just shrugged.

I wished he'd just drop the subject of my sleepover. I searched in my mind for a neutral subject, anything but last night and Adriano's frustration at being here with me.

"So where is he?" I asked casually.

He forced a smile. "Making the cartel curse the day they were born. He's hunting those Venezuelan motherfuckers—" He cut himself off, realizing he had said too much.

"I thought he killed the one that shot your..." I swallowed hard and realized how insensitive that sounded. I worried about Santi. If he was going for the head of the Venezuelan Cartel, he could potentially get himself killed. I had seen firsthand how cruel they were. The Cosa Nostra had some honor and lines they refused to cross; the Venezuelan Cartel didn't. They killed children, women, men, elders... it was all the same to them. "Isn't it dangerous?" Suddenly my heart was thundering hard, and my voice came out hoarse.

"Forget what I said." He pressed his finger against my mouth. He glanced around, seeing the house empty. "Where is your dad?"

"In his office."

Fuck! I had to talk to DeAngelo. We had to get rid of the Venezuelan Cartel in New York, and anywhere else, once and for all. Grandpa was killed for his position in the Venezuelan Cartel. Considering what happened to our family, I was almost convinced they wanted to kill our entire line. They killed Mom and wanted me dead too. They also killed Mr. Russo.

If they hurt more people, I couldn't live with it. My brothers, father, uncle, Adriano. And just the thought of Santi being killed had my heart shattering into a million pieces. That would utterly destroy me.

"But her favorite uncle is here," Uncle Vincent's voice came from behind us, startling me. I hadn't heard him walk in.

I smiled at him.

"You absolutely are my favorite uncle." I didn't bother pointing out to him that he was my only uncle. It didn't take away that I loved him, and he would probably have been my favorite uncle anyway. He disappeared into the kitchen, probably hunting for some cannolis.

Once he was out of earshot, I turned my attention to Adriano. "Why is Santi hunting for more Venezuelan Cartel members?"

He regretted saying anything and was probably scolding himself. "Amore, let it go. I was stupid to let it slip. I'm just so mad. I wanted to go with them, make those assholes pay. He wanted me here with you."

"Oh. Why?"

He inhaled deeply and let out a heavy sigh. "Just forget it."

Letting go of my own selfish inquisition, I wrapped my arms around him and squeezed gently. "He is probably trying to protect you. Just talk to him. Explain that you want to help and do your part. And tell him that I don't need a babysitter."

"He won't listen," he grumbled.

"Have you tried?"

"No, but—"

A beeping sound from the television distracted both of us.

Breaking News.

The words flashed across the bottom half of the screen and a newsreader came on with the details of a shooting in the Bronx between the cartel and the Cosa Nostra. Nobody has been apprehended, no witnesses, and one dead body.

I tensed, forgetting about Adriano next to me. *Please don't let it be Santi,* I prayed silently.

Then I remembered Luigi was with him. *Or Luigi.*

Jesus, I was quickly becoming the worst sister, friend, and daughter.

"Fuck," Adriano cursed next to me, and my head whipped in his direction. He was staring at his phone.

"What?"

"Santi killed another high-ranking member," he muttered, his eyes never leaving the phone.

"How do you know?" I questioned him in a whisper.

He showed me his phone, and my eyes skimmed over the pictures and the article with a timestamp from thirty minutes ago. News traveled fast in New York city.

"He's going to get himself killed," he muttered under his breath. Adriano and Santi loved each other, despite their differences. Adriano just didn't want to be treated as the younger brother. But the Venezuelan Cartel was ruthless, leaving a trail of blood, bodies, and destruction everywhere they went.

My mothers screams pierced through the rainforest, driving creatures to respond in protest to the unnatural sounds. I was locked in a cage, like an animal, tears streaming down my face. The bars left an open view of the compound. I should plug my ears like Mom demanded and stare at the sky, but I couldn't tear my eyes from my mother's beaten form. Fire burning her flesh.

I wanted them to bring her back to me. I wanted to hug her, to tell her I was so sorry. Her hair, so much like mine, except blonde, glimmering under the moonlight. The first night, it shone like gold; tonight, her hair hung rusty, dirty, a dull color.

They held her down, as they pushed a hot iron against her skin. The metallic smell of blood and burned skin carried on the breeze. It took all I had not to gag.

Another piercing scream.

"Mom," I screamed. "P-please, stop! Mooooom!" I fell to my knees, both my hands gripping the bars, my lungs burning with my screams.

They asked questions that made no sense. We didn't have any answers. I couldn't even understand their questions. These men knew more about our family than Mom and me.

The torture went on for days and nights.

They did it in front of me, making sure I could see her pain, hear her screams, and know it was all my fault. George was taken to the other side. We haven't seen him since we arrived, but his screams were just as terrifying and agonizing. The screams shattered through me, imprinting into my soul and my brain.

My breathing was erratic, and my brain buzzed from exhaustion, or lack of oxygen from my screams. But I refused to pass out. I'd stay strong.

For Mom. For George. I kept begging them to stop. I would have given them anything, everything. Just to bring her back to me.

Two blonde men, with cruel eyes and even crueler smiles, stood over my mother's battered body, watching without any remorse. In fact, I was certain they enjoyed seeing her in pain.

Mom passed out from the pain, her frail body sliding onto the dirt. None of them even attempted to catch her. My throat choked, and my heart squeezed in my chest while dots swam in my vision, darkening.

"Can't pass out," I whispered to myself.

I breathed in, then slowly out. I had to wait for Mom. I had to take care of her.

Breathe in. Breathe out.

The dark haze slowly started lifting and I spotted a man walking this way. They carried Mom back to our little cage. It felt like hours, though it was mere seconds, a minute tops, until they reached the cage. The moment they threw her body inside, I crawled to her and lifted her withering form into my arms.

"Please, Mom," I whimpered, holding her battered body. "I am so sorry. Don't leave me."

I hadn't heard George's screams today. They killed him and left him in the ditch, one of the men said. They'd start torturing me soon; I knew it.

I rocked back and forth, my mom in my arms and scared out of my mind. We wouldn't get out of this alive.

"He'll come for us," she rasped through her cracked lips, blood seeping from the corner of it.

"Who?" I cried in a low whisper.

"Your father."

George was dead. He wasn't coming. Except I didn't have the heart to tell her. So, I rocked her like a baby, hoping I soothed her.

I swallowed hard. "I'm sorry, Mom," I whispered against her hair, my body rocking back and forth. "I should have listened to you." My voice cracked. "P-please... I'm so sorry."

Her bloodied hand came to my face. "Set up," she rasped. "You will avenge us. Your father will come, Amore."

The tears burned against my cracked lips, and I worried they'd hurt Mom's cuts too. So, I buried my face in her hair.

"I will," I promised. "If we get out of here, I will. I'll make them pay."

The moon glowed, the stars glittered, and the night creatures piercing calls filled the air as both of our bodies trembled with the cool night temperatures. I held her body all night as she slept in my arms, and I prayed to anyone that listened... just to get us out.

The next morning, they came back for her. I cried, trying to hold on to her. I screamed, begged, and pleaded to let her stay with me.

"I need you to be brave, Amore. Be strong." Those were her last words.

A young blonde man came over, something was familiar about him, but I was so distraught, I couldn't think clearly. He grabbed Mom's hair and placed his knife against her throat. His eyes locked on me, not sparing her a glance. I kept shaking my head, pleading with every fiber of my being.

"Don't! Please don't," I mouthed. I tried to speak, but my throat was too dry, too raw. Then he sliced her throat and took her away from me. She gurgled, desperation in her eyes, her will to live strong. Her eyes sought me out, and I held her gaze as tears streamed down my filthy face.

"Mom," I whimpered.

Her mouth opened but no words came out. Only blood. I watched the light in her beautiful, green eyes extinguished in front of my eyes. My mother's hair stark against the dirt and the crimson red soaking the earth. She was forever gone.

I stood frozen, unable to scream, to move. I wasn't sure whether my heart stopped or whether it raced so fast that I couldn't hear anything. I just stared at Mom's blank eyes that used to shine and smile as she read me stories or drew her next dress designs.

They left her there, in front of my cage and disappeared into their building on the other side of the compound.

Her whispered words rang in my ears. 'Avenge us'. The two words reverberated through my blood.

If I stayed, did nothing, I'd be dead soon too. I had to try. I had to survive to avenge.

I dug and dug, my nails turning bloody. It didn't matter. The pain didn't compare to the one in my chest. The moment the space was big enough, I snuck through the dirt, under the cage and ran. I didn't stop.

The sounds of the jungle were scary and dangerous, but those didn't compare to the men I had left behind.

The Perèz *Cartel. If it was the last thing I did on this earth, I would find them and kill them all.*

The Carrera Cartel found me in the woods, slumped in a ditch two days later, barely alive. They took me to a hotel in Bogotà where one stayed with me along with his guards for five days.

We never spoke a single word to each other. Until I went to sleep and woke up screaming from the nightmares that plagued me. Again and again. He'd come in the room and soothe me, speaking words in Spanish.

Until I learned that I had a father who had been looking for me for the past two weeks. In Venezuela.

Yes, the Venezuelan Cartel was full of monsters. Santi was protecting Adriano by keeping him away from them.

But what if they hurt Santi or my brother?

I stood up and rushed to my father's office, my phone in my hand.

"Dad, have you heard from Luigi?" *Or Santi?* I added silently. My throat tightened at the thought of either one of them being hurt.

My father set his pen down and filed away a piece of paper. "No, why?"

The memory of Santi's kisses from last night and the way he felt inside of me burned through my body along with the fear I'd never have it again. Of course, I was worried about Luigi too. My older brother was too rash, but Santi was too brave, too reckless, too hungry for revenge.

My back tingled in awareness, and I whipped around to find Santi and Luigi behind me. A sharp inhale echoed through the room. It was mine. Relief washed over me like a cool breeze on a hot, humid day.

The assurance both were safe and sound, here in front of me, was priceless. Both my grandma and father prized power and wealth. I didn't give a shit about either. Not if it meant losing the ones I loved.

My gaze locked on Santi, examining him for any injuries. I watched him in his dark, three-piece suit, a phone in one hand while with his other he unbuttoned his jacket. His gun in the holster. His black vest hugged his strong torso, and his tie tucked perfectly inside the vest. I watched those expert fingers move gracefully, and my cheeks flushed crimson remembering how they felt on me.

"Hey," I greeted them both. I was careful not to keep my eyes on Santi too long. Luigi was very observant when he wanted to be.

There wasn't a scratch on Santi. Nor on Luigi. That was all that mattered.

"Hey, sis. Everything okay?" I nodded. My cheeks were hot, and Santi's proximity made me weak in the knees. There was nothing more I wanted than to wrap my arms around him and feel his strength against me.

"Yes, everything is fine," I answered, my voice slightly breathless. "I just saw the news."

"News is not for girls," Luigi repeated the same thing he had been telling me for years. "Russo wants to talk to Pà." I just rolled my eyes and went past him.

"Hey, Santi."

Our shoulders touched as we passed each other at the doorway, his fingers brushing against my knuckles, and heat instantly ignited through my veins and made me burn for him. Light scruff covered his jaw, and I was dying to trace it with my fingers. His dark, soft expression burned right through me, and butterflies fluttered in my stomach.

I had a feeling he purposely moved as I was leaving the room so that he'd brush against me. Though it seemed out of character for him.

"Amore." Jesus, my name on his lips could make me combust. When he said it, all I heard were his groans from last night; Santi crying out my name as he spilled inside me.

Great, now my cheeks were on fire and probably matched the color of my hair. The door softly clicked behind me as I left Dad's office. I went back to the couch. Adriano was gone, nowhere to be seen. *Shit!*

I dialed him up, but his phone rang and rang. There was no doubt in my mind he let it go to voicemail on purpose. Why did it seem like I was losing my best friend as I was getting a boyfriend?

My phone dinged and I slid the message open. It was from Santi.

Dinner. You and me. Tonight.

A giddy smile broke on my face. Of course, Santi wouldn't ask. He would demand. That's okay though because I'd demand sex later.

Yes. Where do I meet you?

I headed to my room, digging through my closet to find something adequate to wear. Most of my latest designs were left in Italy. I never dreamt that such a tragic reason for return would turn into this. A night with Santi.

Digging through my closet, I pulled one dress out after another. Soon enough, my bed was a big pile of clothes, the dangers of the cartel on pause. I'd enjoy every single second with Santi I could get.

I couldn't wait to go out with him.

I'll pick you up at five.

I wondered if Dad gave him permission to take me out or were we using Adriano as an excuse. Dad never denied me hanging out with Adriano, but I had a feeling his answer wouldn't be the same when it came to Santi. I had nothing to base my opinion on except a gut feeling, and I have learned to trust it over the years.

I shot a quick message to Adriano.

You left without saying goodbye.

His reply came right away. ***Sorry. I'll make it up to you.***

Another message from him came in immediately after.

I have to do something. We'll hang out tomorrow.

Probably a woman, not that I could blame him.

Tomorrow was my flight back to Italy, so I'd spend most of the time with Dad and Luigi. Adriano was welcome, but if there were things brewing inside of him, it might be better he talked to his brother.

Maybe take tomorrow and talk to Santi.

The moment I pressed send, I regretted it. Adriano didn't exactly like for people to tell him what to do. It was the reason I couldn't comprehend why he was so desperate to work for his brother.

I quickly sent another text. ***Or we can hang out. Whichever you want.***

Glancing at the clock, I saw the time. I had two hours to get ready. Plenty of time. Despite loving fashion, I was efficient when it came to getting ready. Tonight was different though. I didn't want to look younger than my age, and all the dresses here were at least two years old.

Two hours later, right on the dot, Santi came through the foyer and before Dad or my brother could come out I rushed to him.

"I'm ready," I told him.

I didn't dare take his hand, so I walked past him and into the cool evening air. He came behind me and caught up.

"Where are you running to?"

"Your car."

When he stopped, I did the same. His hand scratched his chin pensively, and I found the move oddly erotic. Made me want to lean into him and kiss his chin. Oh God, he had really turned me into a sex monster.

He remained on the spot, waiting for me to elaborate. I thought it was obvious but maybe Santi thought Dad would be okay with this.

"I don't want Dad to throw a fit if he sees me going out with you," I admitted.

"He knows."

"Oh."

"Of course, he assumed I was taking you out and Adriano was meeting us there. I debated correcting him but then decided against it. I killed enough today."

I shook my head, though a stupid smile tugged on my lips. "You better not shoot my dad or brothers. Now let's go."

He took my hand and opened the car door for me, letting me slide into the seat of his Maserati. I wasn't a stranger to luxury, but Santi seemed to go to extremes when it came to his cars.

He shut the door and came around as I buckled my seatbelt.

"Jesus, Santi. How many cars do you have?" I asked him as he started up the car. Suddenly, I wished he had an old truck, like I'd see in the old movies. With the whole front being one seat, so I could sit next to him as he drove.

"A few."

Leaving the driveway behind us, I couldn't help glancing in the rearview mirror. I half expected my father or Luigi to come out and call out Santi on what we were doing.

"You should get one of those old trucks with a bench seat," I told him. "That way I could sit next to you."

He threw his head back and laughed. "I will be sure to look them up and get one."

I couldn't hold back my smile. It was too easy to feel giddy around him. As he sped down the road and towards the city, I turned my head to watch him.

"Did you have a good day?" I asked him, not really expecting an answer. Nobody ever answered questions on their activities. It was either a good day or a bad day. That was as far as it went.

"Good enough. We eliminated a high member of a rival cartel." My mouth parted at his explanation. He actually answered. "Would you rather I didn't tell you?" he questioned, seeing my shocked expression.

"No, I'm okay if you tell me," I responded quickly. "I just didn't expect it. Nobody ever answers or tells me what happens."

He shrugged. "I want you to know what's going on."

The knowledge he found me worthy and trustworthy for him to confide in made me melt even more for him. It was uncharacteristic for men of the Cosa Nostra. Usually women were oblivious to the activities of the men of the underworld. Or maybe a better term was they turned a blind eye.

"Santi?"

"Hmmm."

"I want you to fuck me again."

He glanced at me sideways with a dark, hot expression, and fire burned in his dark ambers, setting my pulse into hyperactive mode. Slowly, his eyes trailed down my body, over my babydoll style green mini dress. Since it was April, it had quarter sleeves. Too much clothing, if you asked me.

I felt the flush travel over my body, the need for him throbbing. All this man had to do was trail his eyes over me and my skin ignited.

I bit my lower lip, a pulsing ache between my thighs.

"After dessert," he growled.

God, I wanted to feel him between my legs now.

"Or we could start the night off right." I peered at him under my lashes. "And warm up on our way there."

Who was this woman flirting with Santi? I could barely recognize myself. It was as if a switch was flipped, and my seduction went into turbo mode. Seeing the burning hunger in his gaze was my fuel.

"Fuck, Amore." In one swift move, he shifted the car to the right lane and then down a side road to a dead-end road in the middle of nowhere. There was nothing around us, just bare fields with a large industrial *'For Sale'* sign.

My pulse raced in anticipation and the sweet ache throbbed between my thighs. Once he parked and turned off the ignition, my slightly labored breathing and drumming heartbeat sounded loud to my ears.

Will he touch me? Here?

There was something so exciting about the possibility of being caught or seen. The ache between my legs intensified. Santi made me want to be reckless. Somehow I knew he'd always catch me no matter what stupid thing I might do.

"Inside the car or on the hood?" he asked in a hard, possessive tone.

My eyes just about bulged out of my head and my insides burst into flames. It hadn't occurred to me that he could fuck me on the hood of his car, but now that the idea had been planted, I wanted to do it. I was all for it. And today seemed to be a perfect day for it. The outside temperature was mild, although I was feverish with need for him on the inside.

"Hood," I breathed out, unbuckling my seatbelt and pulling at the handle of the car. He was outside before me, desire burning hot in his eyes. It was enough to ignite me into flames. All he had to do was look at me that way and desire soaked my panties.

No foreplay needed.

I glanced around us, and the area was mostly quiet but for the chirping of birds in the distance. Uncertainty slid down my back that someone might see us. We'd be vulnerable out here in the open. While the idea of recklessness excited me, it wasn't something I wanted the whole world to see. And certainly not my father or brothers.

"Come here, Amore," he purred. "Let's finish what you started."

My feet obeyed before my brain even processed his words. I moved to him, and he wrapped his hand around my throat, not hard but with enough force to show his strength. And just like that, the fear evaporated, and a thrill shot through me. The darkness that lurked in him, pulling me in. My body tingled. My blood sizzled. And wetness pooled between my legs.

He nudged me against the hood of the car, his free hand connecting with my thigh. His calloused palm felt rough against my skin. Rough, but right. Every cell within my body was set on fire and only he could extinguish it.

I spread my thighs wider, the throbbing ache there consuming me. Once his fingers reached my sweet spot, a moan left my lips and surprise flashed in his eyes.

I pressed my neck harder against his hand and his grip tightened.

"Fuck, you like this," he groaned, as his other hand slid inside my panties.

Like! I loved it. Needed it. Craved it.

"Is that bad?" I breathed out, my eyelids heavy and fire spreading from my stomach to my lower belly.

"No." He swallowed my next breath with his mouth, his lips demanding I submit. There was no room for debate there; not that I wanted to fight it. My body craved to submit, but only to him.

All the while, his finger rubbed my clit, taking my body higher. I wanted him so badly I trembled, and shivers of anticipation ran down my spine. My pulse drummed in my ears and the entire world faded.

There was only him and I.

I brought my hands up to his belt buckle, my fingers worked eagerly to undo it. Unbuckled, I slid my hand inside, cupping his erection. He hissed against my lips, his body hard against mine. He was conquering me without even trying.

All the fantasies didn't come close to the reality with this man.

His mouth devoured me, hard and merciless, nipping hard at my bottom lip before licking it, soothing the sharp sting with his tongue. Kissing Santi was sex; pure sex that I'd never get enough of. He slid a finger into my slick entrance, and I moaned into his mouth.

"Please," I breathed out, grinding my hips against his hand.

His hand around my throat was unyielding, and his lips trailed down the side of my mouth, then he nipped and sucked at the sensitive flesh at my throat, then my collarbone. His gaze dropped down my body and heat shot through every cell of me, settling in the marrow of my bones. I lifted my hips in encouragement, needing him to relieve this ache inside me. Only he could do it.

"Santi, I need you inside me," I pleaded on a whimper.

Both his hands grabbed my ass and sat me on the hood of his car.

Without prompting, my legs wrapped around his waist. Languid heat rushed through my veins, the need for release like a burning fever under my skin. I felt empty without him. Rolling my hips against him, I was shameless, showing him what I needed. What I wanted.

Fisting my thong, he ripped the material from me in one swift move and threw it on the ground.

He lined his erection up at my entrance, the heat of it bringing another wave of lust. In one thrust, he was inside me, and a growl of satisfaction sounded in his chest. I could feel it vibrate through his chest and straight through my soul.

My eyes, half-lidded and hazy, met his darkness and I drowned in it. I wrapped my hands around his neck, holding on to him. A tremble rolled through me, my panting uneven. I was slightly sore from last night, but I'd rather die than stop him. The pain faded into a sweet, delicious fullness, and I sighed against his lips.

His eyes lowered to where we were joined and a possessive, maddening look entered his gaze. Then with a growl, he started moving. I could feel him so deep inside of me, I wasn't sure where he started and I ended.

"I was going to be gentle."

Thrust.

"See what you do to me."

Thrust.

Yesterday, he took his time. Today, he was a beast, rutting hard into me. He gripped a fistful of my hair and brought our faces close. Then he fucked me, his lips hard on mine as his tongue slipped into my mouth.

It was so intense, and I could feel my heart and soul kindle a spark inside me in tune with my body. I needed his thrusts to sate it, make me explode into a million, shattering stars so he could put me back together. An orgasm was within my grasp. I was so close I could taste it.

"You take me so good," he praised, and a warm satisfaction washed over me. "So *fucking* good."

His pelvis ground against mine and molten heat spread from my sweet spot outward. My moans turned louder, the pleasure inside me climbing higher and higher, ready to burst into flames.

"Your pussy is made for my cock. So wet." His voice was guttural. "For me"

Another throaty moan escaped my lips. I was so close, so damn close. My nails dug into his bicep, holding onto him. It felt like if I didn't, I'd flutter away into the abyss.

His hand slid into my hair, and he yanked my head back.

"Don't fucking come yet," he growled the rough words against my lips.

A shaky whimper escaped me, and my heartbeat raced. Angling my head to take me the way he wanted, his lips clashed against mine, his other hand grabbed my hips and guided me against him harder as he thrust deeper inside me.

"Fuck, fuck, fuck," I muttered against his lips, as pleasure overtook me, and my pussy clenched around his hard cock. The pressure exploded through my veins like a raging inferno. His flesh slapped against mine, never slowing his thrusts as he reached for his own release.

My moans and whimpers carried through the air, I felt him so deep, and my body convulsed around his shaft. The fire inside me burst and white spots swam behind my closed eyelids. The orgasm was violent, and it sent a shudder through every fiber of my being. It was the best feeling ever, so addictive.

"Amore," he cried out. With one last hard thrust and a shudder, he spilled inside me, groaning out his release with my name on his lips.

He stayed inside me, his thrusts shallow and slow while his lips brushed against mine. It was so intimate, so gentle after the rough way he took me that it made me feel raw. *Vulnerable.* I have always loved him but somehow within the last twenty-four hours, that love has rooted into something deeper.

As we both came down from our highs, our heavy breathing filled the air, and I sighed my contentment into the crook of his neck, inhaling his scent. I had no idea how long this would last, but I was determined to enjoy every single second and memorize every single moment with him.

The truth was part of my heart had always belonged to Santi. But now, he owned all of it. I couldn't stop loving him any more than I could stop breathing.

A warm liquid ran down my thigh and I glanced down between our bodies.

"Santi," I whispered softly against his ear, his body still pressed against mine.

"Hmmm."

"Your cum is running down my thigh," I muttered, nuzzling against his neck. "I have to clean up."

A growl vibrated deep in his chest. I searched his face and found his eyes locked on my thighs. The desire in his dark eyes set me aflame again. The response my body had to him was out of this world. Like it no longer belonged to me and was here just for Santi's pleasure.

Thankfully, my brain was quicker than my pussy, which wanted to rub against him ready for the next round. Jesus! I was losing my mind.

"No, not twice on the hood of the car," I muttered teasingly, nipping at his strong chin. "Maybe a different car."

A laugh rumbled deep inside his chest and something inside me swelled with love. This man could order me to get on my knees and I'd do it without hesitation. The question was whether it would be my doom. This must have been the way my mother felt about Dad. I just wished I had someone to talk to about it all.

Pressing another kiss to my lips, Santi straightened up and tucked his shirt in, then buckled his pants. The loss hit me straight away, and I felt it deep in the marrow of my bones.

I am doomed. At least it would be a sweet doom and I'd enjoy every touch, every word... all of it with Santi. Until we both went our separate ways.

I went to rise when his command stopped me. "Stay."

Without a second thought, I halted. His eyes watched me while I laid with my legs spread wide on the hood of his expensive car. He trailed a finger up my inner thigh, catching remnants of his cum and then pushed it back up into my pussy and heat rushed to my cheeks. My whole body grew hot. This man had taken my body multiple times over the last twenty-four hours, yet my body craved more. One word and my body reacted, bending for him.

"Santi!" I exclaimed. Though even to my own ears, it sounded like a weak protest and more like a moan.

"You fucking like it," he murmured, as my legs opened wider. "Tell me how much you like it." Maybe some women would find it demeaning but I found it hot. "Ask me *nicely* to put my cum inside you."

A throaty moan escaped through my lips and my hips pushed off the hood of his car. Sometime within the past day, my stubborn personality had vanished and in its place was an eagerness to please Santi.

Pulling my bottom lip between my teeth, my breathing shallowed. "I like it," I breathed out, my cheeks burning with my admission. "Please, Santi," I moaned, a shudder running up my spine. "Please put your cum inside me."

My heart pounded against my ribs, my entire body shivering with the intense craving.

"You'll have my babies," he growled in a possessive tone. He ran a finger upward and pushed it back inside me. I was panting by now and throaty, wanton noises left my throat.

Satisfaction flashed in his eyes, his finger curling inside me. He was taunting me.

Devil!

I couldn't resist raining on his parade, at least a little bit.

"I'm on the pill so no amount of cum will make me pregnant." My voice was hoarse, and it didn't take a genius to see that I was turned on.

A slightly sardonic chuckle escaped his mouth, his dark eyes dancing as they watched me. Then he shook his head as if to clear his mind. Could it be that I was affecting him too?

"Maybe I'll tie you to my bed and fuck you for a month until your belly swells with my baby."

Shit, why did that make me so hot? Because I was crazy, that's why. He had made a sex addict out of me.

"You better think twice about that plan," I said with a shaky smile. I tried to compose myself, not show him how strongly he impacted me. Though I had a suspicion that ship might have sailed already.

He studied me for a heartbeat, as if he was seriously thinking about it. His dark gaze found mine, something lingering in its depths that I couldn't quite decipher. Santi, being the ruler of the New York under-world, was good at masking all his emotions. I still had a long way to go.

"Let me get some napkins," he finally said, brushing his thumb over my bottom lip. "Stay still."

He was back within a few seconds with tissues. His rough hand came up to my thighs and gently wiped me clean while I watched his movements.

"You know, Santi," I murmured, as I slid off the hood of his sexy red Maserati. "You can't keep ripping my panties. That's twice now in twenty-four hours."

"You shouldn't wear panties. I kind of like the idea of your pussy open and accessible to me whenever I want to stick my cock inside you."

My cheeks warmed and my temperature spiked. *Again!*

"Don't rip anymore of my panties, Santi," I demanded softly. "Not unless you have a bag of super nice panties for me to replace them with."

He let out a roar of laughter, and I stared at his beautiful face. In all these years, it was the first time I heard him laugh. A full-blown laugh and I was mesmerized. He seemed younger when he smiled. There were almost nine years between us, but I felt older than my age. Not sure if it was due to the manner in which I was raised or the traumatic experience in the jungle that made me grow up. Either way, I felt close with him, but on a completely different level than Adriano or Lorenzo.

"I'll buy you more panties," he promised, helping me back into the car. Before he shut the door, he bent his head and pressed a kiss on my neck, murmuring. "Lots and lots of fancy panties because I intend to rip them off your pretty, tight pussy."

"Fuck!" At this rate, I'd melt before we ever got to the restaurant. He chuckled without another word and shut the door. I watched him as he got into the driver seat.

"You know, Amore," he purred softly, throwing me a sideways glance as he started the car. "I am way too old for making out in the car or on top of the car."

I stared at him for a second, then burst into laughter, throwing my head back. "You are not old, Santi," I told him through a chuckle. "Maybe old fashioned, but not old."

He drove us out of our romping location, his right hand resting on my thigh, while I traced the ink on his hand with my fingers.

"You drive really well," I told him, never lifting my eyes from his hand. The ink there fascinated me. There was more to this ink than Cosa Nostra, God, and family; I knew it. He just didn't want to say it. There was too much ink just to be those three items.

"Want me to teach you how to drive a manual shift?" His offer surprised me after all the horror stories Adriano shared of my driving. I was passable driving an automatic... at best. I couldn't even imagine what disaster would happen if there was more to driving a car than putting it in drive and pressing a gas pedal.

"Maybe one day." For some reason, driving didn't appeal to me. "I'd hate to total your car."

"It's just a car."

I couldn't help but chuckle. "Aren't you, Santi Russo, the one that told me I shouldn't touch his car if I valued my life?"

He shrugged. "I'll buy another one if you damage it. I kind of like the idea of teaching you how to drive." Throwing me a sideways glance, he grinned and then winked. "Kind of like I'm teaching you how to fuck."

"Santino Russo!" I scolded him, my face warming. Cursed red-haired complexion and fair skin. He would be the death of me.

Chuckling, he took his hand back to shift, leaving the spot on my leg chilled.

It was odd how easily we became addicted to touch. Or a person. One kiss and you were never the same again. After this, I knew there would be no going back. No amount of pretending would ever make me forget him.

Once he had shifted and was in the appropriate gear, he placed his hand back on my thigh. The movement was so simple, yet so intimate... so possessive.

I tilted my head to the side, watching his profile. Those beautiful lips that could bring so much pleasure, the sharp lines of his jaw and the determination edged in it. There wasn't a single part of Santi I didn't like.

"What do you like most about Italy?" he asked me. His question came out of the blue.

"Freedom, I guess," I answered.

His brows knitted. "Freedom?"

"Yes, freedom, Santi."

"Amore, you have more freedom than all the women of the Cosa Nostra combined."

I rolled my eyes. I knew that but going around with guards assigned and having someone always with me got old fast. Before Mom died, I'd walk to school alone. I'd go to the ice cream shop alone. Hang out with other kids without someone lurking in the shadows.

"If you... *made men*," I started and he scoffed at the term, "think your way of treating women is normal, you are all idiots."

He chuckled. "Leave it to Amore to put it out the way it is," he announced and I shrugged, rolling my eyes again. "You are right, we tend to keep our families under lock and key."

"It goes against feminism and independence. And don't get me started on equality."

"You have DeAngelo and Lorenzo in Italy, just as you would here," he pointed out the obvious to me. "So it's not exactly different from here."

"It's not the same," I reasoned pensively. "It reminds me of the way I grew up until we..." I paused just for a second, the habit of not talking about South America ingrained into me by now. "Before we moved to South America and everything changed." I took a deep breath and then exhaled slowly, glancing out the window as buildings blurred by. "Before South America, I could come and go with friends as I pleased from a fairly early age."

"What was your favorite place when you were a kid? Favorite place you lived?"

"I think Pàris and Milan are a tie. Though our time in Zimbabwe was pretty cool too."

"How long were you in Colombia?"

I frowned, trying to remember. My time in capture was a blur, and I never talked about it after I got away.

"I guess about a month."

Silence followed.

"Did you know there are the most beautiful and unique orchids in Colombia?" I asked, my mind somewhere far away.

"I did."

"I drew dresses and made up styles for as long as I can remember," I muttered, pictures of Mom and George flashing through my mind. "Every country we found ourselves in, I would come up with a new design inspired by that country. Orchids were always my favorite, so imagine my excitement when they told me we were moving to Colombia. I wanted to see the flower in its natural habitat."

"Do you know why your mom moved there?" Santi's voice was low.

I wasn't sure who knew what, so I kept my mouth shut and shrugged.

It was bad luck. Sheer bad luck that George picked a country so close to my grandfather's ancestors and who wanted to wipe us all out. Mom didn't want to do it, but George insisted, and I jumped on his bandwagon, working on convincing Mom that it would be a wonderful adventure.

"Amore?" Santi prompted, reminding me I didn't answer his question.

"George was a biologist, working on creating a new textile." I cleared my throat before continuing. "Whatever he needed was in Colombia. I was dying to go into the jungle, so it sounded like a great idea to me. There was a camp we had to stay at for a few days, it was close to the Venezuelan border. We were within grasp of seeing the orchid, but my mother forbade me to go. When she had to go into Bogotá for work, George assured me it was okay to go. We were going to be back before Mom, so she'd never know. Besides, it was easier to ask forgiveness than permission." My heart clenched in my chest. The memories still hurt. The sounds of their screams were a part of me as much as their love. I shook my head, clearing my thoughts. "It was George's favorite saying," I explained. "Anyhow, there we were, trotting through the jungle." Goosebumps broke out on my skin at the images playing in my mind. "We ventured too far and found ourselves in the wrong place at the wrong time."

I should have listened to my mother, but I didn't. The price of my disobedience was too high. The worst part was that she paid the ultimate price for it. With her life. George, too. Though when I was prepared to stay put, he encouraged our excursion.

Either way, the guilt was a stain I could never wash away. The least I could do was keep my promise.

Santi was the first person I had admitted any of this to. There was so much more to it than just that. But I kept all the secrets, protecting the family legacy.

"It wasn't your fault." Santi took my hand into his. "You couldn't have known."

"No," I muttered, agreeing with him.

Except, why did it feel like it was my fault?

CHAPTER 22

Santino

We ate at one of my favorite restaurants in the Bronx, a little Italian place. Amore's eyes shone with delight, so I'd say she loved the food and people. My father's ex-girlfriend owned the place and made the best pizza in town. Amore completely agreed.

"They also make the best tiramisú," Amore added, as she took another spoonful of it. I knew a lot about Amore Bennetti, but I didn't know she was such a sugar junkie. When I called her out on it, she threw her head back and laughed.

'Life is sweeter with sugar', she said and shoved another spoonful into her mouth. When she smiled, her whole face lit up. Despite the tragedies in her life, she came out of it with this eternally shining light. I should really call her sunshine, but I loved her name too much.

Coming from a kid that had experienced death at such a young age, it was a miracle she had so much happiness. But somehow it didn't surprise me that she refused to let anything affect her mood. I knew she struggled those first few months living in New York.

It surprised me when she opened up about her time in South America. From what I knew, she never spoke about it. Not to Adriano, not to her brothers, nor her father. Her trust hit me deep in my chest, her sorrow seeped into my heart, and her distress saturated through my skin and touched my soul. I wanted to make it all better for her. When she was that young girl on the sidewalk with shimmering eyes, a runny nose, and tears streaming down her face, to now, as a young woman that remembered the death of her mother and still grieved, I wanted to make it all better for her, comfort her. Make her happy.

I remembered when we first found her, and we came to a truce with the Bennetti family. Her old man would come to my Pà shattered, talking about her nightmares and screams at night. He was at his wits end; she refused to talk about it with anyone. That first year with Amore, I saw Bennetti break down more times than I cared to count. Nobody could accuse him of not loving his daughter.

For the first time, I could understand him because the sadness that lurked in her eyes as she talked about her time in Colombia was a tear-jerker. A lump formed in my throat at seeing her pain. I wanted to take it all away, bear it for her so she wouldn't have to. She still came through it all with such strength.

Mine.

Fierce protectiveness welled in my chest over her and grew by the second. Fuck! I was almost tempted to drag her to the Justice of Peace and put a ring on her finger right now to ensure she was mine and mine alone. Talk about obsession. Nothing had ever gotten to me like her. Ever since that kiss in The Orchid, the irrational craving had seared through my veins.

I had ignored it while she was in Italy, convincing myself she was nothing but a kid. Yet, I couldn't forget her nor our kiss. But a woman came back, and nothing would stop me now that she was mine. I had to tread carefully though. Amore wasn't the daughter that would do what her father or any don of the Cosa Nostra demanded.

She knew her worth; her grandmother had helped her in that department. She had been groomed to take over her empire, and from the sounds of it, her grandmother already thought her ready.

There was no doubt Amore had come into her own. Nobody would make her do what she didn't want to. Including me. Though for some reason, I couldn't handle the idea of Amore with anyone else. It was a fucking first for me.

I watched her shove another spoonful of tiramisù into her mouth with little moaning sounds that made my cock stir to life. I could fuck her all day and night and still need more. Those little noises she made would be the death of me.

Her taste, the trust in her desire hazed eyes as I wrapped my hand around her slim neck, her tight pussy. I had found heaven, and she was it. Nothing on this earth compared to Amore Bennetti.

Her eagerness surprised me, and the way she responded to my touch was fucking exhilarating. Though for my own sanity, I had to get some control when it came to her. I had never been eager to fuck a woman in a fucking field where we could be caught. Yet with her, all I could think about was burying myself in her.

I was hung up on Amore. Probably more than she had been crushing on me during her teenage years. She had outgrown those years, and let me tell you, payback was a bitch because I was lusting after her like a teenage boy.

"You sure you don't want a bite?" Amore offered. "I share." Then her brows pulled together. "Well, some things at least. Dessert is one of them."

Amusement filled me. Was she laying claim? It didn't bother me at all.

"I'll have my dessert later," I told her, smirking. She raised an eyebrow, then shrugged and continued with her next bite, making her little *mmmm* noises. I liked that she had a healthy appetite. She'd need it to survive me.

"I'm done," she murmured softly. "I didn't realize how hungry I was."

"I wonder why." Our eyes connected and I couldn't help my smirk. She flushed crimson understanding the meaning and I chuckled. Shy, wanton, submissive... she was the perfect package.

I placed several bills on the table, took her hand in mine, and we walked out of the restaurant. Our fingers interlocked, and I fucking swore my chest glowed. She was bewitching me.

"Should I take you home, or do you want to get some fresh air?" Fuck, I didn't want to take her back to her father's. I wouldn't see her till June. Too damn long.

She mulled over my suggestion, then eventually lifted her head and grinned.

"Or we could get frisky in the back seat of your car?" she suggested, her green eyes twinkling with mischief.

I let out a breath of amusement. Not that I would ever refuse her.

"You are insatiable, Amore."

We got dressed in silence, but I couldn't help but flick my gaze her way. I was used to women announcing their undying love, but there was none of it from Amore. She gave me her virginity so there was no doubt that she wasn't one to sleep around but words of love, devotion, tenderness... none of it slipped through her lips. Yet, I found that I craved those words. Only from her.

Just the idea of Italian boys buzzing around her had me feeling something peculiarly close to jealousy. It had my blood burn hotter and the need to kill stronger. I'd have to check in with Lorenzo every day.

I knew there were plenty of men from all social circles running after Amore; her father grumbled about it plenty. She was the whole package - smart, beautiful, with a body that was every man's wet dream, and richer than most humans on this earth. Ever since she had gone to Italy to study, anywhere she went became a mecca for models, actors, and fancy parties.

But none of it mattered to me. It was her heart and soul that mattered to me. She mattered to me.

Everyone was intrigued by a woman with connections to the underworld and one of the largest fashion empires in the world. I was intrigued by *her*. Her sharp mind, her soft heart, her strong will. There wasn't a man on this earth that would be so stupid to be blind to her inner and outer beauty.

For the past two years, I hadn't seen any reports or pictures of her in the papers with any man. She usually had DeAngelo, her brother, or uncle with her, unless she was with her grandmother. That dragon of a woman controlled what leaked to the press. She kept her granddaughter's picture out of the media as much as she could. Nobody wanted to piss off the great Regina Regalè. Though every so often, a picture of her would end up in some magazine with speculations on Amore's love interests.

There would be no Italian boys or other love interests for her. She was mine, whether she liked it or not.

This field on the way to the Bennetti residence was becoming too familiar. Twice in a day. I should have taken her to my place, but I was sure the news would have traveled to Savio, and he'd probably have a heart attack.

We drove for the first ten minutes in silence, her hand in mine. Amore had always been comfortable with silence, but right now, I wished she'd tell me what she was thinking, feeling, anything.

We were ten minutes away when I pulled over on the side.

"You'll text. Yeah?" It sounded more like a demand, but I didn't want to beat around the bush.

She tilted her head, watching me sideways. "I will, if you will."

I smiled. "You got it."

I brushed my fingertips over her cheek. "Don't you go falling for some Italian now?"

She chuckled, her eyes shining. "Why not? What's wrong with Italians?"

I growled at the thought of her with anyone else. "Everything is wrong with Italians."

She rolled her eyes. "You know you are Italian, right?"

I grinned. "I'm *the* Italian."

"Ohhhh, I see," she teased, her cheeks reddening. "Okay. You are *the* Italian."

I took her by the nape of her neck and pulled her to me for a kiss. She didn't resist it, her body leaning over the console and melting into mine. By the time I let her go, she was panting, and her emerald eyes dazed with desire.

"I wish I was back from Italy already," she admitted softly, her breath hot against my lips. First words hinting that maybe, just maybe, she felt something too.

"Me too," I said.

By the time I pulled up to her father's house, she had straightened up her hair and we shared a look. Both of us sat still as if neither one of us could bear to leave. I wanted her in my bed, to have her spend the night with me. Every night from now on.

With her, I felt younger, lighter. Something I hadn't felt since I was ten when my mother died.

"You think you could keep those Italian boys at a distance until I visit you?" I teased her, albeit very seriously. If anyone touched her, I'd have to kill them. Tear them limb from limb.

"I'm sure I can manage," she said smiling.

When Amore smiled, she glowed. Her bright smile hit me straight in my chest.

"Good," I told her begrudgingly. I almost wished she'd beg me to visit her beforehand. Two months was a long fucking time. "Not sure if I can."

She chuckled. "If anyone can manage, Santi Russo, it is you."

I exited the car and came around to open her door. Both of us were in the blind spot of the surveillance cameras and outside the monitors. Amore followed my lead, sticking to the shadows. Her eyes locked on me. Her body stood close to mine, her breasts brushing against my suit, and I was ready to take her again.

I lifted my hand and gently brushed her hair out of her face, tucking it behind her ear.

Somebody must be laughing at me up there because for the first time in my life it was hard to let go. I wanted to cage her and keep her with me. But she wasn't like other women in the Cosa Nostra. She'd never forgive me for caging her and throwing away the key. She was born outside the rules of our world and keeping her caged would clip her dreams and her wings.

I bent my head down and brushed my lips against hers. It was a fleeting touch, not nearly enough, but it would have to do.

"No Italian boys," I rasped.

Her smile was soft. "The only Italian is you," she murmured.

"What time is your flight tomorrow?" I asked instead.

"My pilot is taking off at four in the afternoon."

"I'll try to come by and see you one more time."

"What are you two doing?" my cousin Renzo's voice traveled across the yard, and she instinctively stepped back away from me. I remained in my spot, clenching my fists. The urge to pull her close to me was overwhelming.

I fucking forgot I sent Renzo to pick up documents from the old Bennetti. It wasn't like me to forget or lose my head. Goddamn it!

Renzo strode over, a smile on his face, but a cautious look in his eyes. He was my consigliere because he was often my reason too. He was reliable and trustworthy, hence why I kept him as my consigliere.

"Hey, Amore," he greeted. "Are you ready for Italy again?"

"Hey, Renzo." She offered him a reserved, polite smile. The one she posed with for the cameras. "I sure am. Nothing beats Italy in the summer."

"It suits you," he retorted.

She tilted her head my way, a secret smile on her face. "Good night, Santi."

"Good night, Amore." Like a queen, she strode away from me towards her father's house. I couldn't tear my gaze away and stared at the door even after she disappeared into the house.

Once she was out of earshot, Renzo started his nagging.

"Are you trying to start a war?" he asked in a low voice.

"Mind your own damn business," I told him. It wasn't as if Renzo was a saint or something.

"None of them will ever let you have her. You are playing with fire. She brought an end to the feud between our families. Don't throw it away."

"Last warning, Renzo," I gritted out. "Mind your own fucking business."

He shook his head with disbelief and shoved his hand through his hair.

"Don't say I didn't warn you," he muttered.

CHAPTER 23

Adriano

"Santi, I want to fucking help," I gritted out.

I tried hard to keep my frustration at bay. These men threatened Amore. She was *my* best friend, not his. He had no right to keep me out of his hunting. Pà kept shutting me out, hinting to me possibly pursuing life outside of the Cosa Nostra.

Fuck. That.

I loved hustling. It was the best adrenaline. Not even fucking a woman compared to it. And I should know, I got laid plenty.

So, I'd hunt these Venezuelan men with or without him. Since Pà died, Santi had started to include me more, but it wasn't enough. I should be his right-hand man, included in everything.

"She's my friend," I hissed.

"Adriano, this is neither the time nor place." Santi was frustrated. Since Pà had been gunned down, he had been systematically killing every member of the Venezuelan Cartel in the city.

One by fucking one.

It was fine by me. I had been chasing leads and assisting. But when the admission came that they wanted Bennetti and Amore as well, a switch flipped. His aggression went into turbo mode, and suddenly, he didn't want me at the front line. It made no sense. He didn't care about

Bennetti that much. And yes, he didn't want to see anything happen to Amore, but she was my friend. He barely interacted with her, so he should leave protecting and avenging her to me.

"Why am I being kept out of the business? Again!" I spat angrily. "You had no choice in it. Why in the fuck am I being babied?"

"You are not being babied. I gave you a job to do and you did it. You found the men that gave us answers. It is only because of you that we now know they want Amore and Savio too."

"Exactly," I exclaimed, pushing both hands through my hair. "And I got this new location for you. So, I deserve to go tonight. With you."

It was past midnight and Santi had come back from a date. No fucking idea what woman could tolerate his grouchy, psycho killer ass during an entire date. Nobody smart, that's for sure.

It was even more weird that he had a date. He usually fucked and left.

"If something happens to me, it falls on you to take over. You can't do that if you get killed," he growled. "Now stop throwing tantrums. You are not going and that is final."

Motherfucker! I knew him well enough to know there was no changing his mind.

"What-fucking-ever." Without another word, I turned around and fucking left him with Carrera and our cousin.

Whether he liked it or not, I'd get involved.

It was almost eight in the morning when I pulled up at the Bennetti residence. Hopping out of the car, I spotted Luigi.

"Where is Amore?"

"Still sleeping."

I frowned. She was usually a morning person. Though her system might still be fucked up from the time change. Striding through the large manor, I took the stairs two at a time.

She flew back all this way for Pà's funeral, and I had barely spent any time with her. I couldn't believe he was gone. Some days, I still expected to see him in his chair. I had to move out of that fucking house and get my own place or something. Santi insisted I stay, but every time I turned around, I saw Pà.

I opened the door to her bedroom, and sure as shit, Amore was sound asleep. Her fancy bedroom in tones of gold was so opposite of mine. She always kept it in pristine order, not a single thing out of place except for her little creative corner.

Maria called me a pig. It was an exaggeration, of course. But who had time to put shit in its place. The only things that had a designated place in my world were guns and condoms. Everything else could go just about anywhere.

I placed the ice cream on the breakfast food tray that someone had left on her side table. I guess they couldn't wake her up.

"Good morning, Sunshine!" I shouted at the top of my lungs.

Amore shot up, lost her balance, and fell right off the bed. I burst into a fit of laughter, seeing her body twisted on the floor. Her bright red hair was a mess and her sleepy eyes darted around like it was a fucking fireworks show.

The second her eyes landed on me, she glared. "What the fuck, Adriano?"

I threw myself on her bed and grinned. "What are you doing down there?"

"Looking for treasure, asshole."

She climbed to her feet and pushed me off her spot, crawling back under the covers.

"I didn't say you could go back to sleep."

"I didn't ask," she muttered. "Why in the hell are you so happy this early?"

"You are leaving today, and I want to spend the morning with you. I know you have lunch with your dad and Grandma. But at least we can spend an hour or two together." She made some '*mmmm*' noise, like she didn't believe me. "I brought you ice cream," I added.

Lazily opening one eye, she peeked at me. "Isn't it kind of early for ice cream?"

"Didn't you tell me it is never too early or too late for ice cream?"

A soft smile spread across her face, and she sat up, her covers sliding off her. "I did, huh?"

She wore a pink satin tank top and matching shorts. Amore was crazy about anything pink but insisted she couldn't wear it because it made her look like a clown with her red hair. I thought she looked cute. Totally girly.

"You sure did," I told her. "I'll join you."

She watched me pensively. "Did something happen, Adriano?"

"Why does something have to happen?"

"Well, you disappeared yesterday, and I haven't heard from you."

Guilt ate at me. She was right; I disappeared on her yesterday and the day before.

"I know, and I'm sorry." Though somehow I wished I was out there with Santi making the Venezuelans pay. "But I'm here now. So, are you ready for Ben & Jerry? Or are you too good for those men now that you've lived in Italy."

She chuckled.

"I'm always ready for Ben & Jerry. Now, give me my men."

CHAPTER 24

Santino

It was almost noon when I finally walked through my home entrance in Brooklyn with blood on my hands and a knife gouge in my left forearm. I strode directly to my bathroom on the first floor and pulled out a first aid kit. The water ran red as I washed my hands and my forearm.

Red like Amore's mane.

Blood and death had been part of my upbringing. It had never bothered me. It still didn't. It was just a way of life. Though I had to wonder whether it would bother Amore. I knew from her brothers they hid their wounds and cleaned up in their city apartment or the guest house at the edge of the property. They didn't want her upset. I didn't think they did her any favors by doing it though.

That kiss two years ago had changed me. I couldn't put my finger on it, but *something* had shifted within me. The girl with shimmering green eyes disappeared, and in her place was a beautiful woman. A woman that consumed every inch of my soul and my heart. She consumed *me*, without even trying.

Once the water ran clear, I turned off the faucet and pulled out a needle and thread, then started sewing my flesh together. Good thing it was the left arm and not the right, otherwise this would have been a bitch.

Or I could call Amore, I mused. She was excellent at sewing. There was no point in sheltering her if she became my wife. More often than not, this was bound to happen, and I'd rather her fix me up than any other woman. She was the woman I wanted to share everything with—happiness and sorrows, past and present, fears and strength. And most of all love because there would be no hate between us. We might disagree and banter but we'd always have each other. I'd always protect her, no matter what.

It took me five minutes to finish stitching myself up with my mind and chest working overtime. Amore was inching deeper and deeper into my chest.

Putting the first aid kit away, I slid my phone open and shot a message to Amore.

Is my monster awake?

The bubbles showed, and I grinned to myself.

I prefer badass, goddess, heiress. Anything along those lines.

I chuckled and typed back.

You are all that. And an insatiable sex monster.

I chuckled when an instant reply came back. Rolling eye emoji.

Better behave if you want me to swing by.

Next message was a saint emoji. Then more bubbles showed on the screen.

Having lunch with Grandma and Dad at the restaurant.

Another smiling emoji with cold sweat. ***Guns still not drawn.***

Ah, fuck! Bennetti wouldn't be suspicious if I showed up at his house, but it would cause alarm if I swung by while she was with her grandmother.

Give me an open window so I can come taste your sweet pussy.

She was turning me into a horny teenager, but I didn't give a fuck. Her pussy was a heaven I never wanted to leave. Bubbles appeared, and I could only imagine the next thing she would say. Then nothing, the bubbles disappeared, and I put my phone down on the bathroom counter and got into the shower. If she was with those two, she might be busy for the foreseeable future.

The water cascaded over me and images of Amore on the hood of my car with my hand wrapped around her neck played in my mind. She was fucking perfect. Would she let me fuck her mouth? Just the thought of it had my cock hard.

My hand wrapped around my solid shaft and I worked myself, all the while Amore's moans rang in my ears and images of her writhing underneath me played in my mind. Fisting it back and forth, back and forth, pre-cum glistened at the tip.

My grip tightened as I imagined Amore on my bed, her legs open for me, waiting for me to fuck her. I pumped myself from root to tip, hard and slow, back and forth with images of her in the throes of passion as she called out my name dancing across my mind's eye.

"Fuck," I muttered, throwing my head back as pleasure jolted through my spine and my cum spurted all over the tiles.

Stepping out of the shower, I felt somewhat sated. Somehow I had a feeling nothing would ever satisfy me as much as Amore's sweet, tight pussy.

Great, now I was hard again!

My phone beeped and I snatched it off my counter fully expecting Amore's reply. It wasn't. It was Luigi!

Restaurant with Dad has been hit.

Fear unlike anything before shot through my spine. Amore was with her father.

Address.

I was dressed in jeans and out the door within two minutes, fully armed and ready to burn down this city if a single bright piece of hair on Amore's head was out of place.

The attack was in the Upper East Side, one of the Bennetti's restaurants, and it took me ten minutes of breaking every single traffic law to get there.

Cops and ambulances were parked everywhere. I left my car behind a cop car in the middle of the street and rushed inside.

A dead woman was wheeled out, her body covered with a white sheet and a hand hanging loose. Each heartbeat physically hurt as I searched for anything familiar. The sheet slipped slightly, and I got a glimpse of red hair. My throat tightened; my ears buzzed and all other noise faded. I had to take a calming breath, the pain in my chest squeezing the fucking life out of me. I had never felt anything like it.

The paramedics fumbled, almost dropping the cart, and I readied to bellow at them when the sheet slid off completely and overwhelming relief washed over me.

It's not Amore. A deep sigh left me. She had to be alive, well and alive. I needed her.

I strode inside to hear Luigi's voice reach over the commotion, and my eyes traveled over the restaurant. It was a mess. Bullet holes everywhere, turned over tables, broken glass, and plates scattered across the floor along with blood.

I found Luigi talking on the phone. He was sitting in the furthest corner, Amore by his side. I couldn't see her face. I had to see she was alright before I lost my shit.

She's alive. That's all that matters.

Losing Pà was bad, but I had a feeling losing Amore would be devastating. For me and everyone else within this city. Because I would burn this motherfucking city down until I found the assholes that dared to hurt her.

I didn't have time to evaluate the emotions and the intensity of them right now.

I strode over to him, Amore's back to me.

"Luigi," I announced my presence, and he jumped to his feet. My eyes were on his sister though. Amore's head whipped my way, and I skimmed over every visible inch of her. Other than a little scratch on her forehead, she was unharmed.

The relief that washed over me was unlike any other.

Though the look in her eyes shattered me. There was a dull pain behind the depths of her green gaze, and though her lips curved into a smile, it didn't reach her eyes.

"Santi. Thank God." Luigi was shaken up. Having his sister so close to the battlefield probably did it to him. "It was the Venezuelans," he added in a low voice.

My eyes darted to Amore, but she kept a guarded expression. I fucking told Bennetti to keep out of public places. He thought his decades of being Don gave him leverage over my advice. He was wrong. Too careless. Too sure of himself. We had more people that wanted us dead than those that wanted us alive. While she was in New York, he should have heeded my advice. It was the reason he sent her to Italy after all. He should know fucking better.

Shouting from the back of the restaurant reached us, and Amore's eyes shifted towards it. There was a hallway back there that led to the offices. I'd been here plenty of times to know the layout by heart.

"Dad and Grandma are arguing," Amore muttered.

Luigi rolled his eyes. "Nothing new there."

Amore wrapped her arms around her body. She wore slim jeans and a white crew neck blouse combined with white chucks. A smear of blood stained her shirt. She looked younger like this with her hair pulled up into a high ponytail.

I sat next to her, putting my arm on the small of her back.

There was nothing more I wanted to do than wrap my arms around her. My heiress had gotten caught up in mafia wars, and it wasn't a place for someone of her caliber.

"You good?" I asked her.

Her eyes flickered to Luigi, who looked like he wanted to go join his father's argument against Regina.

"Luigi, why don't you go break up that party?" I recommended to him. "Before shit between those two escalates."

The older brother's gaze sought out Amore and she nodded. "I'm fine."

"Stay with Santi," he instructed.

Like I would ever let her get away from me.

Once he was out of earshot, she turned my way.

"I'm good. It was... unexpected."

The Venezuelans were causing too much trouble. I wasn't even sure what they were after anymore. Why did they bother coming after my father, or Bennetti, and Amore? Were they trying to finish what they started thirteen years ago? She couldn't possibly be in their way.

My gut feeling was telling me I was missing something, though I couldn't imagine what it could be.

"You are safe, that's all that matters."

She blinked her eyes and sadness crossed her features.

"A woman died," she muttered. "Shot through the window." Fuck, it sucked that she had to see that. It was her first true exposure to the war happening in New York City. "She had red hair," she whispered.

Confusion washed over me at her odd comment. But then, women and men reacted differently to death. Fuck, men like us and normal men reacted differently to death. Most of the time, I didn't even blink an eye and moved on. Unless it was someone very close to me.

But then I remembered the container with red-haired women. I eyed her, worried she heard something about it.

"What are they arguing about?" I tried to steer her mind away from death.

"Whether I should stay or go," she mumbled. "Dad wants me to stay. Grandma wants me to go. If Dad wanted me to go, I'd bet you Grandma would want me to stay."

She was right about that. Those two were opposites and always at war with each other. Though they both agreed to send her to Italy the last time. It was probably safer for her there than in New York City right now.

I took her hand in mine. Amore's eyes flickered around us to ensure nobody was around. I didn't give a fuck, she was mine, and I'd draft up a contract soon.

"What do you want?" I asked her.

Her father and grandmother were both too stubborn and too blind. They failed to see that Amore had grown up and could make her own decisions.

"I want to go," she admitted. "It wouldn't break my heart if I had to stay now that you—" She cut herself off and her eyes trailed away from me. I rubbed my thumb over a pale vein on her wrist, her skin soft under my rough thumb. "But I want to finish college there, and my work rotation through Regalè Fashion."

"Then we'll make sure you go," I told her firmly. I wanted her protected and happy. "My little sex monster."

Her lips curved into a soft smile, and this time it reached her eyes. Just a simple smile from her, and I'd do anything for her. Burn the world down, kill men, just to see her happy. By the time we get married, I'd be eating out of the palm of her hand.

It was dangerous to have a weakness in our world, and she was quickly becoming mine. Or maybe it was too late and she already was.

I stood up, pulling her to her feet. "Now, let's go tell your family what you want."

"Are you sure about that?" she asked hesitantly. She'd hated seeing those two argue for as long as I'd known her.

"Yes."

We strode to the back of the restaurant, and before we reached the doorway, she pulled her hand out of mine and pushed them into her pockets.

"Don't you fucking dare blame this on me, Bennetti," her grandmother hissed. "She was never supposed to be in South America."

"You should have warned her," he growled back.

I frowned at the odd comment and before Regina could say another thing, Amore cleared her throat.

"Ummm, Dad." Everyone's eyes turned to us. Amore took a deep breath in and raised her head high, determination on her face. "I'm going back to Italy to finish my studies and work training."

"Honey, you don't have to go back for work training." Regina surprised me with her reply. "You've learned enough to take over."

"I know I don't have to, but I want to." She pushed her shoulders back, standing her ground. "I want to take over the business my way and when I am ready. Not when you two think I should."

It was a bit comical to see her oldest brother's reaction to his youngest sibling. She had a way of surprising everyone. She had come into her own beautifully, and one day there would be nobody to rival her. She was a strong woman.

Bennetti's eyes shone with pride and the corner of my lip tugged upwards. This young woman would be a kickass heiress one day. I couldn't wait to see it from a front row seat.

Regina glanced at Amore's father, questions in her eyes. "What do you think, Bennetti?"

He nodded. "If that's what you want, daughter. We'll tighten up the security."

"I have my men there too," I told them both. "I'll rotate two of my most trusted ones and put them in Milan."

"DeAngelo and Lorenzo are always with me," she retorted. "I don't need to be suffocated."

"They will be on standby," I assured her.

After a fleeting gaze my way, she looked at her family. "I'll follow the protocols," she promised. She usually did, except when she and Adriano got together.

A cop interrupted at that moment. "Mr. Savio Bennetti, Mrs. Regina Regalè, and Mr. Luigi Bennetti, we need to talk." His eyes traveled to Amore and me.

I recognized the cop. He was on my payroll. He acknowledged me, then turned his attention to Amore. "And you are?"

"That's my granddaughter," Regina chimed in. "She needs to catch a flight. She didn't see anything as her back was to the window."

Regina was lying, I could tell by her posture. In my line of business, reading people was a life-or-death skill, so I became good at it. She was trying to protect Amore. Shield her from the cops, questions, or any possible press coverage.

"You don't need her then," I told the cop. He immediately agreed. "I'll take Amore to the airport," I offered to Savio. They had no other options anyhow. Where in the hell was Vincent?

"Vincent had to run an errand and will meet her at the airport." Bennetti must have read my thoughts. "He can meet you in two hours. Where is Adriano?"

Now that was a question. He said he'd go say goodbye to Amore this morning and be back. He changed his mind though because he went to my underground casino.

"Busy at the casino," I told him.

Need to get work done, Adriano texted. Bullshit, he avoided me.

That was fine because when that text came in Renzo and I were just finishing up our torture of a member of the cartel. I could use Adriano's help and planned to use him in the Cosa Nostra business, but I didn't want to throw him to the front line. After all, I'd promised Pà I'd always take care of him. He had been keeping him out of our business thinking he would pursue other avenues, but clearly Adriano wasn't interested in that.

After a round of hugs and kisses, Amore and I left the chaos, and I put her safely into my own car.

"Another new car?" she muttered teasingly, though exhaustion caused her shoulders to slump.

I drove my black Range Rover today. It had bulletproof windows and was usually what I resorted to when doing work.

"More like a work car."

She glanced around, then her eyes came back to me with a tentative look in her eyes. "Has Adriano talked to you?"

Surprised at the offhand question, I raised my brow. "What about?"

She shrugged, avoiding my eyes. Amore excelled in a lot of things, lying wasn't one of them.

"Amore," I warned her.

"He's upset," she muttered, peering at me under those long eyelashes. "He feels like an outsider but wants to help you."

I knew Adriano hated not being more involved. Why Pà thought Adriano wouldn't want to be in the Cosa Nostra was a mystery to me. He'd never have guessed he'd want to be knee deep in it. It took Adriano a bit longer to get interested, but then he was all in. Except Pà slowly started keeping him on the sidelines for a few years now. I questioned him about it a few times, but he insisted it was better for Adriano.

"I promised Pà I'd keep him safe. He didn't want him pulled into this life."

She nodded, understanding in her eyes. "I can understand that."

"But?" I asked because I knew there was a but in there.

"He should have asked Adriano first what he wanted. You too."

I scratched my chin. "Yeah, we should have," I admitted. Though I have been using him this week since Pà's death. "But I can't break my promise."

She took my inked hand in hers, the color stark against her skin. "Then find a way to keep your promise and keep him engaged. Adriano just wants to feel useful."

I considered her words. Adriano had started to resent the fact he wasn't being included more and more. Pà had misread Adriano. Yes, he got into trouble a lot, even pulled Amore into a few of his shenanigans too.

She let go of my hand, and I put the car into reverse to get us out of here. The street was still closed off and empty of all traffic.

"I'll find something." Her whole face brightened up with a soft smile curving her lips, and she wasn't even asking anything for herself. "Now, tell me honestly," I demanded. "How are you?"

"And here I thought you came to taste my sweet pussy," she muttered, her cheeks flushing crimson. I immediately slammed on the brakes, leaned over and took her face with both my hands.

She constantly managed to surprise me.

"Filthy mouth," I groaned and clashed my mouth against hers for a quick kiss. "I will taste your sweet pussy and hear you scream my name as you climax, then I'll bury my cock so deep in your tight little cunt, you won't be able to walk for days."

"Mmmm." She brushed her tongue over my bottom lip. "Who has a filthy mouth now?" She closed the distance and took my bottom lip between her teeth. My girl was learning quickly.

I pulled away. "But first we talk," I told her firmly.

She exhaled heavily, then leaned her forehead against mine.

"Do we have to?"

"Yes. I want to know who I need to kill." She closed her eyes for a moment. When she opened them, the dull pain in them hit me right in the chest. Damn it, I wanted to take her pain away. See her smile happily. "Talk to me, baby."

Another sigh left her. "I sat facing the window." It was as I thought. "A motorcycle went by. The guy wasn't wearing a helmet and I recognized him. It gave us enough time to duck before bullets started flying."

Silence. Just her slightly elevated breathing.

"Where did you recognize him from?" I asked her quietly.

"South America." Her lip quivered slightly but she got herself together quickly. "I-I think he's related to the man at NYU." I stilled. This couldn't be a coincidence. "The one that attacked me."

When I get my hands on him, I'll dig him a deep grave and bury him alive.

"I'll find him," I vowed. "And I'll kill him nice and slow, make him regret the day he was born."

Surprisingly, she didn't flinch. Her lips curved and her eyes softened.

"Ah, Santi. I love the sweet things you say."

I brushed my nose against hers. "Let's go get your suitcase and get you cleaned up. I want to make you come at least three times before I take you to the airport."

"Only three, huh?" she teased. "That's kind of disappointing."

I grabbed her nape and brought her closer, then nipped her chin.

"I'll make you pay for that comment, Amore."

Her hand came down to my crotch to find me hard already. There would never be a time where I wouldn't be hard for her.

"I can't wait," she murmured softly, her little hand cupping my cock over my jeans.

CHAPTER 25

Amore

We were at Santi's place. I hadn't been to his place yet. Not sober anyhow. That time Adriano and I got drunk didn't count. But I'd seen it from the outside plenty. His red-brick home had a decent size yard with a large garage in the back. Adriano had snuck me in there once or twice when I dinged Dad's cars. I could do College Algebra and Calculus with my eyes closed, but driving... Well, let's just say I still struggled. I have spent a significant amount of time in car garages over the last year. Santi's was by far the coolest - the back wall of it was all glass and it overlooked the Brooklyn Bridge and the river. I couldn't even imagine the view Santi had from inside.

"Fuck, I could get off on the noises you make." His breath ghosted against my neck, sending shivers down my spine. Santi's scruff tickled my neck, his lips touching the curve of my ear.

"Touch me," I begged, grinding against him. "Please, touch me, Santi."

He had someone else go get my suitcase and took me to his place to deliver the three promised orgasms. I was on my fourth.

We were on his bed, both of us naked, with me straddling his lap. He dragged his middle finger along my entrance. I shivered, grinding myself harder against his hand and his pelvis. He moved too slowly, gliding his hand down to cup my pussy and a loud moan slipped through my lips.

A soft curse left his lips. "So fucking wet."

His grip tightened on my pussy, while his other hand moved to my throat, bracketing it and holding me in place. He pushed two fingers into my pussy, and my brain went hazy with pleasure.

He began to move his hand, his fingers finding my G-spot and stroking it.

"Please," I breathed over and over again. Each stroke of his finger drove me closer and closer to the edge. My hands wrapped around his neck, my fingers pushing into his hair.

He traced circles around my clit with his thumb, driving me wild with need. Lust pounded through my veins and need consumed me. I needed him more than anything else.

Our tongues tangled, rough and desperate. He tasted like sin, a temptation that would never ease. Straddling him, I couldn't resist grinding against his hand, brushing against his hard cock.

Removing his hand, his fingers dug into my hips and yanked me forward. In one swift move, he thrust deep inside me, filling me to the hilt. Everything and everyone faded. Nothing mattered. Right now, in his home, his bedroom, it felt like a safe haven that I could stay in forever. I just needed him.

"Ride me, Amore," he groaned. "Make yourself come."

My pulse thundered frantically. Santi was the type of man to always be in control. Yet, he was giving it to me.

I rode him slowly, working myself up and down his hard cock. The sensation was new to me. And as he demanded, I moved up and down, winding my pleasure higher and higher. All the while, I kept my eyes on Santi.

His gaze roamed over my body, locking on where we were joined. He stared at our connected bodies with a dark, possessive look. His hands clenched my hips, almost painfully, but none of it mattered when this pleasure took me to new amazing heights.

My orgasm was drawing closer with each move. I never wanted this feeling to end. His hand returned to my throat. His grip was firm as his thumb stroked my pulse.

It was so constrictive, yet it was exactly what I needed. His other hand skated down my stomach, searing a trail down to my clit. He lightly circled my clit as I moved up and down his cock, little sobs escaping my mouth. Each time I moved, his finger brushed against it.

"Santi," I moaned, fisting his hair and arching my back. Increasing my tempo, I kept riding his cock, my clit rubbing against his fingers. Pleasure coiled tighter and tighter through me, both of us grunting and moaning. Losing myself in my own pleasure, I closed my eyes.

He tightened the grip around my throat and every single nerve within my body exploded as I fucked him. My orgasm shattered through me, languid heat spreading like waves. Incoherent words poured out of my mouth as my body shuddered in Santi's arms. As the cresting waves slowly receded, my senses slowly came back, and I met his dark eyes drinking me in.

I was feeling weightless and exhausted, and before I could just cuddle up to him, a realization hit me. "You didn't finish?"

"No, I didn't."

Insecurity snaked through me, dampening the experience. I wasn't experienced like Santi and others he'd probably had.

"Why not?"

"Because we are not done." My eyes widened. "Your pussy is ready for another round."

The sweetest exhaustion still lingered in my bones. He was still inside me and somehow his words set my body aflame.

"Your pussy is clenching around my cock," he purred with a knowing look. "You like my dirty words."

He bent his head and took a nipple into his mouth, tugging on it with his teeth. A gasp left my mouth, and my back arched.

"These tits," he rasped. Then tossed me onto my back, thrusting hard and deep inside me. His hips worked like pistons.

I cried out, my back arching off his bed. I felt full of him, and he was so deep inside me, I could feel him everywhere.

"You will be the death of me, Amore." He nuzzled my neck, his voice warm and smooth. "I'm addicted to you now."

He might be addicted to me, but I was addicted to him too. His hand came to my hair, fisting a handful as he started to fuck me. The weight of him became a familiarity. Skin slapping against skin. He fucked me so intensely, I fought to find air.

His thrusts were hard, deep, rough, setting sparks inside of me. His name left my lips in chants, over and over again. My body molded to his, welcoming his every thrust.

"So *fucking tight*," he growled.

His breath against my ear was hot, his voice a deep rasp.

"So *fucking* wet. For me," he praised.

Thrust.

"Fuck, you take it so good," he rasped. "Your pussy is heaven."

Warmth blossomed in my chest with his every word. Heat spread from my clit outward. He pounded hard and deep, his pelvis grinding against mine. Every time with Santi, it was intense and earth-shattering. Heat pulsed in every cell of me, moans leaving my lips.

"Ask me to come inside you," he rasped, as he pushed deep inside of me. His gaze was dark and possessive. "To fill you with my cum."

I shivered, my orgasm within reach. He plunged inside me again, pushing a throaty moan out of me. He thrust again and a shudder rippled through me.

"Please," I breathed out. "Fill me with your cum."

A rumble of satisfaction came from his chest and the orgasm was immediate and so violent, stars exploded behind my eyelids. His body shuddered above me, his thrusts slow and shallow, as he threw his head back and found his own release, my name on his lips.

This man would stay inside me. Forever.

CHAPTER 26

Santino

Amore and I walked towards her private plane, her Uncle Vincent already there along with the pilot. I should have known Amore already had her own plane. Initials in cursive with capital A and B plastered on the side of it.

We didn't hold hands, but every so often her hand would brush against mine.

"Are you really going to come in June?" Her head tilted, eyes hidden behind her large Gucci sunglasses. I could practically see her whole posture change as we approached her plane.

From a young woman to an heiress.

I started to sense there were a lot of layers to Amore, and I'd peel back all of them. I'd know every single inch of her body and soul.

"I promised you," I told her. "The only thing I'm unsure of is whether I'll make it until June."

Her lips tugged into a smile. "I can wait."

I groaned. "You realize that is two months away."

"I'm not opposed to you coming early. At. All," she gushed and then added, with a mischievous gleam twinkling in her eyes. "But the internet is reliable, and I heard phone sex can be hot."

"Jesus, Amore," I muttered. "Where have you heard that?"

"A porn site." I narrowed my eyes on her, trying to figure out whether she was joking or not. Then she grinned. "I'm joking. Girls talk, you know. And your brother has shared more information than I care to admit."

Without thinking, I grabbed her hand, and we both stopped. She cocked one eyebrow in surprise.

"Has he touched you?" I growled darkly. My voice was possessive. When it came to her, all my emotions were amplified. It was hard to keep a clear mind. The word *mine* was seared into my chest, and I wanted to demand the same of her. I'd be *hers*. Was it rational? Fuck no, but who gave two fucks about that.

I knew she hadn't slept with my brother, but it didn't mean they didn't fool around. Just the thought of it had me burning with rage. I was never much for sharing what was mine, and I certainly wouldn't be sharing her. "Has he ever kissed you?"

She didn't pull away as she tilted her head and answered without a trace of deceit. "No, Santi. Adriano never touched me the way you do. He has kissed me on my cheek and my mouth, but only as a friend." She shook her head and stepped closer to me. "Gosh, Santi," she said in a soft voice, her hand covering mine. "Don't you know I've had a crush on you since I was thirteen?"

The jealous beast inside me eased with her words. *Jesus Christ!* I was losing my mind. Sharing has never been my thing, but neither has jealousy. I'd have to control it around her.

"Miss Bennetti," a voice interrupted and both of us turned our heads. It was the pilot, along with her uncle. Her uncle narrowed his eyes on us, then glared at her hand on me. "May I take your bag?"

Her hand faltered, and she was back in her reserved mode.

"Thank you so much." She handed him her luggage and the pilot walked away while her uncle remained.

"Everything okay?" Vincent asked, a narrowed look in his eyes. He glanced at my hand around Amore's wrist, but fuck if I would let it go. Let him try and shoot me. I was a better shot than him.

Besides, she was mine. I'd keep her for myself, to protect and own.

"Yes, Zio." She offered her reserved smile.

"I should have come and got you," he grumbled. "But your dad said Russo was bringing you. I assumed it was Adriano."

"Well, it's done now. Are we ready?" she answered him, smiling and lifting her sunglasses to the top of her head, giving me another glimpse of her emerald gaze.

"I'll walk you to the plane," I told her, unwilling to let her go just yet.

Her uncle turned around, and we followed. Amore slid her wrist from my grip and took my hand. We were playing with fire, but I was confident that in a few days, we could do whatever we wanted.

I brushed my thumb over her soft skin. Then as her uncle came to a stop, she quickly slid her hand out of mine.

"Thanks for the ride, Santi," she murmured softly, her eyes twinkling with double meaning. She would be the death of me. At this rate, I'd be flying to Italy tomorrow just to get inside her. And that sexy voice of hers? I couldn't wait to hear her moan my name over FaceTime.

"Anytime," I retorted, smirking, then added in a lower voice. "I know how you like fast and hard rides."

A choked gasp sounded from her lips and her cheeks flushed bright red.

"You coming, Amore?" Her uncle sounded agitated, probably sensing something going on but couldn't quite put his finger on it.

She answered him, her eyes locked on me with a cute little smirk on her face.

"Yes, coming." Her voice was throaty, and instantly I was fucking hard. Oh, I'll get that little minx for that one!

"Well, I..." Her voice trailed off, while remaining in place as she hesitated in taking the first step towards her uncle. She didn't want to go anymore then I wanted her to go.

"Soon," I promised in a low voice. On an exhale, she dipped her head, then started to climb the stairs. Before entering the cabin, she cast another look over her shoulder. I was still there, waiting for her to enter the safety of her cabin. A shared glance, another nod, and she disappeared from my view.

The same second my phone rang, and I answered without looking.

"Yeah?"

"Santi?" Lorenzo's voice came through. "Have you heard from my dad or Amore?"

"Yeah, Amore just got on the plane." A deep, relieved exhale sounded through. "Your dad had to deal with the police."

"I almost had a fucking heart attack," he muttered. "I saw the news and neither one of them were answering. Neither was my damn brother."

I started to walk back to my Range Rover. Would it still smell like sex and Amore?

Her phone rang while I was eating her pussy, but we were a bit too busy to answer it. I smirked remembering her comment that she'd kill me if I stopped. My little minx was sex hungry. I'd never obeyed a woman in my life, besides my mother, but when Amore breathed out her command, it didn't even cross my mind to stop. If the world was burning, I'd ensure my woman got her pleasure first.

I had to get a grip, at least act rationally.

"You there?" Lorenzo asked.

"Yeah, I'm here."

"When are you coming to Italy?" he asked. "I never want to fucking leave. Women are plenty, food is awesome. Forget New York and the Cosa Nostra there. Come to the motherland."

I chuckled. It was exactly how I felt when I visited there in my early twenties. Now though, I wanted to go for a different reason.

"I might come soon," I told him.

"Better make it sooner. Once you get hitched, Italy won't have the same appeal." He chuckled. "I know Amore probably won't be back once she is hitched."

My step faltered. "What?"

"Come before you get married," he repeated, but that wasn't the part I cared about.

"No, you said before Amore gets hitched."

"Yeah, she's promised."

The hell she is. "To whom?"

The rage burned hot in my bloodstream. Whoever it was, they would never have her. Just the idea of anyone laying their hands on her had jealousy snaking through my veins. The aversion I had to even the thought of any man standing close to Amore, never mind touching her, made my chest twist into something cold.

"I don't know. I told my father it was a bad idea, obviously he didn't listen. She even made several offhand comments that she'd rather cut off both her hands than get married through arrangement." Lorenzo didn't sound pleased about his father's arrangement. "Pà just refuses to be reasonable. He's got it in his head that he is protecting her somehow this way."

I couldn't believe Savio made a marriage arrangement for his daughter. A flash of anger pulsed through my chest that he would have offered her to anyone... fucking anyone but me. From the moment she stepped onto Russo territory and I found her in front of the restaurant, she was mine. Back then, she was a girl under my protection. Now she was a woman under my protection.

"Would he consider changing the contract?"

The line went silent. "Why?" I didn't answer. "Fuck, Santi. Don't answer that one. I can tell already. I don't want to know."

It was right there and then I decided it didn't matter. I'd kill whoever it was.

"See if you can get me a name," I told him. "I'll owe you a big one."

And when a Russo owes, we always pay up.

CHAPTER 27

Santino

It had been two fucking days... Two! And the need to fuck Amore was like a burning itch under my skin that I couldn't get rid of. I didn't know how I'd get through two months. Thoughts of her were a constant in the corner of my mind. It was a struggle to think about anything but how soft her skin was, how sexy her moans were, and how tight her pussy was.

Lorenzo hadn't been successful in getting a name. Neither was Luigi. The latter owed me a long list of favors, so I decided to collect. Fuck, I'd consider them all gone if he could only get me that one name. One man to kill.

"Are you sure she saw his face?" Gabriel asked me.

Both of us were seated in my office at The Orchid. It was usually where we met. The smoke hung thick in the air and irritation practically steamed off both of us.

We had been hunting for the fucker that did a drive-by and attacked Amore. Unsuccessfully. It was as if he'd disappeared into thin air. I'd found the Venezuelans that were in on the drive-by, but the main fucker was still breathing and walking.

It. Just. Won't. Fucking. Do.

The urge to roam the streets, killing every member of the cartel drove the restlessness that ghosted under my skin. It did nothing for either one of our tempers.

"Yes," I gritted out. The need to protect Amore was like breathing. I needed her more than oxygen.

Gabriel questioned me several times, doubting Amore knew what she saw. The whole attack was a blur, not even the other Bennettis saw the man. But there was no hesitation when Amore answered. She knew exactly who it was.

He had been slipping through our fingers for far too long. He had fooled Gabriel, and Carrera wasn't too thrilled about it. The man that tipped him off was found dead in the house we raided.

"Can't you at least find out what his fucking name is, so we are not chasing a ghost?" It was a joke that we couldn't even get that much.

"And what the fuck do you think I've been doing? Twiddling my thumbs?" Gabriel spat back. He was just as annoyed as I was.

"Try fucking harder." I clenched my teeth. "Amore's life is at risk. Not yours."

Gabriel's fingers clenched into fists and his lips pressed into a grim line. He was a good ally, a reliable supplier, and a reluctant friend.

"Santino, she's safe in Italy," he finally said. "It is the best place for her until we resolve this situation. No cartel, including my own, will ever dare step foot in that country."

Except that I wanted her here, with me.

But he was right. She was safe there. The motherland was too high of a risk for the cartel. The mafia in Italy was deeply ingrained into every aspect of civil, political, and commercial life. The members of the cartel often got killed before they even left the airport. The mafia didn't want to offer any window of opportunity to them to expand on their territory. Kind of like the Cosa Nostra here in the States.

Glimpsing at my clock, I noted the time. Savio was meeting me in my office.

I got up and turned to leave, buttoning my jack.

"I have to go. Let me know if you find anything."

Ice clinked in Savio's glass. The atmosphere was tense; the air was so thick you could cut it with a knife. It didn't bother me in the slightest.

Sitting behind my desk, I watched him closely.

"What is this about, Russo?"

I refused to tell him over the phone what the meeting was about. Face-to-face meetings were best conducted for this kind of conversation.

"I hear you have a marriage contract for Amore." My jaw ticked. Saying those words out loud were enough to turn my blood to ice and freeze my heart.

Surprise flashed in his eyes, but he quickly got himself together. "So?"

"Void that contract." My gaze found Savio's. There was disbelief in his eyes, then he let out a sardonic breath.

"What?" Savio asked, playing dumb with me.

I thought I was rather clear. "I want her. Name your terms and I'll have the marriage contract drafted up within twenty-four hours."

He tossed the rest of the liquor down his throat and brought down the glass onto the table somewhat forcefully. I watched him closely for any telltale signs.

"I'm afraid that is not possible," he finally said.

A glint of satisfaction shone in his eyes and something violent spread through my veins like poison. *We shall see.* I would not lose her.

"Everything is possible," I replied. "I'll bear your cost for breaking the contract."

"The contract can't be changed." The words cut through the tension between us.

I ground my teeth with frustration. I fucking hated hearing something couldn't be done. There was no such thing, and what I wanted, I always fucking got.

Savio's gaze narrowed as we stared at each other. I got the sense that he enjoyed telling me *no*, though it showed he didn't know me at all. If I was anything, it was persistent and being denied made me more determined.

I never had anything against Savio, even before our truce brought on by Amore. We had reluctant respect for each other, but I would never put up with any of his shit. The Russo territory and profits were bigger, and I never tolerated anyone encroaching on our territories, no matter who they were. You give a finger, they take a hand and all that.

"Who?" I wanted a name. They'd be dead by the morning. One way or another, Amore was mine.

He studied me for a heartbeat before he shook his head.

"I can't give you that," he finally said. Ice snaked through my veins and straight to my heart. He was worried I'd hunt the man down and kill him. Damn fucking straight. "Santi, you can't have her." *Watch me, old man!* He must have seen it in my eyes because he added in a hard tone, "Try forcing my hand and you'll start a war."

I stood up, signaling this meeting was over and Savio followed.

He strode out of my office and my chest hardened.

Amore would marry someone else over my dead body. And I wasn't fucking planning on dying anytime soon.

War it is!

CHAPTER 28

Amore

June. *Finally!*

I was so eager to touch Santi, feel his hands on my body. Face-Time and phone sex were exciting for the first few weeks, but it got old fast.

It had been over two months since I'd felt him inside me, felt his mouth on my skin. He almost came for a weekend in May, but Cosa Nostra business got in the way. It was the only objection I had in dating a don. But he couldn't change that any more than I could change who I was.

Lorenzo and Uncle Vincent had to travel back to the States to take care of some business. DeAngelo was taking some personal time after our last mission in South America. Frustration crawled up my spine remembering our search mission through the jungle. We tried to locate the Perèz camp in the jungle. It was where they kept their product before sending it off for distribution to their suppliers.

DeAngelo believed it was where they kept me all those years ago. He got in touch with a Carrera Cartel member and obtained the information about the area where they'd found me. He was able to conceal the reason for the inquiry, but it was for naught. We trekked through the jungle and hadn't been able to find any trace of the camp where Mom died. The burning anger and sadness mixed in my chest as I remembered how cold the killer's eyes were when he ordered my mother's throat to be sliced. I wanted him dead. Santi had killed one; I wanted the other one dead too.

After three days of nothing but sweat, dirt, and bug bites, we had finally called it quits. Knowing DeAngelo was from Colombia, I suggested he stay behind and visit with his family. He took guarding me seriously and initially refused. It took some convincing and coordinating of security before he finally agreed. I had him arrange my security coverage with Santi's men in Italy.

So, it worked out perfectly.

Glancing down at myself, I smoothed the wrinkles out of my dress. The white top with a deep V cut looked modest and the rusty copper color of the bottom half matched my hair, which I had pulled to the side and braided into a fishtail braid.

"We are here," the driver announced, pulling over inside the private airport. One of Santi's men drove me here.

I didn't bother waiting for him to open the door. Sliding out of the car, I shut the door behind me. My eyes traveled over to the private airplane parked in the middle of the runway.

And just in time as the door to the plane opened and Santi stepped out of the cabin. As if he could feel me, his head turned in my direction and my heart fluttered into turbo speed. We'd talked almost every day since I left New York, but it still felt like a dream. He had been my crush for so long, and then, seemingly overnight, he went from being my best friend's brother to my lover. My boyfriend. Some days I almost expected him to revert back to *'you are just a kid'* status.

I loved him. Every single thing about him. His rare smiles. His direct, demanding ways. His darkness. Everything!

He descended the stairs of the plane in rushed movements, a lone dark figure against the white of the plane. Of course, he looked so damn hot in his crisp, white shirt and dark pants. I rarely saw him dressed in casual attire. Well, except when I'd ripped at his clothes, eager to touch him.

His aviator glasses hid most of his face, and the familiar butterflies fluttered in my lower belly. It was always the same, even when he'd call me. I'd get all flustered and excited.

I started walking towards him, but the second I saw that tug of his lips signaling a smile as he put his sunglasses into his pocket, I broke into a run. I didn't give a shit who saw us or how eager I looked. I missed him so much.

It took no time to reach him, and I threw myself at him, my arms closing around his neck. He caught me with both of his hands and twirled me around. Maybe he missed me too? Santi didn't do carefree or goofy. That was more Adriano and I. Santi always acted too mature, too much... well, like a don.

"Oh my fucking God, Santi," I murmured against his skin, showering his face with kisses. He smelled even better than I remembered. "I can feel you."

My legs wrapped around his abdomen while his hands grabbed my ass. His mouth sought out mine, the kiss hard and demanding. A moan escaped my lips, hungry for the taste of him. He captured my top lip between his and my mouth parted, wanting him deeper. I wanted to taste him, feel his tongue brush against mine. It made me feel alive. His hard body against mine felt amazing, his heat blazing through every single fiber of me.

"I missed you," I admitted softly. A desperate, sweet ache traveled through my veins and ended with a throbbing pulse between my thighs.

"Not as much as I missed you," he rasped. "Best fucking welcome. Ever!"

His one hand wrapped around my nape and angled my face so he could kiss me deeper, his tongue tangling with mine. He tasted so good. Like sin, whiskey, and my man. A groan came from deep in his chest, his hands tightening on my hips. His fingers dug into my flesh as I moaned into his mouth. I licked the inside of his mouth, loving the taste of him. The kiss was rough and consuming. My blood thundered in my ears and rushed through my veins, feeding the flames of passion.

I shifted and accidentally ground against his hard cock. A shiver rolled through me, the heat sparking through every cell of my body.

"Careful, baby," he groaned. "It's been a while for me."

That was the best part. Santi was faithful to me. The don of the Russo family, one of the most feared men of the Cosa Nostra could have sated his need with any woman. There were more than plenty that wanted him. Yet, he didn't. Instead, he'd have a virtual date with me. He was just as demanding during virtual sex as he was face-to-face.

Santi couldn't even fathom how much it meant to me. Men of Cosa Nostra weren't faithful, but Santi Russo was. He was mine, and I was his.

"It has been a while for me too," I whispered against his lips. My breathing was already labored. "Can you fuck me in the car?"

"Sex monster," he groaned.

"Only when it comes to you," I moaned, rubbing all over him.

Someone cleared their throat, and I remembered we were in the middle of the runway. We'd both lost our heads. I buried my face into Santi's neck but stayed in his arms. There would be nothing stopping me from touching him for the duration of his stay.

"Yes?" Santi's voice sounded annoyed at the interruption, and I smoothed my palm against the back of his neck, running my fingers through his thick, dark hair. God, I loved touching him

"Your bags are in the car, sir."

Santi didn't even acknowledge him, and I gently nipped his neck. "Thank you," I whispered against his pulse. "Say thank you."

Of course, he ignored me, so I glimpsed behind me with a small smile. "Thank you," I said.

With a nod of acknowledgement and crinkle of amusement dancing in his eyes, the pilot walked away with a nod. I slid down Santi's body, and we walked towards the car hand in hand. It seemed unreal to have him here, with me.

"You look beautiful," he complimented, his eyes flashing like lightning.

Heat rushed to my cheeks. It was the curse of my complexion. He chuckled in dark amusement.

"All the filthy things we did over FaceTime, and you blush at me complimenting you."

"I can't help it," I breathed out.

His hand gently tightened over mine. "I love that about you, Amore." His gaze traveled down my body, and it made my pulse race all over. "There isn't a single thing I don't love about you."

My heart glowed with his admission. It wasn't exactly a declaration of undying love, but the dreamer in me glowed at hearing those words.

The driver held the door open for both of us, and I slid into the seat, Santi right behind me. Once the driver was behind the wheel, Santi issued a command. "To my villa."

He pressed the button and raised the partition, separating us from the driver and the guard. I never bothered with the privacy screen in the car, but now I was thrilled to have it. Before I could move or say anything, Santi's big hands came to my hips, lifted me, and sat me onto his lap.

"Fuck, you smell so good," he murmured, trailing his lips down my neck. "Feel so good."

My insides clenched with need, and my heart raced with excitement. My eyes lowered to his hands on my thighs and noted the red, busted knuckles. Some things never changed. My fingers gently brushed across them.

His scruff tickled my neck as he trailed downward, pausing over my collarbone. "Santi," I sighed. Languid heat spread through my veins, and I shivered.

He ran a thumb across my skin, his calloused fingers a contrast to his gentle touch. His other hand cupped the back of my head, his fingers lacing through the strands. He pressed his mouth on mine and a shuddering breath left my lungs.

"Zio and my brother are gone," I murmured against his lips. "Only your guards are keeping an eye on me."

A dark chuckle left him. "Only I am keeping an eye on you." His breath was hot in my ear. "For the next week, you are all mine."

I have always been yours. The silent words vibrated through me, and nothing had ever rung more true.

His teeth nibbled on my earlobe, sending shivers down my spine. Tilting my head to the side, I gave him better access to it. His right hand came up the front of me, his fingers wrapping around my neck.

It was exhilarating. So constrictive. So thrilling.

"Mmmm." I leaned into his hand and his fingers squeezed slightly tighter.

"Harder?" he grunted the question into my ear.

"Please," I begged. My palm pressed against his chest, his crisp white shirt the only obstruction between my fingers and his skin.

"Such a proper, greedy sex goddess." It took two heartbeats for me to realize he hadn't called me a sex monster. I pulled back just an inch and smiled.

"Now, that's better," I whispered as my fingers tangled through his hair at the back of his neck. "More fitting for me than a sex monster."

The corner of his lips tugged upwards. "Is it now?" He pulled the back of my knees, pulling me closer, so I straddled him.

Adrenaline pumped through my veins; the sexual tension burning like an inferno between us. I could practically taste it. Our heartbeats synchronized. Chest to chest. The pressure boiled inside me; my breathing labored.

It felt right being in his arms. Yes, we were opposites in every aspect, but we fit perfectly.

His sharp clothing to my creative style.

His big size to my petite one.

His hardness to my softness.

His lips ran down the length of my throat while his grip tilted my head to the left, my body submitting to him. His scruff scraped my skin and shivers ghosted up my spine.

I sighed, enjoying his touch.

"You earned yourself a bonus." I felt his lips curve into a smile against my skin. "I was thinking..." A soft moan slipped through my lips, and he lifted his head, his eyebrow cocked as he waited for me to continue. "Umm... I didn't thank you properly for my birthday present."

He sent me the most beautiful gold necklace with a handmade gold orchid pendant and engraved with our initials and the words.

From our first kiss.

To the end of our lives.

"Yeah?" He ran a thumb across my bottom lip, my hands running down his chest. "What did you have in mind?"

My hands slid down his body, his abs strong and hard under my palms. When I got to his belt, I traced it with my finger.

"I want to give you a blow job," I whispered. His eyes flared, tension radiating from his gaze. Nerves shot through my veins. Santi had probably had women on their knees hundreds of times before. I didn't want to be just another one of those random women. But it was something I had never done before.

Slowly leaning forward, I pressed my lips against his neck. "I hear men love blow jobs," I murmured against his skin.

He suddenly grabbed a fistful of my hair and tugged my head backwards, his gaze full of tension and turmoil as it pierced me. "Who told you that? Have you done it with a man?"

His possessive tone sent vibrations through my veins and a breathless haze filled my brain. His claim hit me right through my chest. Some women hated possessive men. I found that I loved it. Or I just loved Santi's possessive ways. I was his, would forever be his. But he would be mine too.

I licked my lips, feeling breathless. I couldn't get enough air into my lungs. Santi's gaze darkened, focused on my face.

"No, but I did my research." His fist loosened lightly, but I had a feeling he'd leave his hand in my hair and control the blow job I was about to give him. I was fine with it, since his pleasure was the best shot of adrenaline ever. I didn't stand for being controlled, but when it came to Santi... I was all for giving it up. If he'd order me to strip right now, I would.

I slid backwards to my knees in front of him. His hungry gaze tracked my every move. He lazily stretched out, his legs widening, and my heart thundered in my chest. There was so much turmoil and raw, hot desire, I thought I'd burn out right here.

Our eyes locked. His hooded and hungry gaze burned, telling me he wanted to fuck my mouth.

"Do it," he demanded, his bossy tone sending shivers down my spine. He looked like a ruthless, demanding lover. Wetness pooled between my thighs with a throbbing ache that was almost unbearable.

As a don, Santi was used to people pleasing him, obeying him. I couldn't care less about obeying him as a don. But as a lover, I wanted to give him everything.

I unbuttoned his pants, then the zipper followed. The sharp sound loud in the silence of the car, and my heart thundered against my ribcage. I swallowed hard as I pulled his briefs down and wrapped my fingers around his erection. When I did my research, I thought this would feel demeaning, but I was eager to give Santi pleasure, so I was determined to try it. At least once.

But now, seeing the tightness in his shoulders and hunger lurking in his eyes, it felt oddly empowering. His cock was so hard and thick, smooth and warm. The spot between my thighs throbbed with need, and I clenched my legs together. I leaned in and his thighs spread further.

My mouth watered, my stomach tightening as I swiped my tongue out and licked the tip of his cock, tasting his pre-cum, then experimentally licked from the base to the top. A hiss slipped through his lips, and a thrill traveled straight to my core. A hum of satisfaction traveled through my veins, intoxicating and hot. Encouraged by his reaction, I ran my tongue around the head of his cock, taking my time, tasting him. He tasted musky and salty. Addictive.

His fist in my hair tightened to an almost painful grip, but I didn't give a shit. This empowering feeling was such an adrenaline rush. I flicked my eyes to Santi's face, who watched me with a half-lidded gaze, an unhinged look in his eyes.

"Suck," he ordered, his voice hoarse. His free hand rested on the armrest of the backseat, looking like a king getting serviced. In a way, he was.

My eyes locked on him. The tension on his face and body was unparalleled to anything I had ever seen on him before. He was barely hanging on by a thread.

All for me, I thought victoriously, as a warm wave traveled down to my sweet spot.

I obeyed, sucking his hard shaft into my mouth and immediately his head fell back with a loud groan. Encouraged by his reaction, I sucked him again, taking him deeper, gliding up and down. He tasted like sin, his salty taste forever my drug. Both my hands were on his thighs, my nails digging into his muscles.

"Fuck, yes. Just like that, baby," he groaned, his hand in my hair moving my head, controlling the rhythm. I knew he couldn't resist taking control. My head bobbed up and down, taking him deeper every time.

"Look at me," he demanded in a hoarse voice, his grip in my hair tightening further.

My gaze flickered to him, and he pushed himself deeper, hitting the back of my throat. I moaned, relaxing my throat and following his unspoken demand to suck him harder and faster. His noises guttural. His breathing heavy as he watched me with a half-lidded gaze.

"Fuck, that's it," he hissed. He pushed himself deeper, hitting the back of my throat again. My eyes watered but seeing him like this sent pleasure fluttering through me. I sucked him harder, taking more of him into my mouth.

My pussy throbbed, the sweet ache tempting me to reach my hand between my legs. But this was for him. For his pleasure, not mine. So, I clenched my thighs together and a hum of satisfaction traveled up my throat. His thrusts became rougher, deeper, but I couldn't peel my eyes off his face. His jaw ticked, his hooded gaze full of burning desire, threatening to turn us both into ashes.

My breast rubbed against his thighs, the material of my dress stroking my sensitive nipples. I forewent a bra, hoping he'd fuck me in the car. But this was so much better. The friction of the soft material rubbing against my nipples sent sparks of pleasure fluttering through me.

"Stay still," he said harshly, his fist holding my head immobile. I immediately stilled at his command. I couldn't move even if I wanted to. His unraveling was so hot, I'd thought I'd orgasm just watching him lose control. "Keep that pretty mouth open."

I dug my fingernails into his thighs, moaning with need, as he lost control. His hips thrust up off the seat, fucking my mouth rough. He held nothing back. His breaths came out heavy. His free hand clenched the backrest of the seat. As he hit the back of my throat harder and deeper, I gagged, but he never stopped.

"Fuck," he muttered, his expression tightening. I tasted more of his cum, and I eagerly swallowed him. I wanted to see him fall apart. For *me*. "Swallow every drop," he rasped. I hummed my agreement, unable to do anything else, eager to do as he ordered.

Another thrust and he spilled inside my mouth with a masculine groan that sent shivers down my body. I swallowed, again and again, the saltiness of his cum filling me.

His gaze burned hot and lazy, the tension seeping out of his body. He watched me mesmerized as I sucked him clean, eager and greedy, until there wasn't a drop of cum left.

Sitting back on my knees, our gazes connected as I licked the remains of the salty taste off my lips. A drop of his cum trailed down the side of my lip, and he leaned over, reaching with his free hand, he wiped the cum with his index finger.

"Open, goddess," he purred. I obeyed and he pushed his finger with his cum into my mouth. Fever-like hotness shot through my bloodstream. I closed my lips around his finger and sucked it clean. "You listen so well," he murmured his praise and I flushed.

I gently nipped his finger. "Only when I want to."

He smirked, though the lines of his face were relaxed.

"So, you want to please me?" he drawled, and I nodded, still on my knees. It went against all reason. I'd been taught to lead as the future head of Regalè Fashion. Yet, with Santi, I wanted nothing more than to submit. My love for fashion and our legacy faded in comparison to what I felt for him.

Santi pulled up his pants, then fastened them while I tracked his every move. Both his hands came to my waist, lifting me back up onto his lap. Straddling him, I made myself push against him. The unsated flames burned through my bloodstream, and he was the only one who could extinguish them.

Folding me into his arms, his lips hovered over my ear and whispered in a soft, almost worshiping voice, "Amore, you just might be the woman to break me."

I would never break him; I just wanted to love him.

The car came to a stop. I went to move, but his hand tightened on me.

"He'll see," I whispered.

"Let the whole world see," he rasped against my mouth. "Because you are mine."

CHAPTER 29

Amore

Santi held my hand in his as we exited the vehicle. Shyness overcame me and I avoided our driver's and bodyguard's eyes. I hoped they didn't get wind of what we were doing. I was so lost in our act, that I couldn't swear we had kept our grunting and moans to a minimum.

My eyes roamed over the vast property. Glancing behind us, I saw a long driveway cutting a path between the trees. The large marble villa shone bright under the sun, the azure sea beyond it shimmering. The shutters of the humongous villa mirrored the color of the sea. There were fruit trees - lemons, oranges, cherry, and fig groves.

The Mediterranean villa was picture perfect luxury, but before I could admire it further, Santi picked me up into his arms. Wrapping my arms around his nape, a giggle escaped me as he strode through the entrance. It reminded me of a groom carrying his bride over the threshold.

The second we passed through the door of the magnificent villa, he had me pinned against the wall. The front door slammed behind us with a loud thud before his lips pressed hungrily on mine. His tongue parted my lips and thrust into my mouth like it belonged there. Our kiss was fervent, wet, and messy.

My hands pulled hard at his dark hair, clutching him harder to me, parting my lips wider to allow him to consume every inch of my mouth.

His stubble against my cheek was rough, and I loved it. His roughness to my softness.

"I'll never get enough of you," he rasped into my ear. "I'm ready to bury myself inside you."

Desire ignited into a full-blown inferno, shooting flames through my veins. I needed him inside me. The ache pulsing between my legs demanded to be eased. And he was the only one that could do it.

With my legs wrapped around his waist, I rocked against his hard length, riding the friction, desperate for relief. His hands flexed against my ass before he ran one down the front of me and dove beneath my dress. Desperation coursed through my veins and the throbbing ache drove me wild.

"Please, Santi," I pleaded. "I need…"

He understood my body better than I did. The rough pads of his fingers trailed up over the soft skin of my inner thigh and straight to my core. Wetness flooded my sex, and I rubbed against his fingers, twisting my body against him. Our hearts beat as one, frantically, and our breathing erratic.

"Ahhhh, yes," I panted, the second his finger touched my clit. "Santi. Oh, God!"

Unashamed, I ground against his rough hand while his finger worked my clit. My whole body lit up, flames licking at my skin. I was so close and white-hot pleasure ignited through my bloodstream.

His finger rubbed my clit roughly, and I gasped against his lips. My heart beat hard and fast, my skin burning. I rolled my hips against his palm, his mouth hard on mine. Our breaths mixed together, and the pressure built within me.

This sensation was like hot embers boiling in the pit of my belly. And I fucking loved it.

From the corner of my mind, I realized he was walking. I needed him inside me. *Now!* I didn't give a shit if he wanted to take me on the hard tile or desk or couch. As long as he took me.

We both fell onto something soft, and my eyes shot open.

A bed. In a large, airy bedroom with a view of the sea. None of it mattered to me; except the sight of the man in front of me. Frantically, I fumbled to take his shirt off. I wanted to touch his bare chest, feel his hot skin under my fingertips. Santi cursed savagely and ripped his shirt open, buttons popping and scattering all around us.

In one swift move, he pulled my dress over my head. The shredding sound of my panties followed. He touched me everywhere, rough and urgent. The fire spread through me and pooled at my entrance.

"Fuck," I hissed, my sex flooded with an aching need for him.

His mouth latched onto my nipple. His teeth nipped the sensitive bud before easing the sting with his tongue. My back arched off the bed, a loud moan escaping my throat.

He alternated between sucking and nipping. My skin burned and pressure built, ready to explode into a million stars. My fingers tangled in his hair, gripping him closer, desperation clawing at me.

"I need you inside me," I moaned throatily. A tremor ran through me in anticipation. "Now, please," I begged, undone by the burning sensation in every cell of my body.

My hands reached for his belt, undoing it, then his hands pushed the material down his strong, muscular legs. He kicked them off. His socks and shoes followed. My mouth watered at his beautiful golden skin. His strong body was ripped with muscles. He discarded his clothing, standing above me naked and a shudder rippled through me.

Taking a shaky breath, my fingers traced his abs as he leaned over, his body blanketing mine. His skin was as hot as fire. As I wrapped my arms around his shoulders, I hooked my legs around his waist, his cock against my slick entrance.

The feel of him hard and pulsing hot against my center created a longing, which burned through my body as hot as Hades.

"My cock will tear your tight cunt," he growled, and my skin inflamed. I wanted to scream, *yes, yes, yes.* A shiver rolled through me, and heat sparked as he inched his way forward.

He thrust inside me, straight to the hilt and pleasure exploded. My breath caught in my throat as my pussy tightened around his thickness.

"Mine," he groaned against my lips. "My Amore." The way he claimed me made my heart ache and sing at the same time.

One hand moved to my throat, the placing of it so familiar, possessive, and exciting. It was a reminder that only Santi could do this to me. He pulled out only to thrust deep again.

My walls clung to his cock, needing him deeper, claiming me. "Yes," I gasped. "Yours."

Pressure and heat sparked through me as his pelvis ground against my clit. He pounded into me harder and faster. Each thrust took me closer to the edge.

"Santi, Santi," I chanted. "More."

He moved his hips like pistons, burying himself deeper inside me as he squeezed my throat. A shudder shook me as my inner muscles clenched around him.

"Your pussy was made for my cock, he groaned, his hands tightening around my throat. He pressed his lips hard against mine. Then as if he lost all his control, he powered hard, his lips sucking and kissing the curve of my jaw.

"Santi," I breathed out, the dots swimming in my vision from the intensity.

He was riding my body, driving deep inside of me. His flesh slapped against mine, our grunts and moans mixing. Nothing mattered but this amazing pleasure he was giving me. He ignited my body, set flames through my blood, and my pussy clenched around him.

He flipped us over, my body on top of him then yanked me back down to his lips.

"Don't you fucking dare come until I give you permission," he hissed against my lips, his grip snaking up to my hair and tightening. My response was a moan as I rolled my body against him, grinding against his pelvis.

It drove me crazy when he ordered me around as he fucked me. Maybe something was wrong with me, but I loved it. Thrived on it even.

I was so close, so damn close.

My muscles tightened and my vision blurred. "Santi," I begged for release.

His fingers dug into my hips, holding me in place as he drove his hips up to mine. His cock thrust deep inside me, my inside muscles clenching around him. Our bodies covered in sweat; my hair stuck to my neck. He was so deep inside me that I felt his cock twitch and white-hot pleasure shot through my spine.

"Now, Amore," he groaned, thrusting up hard, his lips grazing against the shell of my ear. As if my body waited for his command, it unraveled, pleasure shooting through my body. My pussy clenched around him, his seed spilling inside me, my muscles shaking with the intensity of the orgasm.

"Fuck," he rasped into my ear. "That's it, baby. Let it go."

His hands wrapped around my lower back, holding me tight as my body shuddered in his arms as the remnants of my orgasm ravaged me and wrung me completely dry.

The next morning, I reached for Santi but found the spot next to me cold. Slowly, peeling my eyelids open, I confirmed that Santi was not in bed. I lifted my head from my pillow, my hair falling on my face. I pushed it out of my face.

"Santi?" I called out, worry lacing my voice.

"Out here."

I slid out of bed, wearing only boyshort panties and his shirt.

"I'll be right out," I murmured.

Quickly, I made my way into the bathroom, combed my hair and brushed my teeth. I padded towards the soft noises and found Santi out on the balcony.

Stopping short at the doorway, a sharp inhale escaped me. The balcony overlooked the Ligurian Sea, the sparkling water view stretching for miles all around. Right off the Italian Riviera, the azure water stretched for miles, tranquil and crystalline. The villa had a stunning location, and I found myself wishing to remain here forever. It was magnificent.

Santi sat with a cup of coffee in his hands, skimming something on his phone. My heart skidded to a halt, then rushed forward in the next second. Heat flooded my body and an ache settled between my legs.

He was handsome, no doubt about that. I found him downright sexy. His upper half was completely bare, showing off his tanned and chiseled muscles and abs defined and mouthwatering. His body was pure perfection, the only disruption was the ink on his right hand, snaking up to his shoulder.

But it wasn't the only thing that attracted me to Santi. On the outside, he was all hard, ruthless, and powerful. But on the inside, there was fierce protectiveness, caring for people he loved. Like the way he loved his Pà or cared for his brother. Even me. When I was with him, I felt like I could fight the world and still be safe because he would ensure it. Not that I wanted to fight the world. Just avenge my mother.

Santi set his phone down, his lips lifting as his dark eyes traveled over my body, commencing at my bare toes painted pink.

"Good morning," he drawled. "Sleep well?" Delight danced in his eyes as he watched me blush at the question. We didn't do that much sleeping.

While my body ached in the sweetest way and my muscles were sore, he looked refreshed and well-rested, like he'd slept for days. His dark hair was damp, and my fingers twitched to touch him.

Butterflies danced in my stomach, my eyes glued on his bronze skin, and on his lower abs was a faint trail of hair disappearing into his pants. *Oh Gosh!* My cheeks grew so hot with thoughts of licking that trail that I thought I'd catch on fire.

"Morning," I finally murmured, unable to say anything else. I pushed my hand through my hair self-consciously. He looked put together while I was a frazzled, melting puddle of wantonness.

Swallowing my desire, I headed to the empty chair, but he grabbed my hand. We couldn't be touching and having sex all day and all night. After all, it wasn't practical.

"I don't think so," he said, as he pulled me onto his lap, and I squealed in surprise. "I want to feel you every second of the day. The last two months were too long." My heart danced in delight that he wanted me as much as I wanted him.

"They were," I agreed softly. I raised my hand to his cheek, then rested my palm against his scruff. "Much too long."

As I sat on his lap, he poured me a cup of coffee. I watched his graceful movements, those hands that could bring me so much pleasure.

"Cream, no sugar. Right?"

I smiled, my chest warming. He remembered how I liked my coffee. I have watched him for so long, I felt I knew everything about him. His favorite gun. His favorite food. His favorite car. How he drank his coffee. I never imagined he paid attention to me too.

I nodded and he poured in a bit of cream then handed me the cup. "How did you know?" I asked.

His smile was charming, mischievous, and wicked. "I make a point of learning all your likes."

Oh.

My heart glowed at his words. I tried not to read too much into it, but it was too late. My heart shuddered with feelings.

"Okay, then." I'd test him. Not even sure why. "What's my favorite color?"

"Pink." No hesitation. "But I love you best in green. Like your eyes."

I swore my heart shuddered in the best way possible.

"Favorite ice cream flavor?"

He chuckled. "Strawberry Cheesecake." Right again. "Ben & Jerry's. Those men will have to go, though," he half-joked. "There is room for only one man in your life."

Raising the cup to my mouth to hide a smile, I took a sip. The warm liquid traveled down my throat and a little moany sigh escaped me. The coffee was the next best thing to sex and ice cream.

"You fix good coffee," I said, licking a tiny drop off my lower lip. A low groan sounded off Santi's chest and I twisted around to search his face. "Everything okay?"

His gaze darkened and my pulse skidded to a stop. The groan came from deep in his chest and his hands tightened on my hips.

"I can't get enough of you," he purred, his breath hot against my ear while my back was against his chest.

Butterflies erupted in my stomach. A small smile curved my lips. It felt good to know he craved me as much as I craved him. Slowly, I took another sip and moaned again, grinding myself against his groin. I couldn't resist taunting him, drunk on his desire for me. Or was it my desire for him?

"Minx." He nipped my earlobe. "Stay still. You are going to eat, and then we are doing something fun."

I turned my head around and our eyes met. "Sex is fun," I muttered.

He laughed. Softly. "It sure is, but we'll be doing something else."

"Like what?" I asked.

"Swimming. Maybe do some sightseeing on my motorcycle. Go dancing."

My eyes widened. "I like it all but the motorcycle. Not sure—"

"I'll keep you safe. I promise." When I didn't say anything, he took my chin between his fingers. "Do you trust me?"

"I do," I told him without any hesitation. I have trusted him for as long as I've known him. He made me feel safe. "Motorcycle and a date it is then."

He rewarded me with a kiss on the tip of my nose, instantly sending shivers down my spine. *This man!* I had to get a grip around him, otherwise I'd turn into a doormat for Santi.

Looking back out to the sea to admire the view, I tampered down my reaction to him. "This place is amazing," I uttered softly. "Do you come here often?"

His grip around my waist tightened slightly, though I was unsure if it was intentional. "No, I haven't been in years."

My eyes searched him out, but it looked like he wouldn't elaborate. "Why not?"

He shrugged. "When my mamma died, Pà didn't like coming back here. Honestly, neither did I."

There was no emotion in his voice, but I sensed sorrow underneath it all. After all, I experienced it firsthand. Adriano, Santi, and I had that in common. All three of us lost our mothers young.

I laid my hand over his big one and gently squeezed it.

"I'm sorry," I said softly.

I remembered Mr. Russo's comment about my mother all those years ago. I assumed he wasn't a faithful husband, though when it was your own mamma it was probably different. Adriano wouldn't have known about the infidelity since he was too young when she died. But Santi wasn't too young. He would have picked up on his father's infidelities.

Except, I couldn't ask him about it. I didn't want to cause him pain. He loved his mamma, there was no doubt about it. Most of the men of the Cosa Nostra were unfaithful. After all, it was how I came to be. My father was unfaithful to his wife. Though, it wasn't something I wanted repeated. I wouldn't be anyone's side piece, nor could I live with a husband that would be unfaithful.

"Eat," he instructed. "You'll need your energy."

Without hesitation, I reached for a croissant and bit into it. The flavor burst on my tongue as I chewed, then I eagerly took another bite. Suddenly, I was famished.

"Jesus, this is the best croissant I've ever had," I uttered, my mouth half full. The food practically melted in my mouth.

"It's my mother's recipe."

"Holy shit, it is so good." I leaned forward and grabbed another one. "Don't tell me you baked it."

He chuckled. "No, the cook came early this morning and prepared it all."

"Ahhhh. If it's a man, tell your cook I'll marry him," I teased.

He gently pinched my thigh, his gaze darkly amused. "Then I am lucky it is a woman. Or I'd have to kill my cook."

I pecked his cheek, then brushed my lips against the corner of his lips. It was positively wrong how my body warmed up whenever he behaved possessively. It *had* to be unhealthy. I sensed he wasn't entirely joking and a big part of me liked it.

Downing my coffee, I slid off his lap.

"I'll take a quick shower."

I almost wished he hadn't taken a shower already so we could do it together. *Next time*, I thought to myself. As if he read my thoughts, his eyes darkened.

"You better go before I change my mind and we spend all day in bed."

My stomach fluttered.

"I wouldn't mind that one bit," I teased, then hurried back inside. I grabbed a few of my things and rushed into the shower.

CHAPTER 30

Santino

I watched Amore disappear through the door and not long after, I heard the shower water running. I pictured her stripping off my shirt and those sexy boyshorts and had to fight the urge to go after her.

She was my temptation. My obsession. My addiction. My everything.

I crossed the line the second I landed in Italy. A better man would have come clean with Amore and ended this thing we had going. I was far from a good man. The wrong side of the law was where I was always meant to be. The Cosa Nostra was home. I thrived in it. I was exceptionally good at it too.

As I'd always known though, I was fucking selfish. I would have Amore as my wife, even if it meant war with the Bennetti family. I didn't fear them. I gave the old man a chance to see it my way. He fucking refused. Starting a feud was the only thing left because giving up Amore wasn't an option.

I had Renzo, Lorenzo, every New York lawyer on my payroll, and even Gabriel fucking Carrera digging for the contract that named the man she was promised to. So far nothing. I had governors, senators, and a shitton of high officials in my pocket due to their secrets. Yet, a single fucking name from a marriage contract could not be found.

The anger burned and twisted inside me. I'd lose my goddamn mind if any other man touched her. The war with the Bennetti's would be the least of our worries.

I even had half a mind to ask Adriano to attempt digging for the information. But he'd tell her, and it was the last thing I wanted. Besides, I couldn't ask him without revealing that Amore and I have been sleeping together since Pà's funeral. And she wanted to tell him when he came to visit her in a few months. Face-to-face.

If the name was not found by then, I'd talk to him. Adriano had a keen way of digging up information.

Fuck! I would sleep better if the man was dead already. Then I'd sign that contract and countdown the days until Amore was mine.

My phone rang. It was Carrera.

"Yeah." He better have a fucking name for me. I was worked up, my shoulders tense with pent-up need to get this obstacle eliminated. Until Amore's intended lay dead with a bullet in his skull and the threat from the Perèz Cartel was eliminated, I wouldn't rest.

"Did you know Amore was in Venezuela?" The question caught me off guard and surprise washed over me. The feeling was immediately replaced by a fear for her. She was safe, here with me right now, but the dread of what could have happened to her hit me straight in the center of my chest.

"No." Amore hadn't mentioned leaving Italy.

Why would she go to South America? The Perèz Cartel attacked her in the city and had been haunting her. She knew that; she acknowledged that much. Though the reason behind the attack remained a mystery. Amore wasn't a threat to the Perèz Cartel. My gut feeling was telling me her father and grandmother knew why. It had something to do with the Andersons, I was sure of it.

"Is your source reliable?" I questioned him. Amore wasn't reckless.

"Yes."

"When was she there?"

"Last week."

What the fuck was going on?

"Alone?"

He only hesitated for a fraction of a second, but it was enough for me to notice it and become suspicious. "I believe so."

That was all it took to lose my trust. However, I wouldn't let him know and acted as if I hadn't noticed.

"Anything on the attacker?" I knew there was nothing. All my men were on it.

"No."

"Okay, keep looking." I ended the call. That man was the key to finding out the connection to the attacks on Amore. I just needed a fucking name. He was like a damn phantom.

Hearing the shower water still running, I dialed up Adriano.

"What's up, *fratello*?" Adriano answered.

He didn't call me *fratello* as an endearment. It was Adriano's reminder that I should trust him more than anyone else. He wanted back into the hustle of the Cosa Nostra business. Much like me, and every other Russo, he lived for it. After all, we were the sons of our father. Just like his father, and his father's father, we were all hustlers, ruthless cheaters, and selfish bastards. It was what caused the first feud between the Bennettis and Russos.

Margaret Regalè.

Both my father and Savio wanted Margaret Regalè for her connections to the Venezuelan Cartel. Like I said, selfish bastards. And both were willing to seduce her for it.

Why?

It was simple. For power and connections. Regina's husband, Amore's grandfather, was running the Perèz Cartel. From what Pà told me, she walked into their restaurant by mistake, and they both saw the opportunity. It didn't take long for her mother to fall in love with Savio. And then she disappeared, married George Anderson, and left for Europe. Now we knew it was because she found herself pregnant. It wasn't long after her wedding that Margaret's father was gunned down and murdered.

"I need you to run something down for me," I told him. "For our *business*. Nobody can know about it."

I needed to know what Amore did in South America. Her heritage had connections to the Perèz Cartel, but her father and grandmother were adamant about keeping her out of it. The question was how much did Amore know?

"About fucking time," he replied.

"Amore Bennetti went to South America last week," I told him and heard his sharp inhale over the line. So he didn't know either. She was his best friend. It was natural he'd worry about her. Yet, something inside me twisted and irrational jealousy slithered through my veins. I ignored it. "I want to know where she went, who she was with, and what she did. This is just between the two of us."

"Leave it to me," he promised, and our call ended. He knew the deal. Our loyalties were to the famiglia first and foremost. Though, I knew giving up Amore wouldn't be an option. No matter what the fuck she was doing.

When Regina's husband died, the family's connection to the Perèz Cartel died. There should have been no reason for the cartel to go after them. Unless they took her visit to Colombia as a way to get back into the business. From all the information I had received, neither mother nor daughter had an interest in that life or hustle. Unlike Regina.

The question was what was Amore doing?

CHAPTER 31

Amore

"Where are we sightseeing?" I asked him with a smile. Now that I thought about it, I should have worn shorts, but I was too focused on looking good for Santi versus practical. Though I questioned myself now as I eyed my short dress and debated whether I should go back in to change.

I wore a sleeveless sky-blue dress that came down to my knees. Santi liked it; I could tell by the look in his eyes. Our little vacation had started off amazing, and I felt like I glowed like a hundred-watt bulb.

He was tense when I came out of the bathroom. When I questioned him, he said it was business back home, but something was amiss. Though he got himself together quickly and here we were.

"You'll see." He handed me a helmet, and I eyed it suspiciously.

"Is this a girl's helmet?"

"Yes."

I narrowed my eyes, jealousy suddenly very real in the pit of my stomach. "Have you taken other girls on your motorcycle?"

He laughed. "It's new, Amore. Just for you." He shook his head as if entertained. "Put it on your head. We are going for a ride."

He stood next to a motorcycle. I knew he could ride a motorcycle and often went for rides with his own sport bike back home. Although,

I had never had the pleasure of seeing him ride it. He usually preferred his fast, expensive cars.

"You're not scared, are you?"

I raised my chin up. "Of course not. I just know that Italians drive like crazy, and I don't want to get into an accident."

"You trust me. Yeah?" It was an innocent question that he seemed to keep asking. Yet, it hit me hard every time because I trusted Santi. Explicitly. Deep down I trusted him and would do anything he told me. It probably showed how stupidly naive I was.

Or maybe not. Because I hadn't told him about my little side operation I had going with DeAngelo. I wanted to avenge my mother. I made a promise, and I intended to keep it.

"Yes, I trust you," I finally said. He tilted his head, and a strange expression passed his face. It almost felt like he could read my mind and was wondering why I was not telling him about my expeditions to South America.

Extending his hand, he helped me put the helmet on before putting on his own. He swung his long, muscular leg over the seat and mounted the bike. He looked good. He was wearing a white t-shirt that showed off his impressive biceps and muscles outlined underneath it, a dark pair of jeans and leather boots. I loved watching his right arm, covered entirely in ink.

"Sit close to me." He smiled wide. "I don't want your dress flashing everyone. Only me."

"I should have dressed appropriately," I told him, muttering more to myself.

"But this is so much more fun," he retorted with a smile. This Santi was so different from the man I thought I knew. He was less intense, more fun, and so damn sexy, it made me ache.

I looked down at myself. My sundress and a pair of leather sandals with crisscross straps wasn't an outfit for a motorcycle ride. But I looked good, if nothing else. I secured my shoulder bag on my hip. It had a little bit of everything, my sunscreen, bathing suit, phone, my sunglasses, fashion magazine. Because the latter was very important.

The air between us was relaxed, unlike ever before. I wasn't sure if it was Italy or the fact that it was just the two of us and knowledge that my family was across the ocean. There was no danger of running into them by accident. Eventually, we'd come clean. Adriano was coming in August, and I wanted to tell him in person. I'd tell my family then too, starting with Lorenzo. He was the easiest to talk to. Dad and Grandma would be the hardest, but I wanted to come clean with both of them too. Maybe I should give the news to both of them at the same time, so they could just start arguing, and I'd sneak out. Just thinking about it made my skin perspire and sent my anxiety into overdrive.

But I wouldn't worry about that now. For right now, it was just us and I'd enjoy that to the fullest.

I sat behind him and scooted closer, wrapping my arms around his waist. He started the bike, and I felt the vibrations beneath my legs. The second we drove off, my fists tightened around him, holding on. It was my first time on a motorcycle. Adriano was very fond of them too, but I never had the urge to ride with him. He was reckless on a bike.

The idiot that rode on the back tire down the highway, being reckless... Yeah, that was Adriano. So, it was a 'no thank you' from me whenever he offered me a ride on his motorcycle.

After five minutes, I slowly started to relax, though my grip around Santi didn't. He drove really well. Enough so that I lifted my face from being pressed against his back and allowed the wind to whip around my face and hair, the feeling of freedom racing through my veins. I liked being pressed tightly against him, my hands around his waist. With each mile behind us, I felt more and more relaxed.

Santi took the scenic route from his villa through small, charming towns. I hadn't been to this part of Italy, so I eagerly soaked it all in. We rode for a while before I saw a sign for Genoa. The roads twisted and turned, the glimpses of sea in front of us and mountains behind us. It was breathtaking. The scenic route would stay with me forever.

Finally there, we stopped in one of the parking spots right in the middle of the city. Santi turned off the bike, and I got off, a wide grin on my face.

"Genoa?" I asked him, taking off the helmet.

He nodded.

"We can grab lunch, then go to the beach. Maybe some dancing."

He grinned wide, his dark hair shuffling under the wind. "The day is young."

"I didn't pack a dress for the evening," I murmured with regret.

Dark amusement danced in his eyes. It was silly in the grand scheme of things, but I liked nice clothes. So sue me. I lived for fashion; it was ingrained in me. And wearing a beach dress for dancing just didn't seem right.

"There are plenty of shops here. We'll get you dresses."

"The price tag will be crazy expensive," I complained, which sounded even sillier than complaining about the dress.

A booming laugh left him, and he shook his head with disbelief. "Don't worry. I got you covered, heiress."

I rolled my eyes and shoved my shoulder into him. "You will have to foot the bill for everything. I didn't bring my wallet."

"I got you," he drawled, pressing his lips to mine. *This! This is what I want,* I thought as his mouth devoured me. "I'll always take care of you."

We headed towards the old part of the town. Santi knew his way around and held my hand as we strolled through the city of Genoa. The smell of the sea drifted through the air, along with sounds of the waves crashing into the shore. The city buzzed with life, the sounds of the locals chattering and laughing. It always brought a smile to my face hearing the locals in their vivid and passionate conversations.

With all the time on our hands and no schedule, we strolled through the old city of Genoa for the better half of the morning. We'd been to Le Strade Nuove and the Pàlazzi dei Rolli, then to Cattedrale di San Lorenzo, Via Garibaldi. The streets were full of tourists, but nobody and nothing mattered but the man beside me. It had been, hands down, one of the best days ever so far.

We laughed, talked, and ate ice cream. Santi was the best guide. He knew a lot about this city, a result of spending time here with his mother when he was a kid. I wanted to learn everything about him.

"Ahhh," I moaned, taking another lick of my melting strawberry flavored ice cream. "Italy has the best ice cream."

Santi chuckled, leaning over close to me. "You better like me more than your ice cream."

"I like you more," I rasped softly.

He licked the corner of my lip and then locked eyes with me. "Ice cream is okay, but I know one thing that is even better."

"What?" I whispered in a shaky breath, heat climbing up my cheeks.

He chuckled, knowing exactly what he was doing to me.

"Your pussy." His hot breath against my ear got me all flustered, sending languid heat through my veins. Rattled, I dropped my cone.

"Santi," I complained, all flushed. "You made me drop my ice cream."

His hand came around me, pulling me closer. "I'll get you another." He nudged me to the right. "There is an even better ice cream place at the end of this road."

I glanced at him curiously. "Did you spend a lot of time here as a kid with your parents? You know this city well."

"My mother was born here." He nudged me forward, and I side-stepped my ice cream mess on the ground. "I spent good parts of my summers here with my grandparents and my mother."

"Oh." It wasn't what I expected for a response. Somehow I assumed that both his parents were born and raised in New York. "Was your dad born here too?"

He shook his head. "No, but his ancestors were from this area."

I thought about that for a few seconds. Lorenzo and Luigi never talked about their mother due to what happened.

"Your parents' marriage was arranged?" I knew it was as Adriano had told me so. Just as he told me that my dad's marriage to Elena was arranged too.

"Yes, but they fit well together."

I tilted my head, watching him. I recalled Mr. Russo's comment that it was my mother that drove a wedge between the two families. There was no way Santi forgot that. He wasn't the forgetting type, but I refused to be the one to remind him about it.

He held my gaze as if waiting for something. I wasn't quite sure what.

"Amore?"

"Yes?"

"How do you feel about marriage arrangements?"

My lips parted in shock. It wasn't a question I expected. "You want my honest opinion?" I added.

He nodded. "Whenever possible."

I shrugged. "Marriage arrangements are ridiculous. I mean, we are in the twenty-first century. The whole act is barbaric if you ask me." He cocked his eyebrow. "Seriously, Santi, please don't tell me you actually agree with them?"

He held my gaze, but it was hard to tell what he was thinking. I guess this was his poker face.

"It's a tradition. Certain marriage arrangements keep territories and wealth within the Cosa Nostra."

I rolled my eyes. "It sounds to me like it is just a power play."

"It happens more than you know. Even outside the Cosa Nostra. Among the society that your grandmother prefers too."

I took a deep breath and released it slowly. It was odd to be having this conversation and that he even brought it up. I knew from Adriano that contracts were usually signed between the groom and the father, which seemed barbaric to me.

"Maybe," I told him. "It seems primitive to me. And certainly not fair to the women of the Cosa Nostra." I narrowed my gaze at him. "What is all this about, Santi?"

His expression remained unchanged. "Does your father have a marriage contract for you?"

I blinked my eyes, a heartbeat of confusion and then burst out laughing, hard. He didn't seem to share the amusement.

I tried to get myself together, though I couldn't stop smiling. "No. Grandma would eat him alive." I shook my head, imagining that fiasco and couldn't help but laugh again. "Honestly, so would I. There is no way in hell anyone is telling me who I should marry."

A dark expression passed his eyes. "You seem certain."

I studied his face, something nagging at me, but I couldn't quite figure out what. He seemed rather somber.

Is he— I cut off my train of thought. He wouldn't be thinking about marriage with me. There was no way he'd do a marriage contract for me. Despite my brain being reasonable, my heart fluttered with hope. *How stupid!*

Marrying someone of the Cosa Nostra had never crossed my mind. *Until now.* Damn it, I couldn't think about that. Everyone knows you don't marry your first boyfriend. Even if he was handsome, gave me the most amazing orgasms, was the most eligible bachelor of New York City, and women of all ages fawned over him.

"I am certain," I finally said. There was no sense in getting myself worked up. Besides, I knew from Adriano that men of the Cosa Nostra didn't really look at me the same way as daughters of other families. My upbringing and freedom made me unappealing to them, which was perfectly fine with me.

Except that thought didn't sit well when it came to Santi. Maybe he didn't see me as marriage material either?

Goddamn it, I didn't need these thoughts. This was just dating a super-hot man that I loved... A soft groan left me. I was utterly, devastatingly in love with him.

"What?" Santi questioned me, his eyes on me.

I couldn't tell him that it bothered me to think he wouldn't find me marriage material. Besides, it was better I didn't marry. Most men would want to marry me only for my fortune. But not Santi. He had enough money of his own.

I'd always said I wouldn't marry into this world, and I wouldn't die in it. It just wasn't meant to be.

"I don't want to talk about the nonsense of marriage contracts," I admitted softly. Then remembering what we talked about right before this sore topic came up, I shifted the conversation. "Do you know where Dad's family is from?" Santi's dark eyes flashed with surprise. It was odd that I didn't know, I'd give him that. I smiled sheepishly. "We never talk about it. I think he tries to keep all that stuff away from me."

"I can see that," he muttered. "You weren't exactly born and bred in this world."

There we go again. The reminder!

I frowned. "You make it sound like a bad thing."

His hand took the nape of my neck and he pressed a hard, deep kiss on my lips that was over too quick, then hung his arm over my shoulder as we continued walking.

"It's not a bad thing," he continued like he didn't just take my breath away with his kiss. "He probably didn't want to scare you." When I gave him a puzzled look, he explained, "Your upbringing was considerably different. Your mom and grandmother gave you more freedom in your thirteen years than women in our world have for their entire life."

And another *confirmation*. It wasn't the first time he'd said this.

"Which is stupid and chauvinistic towards women in the underworld, if I may add." His lip tugged up at my comment.

"I don't disagree, but it is for their protection. We create enemies in our lifestyle, and those enemies limit the freedom for women born into our world."

"Okay, I'll give you that one," I muttered reluctantly, dragging another smile out of him. "But you could also teach women to defend themselves, you know. Instead of leaving them vulnerable."

He threw his head back and laughed. I was almost tempted to show off one of the moves DeAngelo taught me to show him we could be just as fierce. Or tell him about one of our missions. But I didn't. When he said nothing else, comfortable silence followed, and my thoughts drifted back to last week in Columbia.

DeAngelo booked us a house in Caracas. My nerves danced through my skin, making me antsy. I could practically taste the restlessness and excess energy colliding within me. I had to burn off some of it so I could keep a clear head when we left for our mission tomorrow.

Dressed in my tight black pants and a black tank top, I headed back downstairs to the gym. Earlier today, DeAngelo and I went over the plans and the map of the area we would target tomorrow.

I was doing this to avenge my mother's death. To make them pay. But this wasn't me. Being a badass warrior woman just wasn't part of my DNA. I somewhat enjoyed the physical part of the training, but that was where it ended for me.

Torture, blood, killings... it just wasn't me.

"Where are you going?" DeAngelo's voice startled me and sent my heart into overdrive.

"Jesus, DeAngelo," I mumbled, holding my hand against my chest. "You scared the living daylights out of me." I took a deep breath, trying to

calm my heart. Then another. "I was going to do another thirty minutes in the gym. I'm too worked up."

He nodded in understanding. He had been around me for a long time. By now, he often understood me without any need for explanation.

Together, we continued to the gym.

"Hand-to-hand combat training?" he asked.

I groaned. It was my least favorite form of exercise and training, but I knew he was right. I had to work on it.

"Sure, why not?" I answered, though reluctantly.

Both of us took our positions. Locking eyes, I waited and watched. DeAngelo always warned that you could tell by a man's expression what the next move would be. So, I waited, keeping a keen eye on his every move. No matter how small.

His gaze flickered for a second to my shoulder and he went to attack. I sidestepped him and avoided his assault. He was going for my right shoulder and was probably going to flip me and land me on my ass.

I chuckled. "Well, well, DeAngelo," I teased. "You are getting slow."

His left foot swept across the floor. I had gloated too soon, tripping over his foot and landing flat on my back.

"Ouch," I muttered.

"Not so slow, huh?"

"Jerk." Though it was all in good humor. He reached out his hand and I took it, lifting me back to my feet. Seeing my opening, I twisted his arm and flipped him over. As if in slow motion, he landed belly down, and I couldn't help my victorious exclamation.

"Don't mess with a Bennetti," I purred, pushing his hand slightly harder.

"I'm impressed," he commended. "You could be lethal if you wanted to. Just like a Carrera."

Instantly, I let go of his hand and sat on the floor of the gym. Coming from DeAngelo, that was a compliment.

Our eyes met and I exhaled before shaking my head. "Except, I don't want to be Carrera, nor Perèz, or even Regalè." He watched me pensively. "I just want to be me, DeAngelo. I want to make them pay, but this is not really me."

"It could be you," he tried to reason.

"But it isn't," I retorted stubbornly. *"Tell me honestly, DeAngelo. Could you ever see me thrive in this world?"*

"No," he answered reluctantly. *"You would be miserable."*

We sat in silence for a while, both of us lost in our own thoughts. "Amore, you realize that you are next in line for a cartel empire?"

Yes! Except I didn't want it. My mother didn't want it, my grand- mother didn't want it, though she reluctantly took it to ensure our safety. Wouldn't it be better if it all just burned to hell?

Santi's finger traced the line of my nose, bringing me back to the present. To him.

I wasn't ready to reveal all my cards to him, so I just smiled. It was too early to show him that invariably I had been turned into a weapon by force of circumstance. I had a promise to keep.

His fingers gently tugged on a strand of my hair. "You know, Amore, I am convinced even if you were born and raised in this world, you'd still be you."

Tilting my head, I studied him unsure how to take his words. "Is that good or bad?" I asked him.

From the little I knew, from Adriano's references, it was hard to gather what Santi preferred. However, I knew one thing for sure. Usually, he went for a completely different type of woman. Curvy, meek, blonde women that kept their mouths shut and only opened it to suck his cock were Santi's type. Adriano's words not mine.

Needless to say, I was nothing like that. Though sucking his cock... hmmm, I was getting hot just thinking about it. His taste was addictive. Or maybe it was just the fact that it was Santi.

"It's good," he rumbled. "You are soft. Untainted. So damn honest."

"I can't quite decide if that was a compliment or not," I half-joked, my cheeks blazing hot. The truth was that I wasn't that honest. And I certainly wasn't untainted. Not since seeing my mother tortured.

His teeth nipped the sensitive spot on my earlobe. "It's a compli- ment." My chest swelled with satisfaction while my cheeks burned harder. "Now back to your question. Your father's family is from Capri."

"Capri, huh?" I guess that was good to know, though somehow it meant nothing. "And of course, you know where your mother's family is from."

My heartbeat faltered for a fraction of a second before it resumed beating.

My heritage from Mom's side was a bit more complicated.

CHAPTER 32

Adriano

Fucking finally!

Santi was finally letting me back into our business. There was no better place for me than the Cosa Nostra, but Pà had insisted I go to college and study business.

Be normal! Boring!

I fucking hated it. All I wanted to do was hustle. It was the only puzzle that fit perfectly in my whole existence.

Nothing compared to it. Not even sex... and I fucking loved sex.

Pà could have insisted I become a doctor, a fucking saint; it wouldn't have mattered. I would have found my way back to the wrong side of the law. Why? Because I fucking thrived in it, just like any other Russo. It was ingrained in my brother; it was ingrained in me.

Santi went to NYU, studied business too. But unlike me, he breezed through it. I only passed thanks to Amore's help.

Amore. My best friend, who happens to be a girl.

People didn't understand our dynamic, but the truth was that my best friend saved me as much as I saved her. As much as I loved the hustle, the killings weren't my thing. Killing men stained me and somehow over the years since my first kill, I lost my way.

I killed my first man when I was fifteen. I watched the void fill his dying gaze. It hit me all wrong. Santi told me there was no sense in regrets. It was a waste of time and energy. But for some reason, the regrets kept piling up and eating at me, one by fucking one.

They didn't seem to bother Santi, but they ate at me, slowly and painfully. Like a slow killing poison, weakening me. *Until I met Amore.* Something about her calmed me and eased the pain of regret, it faded into a fog that didn't matter as much.

Maybe it was the fact that both of us hurt and that neither one of us liked cruelty and had seen enough of it first-hand. She had never uttered the words of what she had experienced, but the glimpses of her nightmares and panic attacks revealed plenty

And now... this task that Santi had put me on was easy, digging up information was my expertise. Yet, it felt like a betrayal.

It was a crossroad.

I could dig up the reason behind Amore's trip to Venezuela. But my gut feeling was telling me it couldn't be good. It had to be connected to her history, to what happened to her mother. I thought we were best friends, that we'd shared everything.

Well, except for Russo business, I thought wryly.

I never shared the Russo or the Cosa Nostra business with her. Not that she ever seemed even remotely interested.

Unlocking my phone, I searched her up in my phone book. She should be available.

The line rang and rang. Just as I thought she wouldn't answer, her voice came through.

"Hey, Adriano."

A soft emotion glimmered in my chest.

"How is my favorite girl?" I asked.

A soft chuckle traveled over the line. "Good. And you? Any stalker ex-girlfriends need a call from me?"

It was what we did. She always jumped in to pose as my steady girl-friend. We got along so well, sometimes I wondered how we'd get along as a real couple. Those ideas were more frequent in recent months. Amore Bennetti was a gorgeous, sweet ass. Sweetest ass I had ever seen, and I've seen my share.

"I'm safe from any stalkers," I assured her with a chuckle. "I just wanted to check on how you are doing. You were never fond of downtime."

"I'm doing great," she replied. I could hear lightness and happiness in her voice. I frowned. She sounded different. Happier than ever before.

"Any reason why you are doing great?"

She chuckled. "Should there be a reason?"

"Usually, women are doing great when they are in love," I grunted. Something about Amore being in love rubbed me the wrong way.

"You should know, huh?" she teased. A light bitterness swelled inside me. I guess I deserved that. After all, how many times had I left her alone for a quick fuck? But I always came back to her.

It was better not to elaborate on that.

"What have you been doing?" I asked her instead.

"Not much," she answered. "I went to Genoa and the beach yesterday. I'm going to the beach again today."

"Alone?"

"No, with a friend," she answered. My first inclination was to think she was going with a man and a growl crept up my throat. Smothering it, I shoved the urge to demand to know the name of who she was going with down.

"Have fun," I said instead. It sounded fake to my own ears, but if she picked up on it, she didn't comment on it. "What did you do last week?"

It was the last week of her semester. I found out she took all her exams the week before last, earlier than planned. Her professors allowed it, marking down a family emergency. There wasn't one. Lorenzo and her uncle Vincent flying home to help with business was hardly a family emergency.

All the Bennetti strip clubs were raided. Savio had been having issues with his suppliers. The Perèz Cartel had it out for him. For everyone in the Cosa Nostra, although Bennetti seemed to be at the top of that list. Santi had been helping him, but the two had a falling out. Not that he could help him even if they were on good terms since Santi was out of the country.

Vacation, he said. It didn't make fucking sense. He hadn't taken a vacation for as long as I'd known him.

"I had exams last week," Amore replied. "So, all my focus was on that."

Lie.

"How did you do on your exams?" I questioned her. I knew she was in Venezuela, but she just confirmed that the reason for her travel wasn't a mere visit.

"Good," she stated. "I have to go. You are still coming at the end of the summer, right?"

"Yes."

"Wonderful. I can't wait." I heard a distant voice in the background. Definitely male. I gritted my teeth. I had no right to be jealous, especially considering I had been changing women like underwear for years. Right in front of her eyes. Except, Amore never dated or even entertained going out with anyone but me.

"Got to go. We can talk tomorrow. Love ya."

The phone still to my ear, I was left listening to the beeping sound, signaling she was gone.

So, this was how it felt.

CHAPTER 33

Santino

My phone beeped and I glanced at the message. It was from Adriano.

Venezuela with DeAngelo.
And three special ops men.
No word on why.
Official story is hiking trip.

Lifting my head, I observed Amore. She was looking through some designs on her computer, completely immersed in it. She was hiding something. I knew she didn't do hiking; that was a bullshit excuse. And what the hell was she doing with special ops men?

Earlier, as we had headed out, she got a call and rushed to her computer. Watching her focus on her work, I saw firsthand how much she loved fashion.

The world around her was forgotten. She jotted down notes after each design, marking up the touchscreen. Her eyes shone with excitement, cheeks lightly flushed. It was a look I had come to know well. It was the expression she wore when I kissed her, and it only grew more intense when I buried myself inside her.

Jesus! I couldn't think about her hazed green eyes when I fucked her, or about her pale, milky skin flushed with excitement. The heat ran straight to my dick. She was insatiable, just as I was. I've been buried inside her more than not. Yet, my fascination and need to fuck her grew each time I had her. I couldn't afford to be distracted, but all this fucked with my head.

Her marriage contract. Whatever Amore was doing in Venezuela.

I had to get to the bottom of it all. I wouldn't fucking lose her to either one of those things.

"I'm almost done, Santi." Her soft voice pulled me back. A soft smile curved her full, red lips. God, what she could do with her mouth! Her lack of experience was irrelevant when it came to sex. She was pure perfection, molding into my every need. "Sorry about the delay."

"Take your time."

From the looks of it, she was making changes to the designs. She was in her element. Fashion was her life, her passion. Not hiking through the jungle. Bullshit story. The fact that DeAngelo went along with three special ops men told me she was doing something more. Something dangerous, and he wanted to ensure she was safe.

There was only one conclusion left.

Revenge.

Amore Bennetti was after revenge.

But I struggled to see her going after the cartel. It wasn't part of Amore's DNA. Mine, yes. But hers, no. She didn't have a mean bone in her body. And the thought scared the living daylights out of me. Just the idea of her getting hurt rattled me straight to my core. Drove me fucking nuts!

Me! A damning hustler that tore through the Cosa Nostra, ruling it and conquering anyone that refused to bend to my will. I'd lost count of the men I'd killed, beaten, hustled, tortured. Truthfully, there wasn't a single man that didn't deserve it. Adriano wasn't cut out for killing. I, on the other hand, didn't give a crap. It was kill or be killed in the world of the Cosa Nostra.

But this woman!

A simple, sorrowful expression in her eyes and she'd bring me to my knees. Someone hurting her would send me into a raging inferno, and not the good kind.

It had finally happened. I had found my weakness. Amore Bennetti had become my weakness, in flesh and blood. Worst of all, she was vulnerable. I wanted to put a titanium suit on her, close her in the highest tower, surround her with the strongest, trusted men... just to ensure nothing happened to her.

Yet, I knew if I did all that, Amore would rebel. She loved her freedom, her independence, her life. How in the fuck would I survive to thirty worrying about her safety?

Amore's soft voice carried over to me. She was talking to someone on the phone.

"I sent you my changes," she said, the young woman gone and in her place a confident heiress. "I think we are on target with all of them. Let me know if you agree and we can send them into production." The room went quiet, then a soft chuckle. "I know. We really did great. I'm so excited to show them off."

Another second and she hung up. Striding over to me with her eyes twinkling like emeralds with excitement.

My lips curved up. "New fashion line?"

Her whole face lit up. "Yes. I'm excited for it. It isn't Regalè Fashion. Something I started on the side."

You couldn't help but admire her. She hustled too, just slightly different than me. We were opposites, yet we fit perfectly.

She looked beautiful wearing a white summer dress that came to her knees with light pink polka dots and matching sandals. Her hair was pulled up into a loose ponytail, a few unruly strands falling free. And her skin... smooth, pale, and so damn silky. I wanted to run my palms over every inch of it. Again and again.

I couldn't find a single thing I didn't like about this girl. I loved it all, inside and out. She was smart, funny, beautiful, and so damn loyal to the people she loved. Irrationally and selfishly, I wanted all her loyalty for myself.

"Now, Santi," she whispered, pressing her body against mine and offering her mouth for a kiss. "Where are you taking me?"

For a woman that didn't have a man before me, she sure knew how to arouse one.

"We are going to eat at a nice restaurant," I told her. Grabbing her gently by the nape, I bent my head down, our lips inches apart. "I'm going to show all the Italian men you are mine. Then I'm bringing you home and bending you over the balcony and fucking you until you are screaming my name out to the sea."

I watched in fascination and self-satisfaction as her cheeks turned crimson. It didn't matter how many times I uttered filthy words to her, she blushed every single time. I lowered my lips to hers, and instantly she parted for me, our tongues dancing together in perfect harmony. Her response to me was so genuine, so soft, so addictive. Like all she ever wanted to do was please me.

And all I wanted to do was back her up against the wall, place my hand over her throat or her mouth, and watch her green eyes haze with lust as I rutted her hard and ruthlessly.

"Well, the night seems promising," she purred softly, and I couldn't resist a chuckle.

"I can't quite decide whether sex goddess or monster is more appropriate."

"Stick to goddess," she retorted, her eyes twinkling mischievously. "And I might reward you."

I shook my head with amusement. "Let's go, sex goddess."

The evening was going great. Amore entertained with stories of her childhood with her mother. It would seem even as a child, Amore was stubbornly independent. The ambiance in the restaurant, Santamonica, was great, the view over the sea and the sounds of waves were relaxing.

Going over the events of her first participation in the fashion show when she was nine, she couldn't hide the soft expression in her eyes. It was a good memory, but memories of her mom came hand-in-hand with sadness.

"I wanted pink," she continued her story. "And unless she gave me pink, I was determined to wreak havoc upon the fashion show. I threw a fit, adamant that nobody would go on the runway unless I was given something pink to wear. Anything, but it had to be pink. It was my favorite color." She chuckled softly. "Pink clashed with my hair, and I knew that, but I loved the color."

"I bet you got your way," I mused. I loved hearing her talk about her life before I met her. It gave glimpses of who she was before she was sucked into the Cosa Nostra.

"Well, Mom was rather clever too," she retorted dryly. "After none of the promises of ice cream worked, she finally had me promise that if she let me wear something pink, I would go willingly and with a smile onto the runway. Thinking I won, I eagerly agreed."

I cocked an eyebrow, waiting for her to continue.

"She handed me a pair of pink socks." She rolled her eyes, annoyed, but a wistful look entered them. She still missed her mother. "So, if you really wanted to, you'd find a picture of my mother and I at the end of the big fashion show where I'm wearing a blue dress, odd pink socks with black Mary Jane shoes." A laugh boomed in my chest, and she pretended to be offended, though a soft smile curved her lips "Not the best fashion statement."

"I'm sure you looked adorable," I teased. "Though knowing how much you love ice cream, I'm surprised that blackmail didn't work."

She chuckled. "She wouldn't have upheld the threat of denying me anyhow and I knew it."

"Why not?" I asked curiously.

"It was our daily routine," she said. "It is the reason I love ice cream so much. Mom and I would have ice cream every day, no matter what was going on. We'd talk about fashion, school, books, boys... anything. It was our time."

I didn't have to ask to know she didn't get that when she was thrown into the Bennetti life. Initially, Savio's wife made her life hell by hurting her, and knowing Savio's schedule, he probably didn't have a similar routine.

"I'm guessing you didn't continue that tradition with your dad?"

She tilted her head. "No, he and Luigi worked a lot." I nodded, understanding that too well. Being a don and staying on top required a lot of hours away from home. "But Lorenzo and I got into a routine. More frequently than not, we'd each have a bowl of ice cream, sit in front of the TV and chat about stuff."

I knew Lorenzo and Amore had gotten close. Both brothers were protective over her, but Lorenzo took more time than Luigi, and even Adriano, to talk to Amore and get to know her.

"Well, well, well." A familiar voice came across the restaurant, and I recognized it before I spotted her.

Fuck! Of all the people, why her?

CHAPTER 34

Amore

"Grandma!" I exclaimed, jumping to my feet while the chair fell behind me with a loud thud. "Where did you come from?" I blurted out stupidly.

My eyes ping-ponged between her and Santi. He didn't seem bothered, though annoyance lurked in his dark eyes. I didn't anticipate running into anyone during this week. I wasn't prepared nor ready to start explanations. I've been meaning to talk to Santi about coming clean to my dad.

Grandma stood next to our table, looking stylish in her black Chanel dress, white pearls around her neck, and her silver hair perfectly styled. She looked pristine and Regalè, like a queen.

"I could ask you the same," Grandma replied. I noticed her two guards hanging back, and she probably had a few more outside. Considering our family history, she was adamant about protection. "What are you doing here alone?"

I swallowed, my pulse racing. "I-I'm not alone. Santi is with me." Santi came behind me, startling me. I hadn't even realized he'd stood up. He had already picked up the chair. He placed his hand on my shoulder, his touch gentle but firm. Our eyes connected, a possession in his dark depths. I returned my gaze to Grandma's and forced a smile. Something about the confident and unperturbed way he was moving gave me my own strength.

It wasn't like Grandma could regulate my life. I was twenty-one, had my own money, a new business that I had started with Maria. This was my life, not hers. Not anyone else's. "You remember him, I'm certain."

Santi had already returned to his chair and sat down, leaning back with one elbow on the armrest. He focused on my grandmother with sardonic, dark eyes, challenging her to say something.

Her green gaze, so similar to mine in color, watched him with narrowed eyes, and I held my breath. This was not exactly how I expected to break the news to my family.

She pulled out a free chair and lowered herself onto it.

"May I join you?" she asked, though she was already seated.

"Would it matter if we said you may not?" Santi drawled, his voice dark and matching his expression. "Seeing how you've already sat down."

Nobody ever spoke back to my grandma that way - except for my father and Santi. Even Luigi, Lorenzo, and Adriano avoided Grandma like the plague because of her whiplike tongue and difficulty holding their own against her.

Ignoring Santi, Grandma's eyes returned to me. "Where is your brother? Your uncle?"

"They had to fly back to New York," I murmured, throwing a fleeting glance Santi's way.

"How convenient," she scoffed. Sometimes, I wished she would just act a little bit softer.

"It was, until you showed up," Santi deadpanned.

My eyes snapped his way, and he winked. Actually winked! A ruthless don of the Cosa Nostra who had killed hundreds of men winked at me. I had to bite the inside of my cheek or risk laughing.

"Amore, what is this nonsense I hear about a new company you started?" Grandma turned her attention back to me. "Keeping secrets?"

Yes, there was a double meaning to that jab. "Grandma, the new business has nothing to do with Regalè fashion. While it is a fashion company, it is a completely different brand of clothing. You don't have to worry about a conflict of interest."

She waved her hand. "Regalè is yours," she said. "I'm not worried about any competition. But why do it, Amore?"

I chewed on my lower lip. The truth of the matter was that I loved creating designs with Maria, Mr. Russo's housekeeper. We had been doing it for so long, and within the last year, we finally decided to make it official. It took me a bit of convincing her since I was the only one with the financial capital. But we finally came to an agreement. With my obligations to the Regalè company, I wouldn't have as much time to work on our company.

"Amore?" Grandma's voice sounded slightly agitated. "Didn't I teach you anything? You do not start a business with a stranger."

I knew she'd harp on about it. It was part of the reason I refused to ask her for her opinion.

I shrugged. "I used a lawyer to draft the paperwork and I trust her."

"She is a stranger, Amore," she hissed under her breath. "We are Regalè."

I couldn't resist rolling my eyes at her snobbiness.

"She's not a stranger," I told her, keeping my cool. "I've known her for years. And I trust her, so that's that."

Two heartbeats of silence, then Grandma transferred her frustration to Santi.

"And I'm guessing you encouraged it, Russo," she spat.

He didn't even flinch, his gaze unchanged. His lips tugged up in an almost cruel smile.

"Amore can do whatever she wants," he drawled. "She's good at her work and knows what she's doing."

His vote of confidence meant a lot.

"Grandma, the business was my decision," I told her. "Maria and I came to terms, and I ran with it. Nobody else has a part in it and it is none of their business." I let the words sink in, then added. "Including yours."

"And this?" she retorted, her eyes ping-ponging between the two of us. "Is this nobody's business as well?"

Before I could answer her, Santi spoke up. "Mind your own business, Regina." His voice was cold as a whip.

"Wrong, Russo," she hissed under her voice. "So fucking wrong."

My head whipped in her direction. My grandmother rarely ever cursed. "She doesn't belong in your world."

"The fuck she doesn't," he growled low, and the look he gave her turned my blood cold. This was the ruthless, cold Santino Russo.

My hand reached out and I placed it over Santi's before he could say something else or even worse, shoot my grandmother.

I locked eyes with her. She had been overprotective ever since Mom died, and I loved her for it. She had big dreams for me of taking over the company, and I was onboard with them. I loved her company as much as she did. She'd also sacrificed a lot. But I also wanted to make my own mark, my own legacy. And I certainly would not be loving or seeing men that either she or my father thought good for me.

"Grandma, it is my business who I see or what I do," I told her in a firm tone. "Why are you here? You weren't scheduled to come to Italy until next week."

She wasn't pleased with my answer, but there was something resembling pride in her eyes. Getting up, she tilted her head. Just like the queen she was.

"I will see you next week then, Amore."

She strode away without another word. I didn't realize I was holding my breath until a heavy sigh left me once she disappeared from my view. My head snapped to him. The cold, dark expression was gone, and my eyes lowered to my hand still covering his.

I slowly pulled my hand away. "Well, that went well," I muttered with disbelief. "You hid your surprise well. I just about had a heart attack."

"Why?" He seemed genuinely surprised. I shrugged, at a loss for words. Legally, nobody could tell me who I could or couldn't see. "You are her only grandchild. And she loves you."

Smiling, I nodded. That she certainly did. "I know you don't like her much, but she is actually very fun. Just a tiny bit overprotective."

"Understandable," he said. "But you always hold your own well."

I shook my head, not believing he was sincere. "Are you making fun of me?"

"I'm dead serious," he retorted dryly. "Though, I wonder how fast she'll tell your father."

"She won't," I told him. "She'd rather keep it from him than share it with him."

It was true. She'd never give ammunition to Dad to push me away from her. She'd find a way to use this to pull me away from him. She had been dreaming of the day I'd leave the Cosa Nostra behind me, buried, and take my rightful place in the tower. Away from all the underground activities.

It seemed like a good time to bring up the conversation about telling my father and brothers. Except, it felt awkward to assume he'd want to make this a long-term relationship. I was never one to just give up on something I wanted so I went for it.

"Santi, I-I've been meaning to ask..." The words failed me. I didn't want to seem too presumptuous that he'd want us to tell my father we were dating. I guess this was dating. From what I'd seen with my brothers and Adriano, men didn't do clingy girlfriends. And somehow, I was certain Santi didn't either. "I want to wait to tell Adriano about... ummm... about us... when he visits, but my family... I don't want to lie to them. I want..."

I trailed off, unsure what words to use. It seemed telling my family would be a firm commitment and I wasn't sure if that was his intention.

"We'll tell your brothers and father then too," he finished for me, and I couldn't help but smile. "Are you in agreement with that?"

"Yes. Absolutely."

CHAPTER 35

Amore

Days were flying. Way too fast! Santi had another two days left before our week was up. I got to know Santi more this week, and we settled into a routine. I'd wake up to the smell of coffee and his mother's croissants. We'd spend the morning making plans for the day, kissing, cuddling. I loved Santi's dominant side, but when he was soft, I melted. Then lunch time would roll around, and I'd make us sandwiches while he was catching up on his emails. Afternoons, we would roam the city or head to the beach. Though dinnertime was just the two of us at home, and both of us in the kitchen preparing food was my favorite time.

It was way past midnight, and for some reason, sleep wouldn't find me. I couldn't stop thinking about his upcoming departure. I didn't want him to go. I released a deep sigh, knowing it was irrational. I turned over for the hundredth time and faced Santi's sleeping form. I was usually the first one out and had no problems sleeping. In his sleep, he looked less intense, his features were more relaxed.

Reaching out, I couldn't resist tracing my fingers over his lips. He was a light sleeper, so I was surprised he didn't wake up. He'd had to handle some work calls early this morning, and from the sound of it, there was shit happening back home. I knew he was capable and could hold his own, but just the idea of him hurt rattled my bones.

Gosh, it was scary to love someone so much. Feeling only lust would be so much easier. But this squeezing in my chest each time I thought about something happening to Santi... that was unbearable.

There were so many thoughts swirling in my head. My gut feeling was telling me that Dad wouldn't take the news of me dating Santi well. Eventually, he'd come around though. And then there was a lingering fear that Santi would wake up one day and call us a mistake. Or he'd opt for another woman, more appropriate by the rules of the Cosa Nostra. It would leave me in the same spot my mother was with Dad. Minus a child. No chance I'm going off birth control.

God, to be Santi's forever. It sounded like heaven. To have a home together, knowing we'd both find our way back to it no matter how hard the day. Little Santis running around in our future. Making life-long memories here in his villa. Flutters filled my chest, a buzz of warmth spread through me, and I breathed out a shuddering breath. I was so deep into Santi, there was no way out.

My fingers lightly brushed his dark hair off his forehead, tenderness swelling in my chest. I pushed my hands lightly through his soft strands when his eyes slowly opened.

"Sorry," I whispered. "Go back to sleep."

His hand came around my waist and pulled me closer, leaving our bodies flush.

"What's wrong, Amore?" His voice was low, raspy, sleepy. "Don't say nothing."

"I can't sleep," I admitted softly.

With his free hand, he cupped my left cheek softly. "Tell me what's on your mind."

"I don't know," I murmured. "Everything, I guess. I'm worried about Dad and how he'll take the news. I don't want to spend months without you, but I know you're busy back home."

He tucked hair behind my ear. "Your dad loves you and wants to protect you. Savio might be upset, but he'll get over it." His reassurance didn't settle my nerves. "I won't give you up, Amore. We'll get through it. Together." A ball of emotion curled in my throat and refused to budge.

I swallowed hard, trying not to let my emotions swallow me whole. "Together," I repeated, my voice hoarse.

"That's right." He pressed a soft kiss to the tip of my nose. "Always. Now get some sleep. You need rest after our *extra-curricular* activities right before dinner today."

My lips curled into a smile. Earlier tonight, in between preparing our dinner, Santi and I got sidetracked. I'd never be able to look at lasagne with a straight face again. I thought back to it as I closed my eyes.

Bare feet against the cool tiles felt good. It had been hands down the best week so far. Santi, his scent, felt like home. He was home. I wanted to stay with him forever.

I followed Santi's directions, put all the ingredients in a bowl and mixed it. He had me fixing sauce for the lasagne al forno. I couldn't stop my eyes flicking to him every so often. He wore a plain white t-shirt and a pair of worn-out jeans that molded perfectly to his thick, strong thighs. God, his muscles! They bulged with every move, and it took all my self-restraint not to reach out and run my fingers down his biceps.

You'd never guess he was a mobster dressed like that in the middle of a white, airy marble kitchen. Just looking at him made me ache. The only time I felt whole was with him inside me, his raspy voice in my ear mumbling silly words, claiming me forever.

His eyes caught me gawking at him again, and his grin had butterflies running wild in my stomach. The smell of the sea mixed with our cooking drifted through the air. The windows were wide open and the sounds of the waves along the shoreline mixed with the banging of the pots and pans. But all those noises were drowned out, and the only thing I heard... the only thing I felt was the thundering of my heart and blood rushing through my veins.

I dreaded this week coming to an end. I couldn't go weeks, months without him.

"See something you like, baby?" he asked, never stopping rolling pasta with his big hands. It would be a comical sight, if somehow he didn't look so damn sexy even in the kitchen. First night we stayed in, I couldn't stop staring. I have never seen a man of the Cosa Nostra in the kitchen, except

to sneak in some food. Dang it, even outside of the Cosa Nostra, I haven't seen a man in the kitchen. Not unless he was a cook.

"Amore?" he purred. His voice was deep, slithering down my spine with a rough caress. I loved what he could do to my body. Just the tone of his voice had every cell within me shaking for him.

Was it healthy? Probably not, but I didn't give a shit.

I felt my lips curve into a smile as my eyes traveled over him. Now that I'd kissed him, felt him inside me, tasted him, it would be impossible to get over him. He was my missing puzzle piece. Yes, I was only twenty-one, but he felt so right. Not only on a physical level but emotionally too. He was my safety blanket, my savior, my rock.

My everything!

A small, knowing smile spilled across his face as he strode to the sink and washed his hands. Of course, he knew what he did to me. I was an open book to him. There was no sense in pretending. I loved him; I wanted to give him my all and wanted his all. When it came to him, I was just as selfish as the men of the Cosa Nostra. I didn't want to share.

I just prayed Santino Russo would take care of my heart because somehow I knew deep down, I'd never survive if he broke it.

"I love..."—my courage faltered, and 'you' remained behind my lips—"everything I see right now."

Santi's electric eyes locked on me with something dark and intense, and my stomach fluttered. I knew that look. Our eyes glued on each other, the attraction and need sizzled, ready to bake the pasta laid out on the kitchen counters.

"I need you," I whispered, the throbbing ache between my thighs demanding to be sated. I had no shame when it came to Santi.

He is mine. He completes me! These two thoughts echoed so loud in my brain.

I'd be an empty shell without him. And the truth of those words stole my breath.

Santi stalked closer, pinning me against the counter. He took the bowl out of my hands and placed it behind us on the counter. I was doing a shitty job of stirring anyhow.

Reaching up, I pushed my fingers through his hair, tugging on it to bring him closer. He was too tall, and I wanted his lips on mine.

"I don't want this week to end," I said, my voice soft. I wasn't brave enough to admit I was hopelessly, completely in love with him. He bent his head, his lips brushing against mine. It was the softest kiss he had ever given me.

"It's just the beginning, Amore." It sounded like a promise. Santi kept his promises.

My hands pulled him closer to me, starved for his touch. For more of him. When my nails scraped against the skin on his nape, a groan vibrated in his throat and my eyes fluttered shut. His tongue pushed through my lips, deepening the kiss.

This was the way it was every time with him. Every time we kissed, everything seemed to fade. A soft, whimpering sound escaped my lips as I rubbed myself against him, needing more of him. His hands came down to my ass, lifting me and my legs instinctively wrapped around his waist.

"Bedroom," I breathed out, panting. My hands fisted in his hair, our mouths clashing hungrily.

He took a few strides, but we never made it outside the kitchen. Instead, my back slammed against the wall and the kiss broke. But his mouth remained on my skin, trailing kisses down my neck. His scruff burned my skin in the most delicious way. His teeth nipped, his tongue licked, and my skin tingled with embers.

From the far corner of my mind, I realized we were on the balcony. Ironically, the sounds of crashing waves matched the wave of passion between us. His fingers dug into my flesh, keeping me pinned against him

"You are so fucking beautiful," he rasped, raking his lips over my bottom lip. I craved him with a desperation and fire that couldn't be extinguished. He consumed me.

Lifting my arms, he removed my t-shirt. Actually, it was his. More often than not, when we were home, I wore his shirts. I loved what it did to him. Something dark, primal and possessive would flare in his eyes and it sent shivers through me. Every. Fucking. Time.

"And mine," he growled. "Just mine."

His mouth was greedy on my skin.

"I'm yours, Santi," I barely breathed out. His mouth moved to my neck, and I tilted it to allow him better access. He bit gently and a hiss left *my lips, prompting him to suck at the skin there. "But you are mine too," I added breathlessly. I would lay claim too.*

"Damn straight."

He ripped my pink boyshorts, the shredding sound filling the room. At this point, I was used to my panties being ripped to shreds. I fumbled with his shirt next. I needed to feel his hot skin under my palms. Somehow I always ended up naked and bare while Santi kept some piece of clothing on.

His shirt discarded on the marble floor, I started unbuttoning his jeans. This desperation was clawing at me, igniting fires through my veins. The ache between my legs begged to be eased and only he could do it.

"Please, Santi," I pleaded breathlessly. His hand reached between our bodies, his fingers brushing over my clit and a shudder ran through me. He whispered words in Italian into my ear. I was too far gone to grasp the meaning, all I got was something about wet and hot.

"I want you," I cried out, working myself against his hard touch, grinding myself against him. Whimpering noises trembled from my lips and he seemed to eat them up. "Please, please," I begged mindlessly.

I hungered for him, ready to shatter into a million pieces for him. His dark gaze found mine just as he took my nipple into his mouth. All the while, my hips rocked under his touch. His mouth was hot as he licked and played with my breasts, my veins blazing with an inferno only he could extinguish.

I could die now and go to heaven. He was making me delirious. A look. A touch. And I was soaking wet for him.

When his mouth left my breasts, I wanted to scream in protest, but then I felt the tip of his hard cock at my entrance. He entered me slowly, driving my need wild.

"Santi!" I hissed. He was being too slow. This pulsing ache was driving me wild. He had made an addict out of me.

"My sex goddess," he grunted, his smoldering gaze penetrating me to my soul while he thrust deep and hard into me.

"Ahhhh," I cried out. A deep rush of pleasure flooded all my senses.

A deep groan sounded in his throat, and I buried my face into the crook of his neck, inhaling deeply. "Oh God," I panted, as he pulled out and thrust again.

"Not God," he grunted, sliding out of me only to plunge deep inside me again, filling me to hilt. "Me, baby." He hit the spot, over and over again. He plunged deep inside me, every inch of him filling me. A soft, needy whimper escaped my lips. "Who's fucking you, Amore?"

"You, Santi," I screamed, reaching for my orgasm. I was so close. So damn close. Heat and flame swirled through every cell of me. A loud, throaty moan left my lips with his every thrust. I couldn't stop them; it was like oxygen that my lungs needed to survive.

"Your pussy is mine," he grunted.

As if he lost all control, he pumped faster and harder, each thrust stretching me. Accommodating him. My body was his.

"Going to fuck you until the entire city hears you scream my name. Take it all, baby," he praised as he screwed me. "So good. I want to see you come for me."

His pelvis ground against mine with each thrust, spreading fire through me. I never wanted it to end, waves of pleasure making me delirious.

He covered my mouth with his palm, muffling my screams while his other hand pushed into my hair, fisting it roughly. He angled my head up, his smoldering, dark eyes watching me with each powerful thrust.

I needed this. Domination by Santi Russo. His darkness. His possession.

My submission was only for him.

My orgasm burst suddenly and violently, sending a shudder and white pleasure through me. It was so strong, tears pricked behind my eyelids. My pussy pulsed with heat, convulsing around his cock. His thrusts shallow and slow, he found his own release right behind me. A deep grunt came from his chest. My body trembled with my own release, and I watched him through heavy eyelids as his head tilted back. All his muscles seized, and he spilled himself inside of me.

As we both slowly came down, I met his gaze, dark as night. He pulled his hand from my mouth, and I realized there were teeth marks imprinted on his hand. Mine. I must have bit his hand when I orgasmed.

I leaned over and placed a soft kiss over the marks. "Sorry," I murmured softly, my body placid and limp after the intense release.

A deep rumble sounded deep in his chest. "I'm not." He kissed my forehead, making me close my eyes.

I love you! *The words screamed in my soul, heart, and brain. Yet I couldn't say them out loud. The fear of rejection held it all back.*

Santi's hand tightened on me, pulling me closer to him and my thoughts dispersed as I glanced at his face. Strong jaw. His full lips that could do so many sinful things. I dreaded losing him. It was difficult to keep my doubts and insecurities at bay. I wasn't usually the girl filled with insecurities. He'd rejected me once. Even my own father rejected Mom in a way. She was his sidepiece. The men of the Cosa Nostra didn't like independence in their women.

Santi hadn't mentioned love. Yes, we had a lot of sex. Lust was not in short supply between us, but love... He said nothing about love.

Neither did you, idiot! My mind whispered. Though he assured me of our future. He planned on talking to Dad. If he wasn't serious about us, he'd never talk to him. It was a good sign that he didn't consider this a passing fling.

Ugh! Just stop it. I'd enjoy our time now. There was no reason to borrow trouble.

Yet, the feeling of worry didn't fade. A sense of dread lurking somewhere in the shadows. Just like the man that wanted me dead.

It was ironic, really! Until recently I was certain, without an ounce of doubt, I'd never be part of the underworld. My goal was to finish college, kill the men that killed my mother and haunted me. Then I'd take over Regalè Fashion.

However, ever since Mr. Russo's funeral, all my priorities had shifted, and they all revolved around Santino Russo.

Placing my hand over his chest, I focused on Santi's even, strong breaths and clearing my mind. Slowly, as I matched my breaths to his, sleep pulled me under.

CHAPTER 36

Amore

Santi's motorbike came to a stop. He parked in the designated spot for motorcycles, and I slowly climbed off the back, then stepped onto the blacktop. This place became our favorite beach spot. It was right on the edge of the city and, more often than not, it was a fairly empty beach.

Taking my helmet off, I handed it to him. He secured it alongside his and climbed off the bike. We made our way to our spot, which was secluded, hand-in-hand. I could get used to a life like this—away from the Cosa Nostra, away from the Regalè empire. Just the two of us against the world.

Or with the world. It didn't matter to me. As long as we were together.

A few of the locals I recognized from our earlier visits to this beach glanced our way and waved to us like they'd known us forever.

"Buon giorno," they greeted us.

"Buon giorno," both Santi and I responded in unison, waving back.

I could practically see us doing this for years to come, until we were both gray-haired and wrinkled. I shook my head at myself; I was too young to think that way. I had been falling for this man for years, but now, I was spiraling.

We came to the designated bathrooms and changing area. I had my swimming suit in my bag instead of wearing it since we stopped in Boccadasse, a tiny romantic village outside Genoa. Each time we visited that city, I saw it through new eyes. It constantly surprised me with the labyrinth of alleys and hidden gems, Boccadasse being one of them.

No wonder Richard Wagner, a romantic opera composer, fell in love with the city. So did I; this city and a man within it captured me completely and deeply.

Santi took me to taste gelato in the historical gelateria located by the beach. We hung out there for an hour, savoring our ice cream and watching the locals. He offered up stories of his childhood here and his grandparents that brought him here often.

"You did not do that?" I said, throwing my head back laughing.

"Unfortunately, I did," he admitted with a smile, his dark eyes amused. "I went to the back of the ice cream shop, took the whole tub of ice cream and sat myself on the floor and ate directly out of it. One of the customers caught me and screamed like she just saw a cockroach."

I laughed so hard that tears pricked at the corners of my eyes picturing five-year-old Santi in my head gorging on the ice cream.

After a few hours there, we found our way to the water. This beach was smaller and less secluded than our other one. We just wanted to dip our toes, then go back to our regular spot in the other town. I slipped my sandals off, held the hem of my dress, then stepped into the cool water. Playfully, I kicked water his way, wet drops getting on his shorts. He gave me a warning look, but a big smile ruined the threat.

I never wanted to leave the place. This was happiness and I wanted to grip it tightly, never letting it go.

His hands grabbed me by my waist and lifted me up into the air as I kicked my feet and giggled.

"Okay, okay. I won't splash you anymore," I chortled, grinning like a fool. "Take us back to our other beach, Santi."

That beach would forever be ours, and my most favorite place to go to. This was nice but it wasn't ours.

"As my woman commands," he purred softly. God, I loved it when he called me his woman. So barbaric and chauvinistic, but so damn hot.

Fifteen minutes later, we were back at our favorite beach. We walked towards the changing rooms, hand in hand, our fingers twined together. Just a boy and a girl. Man and woman. His don status didn't matter here. Neither did my heiress status. No past or future worries. It was just him and I in this city, this country, and would forever be part of us.

"I'll wait for you here." Santi's voice pulled me back from my daydreaming. Glancing at him, I wondered if he was as impacted as I was. He seemed content, relaxed, but I found that I craved his declaration of love.

I nodded and strode into the changing room. Once inside, I put my bikini on and suddenly felt nervous. Santi took me shopping yesterday because he had ripped too many of my panties, but he more than made up for it. He pretty much bought out the store. When I spotted this bikini, I snuck it in.

Though now I questioned whether it was smart. The bikini fit great, but somehow felt too revealing. It was white and the string fabric felt so freaking small. It made me a bit self-conscious.

I immediately scolded myself. The man has seen me naked plenty of times.

"But the rest of the beach hasn't," I muttered to myself.

Ignoring my self-doubt, I walked out of the bathroom and found Santi already wearing only his swim shorts. My eyes were glued to him, shamelessly eating him up. I had seen him naked more than once now, but each time, it felt new.

He was so much taller than me, and all I could see was his six-pack-abs and tanned, olive skin. Every ounce of him was pure muscle. A deep V on each side of his hips made my mouth water.

My breath caught when our eyes met, desire burning in them. His eyes traveled down my body and the longer they lingered on my skin, the hotter I got. He was my own personal sun, scorching my flesh.

"Do you have a cover up?" he purred, voice dangerously low.

"You don't like it?" I breathed the question, the air in my lungs heavy. I adjusted the top to try and cover more of my breast, but it was fruitless. It was meant to be sexy, slightly revealing.

"I love it," he drawled. "But unless you want me to kill every man on this beach, we better put a little something over it."

A choked laugh escaped me. Santi wasn't the sharing type. I dug a little wrap out of my bag and tied it around my waist.

"Is this better?' At least it covered my almost naked butt.

He smirked. "The other way was better, but let's save it for our pool time at the villa."

We had used the pool once when neither one of us could sleep. A midnight swim under the summer stars was exactly what both of us needed. Well, it might have been the sex rather than the swim that did it, but both were nice.

"Let's go," he said. "You better stick close to me."

I couldn't help but laugh. Yet I appeased him because I loved being close to him anyhow. We walked towards the sand. We barely took two steps before a few whistles followed us.

"Ahhhh, mamma mia," a man's voice sounded, followed by more whistles.

Santi glared at the young men who immediately scurried away.

"You are too hot," he mumbled the complaint.

"Oh, and you are not?" I gently shoved my shoulder into his hard biceps. "Can I glare at women when they drool after you?"

His smile practically dazzled me. "You can," he said matter-of-factly. "But none of them compare to you."

My heart glowed brighter than the Italian sun. *Don't read too much into it!*

We found a spot on the empty side of the beach. A few people were sprawled out or swimming on the other end, which was fine by us. This spot was always empty, as if it was just waiting for us.

Santi laid two towels down for us. Peeling off my cover up and discarding it, I sat down on one while he laid down on the one next to me.

"Come here." He pulled me over, and I laid my head on his chest, closing my eyes and putting my face up to the sun.

I smiled dreamily, enjoying the warmth of the sun on my skin.

"I want to stay here forever," I murmured dreamily. "Just like this."

His fingers tangled through my hair. "You'd miss your fashion empire."

"I'd design clothes for you," I suggested jokingly with a soft smile.

"I'd get you out of leather shoes and into environmentally friendly shoes." His chest shook under my head, and I rolled over so I could see his face. He was laughing, his dark eyes twinkling with amusement.

"You are too ambitious," he rumbled. I opened my mouth to protest when he cut me off. "Remember your words. You want it all." His eyes darkened and dropped to my lips. "There is nothing wrong with that. I want it all for you too."

God, I love this man! I couldn't believe he remembered those words. I had uttered them to his father and him almost five years ago.

I grabbed my sunscreen out of my handbag. "Santi?"

"Hmmm."

"Will you put sunscreen on me?" I handed him the bottle and our eyes locked. We both knew that touching each other usually led to frantic sex. We were electric together.

He ran a thumb across his bottom lip, then reached for my cheek. His roughened knuckles ran down my cheek. His eyes softened, desire lurking in his dark gaze, as his thumb skimmed the edge of my bottom lip.

"Amore, do you know how hard it is to touch you and not fuck you?"

Excitement tore through my bloodstream, and I smiled sweetly. "You'll have to try. And if you are good, maybe we can go for a swim to cool you off."

I was playing with fire.

I rolled onto my stomach, and after a heartbeat, I heard the squeeze of the sunscreen bottle and I closed my eyes, smiling happily against the towel. He straddled my ass, his hands rubbing together, then I felt his rough palms slide up my back. He unfastened my bikini top, and he carried his movement up to my shoulders.

"Ahhh, that feels good."

He nudged forward, and I felt his hard erection against my ass. His lips came to my ear from behind and he whispered. "I'm all for pleasing you, baby."

My heart thundered hard against my ribs at the double meaning. He continued his sensual movements up and down my back, not missing a single inch of my skin. It took all I had not to grind my ass against him. My sex throbbed with an aching need for him.

His hand slid down my back, lower over the exposed skin of my ass and down my legs.

"Roll over, baby." His voice was hoarse, intoxicating.

I held my bikini top to my chest and rolled onto my back. He poured some more sunscreen on his hand and re-started the process. His eyes were dark and filled with desire, the same one that burned through my veins.

He rubbed his rough palms down my neck, pausing for a brief moment, and I thought I'd explode. Then he continued his trail down over my stomach and my inner thighs. His hands moved in circles, every so often brushing against my core. I couldn't resist parting my legs just slightly, my insides melting.

This was as torturous for me as it was for him. The sweetest torture.

"Amore," he purred. My name on his lips sounded like an endearment. He leaned down and his lips locked on mine, his tongue parting my mouth. His erection hit my core and I moaned into his mouth.

"Let's go swimming," I breathed out, the throbbing ache between my thighs pulsing.

He tied my bikini top, then stood up, and he helped me onto my feet with his other hand. He was hard, the outline of his hard cock against his shorts clear.

"You wanted to play with the beast," he rasped, attempting humor but his eyes were too dark and feral and focused on me. We ran down to the water, our fingers interlocked, and immersed ourselves in the water up to our necks. Well, it was up to my neck. It only came to Santi's chest.

The water felt cool against my heated skin. It was a welcome relief. My pulse rushed through my veins, buzzing in my ears, mixing with the sounds of the sea. Santi took me into his arms, holding me steady against his strong body. My legs wrapped around his waist.

My hands roamed up and down his shoulders, loving the feel of his muscular body under my fingertips. His skin was warm even in the cool sea.

His mouth crashed down on mine, hard and desperate. He grinded my sex onto his swollen cock, and his fingers dug into my ass cheeks. His one hand moved my flimsy string bikini to the side, and I felt his hard shaft at my entrance.

"Holy fuck," I panted, grinding myself against it. My insides clenched, tiny whimpers leaving my mouth. I was greedy to feel him inside me again.

"You want me to fuck you here?" he breathed against my mouth.

"Please. Yes!" One thrust and he filled me to the hilt. Another moan, a louder one.

His eyes flickered with heat and arousal. His lips pressed against mine, wet, messy, and rough.

"Keep quiet," he growled, then locked our lips again as he pumped into me, his fingers digging into my soft flesh. If somebody was watching, they'd know exactly what we were doing, but right now, I didn't care.

I was greedy when it came to him. Every thrust sparked embers that only the next thrust could sate. Each time he pulled out, he drove deeper inside me, and my nails dug into his biceps as shudders rolled through me.

Both of us breathing raggedly, our movements rushed, desperate. His thrusts turned harder, increasing in tempo, and I ground desperately against him. Throaty moans swallowed by his lips pressed tightly against mine as he pumped furiously. He grabbed my hair at the nape and pulled my face an inch away from his.

"You feel so fucking good," he praised, his breathing labored. "Your cunt wants my cock harder, doesn't it?" His thrusting increased, hitting that amazing spot inside me. My eyes just about rolled back in my head. "Ask me." His voice was hushed and commanding.

"Harder," I panted against his lips. "Please, harder."

His hand fisted my hair, his mouth hovering above my lips. "Mine," he growled. "Your pussy is mine."

"Yes, Santi," I vowed. "Always."

He pumped hard, hitting my pelvis, sending liquid fire straight to my core. I rose up and down, riding his cock. Our moans and grunts mixed together. I was reaching for the stars, aware of nothing but the pleasure that was within my grasp.

His fingers dug into my hips and thrust hard. Once, twice and my body exploded, clenching around him. He buried himself deep inside me and his cock jerked, then he came in a rush. We both cried out and came together, shudders running down my body as he kissed me like it was our last kiss.

Santi Russo fucked me in the Ligurian Sea, and I loved it.

CHAPTER 37

Santino

It was two a.m. and sleep just wouldn't come. Yesterday, Amore struggled to find sleep. Today it was me. One more day and night, then I was due back in New York. I hated the idea of leaving her here. More than anything, I wanted to put a ring on her finger and drag her home with me.

Or if she insisted on staying here... Fuck it, I'd move to Italy if it made her happy. I had known we'd be perfect together ever since that kiss in The Orchid. I resisted it, unwilling to see her as anything other than a kid, that girl with tears glistening in her emerald gaze. But after that little kiss... I couldn't forget her taste, her moans, her soft body under my palms.

She has always been mine. And I'd be damned if I let her father, that dragon woman of a grandmother, or anyone keep me away from her. Something in my chest twisted at the idea of losing her.

My eyes breezed over Amore's sleeping form in my arms. She was sound asleep wearing my dress shirt and a pair of pink panties underneath it. The moonlight shone across her face. Or maybe it was the television. She'd insisted we watch a Marvel movie. *Black Widow* was her favorite.

I couldn't remember the last time I even turned on my tv set at home. Of course, she fell asleep not long into the movie and I let it play out. The volume was muted, so it wouldn't wake her up.

The window was wide open, a light breeze sweeping through the room, lightly rustling the sheet covering her body. She slept on her side, facing me with her thigh hooked over me. Her breaths came out even through her slightly parted lips, her cheeks still flushed.

After our beach time today, she insisted we eat at home. I didn't mind. We fit well together, even in the kitchen, though she couldn't cook for shit. Not even mixing the ingredients. She often got side-tracked, either with an idea for a clothes design or by eyeing me. Damn, what that girl could do to me! My chest ached... actually hurt like a motherfucker, each time I even thought about losing her.

Fuck, I *was* whipped. Utterly, completely in love with Amore Bennetti. Somehow, in all of this, life had become separated into two events, before we kissed and after we kissed.

Ever since our kiss, the idea of her with another man left an acidic taste in my mouth. I hated the idea of her with anyone else. An itch in the back of my head kept reminding me about that goddamn marriage contract. It should have been an easy piece of information to find out.

Yet, nothing. Fucking nothing!

My teeth clenched. I wanted Amore. Forever in my bed. Forever in my life, tied to *me*, because she'd be forever in my heart.

There'd never be another woman for me. She was *it*.

But I also had to resolve her activities with DeAngelo. How in the fucking hell did she find time over the last two years to attend college, work for Regalè Fashion, start her own business with Maria, and run around South America hunting for her mother's killer?

No wonder I had fallen for her. I'd watched her come into her own over the years. Unlike any other woman I had ever met, she had a resilient strength about her. Even when things spiraled out of control, she held her own with her ruthless father and her hard, demanding grandmother. Amore was shrewd and incredibly capable, navigating the world between her father and grandmother better than any other don I'd known.

Unlocking my phone, I read through the message from Carrera again. The family tree of George Anderson was a surprise, not a pleasant one either. He had two sons. One was killed by me. The other was still alive.

Ulrich Anderson was the man that slipped through our fingers. The man that was after Amore.

The man who held her and her mother captive. The question was, why did they want Amore and her mother dead?

CHAPTER 38

Amore

It was our last night together in Italy. I already hated the idea of going back to reality tomorrow. To spend days, weeks, and months without seeing him. And he hadn't even left yet. I had half a mind to drop everything and go back to New York, but DeAngelo had made it clear I was safer in Italy.

At least until Ulrich Anderson was dead.

DeAngelo had intel on him, and I trusted DeAngelo to see me through this safely. I trusted him almost as much as Santi, though the latter would always be the number one in my book.

Jesus, how did everything go so askew? In all those first thirteen years of my life, I never heard George mention he had sons. Even less that those same sons would have killed my mother and want to kill me. They killed their own father.

What the fuck happened? I wasn't sure anymore what I knew, or I didn't know.

The only thing I was certain of was that we had to find him and kill him. Before he killed me.

Santi and I sat outside at a local restaurant on a stone patio that hung over the sea. Night had fallen but the air was comfortable, warm, and breezy. The little white lights lit up the terrace and threw off a beautiful glow across the whole area. I kept glancing out to sea, the lit-up yachts and sailboats shimmering in the darkness, the blood moon barely lighting up the sky.

The dance floor had opened. Young and old couples alike found themselves slowly swaying to the music. Smiling. Laughing. Kissing.

It was a tranquil atmosphere, but deep inside the dull ache had already started to swell. Maybe this was the reason I should have kept my distance from Santi all along. He had parked himself deep inside my heart, and there was no way of pushing him out. Not that I wanted to.

My savior. My rock. My protector.

I could have never imagined these feelings for him would grow so strong. I have always loved him, ever since he brushed my tears away on that hot summer day. But over the last few months, I'd fallen deeper and deeper in love with him.

So deep that I couldn't imagine my life without him.

A faint beeping sound reached my ears and I dug through my purse for the phone. Glancing at it, I realized with a start that it must have been going off for quite a while.

"Crap," I muttered.

"Everything okay?" Santi sat back, leaning casually. The past week with him has been amazing, though he has been uncharacteristically quiet today too. When he fucked me, I was convinced he loved me. I felt connected to him.

But in times like these, the doubts crept into my heart. Maybe because I wanted him so much that it scared me to lose him. Things would never be the same if Santi and I went our separate ways. The life and family I'd known since I was thirteen would go up in smoke. I'd avoid them all in an attempt to avoid Santi. It would hurt to see him.

"Bunch of missed messages," I muttered, lifting my eyes to him. He was now on his own phone. "From everyone."

It seemed like everyone decided to message me at the same time

"Better answer your papà first," he suggested.

I raised my eyebrow. "And how do you know one of them is from Dad?"

He lifted his phone. "Because he just sent me a message asking I check on you." I started vigorously typing my reply. "Though I'm surprised," he added begrudgingly.

My head shot up. "Why?"

A heartbeat of silence.

"We had a disagreement the last time I spoke to him," he remarked dryly.

"Huh?" I couldn't see what could cause disagreement between the two of them.

"Nothing for you to worry about," he deadpanned. "Send replies to the messages so they don't worry."

I quickly shot messages to everyone, one at the time, letting them know I was fine and safe. Dad. Lorenzo. Adriano. Luigi. Uncle Vincent. Santi's men were my assigned guards for this week. Luckily, they all answered to Santi so we wouldn't be ratted out.

Just as I suspected, Grandma didn't say a word. Otherwise, all these messages would have been sent in an entirely different tone.

Finally, I was free of my cell phone and shoved it back into my purse. My eyes landed back on Santi. He was back to wearing his black three-piece-suit with a white dress shirt underneath, right along with the gun holster.

Italy suited him. His tanned skin was slightly darker after all the time we spent in the sun. He had never looked more like a true mobster of the Cosa Nostra. Or maybe it was the stark contrast after seeing him the whole week in jeans or swim shorts.

I wore a long, white dress with a strapless back and paired with silver sandals. I kept my makeup simple and to a minimum while my hair was pulled up into a high ponytail. The only jewelry I wore was the necklace Santi had gifted me.

When I came out of our bedroom earlier, Santi stopped scrolling through his phone when he spotted me. His eyes darkened and his teeth raked over his bottom lip. "Stunning." He called me, lifting my hand to his mouth and placing a soft kiss on my knuckles. "Absolutely perfect."

Why couldn't it just remain like this? Just the two of us in our little world where nobody and nothing else mattered.

"Amore, what's bothering you?" Santi read me too well.

I swallowed the lump in my throat. We've had an amazing week.

Laughed and talked about everything. And fucked. So many times, everywhere. I was convinced that by now, we had covered every spot of his villa.

I dropped my gaze for a moment. It was uncharacteristic of me not to express what I wanted. Yet, I have never been so scared to hear a denial. I craved his words of love like the oxygen I breathed.

"Amore, look at me," he ordered. As if on instinct, I obeyed, meeting his gaze. "Tell me."

I sighed deeply.

"I don't want you to go back," I murmured. "It's stupid, I know. I have to get back to work, then studies will start. I just want..." *You. Now. Forever.* "... more time."

He leaned over the small table, his hand reaching out to take my chin. Instinctively, my body leaned forward too, and his mouth brushed lightly over my lips.

"I want to stay too," he rasped against my lips. "But I have to get back. Shit is happening, and I have to take care of some things. Make it safe for you to come back." My face fell. I didn't expect him to stay anyhow. "But I'll visit often, and I'll send my plane for you too."

"I have my own plane," I told him stupidly.

He smiled. "I know, but this way, I can ensure there are no changes in the plans. Nobody will keep you away from me. Not a delayed flight, not weather, not your father or grandmother. Remember." His languid drawl washed over me like warm water. "Mine forever."

My eyes snapped to him, and my heart fluttered in excitement. Those words sounded permanent. There was no misunderstanding forever.

"Yes," I whispered, the word coming out as something in between a question and a confirmation.

His eyes darkened. "Yes. You are mine. No other man touches you. If they do, I'll kill them."

"Threats of killing are not funny, Santi." Though my lips were curved into a soft smile.

"I'm not joking, Amore. You are mine," he growled.

I took his hand and kissed his knuckles. "Okay, but then you are mine too. No woman touches you either." Surprise flickered in his eyes.

Now that he had opened the door, I wanted to stake a claim too. "It is only fair, Santi. It's a two-way street."

A satisfied smile spread over his face. "Bene." *Good.* His eyes danced with delight and smugness. "Nobody touches me. Nobody touches you."

A laugh bubbled inside me and spilled through my lips. He made me happy, and I was determined to make him happy too. No riches or dangers of the world mattered to me; only this man that sat in front of me.

"I'm all for it," I muttered, grinning happily. "Seal it with a dance and a kiss?"

Santi gave a throaty laugh and stood up, extending his hand. I took it immediately and followed him onto the dance floor. He didn't waste any time, his mouth searching out mine. Our bodies started swaying, harmonized and slow. The old Italian songs played, and he showed me steps while I followed his lead. Our bodies worked well together in the bedroom and on the dance floor.

The song switched to a more upbeat Italian song with freestyle dance moves. Santi was smooth on the dancefloor, an excellent dancer. A sting of jealousy slithered through me to think how many women he had danced with to become such an expert.

"You are an excellent dancer," I commended him. "Must be popular with the ladies."

He chuckled. "Maybe, but only one lady matters."

My cheeks warmed. "Who taught you how to dance so well?"

I frowned and realized too late that I might not want to know about Santi's many women.

"My mother taught me to dance."

"Oh," I uttered, surprised. "She did an excellent job."

Santi twirled me, spinning me around and around. The room spun, but I couldn't stop smiling and laughing. I loved dancing with him. I was practically glowing with happiness. A few of the locals threw glances our way, smiling but I didn't care. I was in heaven and only the man holding me mattered.

The beat changed and the first string of English words played. We both halted and I grinned.

"I know this song," I exclaimed. Santi gave me a blank look. I took his hand and smiled, glad for reversed roles. "Now, I will teach you some steps and words."

"Promiscuous" by Nelly Furtado and Timbaland played, and I lip synced, maybe yelled, the words. Ignoring all the steps, we danced. Santi and I laughed like we didn't have a care in the world. Tomorrow, reality would come, but tonight, we would enjoy our last night together.

Women threw looks Santi's way, hoping for a glance from him. Anything. I couldn't blame them. There was a magnetic kind of energy around him, and he was so handsome, towering over all other men on the dance floor.

But he never looked away from me.

CHAPTER 39

Santino

It'd been only two days since I returned from Italy, and I was already contemplating ways to go back. There was no way I could wait months before I'd see her, bury myself inside her. I had already decided I'd travel every other weekend. I told her as much too this morning via text.

I kept cracking my knuckles, irritation and restlessness flooding my senses. I wouldn't get through the workday, never mind the work week or month, without killing someone in this state. The images of Amore wearing my shirt, her pink boyshorts, or her in the bikini kept playing on repeat in my mind.

However, business piled up and dangers lurked at every corner. I couldn't fucking handle not seeing Amore every single day, but I wouldn't risk her life. Sooner rather than later I would have her back with me.

She belonged in my bed, my home, my life. She was already in my heart.

But Ulrich Anderson had to be eliminated first so she was safe when she came. Then this marriage contract to whoever the fucker was would be burned to ashes. I'd shoot him in the goddamn head. She wouldn't be anyone's but mine.

So, until Ulrich and the man her father promised her to were dead, she'd have to stay in Italy.

Adriano had been helping with my legal businesses. I had promised Pà I wouldn't pull him into the underworld, but Adriano kept finding one way or another to hustle. I'd rather he did it for our family business and the Cosa Nostra, than find his way with the Russians or some other crime family. Keeping him out of the Cosa Nostra and the underworld was almost a moot point since he kept inserting himself back into it. He could help cover for me along with Renzo when I visited Amore. Renzo would keep him on a straight path and steer him from disasters when I wasn't around. I'd leave my legal business to the strait-laced fellas.

Since I got back, I've been swamped with work that had needed my attention during my week with Amore. Going through my documents on my laptop, my eyes flickered to my cell on my desk. There was nothing else on it. I liked my space organized, not in havoc like Renzo and Adriano preferred theirs. If those two ruled New York, the city would burn down by the end of the week.

No message from Amore. I was half tempted to call her up. She was going to work out a weekend getaway schedule with Lorenzo, so he'd cover for her while she was with me.

Fuck! And I was craving Amore so bad that I was willing to leave shit in my brother's and Renzo's hands. Wonderful, I was just as much of an idiot as those two. *I have to kill Ulrich and Amore's unknown intended ASAP!*

My phone beeped and I had never reached for it so fast. Instantly the corner of my lips tugged upward. It was from Amore.

Lorenzo will cover for me and my hot boyfriend.

The door to my office swung open and Renzo strode into my office without knocking, then plonked his ass on the edge of my desk. I locked the phone and shoved it into my pocket.

"Puccini is here." Renzo said, throwing his knife into the air and catching it.

I tucked my gun in the back of my pants. I didn't expect trouble from our family lawyer, but I liked being prepared. The men that wanted me dead came in all shapes and sizes. Though I pondered what the fuck he wanted to talk about. He left me a frantic message my first day in Italy, worried about a document he forgot to share with me. I wasn't too worried about it, but he has called every goddamn day since asking that we meet.

"You put a hole in my desk, it will be your head," I muttered, though for the first time in months, it wasn't a real threat. After a whole week with Amore, I was in an exceptionally good mood. We had a plan, and I'd see her again by the end of this week. Going weeks without her wasn't an option. I was head over heels smitten with that girl, and I didn't give a shit who knew it. If someone dared to hurt her or touch her, I'd lose my goddamn mind. Just the thought of it sent me over the edge.

"I don't think you mean that." He threw the knife up into the air again. "You must have gotten some good pussy in Italy." I ignored him. He hadn't outright said it, but he suspected there was something going on between Amore and me. I trusted him not to say anything to anyone or risk a bullet in his skull. "What about Puccini?"

"I'm waiting for you to bring him up," I told him dryly. "Or are you waiting for step-by-step instructions?"

He rolled his eyes. He was two years younger than me, and we had always gotten along. So, when my role in Pà's organization started growing, I took him along. I never regretted that decision.

Renzo disappeared from my office as I leaned back in my seat. My office was on the top floor of the building. It was the first skyrise I bought, and the entire city stretched in front of me. Each floor below us was dedicated to a different business. I was proud of what I had accomplished. I had tripled our value, and while I wasn't a billionaire like my little sex monster, I could more than provide for her and offer her the same life. I didn't discount the possibility that her grandmother might disinherit her, and I wanted to ensure Amore had everything she could ever need.

"Don, thank you for meeting me so early," Puccini greeted me. The last time we met, the Don title was a painful reminder of my father's loss. Today, it was a recognition. My responsibilities had grown since my father's death, though I carried the majority of them even before the murder.

"Mr. Puccini," I greeted him. "Please just call me Santi," I reminded him.

"As you wish." He bowed his head to the side. My father had used him for years, so I saw no need to change our lawyer. Though he was older, I assumed he'd eventually transfer the reins to his eldest son.

We sat down and he opened his briefcase, laying out the documents.

"After I transferred all your father's assets to your name, per his Will instructions, I did one last inventory." His voice was tentative. The Puccinis have been our family lawyers for as far back as our presence in New York. At least the last three generations. They were loyal and sharp, and that was all that mattered to me. "As discussed, you are your brother's main financial executor until his twenty-fifth birthday, upon which time you will present him with the transfer of the home of your choosing along with his portion of inheritance and..." he paused, hesitancy in his eyes. I already knew all that so there must have been something else that worried him. "And the marriage contract."

I frowned at his last comment, disbelief in my eyes. I knew about all my father's wishes and the marriage contract was never one of those. He'd never dictate to either Adriano or me whom to marry.

"What marriage contract?" I questioned him, a bad feeling pooling in the pit of my stomach.

"I apologize." He bowed his head again, nervous energy practically streaming from him. He was in his fifties, and I stared at the crown of silver hair. "It has been so long, and the document was stored in a separate location per your father's instructions."

He handed me a piece of paper that undoubtedly showed my father's signature. My eyes skimmed over the words. The moment I saw Amore's name and the second signature, my entire world tilted. Fire ignited through my veins and blood buzzed in my ears. Rage rushed through every cell of me, burning everything in its wake while a red haze blurred my vision.

It cannot be! Fuck no! I fucked up by sleeping with Amore Bennetti.

I stared at the words blurring my vision, a single piece of paper that changed everything in one breath. Fucking letters danced in front of my eyes, dangling a woman that would now never be mine. That had never been mine for the taking. I was prepared to kill whoever she had been promised to, but I never counted on that man being my brother.

My very own fucking brother!

Something poisonous slithered through my veins, the burning anger searing through my blood. The images of her naked in my villa, in the pool, in my bed flashed in my mind, and I could practically taste her on my tongue even now.

And now... Adriano would get to see it.

She is mine!

God help me, but at this very moment, I contemplated killing my own brother. He couldn't have her. He wouldn't dare touch her, feel her smooth skin, hear her moans. She wasn't his; she was never his. That notion alone hit me like a punch to the chest. It felt like a goddamn heart attack.

I couldn't fucking handle the idea of Amore and Adriano. This red fury inside me threatened to burn this motherfucking city to the ground. Grinding my teeth together at the knowledge that she'd never be mine again, a bitter taste filled my mouth, and something dark and unwanted slithered through my veins.

Tension crept through the office, and I could practically taste it. So could Puccini because he practically shook in his pants with fear. Fucking let him! Maybe I should start by killing him and burning the contract to all hell.

"Is the marriage contract amendable?" I asked, my voice detached while my heart pounded hard.

Seven years! My father and her father agreed on tying our two families together seven years ago. Seven fucking years and not a peep.

"No."

One answer. One contract. It changed everything.

CHAPTER 40
Santino

T he gunshot echoed through the yard, Bennetti staring at me like I had lost my mind. I fucking did, motherfuckers. A string of curses left Luigi's mouth, but his anger didn't match mine. My rage was strong enough that I thought I'd choke on it. This felt worse than losing my father or my mother. The anger burned in my throat, in my chest, and my heart, while my vision blurred with a red haze.

"What the fuck, Russo?" Luigi spat, gripping his hand. I shot that lying motherfucker in the goddamn hand. He should be kissing my boots for not shooting him in his damn head. Everyone knew you didn't fuck with a Russo, yet that rash fucker kept the name from me.

The air was so brittle with tension it could snap at any moment. These kinds of rash moves got you killed. But somehow dying seemed better than losing Amore. Suddenly, killing all the Bennetti's, except for Amore, sounded like a very good idea.

Unamendable contract. My pà knew better than to agree to a contract that could not be broken. After all, Russos were known for always protecting our own interests and making deals that could be broken if reason called for it.

Well, the reason fucking calls for it.

Puccini indicated only the signatories of the contract could amend the contract. Papà was dead and Savio... I would fucking change his mind. His no would become yes. If I had to beat it out of him.

Renzo was at my back, holding his own gun pointed at Luigi's guard.

"You knew," I hissed. "You fucking knew!"

I called Lorenzo after Puccini left. He didn't know the name. His father kept him in the dark. But he was certain Luigi knew and recommended I reach out to his brother. Except, Luigi fucking Bennetti had owed me that answer for months.

Question was how long did he know? It might decide how many fucking bullet holes he got from me.

"This is about that goddamn marriage contract?" Luigi's jaw ticked. Blood dripped from his hand to the blacktop, a dark expression on his face.

The *goddamn* contract played on repeat in my mind, ridiculing all my plans and taking Amore from me. A burn traveled through every inch of me, demanding I make him pay. Make his father pay.

So, I hit him. It was better than shooting him again. Lucky bastard! Pain exploded through my cracked knuckles the second my fist connected with his jaw.

Savio finally made it outside, a dark expression on his face. He was furious. Good! He should taste a fraction of what I felt.

"What the fuck is going on here?" he shouted, his gaze flickering to me and then back to his eldest.

Luigi immediately stood up straighter. I didn't need to; I towered over both men.

I stepped away from Luigi and faced Savio. His guard had a gun aimed at my head. I held mine by my side. I didn't need to aim it at his head. Before his guard could even pull the trigger, I'd have both of them dead.

Killing them, as tempting as it sounded, would turn Amore against me. She loved both her brothers and her father. She wouldn't forgive me for killing them. Just the notion of earning her hatred, sent a hollow, dull ache throughout my chest.

"That contract is null and void," I gritted out.

Savio stepped closer, his jaw tightening and fury coloring his face. Well, fuck him. "You want to start a war, Russo?"

I ran my hand over my jaw with sardonic amusement. He would never win that war. I had more men, more territory, and a lot more funds to spend on fighting him.

My eyes darkened. "I don't want to start a war," I growled. "But I will. Amore is *mine*."

Savio and I stared at each other. I had just laid my cards down; the old man knew his daughter meant something to me. She meant *everything* to me. I was keeping her. I loved her.

Jesus!

The greedy, selfish bastard in me loved Amore Bennetti. I refused to let her go, even for her own happiness. Or my brother's. Only *I* would make her happy. Only I would touch her.

"Russo, even if that contract was to be voided, she won't be yours," Savio hissed. "My last promise to her mother was that I'd keep our daughter out of the underworld. You are as deep in it as they come."

One heartbeat. Two heartbeats.

"Has anyone asked Amore what she wants?" I gritted out.

It was a pointless question. He didn't. He had never bothered asking her what she wanted.

"Keep away from my daughter," he retorted angrily. "I intend to keep the promise to her mother, even if it kills me."

If fucking might because I was more than tempted.

CHAPTER 41

Santino

The sunrays sparked over the skyrise buildings, reflecting off the glass as I stared out the window. The skyline of my city stretched for miles, my empire suddenly looking gloomy, dark, and empty. Sickening as fuck.

I always knew Amore wasn't meant for this life, but I hadn't even dreamed that her father would make sure she wouldn't remain in my world or give her to my brother.

A promise to keep.

It was the reason my father didn't want Adriano pulled into the Cosa Nostra. Her old man wanted Amore to marry someone with connections to the Cosa Nostra but wasn't integrated in it; had no position in it. When Amore came into my life, I was already knee and elbow deep in the Cosa Nostra.

More than anything I wanted to kill her father. Luigi too. Except, I wouldn't win that way. I'd lose Amore the same as if I let the fucking contract play out. For the first time in my entire damn life, I had no solution.

On my third glass of whiskey, straight up, no ice, I'd gone over every possible scenario to get out of the contract, without killing her family, or my own brother, and marry my girl. I could keep her safe with or without the Cosa Nostra.

I even considered kidnapping her. The more time went by, the better the idea appeared. Or it could have been the whiskey talking. Pouring myself another glass of whiskey, I downed it in one gulp. Except this dull bitterness that swelled inside me refused to go away.

Amore had fucked with my head and taken my heart. She'd created an obsessive monster out of me. I called her my little sex monster; the truth was I was the same way for her. I was so worked up that my shoulders were stiff with tension. My teeth clenched and my jaw ached.

No woman touches you either, Santi. You are mine. Amore's words rang in my ears from our last night together in Italy.

Goddamn it, I was hers. The words *mine* and *hers* screamed in my head.

In one swift move, I threw the glass and watched it fly through the air, liquid spilling out of it like blood spilled, before it shattered against the glass.

Renzo burst through the door, prepared to shoot someone. I didn't even bother looking up.

"What happened?" he questioned, checking out my office as if he expected someone to be hiding in the corner. His gun was pulled out, his shoulders tense.

The image of Amore, her wild red mane flowing through the air as she ran towards me at the airport, her soft smile, her green eyes shining with happiness. Her lush lips wrapped around my cock and a hazed, desire-filled gaze. Her soft admission that she wanted to please me.

Fuck. Even if I wanted to let her go, I couldn't.

I fisted the contract in my hands, tempted to shred it and kill anyone that dared to challenge me when taking Amore as my bride.

Kill her father. Kill her brothers. Kill my brother.

These were all men she loved, and they wanted to take her away from me.

"Santi, what happened?" Renzo repeated.

I lost her, that's what happened.

CHAPTER 42

Amore

I sat on the same beach in Genoa where Santi and I spent days sunbathing, making love in the sea. Everywhere I looked, I saw ghosts of us, his hands on me, his lips on me. I left the Milano office in the middle of a meeting and begged DeAngelo to bring me here. We ran into Lorenzo on our way out of the building and he insisted on coming too.

Unplanned, impulsive actions were dangerous, everyone warned. I didn't care; I needed to be alone. My heart ached worse with each beat. Each breath sent sharp pain through my constricting lungs. I struggled to grasp what could have changed in a matter of a few days. Only two days ago, he sent a message saying he was coming this weekend and now... he'd dumped me.

My first break-up. Yet, it felt like so much more. Like my world and my heart shattered into a million little pieces. My first crush. My first love. My first heartbreak. Santino Russo was really going for first prize in everything.

My face was wet with tears. No matter how many times I dried them, more came. The warm, glowing feelings from the last week were replaced by emptiness and coldness. My mind spun, turning over every text, every word from the last week, desperate to find something to hold on to. Anything that could somehow reverse his message so that all would be well again.

Another tear rolled down my face and I angrily brushed it off.

This... well, this fucking hurt. It physically hurt, leaving me with a large void in my heart.

Sliding the phone open, I read the message for the hundredth time.

This is not working. We are not working. It has to end.*

It was unexpected. We's spent the entire week together; we couldn't keep our hands off each other. He talked about discussing this with Dad. About coming this weekend because he couldn't keep away. Told me we'd work it all out together. And now this.

I gave him my heart, unconditionally and fully. I trusted Santino Russo to take care of it. He'd held it in the palm of his hands for years. And now, he shattered it with one text message. He drove a knife through my heart and destroyed it. But not my love for him. Why couldn't it destroy my love for him? I was such a fool, but I had loved him for so long that I didn't know how not to love him.

I needed him with a desperation I couldn't understand. I felt at home with him, safe and loved. I *longed* for him.

"Amore, what's wrong?" DeAngelo lowered himself next to me and sat down on the rocky beach. I needed time. To come to terms with this anguish, the pain that swelled in my heart.

"Nothing," I rasped out. "Nothing important."

Lorenzo lowered himself down on the other side of me. He looked ridiculous sitting on the rocky beach wearing his three-piece-suit. He unbuttoned his jacket, giving me a glimpse of his holster. Sometimes I thought Lorenzo took showers with the damn gun.

Lorenzo wrapped an arm around me. "If it was nothing, you wouldn't cry."

"Maybe it's that time of the month," I muttered. "And I'm highly emotional."

Both DeAngelo and Lorenzo rolled their eyes, but I ignored them. I wasn't in the mood for their discussions. I didn't want anyone to see me fall apart and now both of them were crowding me. I hadn't cried like this since Santi wiped my tears away all those years ago. I never even dreamt he'd cause the next ones.

The betrayal washed over me. I thought he was better than to break up with me over text. He could have at least FaceTimed me. Anger slowly simmered in my veins, turning my sorrow into bitterness. Who did he think he was?

Pulling my phone out, I scrolled through my phone book until I found his name.

"Nothing, huh?" Lorenzo mumbled, his eyes on my phone.

Ignoring him, I pressed the FaceTime button. The ringing sound vibrated, but it was immediately turned off. He cut off the ring.

Bitterness turned into fury.

That fucking asshole can't even dump me over FaceTime!

"Amore, you—" Lorenzo started but I cut him off.

"Brother, DeAngelo, please give me five minutes," I said, trying to keep my voice even. Those two could be stubborn when worried about me. I didn't want to feed their worry right now. "I just want to call Dad."

It was a partial truth. Those two shared a glance, then without another word stood up and left me to it.

I pressed the call button again, attempting to FaceTime Santi.

Ended. An incoming text message beeped.

Stop calling, Amore. There is nothing left to say to each other.

Rage rose within me, mixing with the pain of his loss. Yes, I loved the prick, but he had another thing coming if he thought I'd take it silently. I still had plenty of fucking shit to say.

He didn't want to watch my face as he broke my heart.

Fine.

He didn't want to see my tears.

Fine.

Russo would get his wish. I would never message or call him again. But if he thought I'd hide or make this easy on him by keeping out of his sight, he had another thing coming. I was the Regina Regalè's heiress, Amore fucking Bennetti. I've survived worse things. I've seen my mother tortured and murdered in front of my eyes; I listened to George's painful screams as he was tortured; I hid in the jungle for days before the Carrera cartel saved me and spared my life.

I was a fucking survivor. I lived the first thirteen years never hearing the Russo name; I sure as hell could live the rest of my life never hearing it. But he'd hear mine.

I wouldn't see him, but I'd be damn sure he saw me everywhere.

Picking up the phone, I dialed my dad. He answered on the first ring.

"Amore, everything okay?"

"Yes, Dad, all good."

I heard a sigh of relief over the phone line. "Where are you? Vincent said you left the office early."

Of course, Uncle Vincent would have told Dad. "Lorenzo and DeAngelo are with me," I assured him softly. All the crying suddenly made me feel exhausted, but I was adamant I was going through with this.

"Is this a good time to talk?" I asked him.

"I'm here with Adriano and Santi, going over..." he faltered, and my heart immediately plunged down to my stomach upon hearing Santi's name. "some plans."

Probably some fucking mob business. Then a thought hit me. Maybe that was the reason he didn't answer my FaceTime?

No, idiot! He sent you a message saying he has nothing to say to you.

It was on the tip of my tongue to ask him to tell Santi to go fuck himself, but I stopped myself. I wouldn't start a war for a petty female revenge though it sounded awfully tempting.

"Say hi to them," I mumbled, trying hard to keep my behavior unchanged. "Want to call me afterwards? It should be quick."

"What is this about?"

Can you beat the crap out of Santi for breaking my heart? I asked silently but would never dare say it out loud. Despite his shitty way of dumping my ass, I didn't want to see him hurt.

"Grandma asked me to be the face of Regalè Enterprise." I went straight to my plan. She has asked me again this week. She even went as far as blackmailing me. She promised she'd keep Santi secret in exchange for me taking over the company and becoming the face of it. I blew her off, but now she'd finally get her wish. And I would fucking be everywhere. "Is that okay?"

Silence followed. Dad always knew I'd take over one day, but it didn't mean he was happy about it. He worried I'd turn my back on him and my brothers, but I would never do that. "I'm still your daughter, Dad. I will eventually be the face of the company, so I might as well start now."

"One day, you'll be married, and your husband can manage it."

"Well, that's sexist," I retorted dryly. "Regalè Enterprise is mine, and I don't need a husband to manage it." The way he grumbled, I knew he didn't agree. "Besides Grandma, there is nobody else that knows the business as well as me. And considering I'll inherit it, I should be the face of it."

"It makes sense," he caved. "Will it require travel?"

"Yes, probably."

"Lorenzo and DeAngelo will go with you. Everywhere."

The threats of the Perèz Cartel were real, so I'd never purposely endanger myself.

"Dad, I'm not going into the battlefield." I chuckled bitterly hearing his grunt, while my heart ached. "I'll let you get back to business then. Love you."

"Love you, too."

I hung up the phone and called my grandma next.

CHAPTER 43
Adriano

I shared a glance with Santi hearing Amore's name. His jaw was pressed so tightly, I thought he'd break it at any moment. My brother's expression told me he was on edge.

Something had happened between Savio and Santi, both wore dark expressions, and I was certain Santino was itching to shoot both Savio and Luigi.

It was only this morning that Santi called me to The Orchid. To give the *wonderful* news. To say the whole marriage contract was absurd was an understatement. Though, it wasn't repelling. I loved Amore and she loved me for who I was.

"When will you tell Amore?" I growled.

Bennetti didn't know his daughter at all if he thought she'd do whatever he said. Another daughter in the Cosa Nostra, yes. But not Amore. She had a mind of her own, and she had said on more than one occasion she'd only marry for love. One word to her grandmother and she'd pluck her out of the Cosa Nostra, never to be seen again.

"When the time is right," he spat back.

"That would be right about now," Santi hissed. He was tethering, ready to snap. I just couldn't figure out what got him so riled up. The fact that Pà had a marriage contract or that he was blindsided.

310

"I know what's best for my daughter," Savio fumed. "She is not your concern."

"Fucking wrong." My brother exploded, getting into Savio's face. His fist gripped his collar, lifting him off the ground.

Santi has lost his fucking mind.

Both of them were dons and shit like this started a goddamn war, marriage contract or not.

"Put him down," Luigi shouted, his gun pointed at Santi. At the same time, Renzo and I pointed guns at Luigi's and Savio's heads.

Luigi's hand was bandaged up, and I gathered Santi did it from the way Luigi greeted him. When he arrived, Luigi spat a few curses at Santi and the latter told him he better shut the fuck up or he'd lose his other hand. Yeah, Santi definitely did it.

"You'll never have her, Santino Russo." Savio's words sliced through the air, the meaning hitting me straight in the chest.

My brother wanted Amore Bennetti for himself.

The drive back to the city after we left the Bennetti residence was tense. Renzo sat in the front seat, chewing his gum and kept spinning the bullet chamber to his revolver. Fucker would shoot himself one day, or even worse, one of us.

My eyes kept fleeting to Santi. He hadn't said a word since we got into his Bugatti. His jaw was locked tight and his fingers were gripping the steering wheel so tight, I expected the damn thing to break off at any second.

Amore and Santi. No, no, no. It couldn't be. She would have said something. She never fawned over him and certainly never chased after him. Maybe it was one sided. After all, Amore had men chasing after her everywhere she went. She was a catch with her wealth and beauty. She was an unparalleled catch. Though to me, she was so much more. She'd always stood by me, supported me. She wouldn't forget about me and chase after my brother like most other women.

Insecurity wormed itself into my heart. Santi was always better than

311

me at everything. There hadn't been a woman in his entire life that rejected him. If he wanted her, he would get her.

The door slamming had me turning my gaze away from Santi's clenched hands on the wheel. Renzo got out of the car.

"Get in the front, Adriano. This isn't driving Miss Daisy." My brother's voice was hard and cold. For a fraction of a second, I debated treating him as my chauffeur but decided against it. In his current mood, I wouldn't put it past him to shoot me.

Exiting the car, I got into the front passenger seat. Without delay, he shifted the car into first gear. I lasted barely a minute without saying a word.

"What was that about, Santino?".

One breath. Two breaths.

"What exactly?" Not a flicker of emotion in his voice.

"You know exactly what," I grumbled in agitation. "You attacking Savio, shooting Luigi. Are you trying to start a war?"

"There are worse things." Typical Santi to answer in short, clipped answers.

"Like what?" I challenged him.

"Like this goddamn marriage contract," he gritted out, his jaw clenching.

"I'm not upset over it," I retorted. "So you shouldn't be either."

"It's not the right move," he snapped.

"Why?" I hissed. "Because you don't like it."

"Fucking straight," he barked. "I'm the don, fratello." *Brother.* "Not you. So deal with my fucking decisions."

"Fuck. You. Don Russo." If he thought he could tell me what I should or shouldn't do, he had another thing coming. "Stop the goddamn car."

Santi didn't even hesitate. He stepped on the brakes, causing me to almost kiss the fucking windshield. Glaring at him, I pulled on the door handle and slammed the car door with a brutal force, hoping the fucking door would fall off.

The door barely clicked before the tires of his Bugatti screeched as he took off.

CHAPTER 44

Amore

I laid on my stomach in my hot pink bikini, reading a fashion magazine. The late August edition. I couldn't believe they had featured mine and Maria's designs. It offered us great exposure. I couldn't wait to celebrate with her.

I was enjoying my last week to the fullest before returning home. Uncle Vincent was already back in the States, getting back to business. Lorenzo was in Ibiza with us, currently having a hot date with a local girl. I still couldn't decide who was a bigger manwhore, Adriano or Lorenzo. I loved them both, but I swore they had a new girl every week.

And I... I had a picture-perfect life and admirers at every corner according to the papers. I hid my heartache behind a dazzling smile. I had come to terms with Santi being my addiction, and this withdrawal would be something I'd have to manage for the rest of my life. It had been two months, three weeks, and four days since he kissed me last. But who's counting?

The saying *'time heals all wounds'* was bullshit. The craving didn't ease. Love didn't diminish, not even slightly. And the nights... God, the nights were tortuous.

My phone beeped and I reached for it in my bag, picking it up. It was Lorenzo, a selfie with a girl. A very beautiful one.

My date. Told her you'd worry if I didn't check in.

I grinned. He was a Casanova. He wouldn't remember her in a few days, but right now she was the love of his life. Maybe that was the trouble with men, they couldn't be faithful. I had started to wonder if even George was faithful to my mother. Though his sons were older than me. They were around Santi's age.

I laid back next to Adriano and took a goofy selfie with my tongue sticking out and a rock-on hand symbol, then sent it to him with the caption.

My date. Tell her to keep her guard up.
Don't jinx me, sis. We have only a few days left.

I sighed. I had bought myself extra time, only because Adriano and Lorenzo were willing to stay with me. Adriano and Santi were having disagreements, so I suspected he wanted to cool off. It worked in my favor. Lorezno only agreed to remain for the chance to see more European girls. I felt sorry for whoever their wives would be one day because I couldn't picture either one of them ever being faithful.

Glancing at my best friend, I smiled. He might be a manwhore, but I still loved him. He took me under his wing during high school, and everyone knew if they fucked with me, he would fuck with them. Girls could sometimes be meaner than boys, and he even had that covered. Half tried to jab at me because they were jealous that Adriano Russo gave me attention, and the other half tried to be my fake friends to get closer to him.

And here he was now, sprawled out next to me with his aviator shades on. He thought he was fooling me by pretending he was sleeping. I knew he was checking out women behind those dark sunglasses. I was half tempted to put sunscreen on his nose and leave it smeared white so he would look ridiculous.

He faked a snore, and my mind was made up. It was a prank kind of day.

"I'm going to put sunscreen on your nose and chest to ensure my best friend doesn't burn," I muttered, just loud enough to ensure he could hear me.

I kept my face straight as I pulled out my sunscreen with titanium dioxide; I used it to ensure my fair skin didn't burn. I applied some to his nose and smeared it. Once his nose was good and white, I put a generous amount on his chest. I bit the inside of my cheek to stop from grinning.

My palm on his chest, I smeared it slowly over his warm skin. Adriano's chest was nothing like Santino's. The two brothers were physically similar but Santi's body temperature ran a few degrees hotter and he was taller. Unfortunately, both brothers were very well built, though for some stupid reason, Adriano's body did nothing for me. He could parade naked, and my heart wouldn't even skip a beat.

Once satisfied that Adriano's tan chest was plenty white, I returned my attention to the magazine. I skimmed through the pages, happy to see over half of the magazine was designer clothing produced by The Orchid, my business venture with Maria, and the Regalè Fashion House. The business was growing, the shares had skyrocketed. There were hurdles I had to overcome when I became the face to the Regina Corporation. There were those on the board that thought I was too young. They might have been right, but I was determined to succeed. Now, I sat on the board of directors right alongside them.

And I had started my own company, The Orchid. There was no board of directors to answer to, and Maria was my partner. It started as a fun project that had exploded. We had a backlog for the next five years and orders kept pouring in.

The Orchid. My first kiss happened there. Officially the name derived from my mother because we wanted to create a spectacular design inspired by orchids. It was only half of the truth. The other half was that it also reminded me of Santi. Despite everything, he had turned my memory of that flower into something beautiful again.

For a long time, the flower represented my guilt. For not listening to Mom. For causing her death with my recklessness. But Santi turned it back into the love Mom and I shared for that flower before all that. Despite the fact that he dumped me and broke my heart.

On top of all that, DeAngelo and the team of special ops men had been cleaning out the jungles of Venezuela. The Perèz Cartel numbers were dwindling down.

The question now was who took over. Somehow George's sons,

which he'd kept hidden, were connected to the cartel and wanted their father, my mother, and me dead.

Truthfully, I couldn't wait for this little side endeavor to be over with. Fulfill my promise and then focus on the good things in my life. Besides, constant excuses and lies for my travels to South America were getting exhausting. To my family, I used Regalè business as an excuse. Some bullshit about meeting suppliers for new material.

With a sigh, I rolled over onto my back, leaned onto my elbows and watched people swim, hang out on the beach, eat ice cream, dance to music. We were in Ibiza, the techno mecca of Europe. I thought Italy was heaven, but nothing quite compared to this little island. The rich and famous thrived here, yet I felt adrift. The missing puzzle piece ruled the Cosa Nostra in New York and without him, nothing felt quite the same.

The summer was coming to an end. Both Grandma and Dad expected me back in New York. Two months since *he* dumped me, and I wasn't ready to see him. I didn't think I'd ever be ready to see him.

Funny how certain life events mark your life.

There was life before South America and after.

Life before Santi and after him.

Time before he broke my heart and after.

I didn't want to be in the same country as Santino Russo, never mind the same city. I'd never be ready, except that I wasn't a coward. I'd shove all the feelings for Santi somewhere deep and put on a happy face.

Girls' giggling pulled me out of my thoughts and my attention turned to two girls in front of us. They had passed us by three times since we'd come to the beach, eyeing Adriano. But now they got to see him with a white pasty nose and chest.

"What's funny, ladies?" Adriano was suddenly awake, lifting himself onto his elbows. He had his normal suave smile on his lips, and I rolled my eyes behind my own sunglasses. I would never understand why women fell all over themselves for him. Just the way he looked at them was a clear indication he was just looking for a passing thing.

But then, so was Santi, apparently, and I was too blind to see. So, who was I to judge!

316

The two women just giggled and took off. Another set of giggling girls passed us by, and I hid my smile.

It took Adriano almost an hour to realize something was on his face. I couldn't help it; it was way too much fun. I burst out laughing at seeing his horror when he grabbed his phone and glanced at his reflection.

"I'm going to kill you," he threatened jokingly, rising to his feet. But I was quicker and took off running and laughing, Adriano right behind me.

"I'll make your nose all white now," he shouted. Giggles escaped me, sand at my feet flying behind me. I picked up my pace, aiming to put more distance between us, but Adriano was quick too.

The sounds of a camera clicking had me faltering and slowing down. It was how Adriano caught me, lifting me up into his arms.

"Actually, change of plans," he announced. "I'll throw you into the sea."

"Stop, stop," I pleaded, laughing. I wiggled, attempting to get free of his grip. But Adriano was strong too. "Adriano, stop—"

Splash! I closed my mouth just in time to not swallow a gulp of seawater. My feet touched the rocky bottom, and I pushed myself up, kicking my feet to get to the surface faster. As soon as I resurfaced, I took a deep breath.

"Ah, sweet revenge," Adriano's voice purred next to me, and I whipped around. He had jumped into the water with me. He was such a kid, despite turning twenty-five in a few weeks.

"You ruined my sunglasses," I complained.

"I'll get you another pair," he drawled. More clicks of the camera, and I groaned. If I could go back to the day I decided to become the face of the company and then take it all to the next level by being a model, spokesperson, and hostess for all the company events, I would have taken a bit more time to re-think the whole plan. Because the paparazzi became obsessed with snapshots of me.

"Come on." Adriano pulled me by my hand. "Let's just swim to the yacht. I'll send someone to get our stuff."

Santi's yacht. It was the last place I wanted to swim to. The ruthless don lent his yacht to Adriano but unknown to Adriano, I hated being on it.

I wanted nothing that belonged to him.

Lorenzo, DeAngelo, Adriano, and I were seated at a local restaurant.

While Lorenzo and DeAngelo were acting like responsible adults, Adriano and I were acting like goofballs. We cracked bad jokes, really bad jokes, and Adriano was on his fourth shot. We celebrated my early graduation and business success, though I suspected it was just an excuse to get drunk.

"What should we toast to?" Adriano slurred. Unfortunately for him, he had started celebrating my birthday three hours ago. It was barely five in the afternoon, and he was already hammered. "How beautiful and smart you are? Or how rich you are?"

Lorenzo, DeAngelo, and I shared an amusing glance. I couldn't remember the last time he got so drunk. I was still on my first glass of wine, while DeAngelo and Lorenzo opted for mineral water. Those two could be boring sometimes.

"I just love white on you," he purred. "You know that. You look so angelic in white."

I grinned. It was actually a golden yellow sundress that came to my knees. And one thing I was certain of, I have never looked angelic in my entire life. Not with my vibrant red hair.

"Thank you."

"Women get married in white," he deadpanned in a slurred tone.

I rolled my eyes. "Do they now?"

An annoyed expression passed Lorenzo's face, but he said nothing.

"Do you want to get married, Amore?" Adriano rumbled on. "You'll be a good wife. We'll be a good-looking couple." My best friend had lost his mind.

"Adriano," Lorenzo growled in warning, and I waved him off.

"He's fine," I assured my brother. It wasn't as if I'd get involved with another Russo. One was quite enough. Lorenzo was too protective and too worried since my crying afternoon in Genoa. I turned my eyes to

Adriano, who was downing another shot. "And you, Adriano, would hate being married."

Adriano grumbled something unintelligible under his breath. It sounded like '*you have no idea*' but I couldn't be certain.

"Let's drink to success," I said, raising my glass. "Old enemies and new friends." DeAngelo and Lorenzo raised their own glasses and Adriano joined in too.

"Excellent toast," Adriano drawled, sliding a shot glass my way. "Now you have to drink with me."

"Fine," I agreed, smiling. "As long as it is not tequila. Salute!"

All of us clinked our glasses and drank. Adriano and I downed the shots, and before I could say anything else, Adriano was already flagging the waiter.

"More shots."

I shared an amused glance with Lorenzo. He mouthed, '*Don't drink too much.*'

Taking his hand into mine, I grinned. "I love you, brother. You know that, right?"

The look in his eyes softened, and he squeezed my hand. "And I love you," he murmured. "Best thing that ever happened to our family was finding you."

A lump in my throat made it hard to say anything else. So instead, I smiled, choked up with emotions. Despite the tragedy that led me to my newfound family and our rough beginning, I was grateful I found such good men.

An hour later, Adriano and I could barely stand on our own two feet. I only had a few shots, but they hit hard. We swayed on our feet, stumbling out of the restaurant, looking like two idiots.

"Goddamn it," Lorenzo grumbled. "Why is it that you two always act stupid together?"

I raised my index finger, moving it left to right and back again, clicking my tongue. "Now, now, brother. We are fun. *Fun*, brother." I stumbled, missing a step but Lorenzo caught me before I could fall forwards.

"Right. Cause this is so much fun," Lorenzo muttered, rolling his eyes and steadying me as I swayed on my feet. "I want to do it every day."

A stupid smile spread over my face. "I miss him, you know."

He wrapped his arms around me. "I know," he whispered low. "I know you are hurting. Everything will be alright. I promise."

I swallowed, resting my forehead against his shoulder. "I'm fine."

He rubbed my back gently, his touch comforting. But at the same time, it made my chest swell with pain. You couldn't win, not really. Be overly nice, it made me want to cry. Be overly cruel, it made me want to cry too.

"We should get tattoos." Adriano's suggestion caught me off guard and had me lifting my head off Lorenzo's chest. "Bestie tattoos forever. So we can remember it if shit hits the fan."

Stepping away from my brother, I shrugged drunkenly. My thoughts immediately went to Santi's ink. I always thought it was sexy as fuck. But now, thinking about it brought me pain and a throbbing ache only he could ease. Unfortunately, he wasn't interested in me.

"It will bring pain." I swayed slightly on my feet. Lorenzo caught my elbow again, steadying me and cursing under his breath.

"No, it doesn't hurt," he slurred. I guess he would know, he had a tattoo on his back. "Let's do it. You and me."

"Orchid flower?" I slurred, my thoughts slightly jumbled.

"Fuck no," he spat. "Let's do something cheesy."

"Like swiss cheese?" I murmured.

"Neither one of you two drunk asses are getting a tattoo," Lorenzo snapped. "I could be getting lucky tonight instead of babysitting you two drunks."

"We are not drunks," I told him slightly offended, immediately followed up with a hiccup. "We are amazeballs." I snickered. "Balls... get it?"

Both Adriano and I burst out laughing. Things were always funnier when drunk.

"We'll tattoo Lorenzo's ass too," Adriano announced, trying to shove his hands into his pockets and missing. "With a donkey. My treat."

"Stronzo," my brother hissed. *Asshole.*

I chuckled. "That's not nice, Adriano. I love Lorenzo."

My brother's hand came protectively around me. "I love you too. My favorite sister."

I grinned drunkenly. "Awww, my favorite brother."

I was too tipsy to point out to him I was his only sister.

"You love me too, though. Right?" Adriano asked, swaying and DeAngelo pushed him upward with an annoyed expression. "You and me together. Forever." I frowned. His brother said we'd be together too. Sharp pain pierced through my chest, just as it always did when I thought about Santi.

"Sure," I muttered.

"If you love me, let's do this together," Adriano repeated. "Matching tattoos. We can show it to our kids one day."

My brows furrowed. *Our kids?*

"You two are drunk as fuck," Lorenzo hissed, breaking my thoughts. "And you want to get a tattoo?" He looked like he wanted to punch Adriano and smash him into the next island. "And you are not having kids with my baby sister," he added with a grunt.

Completely unperturbed, Adriano grinned. "With you or without you, brother."

"I'm not your brother, jackass." Lorenzo wasn't Adriano's fan tonight. Lorenzo turned to me, his dark eyes on me. "Don't do it, Amore," he pleaded in exasperation. "You'll regret it tomorrow."

I pushed him lightly, but he didn't even budge. I was drunker than I thought.

"Perfect day," my words slurred. "Drive us there or we walk."

"You have to make sure we don't get donkeys tattooed on us," Adriano slurred badly, swaying back and forth. "Donkeys are only for you." He reached for my hand and would have pulled me onto the sidewalk if Lorenzo hadn't caught me.

"I hope you are not considering this," DeAnglo warned Lorenzo. "Your father will murder you."

"My father will murder me if they sneak out and do it alone," my brother retorted in exasperation. "And end up with donkeys or something worse on them."

An hour later we stumbled through the tattoo parlor.

Adriano pulled out his phone, showed the artist what he wanted for both of us. His artist went straight to work.

My artist wasn't that lucky. The moment I was situated in the chair, I shot up.

"I changed my mind," I cried out, scrambling off the chair. "I think I want a tramp stamp."

Lorenzo and DeAngelo groaned. "Don't let her. You are her brother," DeAngelo hissed at Lorenzo, but I ignored them both.

"You are a fucking ex special ops badass," Lorenzo retorted back. "You tell her she can't do it."

DeAngelo rolled his eyes. It might have been the first time I saw the man do that. "I work for her, man."

I raised my finger at both of them. "Stop it you two. It is just a tattoo."

A snore sounded and our heads whipped that way. Adriano was in the chair next to me, asleep getting his tattoo.

"I never knew Adriano snored when sleeping," I whispered conspicuously to Lorenzo and DeAngelo. "So unflattering."

"Amore, don't do the tramp stamp," Lorenzo begged.

I swished a lungful of air. "It's just a symbol." I looked at the artist who was a good sport. "Right?"

I fumbled getting off my chair and tripped over the footstool. My knees hit the floor and before my face could hit the tiled floor, DeAngelo caught me.

"Where are you going?" Adriano asked, jolting up as his artist cursed under his breath. I swore he said something about hating drunks.

"Fuck, I almost messed it up. You can't move," he reprimanded him, shoving his body back down with a loud thump.

"Another design," I told him.

"No besties?" Adriano opened his eyes, blinking his long eyelashes like a sad puppy. I couldn't resist chuckling.

"Always besties," I promised. "I think maybe a tramp stamp is sexier for me."

Adriano shrugged. "I'm not getting a tramp stamp."

A dorky grin spread on my lips. "You should. Both you and my brother should get a tramp stamp."

A laugh bubbled out of me and once I started laughing, I couldn't stop. I laughed so hard, tears pricked my eyes. Nobody joined in, guess they didn't find it funny.

Still chuckling and ignoring everyone, I headed towards the wall and scanned through more designs. The interest in tramp stamps was lost quickly, so I looked through other options. I debated between a globe, heart, bird, cross, bullet. I was all over the place. Then I decided on an orchid. Everything always came back to the orchid.

"Okay, this on my butt," I told the artist.

"No," my brother hissed. "No fucking way."

"Yes, on my butt." I sat myself on the chair, turned to my side and pulled my panties aside to show him where to do it.

"Don't you fucking touch her ass," Lorezno growled. "Amore, pull your dress down."

I ignored him. "Just think of my panties as a bikini. That's all." Then I addressed the tattoo artist. "Carry on, please."

The latter shook his head. "Right away, your majesty."

My eyes darted to my brother and DeAngelo grinning. "See, he knows how to treat a lady." I smiled widely. "Maybe I just need to broaden my horizons—"

The moment the tattoo gun hit my skin, I yelped and jumped off the chair.

"What the fuck?" I cried out.

There was a second of confusion on everyone's face and then a loud laugh broke through the tattoo shop. Lorezno and DeAngelo laughed so hard, actual tears came out of their fucking eyes. At that very moment, I couldn't stand either one of them. We got kicked out of the tattoo parlor, with Adriano getting only half of his 'besties forever' tattoo. It only said besties.

Who was laughing now?

CHAPTER 45

Santino

T saw Amore Bennetti more now than I did when she lived in the city and hung out with Adriano every day. Her pictures were plastered everywhere - billboards, Times Square, television, papers, internet. The images of her at worldwide premieres and events were a weekly occurrence, sometimes even a daily occurrence. There were even pictures of her in men's bathrooms, and it pissed me off to think some of my staff jerked off to her images.

I couldn't get away from her face. Her secretive smile on her full lips, her striking green eyes, that body of hers. The worst were pictures of her in a bikini. The whole world gawking at my woman.

No, not yours, I reminded myself. *At least not yet.*

I hated how much I wanted her. I didn't do the sweet and tender kind of fucking, but with Amore it felt like it. She craved my darkness as much as I craved her light. She accepted me for who I was.

My perfect match.

Fuck! This was a lose-lose situation. If I killed the male members of the entire Bennetti family and my brother, I'd lose her. By letting them live, I've lost her. But at least she wouldn't lose everyone else.

"Jesus, she is a real knockout," Renzo muttered, glancing my way.

Jackass was probably taunting me. "Men are on that ass probably like bees to honey."

I purposely ignored the comments my cousin made, gawking at the world premiere of the fashion week in Milan on television like he was into damn fashion. I ground my teeth, fighting the urge to beat the living shit out of my cousin, or say something I might regret later.

She'd be back in New York in another few days. I'd hate to see how he'll act when he finally sees her again. He'll be added to her list of admirers, and she has those everywhere she turns. The only man she has been pictured with more than once is Adriano. The urge to kill every single one of those men clawed at me, including my baby brother.

Amore looked good, too good for her own good. Bennetti has already put wedding plans in motion. He was eager to make her my little brother's wife, and I couldn't get her out of my fucking head. It didn't bode well for anyone because when a Russo fixated on something or someone... blood and sex followed.

Adriano returned earlier this week after spending a week with her. After our falling out about the marriage contract, he ran to Italy to cool off. Amore was good at pulling my brother off the ledge. He came back more accepting, or at least acting like it. It burned me to think how she calmed him down.

Did she wrap her lips around his cock? Or sit her pussy on his face so he could see her writhe under his tongue as he gave her pleasure?

Motherfucker!

"Is Amore back in New York?" Renzo asked.

Her grandmother had been grooming her, and Amore had been an excellent pupil. She had increased the value of the company shares by eight percent within the first four weeks of taking over. Amore learning every aspect of her company had paid off. It was fucking impressive; if only the media and reporters hadn't been so enamored with the face of the richest and youngest heiress in the world, taunting me with her.

"No, she had a few more stops to make before returning," Adriano answered, aloof. Even now, knowing about the marriage arrangement, he never worried about seeing Amore surrounded with other men. I, on the other hand, wanted to gouge their fucking eyeballs out. "She had some business to attend to. In Italy, I think."

I shook my head. It made no sense for her to go back to Italy when all her work had been transferred to her grandmother's office in New York.

"I think Amore and I will get our bathroom towels embroidered with fancy, golden A&A letters," Adriano added randomly. I clenched my jaw so hard my fucking molars hurt. Did he tell her about the arrangement? He wasn't supposed to. "She likes nice stuff," he continued aloof to my sour mood. "Maybe she could even design it. She loves that kind of stuff. She'll probably have our entire house decorated with our initials. Heck, might even name our kids with names that only start with letter A."

"Adriano," I gritted out.

"Yeah?"

"Shut the fuck up."

I stared at the paperwork in front of me, not seeing a single damn fucking word. I was so fucking pissed off that I swear letters were burning in front of my eyes. I fucking hated the idea of their matching letter embroidery. Maybe as a don, I could banish that shit.

"Holy fuck," Adriano exclaimed, and my head snapped up. "She never told me she opted for the emerald dress. My hot little wifey."

He was getting on my last nerve. My fingers itched to reach for my gun and pull the trigger. Pà said to take care of my little brother; that would pass as such. Right?

"What do you mean?" Renzo asked, unable to peel his eyes off the television.

"She couldn't decide between this dress and another," Adriano explained. "I guess she went for the sexy look."

"I'd say," Renzo eyed her like a piece of candy he had been craving. "Those tits—"

"That's enough," I barked out. "I'm not paying you two to watch a fashion show or yap like two fucking old ladies."

Neither one of them bothered to turn their heads my way. They continued gawking at the television as if scared they'd miss a single moment of Amore Bennetti's magnificent appearance.

My eyes darted to the screen, and it was the same as always. Every time I saw Amore's face, it was a punch to the gut. It had been over two months. Two goddamn months and she still got to me. She had the sweetest body around, but that I could ignore. It was *her* I couldn't forget. Her smart mouth. Her creative mind. Her determination. The way her eyes glittered as she watched me or hazed with lust when I touched her.

Amore's love was the most beautiful thing to have and the hardest thing to let go.

Well, fuck that shit. I wasn't prepared to let her go. After the initial shock of learning that she was promised to my brother, I couldn't think straight. But now, my mind created a twisted plan. One that started to sound less and less like a bad idea with every day that drew nearer to the wedding day. I'd steal her from my brother and blackmail her grandmother. If that failed, there was my kidnapping plan. Fuck it, I'd fight Savio, my brother, and anyone else that dared to keep her from me. She was mine and I was hers. Fuck everyone else!

In my life, I had never feared anything. It was probably the reason Pà had me as acting Don despite my age. But losing *her* scared me. It should have been a sign to keep my distance, but I just couldn't. If I was decent, I wouldn't jerk off to thoughts of her; I wouldn't scheme ways to take her for myself.

Good fucking thing I never claimed to be decent.

I watched her on the television, striding with confidence into the event. Her green dress had a deep V neckline, exposing her milky white skin and cascading down her slim body. The dress was stark against her red hair and accentuated her eyes. As always she barely wore any jewelry, only a necklace. The necklace I had made for her. It became her signature.

In one of her interviews, she was even asked about it. She just shrugged and said it was a reminder not to let people fuck with you, causing quite a media stir for her language on live TV. Unlike other women, she didn't need glittering jewelry to get noticed. She had a presence about her, probably got it from her grandmother.

I glanced at my brother. I detested the envy, but it grew hard and fast, spreading through my veins like poison. Those two had gotten even closer over the last two months. Like it wasn't enough they were joined at the goddamn hip. There was pride on his face every time he saw or spoke about her. They texted every day. But he still chased other women.

My hands were bound tight with fucking handcuffs. I hired multiple lawyers to go through the contract and find a way to breach it. It was my first step at fighting this absurd marriage contract. Well, there wasn't a single loose clause, not without starting a war. Or me executing my brother and Amore's family. Fuck, if it were anyone else, I'd fire a bullet and take what I wanted right now. And trust me, it was so tempting.

But realistically, war was something I didn't need right now. I had issues raining down on me with the cartel that was encroaching into Russo and Bennetti territory in New York and causing havoc every time I turned around. Things were escalating. And there was the threat of Ulrich Anderson.

Adriano's phone rang, and I didn't have to wonder who it was. His face had the same expression every time Amore called.

"How is my favorite girl?" he answered, and I gritted my teeth. I wished he'd take his calls privately. It fucking pissed me off to hear his conversations.

I could hear Amore's laugh ring through his headset. What the fuck, did he have it notched up to the max volume? Was he deaf?

"I'm good. I have one final stop, and we should land the day after tomorrow."

"I need my shipment status," I barked, agitation burning down my spine. "Now!"

Renzo jumped but Adriano didn't even move and just put her on the speaker so he had his hands free to grab the documents he had for me.

"I saw the dress. They just aired the fashion show. Excellent choice," he commended her.

"That was weeks ago."

"You looked sexy, totally hot..." he trailed off while his eyes flashed to me. "I miss you, baby girl. You missing me?"

Her soft laugh rang over his speaker. "Of course. Always."

My teeth clenched and hot animosity slithered through my blood. I fucking itched to fight, to kill. It was the only thing that could relieve this tension right now. Either that or fucking, and for the latter, I needed Amore Bennetti. Ever since I'd had Amore, no other woman did it for me.

Fucking trust me, I'd tried. I really had, but I couldn't even get semi-hard for any other woman.

"I'm glad you picked the green dress," Adriano said, locking eyes with me. "It goes great with your eyes and hair."

I narrowed my eyes on my little brother. Similar words were spoken by me not too long ago.

"I was worried my boobs would fall out," she replied, chuckling. "Don't tell anyone, but I taped the edge of it to ensure there were no wardrobe malfunctions."

Adriano chuckled. "I won't tell anyone except that you just told Santi and Renzo. You are on speaker."

Silence followed, and I could picture her skin flushing with embarrassment and agitation.

"You should warn me when you do that," she scolded him. "Anyhow, I didn't realize you were not alone. I'll let you go."

"Don't worry. Santi won't fire me," Adriano teased.

I wouldn't be so sure if I were him. More often than not, we argued lately. I was tempted to fire him.

"I don't know, Adriano. If you slacked at my company, I'd fire you," she retorted dryly. Out of the two, Amore acted more mature for sure. Loud noises and laughter mixed in the background of Amore's call.

"Amore," a man's voice shouted. "Ven aquí, niña. Estamos esperando." *Come here, girl. We are waiting.*

She must have put her hand over her phone because when she replied, "Just a second," her voice was muffled, and a string of English curses poured in. She shushed someone and then her voice came through the line again.

"What was that about?" Adriano asked, but he didn't seem overly concerned.

"Nothing. I have to go. See you tomorrow."

I frowned. I thought Adriano said she had some business back in Italy, though she seems to be in Spain. The realization struck like lighting.

She was in South America.

My phone beeped the same second. Grabbing it off my desk, I read the message.

Venezuela.

Meet me at The Orchid.

G.C.

I threw another glance at the television. It featured Amore in a hot pink bikini in Adriano's arms, both of them laughing carefree and happy. My gaze darkened.

Without another word, I left Adriano behind while Renzo tagged along. My fury blurred my vision as red crept along the edges and simmered hot in my chest like burning coals. He sensed my mood so he kept quiet.

"Jesus Christ," I muttered under my breath as I debated which car to drive. My eyes roamed over my Range Rover, Maserati, older Aston Martin.

My eyes skimmed over to Renzo to find him wiping a hand across his mouth, hiding his amusement. He knew exactly why I no longer drove most of my cars. He found a pair of Amore's ripped panties in one, and I almost lost my shit seeing him hold them.

I went to my new Aston Martin Vulcan. I couldn't stomach driving the cars I had Amore in. The images of her played in my head every time I glanced at them. My heiress on the hood of my car, her legs wrapped around my waist or the two of us inside, fumbling hungrily to rip each other's clothes off.

I had it bad for Amore Bennetti. If it all failed, I might just have to find another city to dominate, so I could keep my distance from her. I had never failed before, but I had never had so much to lose.

It took me only ten minutes to get to The Orchid. Even this damn club was a constant memory of her.

"What was so urgent that we had to meet right away?" I questioned Gabriel, sliding into a seat.

"I got coordinates for Ulrich in Venezuela," Carrera answered. "And if we leave today, we might catch him before he ghosts us."

"How reliable is this source?" I grumbled. "I'm not in the mood for chasing bullshit."

"Very reliable."

"What are we waiting for?" I raised an eyebrow.

"We need to leave today, but my private jet is in Africa, so I kind of need your plane to go after him."

"Not without me, you aren't," I grumbled.

There was a very good chance it was the reason Amore was in South America. The fear for her felt like a knife through my chest. I had never felt such dread before, like lead in the pit of my stomach.

Carrera downed his drink. "I thought you might say that. I have two men on the ground."

We both stood up and headed for the door. "We meet in an hour at the airport," I told him. "My plane will be the fastest way. I'm bringing Renzo. Do I need extra men on standby?"

"No, we'll have everything we need on the ground."

I nodded and headed in the direction of my car.

"One more thing, Russo." Carrera's voice stopped me, and I raised my brow. "You won't like this though."

"There are quite a lot of things I don't like lately," I told him. "No sense breaking the trend."

Carrera seemed to think this news was even worse than all my others. Nothing was worse than losing my woman to a brother I loved.

"Anderson has a price on Amore's head." My jaw locked. "Dead or alive."

It didn't surprise me, considering all the brutal messages he'd sent. But the excessiveness of it seemed extreme.

The obsession of the Andersons went beyond reason when it came to Amore Bennetti. They cost Regina her husband, her daughter, and now they were after her only granddaughter. No wonder she was protective of her.

"Amore's in line to take the Perèz Cartel. After her grandmother."

"And after Amore?" I questioned.

"If she dies without children or a husband," he started explaining. "It goes to the Andersons. It is the reason they want her dead. Her grandmother convinced her late husband to retract the offer to make her daughter's husband head of the cartel upon his death."

I bet Regina didn't anticipate that by taking over the Perèz Cartel she'd bring the war to her front step. And to New York. She might have cost her daughter her life and her decision had put a target on her granddaughter.

Amore was a Venezuelan cartel princess. I couldn't imagine Amore in the Cosa Nostra, never mind in the brutal cartel world.

I'd be damned if I let anyone get their hands on her.

CHAPTER 46

Amore

DeAngelo and I, along with four other men, worked our way through the rainforest of Venezuela. It was hot, especially in the gear we wore. Summer months in the jungle were brutal. Killing Ulrich Anderson would be so much better in the goddamn winter.

In my black lightweight pants, black hiking boots, and a white, long sleeve cotton shirt, which at this point looked off-white and clung to my body, I blended in with the rest of the men. Except that I was smaller, much smaller and my hair was the only splash of color among us.

And then there was the smell. I wasn't sure which was worse, the sweat or smell of the bug spray. I had so much repellent on, it was making me nauseous. But at least it kept the creepy crawlies and mosquitoes away.

We arrived in Venezuela last night and met a few locals that were more than willing to share what they knew. They provided information on the location of the orchids, deep in the jungle where nobody went. Except for them! The Anderson and Perèz Cartel. The moment the villager mentioned the orchids my heart turned to lead.

I couldn't help but be paranoid. About everything. Taking the same road that I did almost eight years ago and costing these men their lives.

The villagers claimed they wanted to overthrow the current men leading the cartel, causing havoc through their villages. Distrust was deep within me. You never knew whether it was a trap.

DeAngelo must have rubbed off on me by now. Or maybe my eyes were wide open, finally seeing clearly. George had sons that wanted to take over our family legacy. Fuck, if only they asked nicely and hadn't killed my mother and their father, I'd have given it to them. Back then neither Mom nor I knew that Grandma had taken over. Well, now I did know, and I'd let hell freeze over before I let those bastards take over. I'd burn it all to ash.

This was the reason I didn't belong among all this crap. Give me a billion-dollar fashion empire, board of directors, cranky models, and a dragon grandmother. I could handle that. This... not so much. But I'd made a promise and I intended to keep it.

My eyes scanned the area.

Orchids!

My step faltered, staring at the tree. The exotic scents, from spicy and strong to soft and flowery, perfumed the air. I'd recognize it anywhere. It was then I spotted them. The Orchids. Trees full of vines intertwining along the trunks and a variety of orchid flowers decorated them from top to bottom.

So beautiful. So wild. So deadly. I swallowed hard. *I'm so sorry, Mom.*

Goosebumps broke over my skin, despite the heat. The memories still hurt like hell. Her painful screams rang in my ears. It would be something that would stay with me forever. Until my own dying breath.

"Do you recognize anything?" DeAngelo asked, interrupting my thoughts.

I cleared the lump in my throat. "Yes. I believe we are on the right path."

"Good. If the villager's information is correct we are five minutes from the camp," DeAngelo warned.

I nodded. To avoid detection, our helicopter had landed a good distance away and we'd had to hike through the jungle for the last twenty miles. Terrain was rough and despite being in good shape, my muscles complained. I was sore. Maybe it was the excess weight of the weapons and a knife, though I didn't think so.

Dread hit me with each step as we approached the camp. Call it a premonition. Or maybe memories. It was hard to orient myself in the rainforest, everything looked alike. Except for the orchids. I distinctly remembered them being close to where we were captured. It was probably the reason this path looked more familiar.

I have been here before.

I took several steps towards a tree. *The* tree. And that was when I saw it.

My initials. A.R.B. that George had carved into the tree right before we were captured by the Venezuelan Cartel.

"What is it?" DeAngelo asked in a low voice.

My hand traced the letters. How did I not remember him putting the wrong letter for my last name?

He wasn't supposed to know I was Bennetti's daughter. God, I didn't know until I escaped. He thought I was his daughter, just as I thought he was my father. Yet, he'd carved a B at the end.

"He knew," I whispered. "George knew I wasn't his."

DeAngelo's eyes watched me carefully, his own brain putting things together. My eyes flicked his way and locked with his.

The other men stood a few feet behind us, giving us privacy.

"Do you think..." I couldn't even finish it. I heard him scream, the agonizing pain of it haunted me for nights to come. No, it couldn't be. He loved Mom. He wouldn't have let anyone hurt her. I saw what they did to her with my own two eyes. The pain and terror on Mom's face as they tortured her, burned her, cut her. Then ended it all by slicing her throat.

I clenched my hand into a fist and shook my head. Not now. Right now, I needed to focus.

"Never mind," I said brusquely. "Let's go."

We continued on foot, but I couldn't erase the bad feeling; my gut telling me to evaluate all the thoughts swirling in my mind. George kept his sons a secret. It could be that he kept many more secrets. His sons killed Mom and wanted me dead.

Except, what could they gain by killing us? Damn it, I needed a clear head. When we get home... I'd think it through then.

Unless we are walking into a trap here, I thought wryly.

"Okay," DeAngelo whispered in a low voice. "Everyone put your masks on."

I groaned silently. I hated wearing it, but DeAngelo knew it was safest. We didn't want anyone recognizing our faces. It would make us vulnerable. Though if they had some brains, they probably knew already. I mean, if you attack, you get attacked back.

Tit for tat and all that bullshit.

DeAngelo pointed a finger, directing the men, splitting us up. "Two men there, two there, and Amore with me. Everyone, sync up the watches. The chopper will get us in twenty minutes. Set the explosive and we get clear. If you see *any* Anderson, old or young"—And there was my confirmation. DeAngelo thought George alive—"kill him and take a picture. Twenty minutes!"

We took two steps into the camp and chaos exploded around us. The whistling sound of an object being thrown was the only warning we had before a grenade exploded. It pitched me and DeAngelo forward, spraying dirt and debris on our faces, and DeAngelo threw his body over mine.

My head turned his way; he was screaming in my face, but I couldn't hear a thing.

My ears were ringing, and I wondered if this would be it. One glance in the opposite direction told me the whole damn camp was on fire, a flaming carcass.

"Chopper now." I could finally hear DeAngelo's voice. My eardrums were finally starting to clear. "Fucking bring the chopper now," he yelled into his watch.

Bullets started to fly, and DeAngelo had me flattened to the ground. Somewhere in the distance I heard a chopper. Commotion, yelling in Spanish and English.

"We just fucking got here," he hissed. "What the fuck?" When he was pissed off, his accent got thicker. It was kind of sexy. Not Santi sexy but still. In the midst of the chaos, I wondered if DeAngelo had a girlfriend.

His eyes roamed the area. I wanted to do the same but he literally kept my head down with his palm on my forehead, so I was left just staring at his hard and handsome face. If it was Santi's hand on my face, and there weren't bullets flying around, I would have totally been turned on.

Priorities, Amore, I groaned silently. This wasn't the time nor place to think of Santi and kinky sex.

"We can't stay lying here," I hissed. We had to help the others and kill whatever members of the cartel were still here. Hopefully, Ulrich was here, and we could end him once and for all. And if George was alive... well, let's just say I knew a few men that were excellent at torture. Starting with my father and brothers.

DeAngelo finally nodded wearily.

"Stick to me and stay low," he warned.

I had no desire to get killed, so I followed his advice. The compound was a battlefield. I aimed and shot at whoever was shooting at us. I couldn't pause and think about their families. Then we'd never make it out of here alive.

These men had to be held accountable for the destruction they caused to numerous families, including mine.

From the corner of my eye, I saw a reflection of light, blonde hair and my head whipped in its direction. *Ulrich Anderson!*

He was here; he was actually here! The other bastard that killed my mother. One nod from this asshole and his brother sliced my mom's throat. My mind was filled with the blood-soaked images of her body, her screams echoing in my brain. They had done that to many others, mutilated corpses, men and women that disappeared forever. My mother couldn't even get a burial because her body was who knew where.

I grabbed DeAngelo by his hand and pointed. He followed the line of my sight and spotted him too. We both started running after him. I was ready to end all this bullshit and make him pay.

DeAngelo was faster than me and tackled Ulrich to the ground before I got to him. As I neared him, I could smell blood before I saw it. It was Ulrich's. His shoulder was bleeding profusely. DeAngelo grabbed him by his neck and held him up in the air, his feet dangling.

I stared at the face, now barely two feet away from me. The man that killed my mother. He was younger than I thought. It was the first time since that frightful night all those years ago that I'd seen him up close. Oh, how the roles were reversed! He was the one that would die today. Though from the looks of it, someone already got to him. His face was beaten and his left eye swollen shut.

He looked like shit.

"Ulrich Anderson," I rasped, my voice shaking. I'd like to think it was because my ears still rang from the earlier explosion, but I knew it wasn't. So many conflicting emotions swirled through my soul.

Make this man pay.

It is not right to be judge and jury.

Make him pay.

The voices screamed in my mind. Why was I hesitating? DeAngelo wasn't. With a sadistic smile, he punched Ulrich in his side, where he was already wounded. The man looked like he had already been tortured.

With a startling realization, I noted the man was crying. He was crying, his entire body shaking violently, whimpers and saliva leaving his mouth. He was pathetic. The cruel man, who ordered men to torture my mother while he watched passively detached, suddenly seemed like a fraud. Not worth my nightmares.

And just like that, years of hungering for revenge dissipated. He didn't deserve to live, but I wouldn't stoop to his level. From the looks of it, someone already gave him a taste of his own medicine.

"DeAngelo," I called out to my bodyguard, who has been with me through so much.

He immediately paused his punching, his eyes seeking out mine.

I returned my gaze to Ulrich. "I want to know why?" I asked in a firm tone while my insides shook. The havoc and battle stirred all around us but in my mind, we were alone. The world faded into the background as I stared at him.

He has his father's eyes, the thought hit like lightning. So did his brother, the one that Santi killed.

"Why?" I demanded again, never raising my voice.

His eyes bore into me, and I saw resignation in them. He had no fight remaining inside of him.

"Your grandfather promised to sign over the Perèz Cartel to the Andersons. Marriage of your mother to my father was supposed to be a merger. He lied."

My brows creased. "But your father was a textile biologist, not—" His maniacal laugh broke through the air and a glimpse of a sadistic smile curved his lips. This was the man I remembered from all those years ago.

"He was a biologist alright, but textile was the furthest thing he conjured. Your mother ran the fashion empire while my father ran the cartel, but only while he was married to her. Breaking that marriage took the power away."

"Breaking the marriage?" What the hell was he talking about?

"Your mother wanted a divorce," he choked out, blood trickling down the side of his mouth. The scent of ash, gunpowder, and decay mixing in my nostrils. "She led him to believe he was your father. Until she was done with him."

Jesus Christ! Did I know my family at all? I didn't remember any of it. Not a single fight or disagreement between George and Mom.

He cackled, his laugh taunting, but immediately started to choke. "She never thought he'd have the balls to get rid of you or her," he rasped, his voice choked up. "She was wrong, on both accounts."

So damn wrong! And I walked right into George's trap.

"Your father, is he alive?" I questioned him.

"No." He only hesitated for a fraction of a second, but it was answer enough. "I fucking hated your guts. Your mother's and yours."

My heart clenched in my chest. The hate in his voice was hard to miss. What could I have done to him to hate us so much? "My father got rid of my mother so he could marry yours," he spat out. How ironic! His father dumped his mother and he blamed us... he should aim his hate at his father.

"Maybe you should have taken that up with your father," I deadpanned, hiding all my emotions. All this was sickening me. "But now you won't have a chance. Any final words I should relay?" I asked, hoping he'd fall for the trap.

"He's dead," he hissed, but his eyes darted away from me for a fraction as he told me that lie. "You know what that means, don't you?" he taunted.

I shouldn't play into it but curiosity prevailed.

"What?"

"When your mother died, the cartel went to you."

My eyes widened with shock. "And if I die?" I choked out.

"It will come to the Andersons." He said *will*, not would... The last confirmation I needed.

I raised my gun and aimed it at his heart. The black heart he didn't have. I wanted to feel the rage, but truthfully, sadness was heavier. DeAngelo lowered him onto his knees. He didn't deserve mercy, but I still gave it to him. I didn't hesitate. I blinked and pulled the trigger. One clean shot between his eyes. The back of his head blew behind him and my stomach churned.

I thought I would feel better avenging my mother's death. I didn't.

CHAPTER 47

Amore

"It's done," DeAngelo put his big hand on my shoulder. "Let's get our men and you back to safety." He glanced at his watch. "Explosives have been laid," he added.

Everything seemed kind of different. My eyes flicked to the dead body. The life that I took.

"I killed a man." I felt something dull and empty inside me. No regret! No tears! No fear of going to hell. Maybe it hasn't sunk in yet.

He grabbed my face and held it firm. I couldn't feel his touch over my mask. "That was not a man. He was a cruel and twisted animal. Erase him from your mind."

He was right, yet I should feel something. Anything! *I'll think about it tomorrow.* I shoved another event into a dark corner.

"Let's go," I told him, leaving the body of Ulrich Anderson to the jungle. He deserved nothing better.

I scanned the area and counted DeAngelo's men. He was doing the same. They were all accounted for. I sighed in relief; I didn't want anyone hurt or dead on my account.

Just as I was about to turn to DeAngelo, I froze.

Santi!

I blinked in confusion and sure my brain was playing tricks on me. I blinked again. He was still there. His presence hit me right away, and I took a step towards him. His friend, Gabriel Carrera, was there too.

What were they doing here? Fighting the cartel? Forgetting my promise to DeAngelo to stick to him, I ran towards Santi. He was holding his own against five men but worry for his safety overwhelmed all my other senses.

I lifted my arm and pointed. *Click.*

One down. The others turned their eyes to me, and Santi took advantage, shooting another one down.

Three more to go.

I aimed. *Click.*

Two more to go

By the time I was by his side, the last two were dead. I turned to face Santi, but he wrestled me to the ground, swishing the air out of my lungs. In confusion I stared up at his face.

Then it hit me.

I was such an idiot! He didn't know who I was. Duh, the whole reason behind the masks. No wonder he attacked me. I maneuvered on top of him, but he quickly shifted me back onto my back with him on top of me.

Part of me wanted to tell him it was me. But the other side of me that was more stubborn prevailed. He had been my savior through my teenage years, and it was easy to fall back into it, but I no longer needed a savior.

I needed a man that would love me. Keep me.

We continued wrestling on the jungle floor. I grunted, trying to overpower him. He was stronger than I was. His body pressed against mine, and I had to fight the urge not to melt underneath him. I loved his weight on me.

I am my own worst enemy. No matter what he had done, I still wanted him.

At least he had no idea who I was. I'd have to remember to thank DeAngelo for insisting we wear masks. Despite the fact that I would probably die due to lack of oxygen because of the damn thing.

"You're a woman!" Santi exclaimed, voice full of surprise. It was stupid how easily he got to me, made my panties soaking wet. Here we were fighting, and my pussy was clenching for him.

Yep, idiot with a capital I!

Using his hesitation and surprise against him, I maneuvered my legs from under him and wrapped them around his waist then swung us over, my thighs spread at his neck. Images of him eating me out in his villa in Italy flashed in my mind, and I had to stop a moan from slipping through my lips.

What was wrong with me? Even fighting him, Santi turned me on. *Me. Complete. Idiot.*

"You like women kicking your ass?" I rasped in Italian, keeping my voice husky and my knife against his throat.

"Depends. You like men slicing your pussy?" He flicked a gaze downward, then back at me, and I followed his eye movement. *Fuck!*

I had no idea how he managed to pull out a knife and press it against my inner thigh, too close to my throbbing pussy. *Jesus!* It turned me on unlike anything else. I had some serious issues.

"Depends," I repeated his earlier answer, pushing my inner thigh into the knife. It didn't cut, but for some sick reason, my entrance so close to him made me pulse with need. The heat from him was making me ache even worse.

He chuckled darkly. "Sorry, honey. Not today."

"Too bad," I rasped and realized too late I replied in English.

His brows furrowed and I cursed myself silently. I couldn't blow my cover. I hadn't seen him or talked to him since Italy and my feelings hadn't diminished one bit.

Maybe if I kill him, I'll get rid of this love for him, I mused silently. Although, it would probably be pointless since just the idea of him shattered me. If him trampling my heart didn't change my feelings, nothing would.

As if I was pulled by an invisible hand, I leaned closer to him. I cursed that I couldn't bury my nose into the crook of his neck and inhale his scent. Two months were too long without him.

"Let's go!" DeAngelo's shouting shattered my lust filled haze.

"Your friends will leave without you," Santi deadpanned in a taunting voice. "You might want to run."

"Do us both a favor," I murmured, ignoring his comment. "Don't do something stupid. I'd hate to slice that sexy throat of yours."

Amusement I hadn't seen since Italy flickered in his amber eyes. "At least it's sexy."

"Don't let it go to your head," I warned, though there was no real threat in my voice. "I could still change that."

Okay, so I wasn't a badass woman and killing churned my stomach. But to use it with Santi... yeah, it was time well spent. I straightened and stood up in one swift move. Just in time, since Carrera approached with his gun pointed at me.

In one swift move, DeAngelo pointed his at him, and I flipped my knife through the air, catching it between my fingers.

"Don't worry, Ink," I muttered. Why in heaven would he have so much ink was beyond me! "I left your sexy friend intact." I glanced over to see Santi already on his feet, his one hand on his gun and the other holding his knife. It was the first time I'd seen him in battle, and I had to admit, his ass was fucking sexy and dangerous.

Makes me want to jump his bones!

"Leave them," DeAngelo shouted again, never removing his gun from the target. Our helicopter was close by the sound of it. I flashed my gaze up and saw it right over the tree line, then looked at the two men in front of me.

My eyes locked on them, my steps shifting towards DeAngelo.

"This has nothing to do with you and your men," I told them over my shoulder. "But you might want to clear out. This place will blow in... hmmm, about ten minutes."

The noise was getting louder, and the wind picked up from the propeller of the helicopter.

With a final nod, I ran towards the helicopter and jumped in, DeAngelo right behind me. I glanced back, hoping those two took the warning seriously. I didn't want anything to happen to them. They were running in the opposite direction.

They listened, I breathed easily.

I pulled the mask over my head, my hair falling loose down my back, and I wiped the sweat off with the back of my hand.

I grinned. "We made it."

DeAngelo nodded.

"We need the last Anderson." Our gazes locked. "You realize he is alive, right?"

I acknowledged him with a nod.

Except, where was he? What if we were chasing a ghost?

CHAPTER 48

Santino

Carrera and I ran towards the jungle. Renzo waited there for us with our Jeep. We'd clear out quickly. The compound was destroyed, thanks to the little team taking off in a chopper. It was not how I envisioned seeing Amore again.

I tortured that fucker Ulrich Anderson when an explosion blasted through the compound, sending me flying through the room. He took off, like the damn coward he was. I recognized her right away. That body was hard to forget. I saw her put a bullet into Ulrich's skull as I fought against the remaining men of the Anderson Cartel.

That was our mistake all along. We were searching for Perèz compounds, rather than the flimsy little Anderson Cartel.

I glanced over my shoulder at the helicopter rising and caught a glimpse of striking red hair cascading down the woman's back.

Soon she'd be mine!

"Start the car," Carrera shouted at Renzo.

We jumped into the Jeep and took off; Renzo's off-road driving jarring every damn bone in our bodies. The vehicle sped down the dirt road, every second away from the camp counted.

"Faster," Carrera instructed. "Before this place blows."

Jesus, we might blow into pieces, and I was rock hard. When in the hell did she learn to shoot and fight like that? It was hot as hell. If I could have, I would have grabbed her and brought her along with us, then buried myself in her pussy the moment we were alone.

"Did you know Amore was going to be here?" he questioned me.

I shrugged. Until he started coming clean, neither would I. He was getting his information from DeAngelo. The question was why was Amore's bodyguard working with Carrera?

Regardless, one thing was for sure. My little heiress was a complete badass.

CHAPTER 49

Amore

I had been back in New York for a day. DeAngelo and I landed last
night and came home expecting everyone. We arrived to an empty
house.

With Ulrich dead, the looming threat felt lighter. Though I couldn't
shake off the feeling that it wasn't over. George, the man I believed to be
my father, might be alive. I had nothing pointing to it, but somehow I
was sure of it. So was DeAngelo.

For the first time in my life, I kept replaying the capture from all
those years ago. I went through every detail, every word, every sound... I
never saw George hurt or tortured. Why hide his torture when they
clearly didn't care if I saw my mother's?

"Where is my girl?" Dad's booming voice traveled over the foyer,
and I jumped off the couch, rushing towards the sound of his voice.

The second I saw him, a wide smile spread over his face.

"Amore," he exclaimed, opening his arms. I walked into them, his
strong embrace and familiar cologne surrounding me. In his mid-fifties,
he was still a good-looking man, though since Elena's death, I never saw
him with a woman. I was sure he had flings, but he kept it well hidden
and private. Which made sense. It wasn't like I wanted to know his sex
life, but I wanted to see him happy.

"Hi, Dad."

"Welcome home," he murmured against my head. "Finally, we get to have you back."

I chuckled against his chest. "It's good to be back." For the most part, and if only I didn't dread seeing Santi so bad. Running into him in the jungle was almost worse because I knew my attraction hadn't eased one bit.

I turned to Luigi, hugging him.

"And don't forget your favorite brother," Lorenzo teased, driving a growl out of Luigi.

I couldn't help but chuckle. "I just saw you less than a week ago."

He pulled me into a hug. "I don't care. I still deserve sister love."

Smiling softly, I returned the hug. "You are both my favorite brothers," I gushed with emotion.

"And what about your favorite uncle?" All our heads whipped around to see Uncle Vincent striding through the door. *Family!* It felt good to have the entire family back. If Grandma and the Russos were here, it would be complete.

I shook my head, pushing those silly thoughts away.

"We expected you back yesterday," Dad grumbled, pulling me back to him. He wasn't overly affectionate but with me, he always tried. And I loved him even more for it.

"Our supplier had some delays," I muttered into his chest. It was easier to lie when not staring into someone's eyes.

Lorenzo pinched my cheek. "You should fire some of those suppliers," he mumbled, giving me a suspicious look.

Ignoring his comment, I changed the subject. "Where were you three?" I questioned. "Causing havoc in the city?"

"I had business in New Jersey," Dad responded. By now, I knew what that meant. He had a shipment he had to take care of. I was rich enough to provide for my brothers, dad, and many others, yet my family insisted on this *business*. Somewhere along the way, I learned that they all thrived in it. They loved hustling and the Cosa Nostra.

There was no changing it. The Bennettis. The Russos. It wasn't something I would ever understand.

The exhaustion settled, though Lorenzo insisted we all share ice cream. It wasn't something I could refuse. So, with Lorenzo, DeAngelo, and I working as a team, we prepared a banana split for all of us.

"Something healthy with unhealthy," I mused as I handed the dish to Dad.

He chuckled. "I'm guessing bananas are the only healthy thing in here."

I shrugged, smiling. "Well, there is dairy in the ice cream."

Settling on the couch in between Dad and Lorenzo, it felt good being home. They talked about a new restaurant they were opening, which I suspected was to launder money through. I told them about my new company The Orchid and how things were taking off quickly.

"Maria is the best partner," I raved. "Unlike Grandma's company where major decisions have to go through the board, we get to just talk through them and agree. I love it."

"Maria, the housekeeper?" Uncle Vincent asked in surprise.

I smiled coyly. I had a feeling he liked her from way before. "Yes. And she is single," I added. "Perfect age for you, Uncle Vincent."

"You want to start a dating agency too," he grumbled though a smile stretched across the planes of his face.

After an hour of catching up, I couldn't fight the exhaustion anymore. I wouldn't be good to anyone tomorrow if I was dead tired. It was barely eight.

"I better go to bed," I said through a yawn. "I have to go into the office tomorrow."

Dad stiffened slightly but kept his words to himself. I couldn't even imagine what kind of curses played in his mind. But I needed to keep busy, especially now.

I'd exchanged a few text messages with Adriano. He'd promised to come later tonight, but I was too tired. The trip to South America had been exhausting.

"Are you sure you don't want to stay up for another hour?" Luigi questioned. "Adriano and Santi are swinging by."

That would be a definite no. Bed was calling to me. I didn't want to see Santi. Not yet. I wasn't ready, which in itself was ridiculous. It was ludicrous that I was still hung up on the bastard.

"Yes," I told him. "I can barely keep my eyes open."

Yes, I was fully aware of being a coward. So what? It was my life, and I'd be a coward that avoided Santi Russo if I wanted to.

I was Amore motherfucking Bennetti.

CHAPTER 50
Amore

Getting situated in my new office at Regalè headquarters, I couldn't shake off the feeling that everything was off. I got acquainted with all the new personnel and hearing them speak English was a constant reminder that we were back. I'd got used to the office in Italy, their constant smiles, long coffee breaks. I could almost feel the corporate feel of the Regalè empire choking the creativity out of me.

It was the reason I thrived with Maria. I needed The Orchid even more than she did. It allowed me to do what Regalè didn't. Be creative and enjoy every second of it. It was the reason Maria was the only viable candidate for a partner when I came up with the idea. She had nurtured it all these years.

"Miss Regalè," the woman's voice came from the intercom. I gritted my teeth. It was another thing that bothered me. They kept calling me Regalè instead of Bennetti. In Italy, I was Miss Bennetti. Here, I was Regalè. How in the hell were you supposed to get used to your last name if it kept changing?

"I'll be right there," I responded.

"You might want to stop growling," DeAngelo joked, and I glared at him. His eyes shone with amusement. "You've been cranky," he remarked.

"I just wish everything was over with," I muttered under my breath as we turned into the hallway. We'd left my office and were walking to the corner of the floor where my grandmother's office was. "And this... This was something that has been drilled into me for so long and now, I just feel..." I sighed heavily. "I just don't want to be here," I finally admitted. "I don't want to do this."

DeAngelo's gaze darted my way. "Do what? Regalè Fashion House? Live in New York? Your side business? Hunt for George Anderson? The problem is that you're doing too much." Well, he might have a point now. "You realize you'll have to take over the cartel. It is the only way to eliminate the constant threats."

I had no desire to run a cartel. Hustling wasn't my thing. I knew nothing about the cartel, Cosa Nostra, nor those kinds of *businesses*. I guess it would be something I'd worry about when the time came.

I seem to say that a lot lately, I thought wryly.

Just as we reached my grandmother's office, my step faltered, and my heart stilled.

Santi Russo.

Why did that name cause such heartache and unparalleled thrill at the same time?

He stood there in his three-piece black suit, his hands in his pockets. It was as if the entire world ceased to exist and left me with the very man that sucked the oxygen out of my lungs, leaving me gasping for air and craving his love.

It pissed me the fuck off!

He looked like he was expecting me, waiting for me. I couldn't help but compare it to the way I ran to him in Italy after not seeing him for two months. Such a contrast to the first reunion.

My eyes traveled over his body and unwanted desire rushed through my veins. He seemed older, harder, colder somehow. But just as devastatingly handsome. There had to be a way to kill it if I was to survive living in the same city as this man. He looked casual, uncaring except when you glanced up and saw the dark look in his eyes.

And it was directed at the man by my side. DeAngelo. He was always by my side. DeAngelo must have sensed the tension in the air because his eyes flicked curiously to Santi, then back to me.

I would have preferred to have had a warning that Santi was going to be here. I haven't heard from Adriano all day, and suddenly, I found myself agitated that Santi Russo was the first Russo man I ran into in New York city.

"All good?" DeAngelo's question was low, but I could tell by Santi's burning gaze he heard it.

Frustration crept up my back. He had no right to look at DeAngelo that way. At this point, Santi Russo was nothing but a reluctant family friend.

I recalled all the times Santi acted downright psychotic and possessive. I used to find it thrilling and exciting. Now it irked me, and I hated him.

Then why is your heart racing? My mind mocked me, but I ignored it. I didn't need this shit right now.

"Yes," I muttered.

Santi's eyes flickered with something dark, and agitation flashed across his face. He had no right to feel agitation. It was he who had shattered my heart into a thousand little pieces and changed me forever. I was done with his rejections.

Yet somehow, he still fascinated me, and if I didn't keep my distance, I'd never make it out of this alive.

My hands felt clammy, and my heart twitched with a dull pain at seeing him. I couldn't help it. I should move on; I wanted to move on. But my heart wanted Santi Russo and refused to beat for anyone else.

"Ah, Amore." My grandmother's voice pulled me out of my thoughts. "Santi and I have to talk to you and DeAngelo."

I tensed. My grandmother never wanted to be around the Russos nor Bennettis. It was common knowledge. DeAngelo and I shared a look, then my eyes darted to Santi. The latter's gaze narrowed on me, hot and dark. And my heart just about fluttered from my chest and straight into his darkness.

Ah shit!

Couldn't I have gotten at least a week of reprieve from seeing Santi upon my return to New York?

DeAngelo went in first after my grandmother and I followed him. Santi didn't move and my heart thundered harder with each step as I came closer to him. I tilted my head his way in greeting and walked by him, my sleeve brushing against his. His masculine scent, just as I remembered it, filled my lungs, and the familiar heat from his body drifted to me. It was worse than I remembered. Or better? *No, no, it is bad.* It shouldn't impact me more than it did before.

Yet, it did. And all the while he didn't seem bothered by my presence at all.

Fucker!

I took a seat next to DeAngelo and crossed my legs, then raised my head just in time to catch Santi's eyes darkening in a way that made my lower belly clench. His eyes were on my thighs. A fleeting feral and hungry expression crossed his face, but it was gone so fast, I wasn't sure if it was a figment of my imagination.

Maybe I wanted him so much that I imagined his desire too.

My hand smoothed across the material of my Gucci dress to ensure nothing inappropriate was showing. The dress was to highlight the latest teaming event for the upcoming show. It was black with a white accented wrap around my waist and a slit that came up to the middle of my thigh.

"What's going on, Grandma?" I asked, turning my attention to her. She was safer than this towering man that was too distracting. He didn't sit down, and I sensed it was on purpose. He liked to show his dominance.

"We are putting extra security on each floor," Grandma started, sharing a glance with Santi.

Ah, and here we go! My gut feeling was telling me something bad was happening in New York. I'd noticed the security around the house was tighter than before.

"Why is that?" I asked.

"There are some big events coming up," she justified. "It is normal to tighten up the security. And with the latest deal you secured with Gucci and Chanel we need to ensure there are no hiccups."

Annoyance flared in me. She wasn't being honest with me. No surprise there, I guess.

"Seriously?" I scoffed. "We've had large names before and never tightened security. Why now?"

My eyes shifted back to Santi, but it was hard to tell what he was thinking. He kept his gaze guarded. I resented him so much right now.

"Amore, your father and I agreed—"

I sat up straight. "Well, that's a first."

My grandmother let out an exasperated breath. "Now is not the time to test your limits, Amore."

"I'm not testing my limits." I narrowed my eyes on her. "I'm asking you to tell me the truth, instead of some bullshit story."

Her hands tightened on the desk, but she kept still. "You have been gone for a while. Certain things have changed. Security is a necessity. You won't leave the building until the driver is out front, and there will be someone with you at all times."

Yes, something is happening for sure!

"DeAngelo is with me at all times," I reminded her.

"There will be someone else," Santi chimed in, his voice behind me. I whipped my head around. I didn't realize he'd come up behind me, his movements like those of a jaguar.

I sat, the tension between us suffocating me. He was the reason I didn't come back. The first time because of that kiss in The Orchid, which he called a mistake, and the second time because he dumped me after promising me forever.

"No," I told him. "I have my own security. If I need another body, DeAngelo and I will pick someone."

"Since when do you have your own security?" My grandmother almost sounded shocked. "I haven't seen those invoices."

I stood up, smoothing my dress with the palm of my hand. DeAngelo stood up right along with me. "I felt it wasn't fair that Regalè Enterprise foot the bill since I hired them. I pay them directly."

"Amore, I understand your need for independence. First this other company, now this." she warned.

"It's just business, Grandma," I told her calmly. "You are reading too much into it."

Before either Santi or my grandmother could say another word, I strode out of the office. I needed to put distance between Santi and me. I had to get over him.

You'll never get over him, my mind whispered, and I silently cursed it.

CHAPTER 51

Santino

"Happy?" Regina hissed in annoyance. "I told you Amore wouldn't go along with it."

"She will," I told her. "And you will ensure that she does."

The woman hated being cornered. Too fucking bad.

"And if I don't?" she growled. The woman had balls, that was for sure.

"The world will know that the Perèz Cartel is run by the same woman as Regalè Fashion," I deadpanned. I wasn't fucking around. I was playing for my queen, for Amore, and nobody would refuse me and keep me away from her. Not her grandmother. Not her father. Fucking nobody! "Imagine that stock price," I drawled with a smirk. "All your granddaughter's hard work increasing the share price will go down the toilet."

"I should have expected as much from a Russo," she gritted out. "Greedy, selfish bastards."

I slipped my hands into my pants pockets. Her fucking opinion meant nothing to me.

"You better watch it, Regina," I warned her in my indifferent voice with the lazy, sardonic stare I was known for. I'd give it to her; she wasn't easily scared. Most men shook in their pants when I got this way. "And imagine what Amore would think... she might even blame you for her mother's death."

The first flicker of emotion passed through her face. The woman was a fucking dragon, but she had a weakness. Her granddaughter.

Regina Regalè had run the Perèz Cartel all these years, fighting against the Anderson Cartel. Inadvertently, she had put Amore and her mother's life in danger. Amore's grandfather intended to merge the Anderson and Perèz Cartel with his daughter's marriage to George Anderson.

Regina convinced him not to because she knew her daughter's baby wasn't George's. And the dominoes rolled for twenty years. One event led to another. With her dumb behavior, she had put Amore's life at risk and caused her mother's death. She knew Amore would never forgive her if she knew.

"The Andersons blackmailed me to turn over the Perèz drug business," she hissed. "Margaret was just a stepping stone for George. He wanted it to become a legacy for his sons." Two brothers. One dead by my hand. The other by Amore's. "Instead of doing that and signing certain death for both my daughter and granddaughter, I gambled. I struck a deal with the Carreras but Amore ended up escaping George's clutches on her own. I lost my daughter. In the most brutal way."

The woman was good at hiding her emotions, but I saw a slight tremor to her hands. "Did it ever occur to you that maybe it would have been better for your daughter to be a single mother? Rather than sign her off to a cartel member."

"I really don't like you," she grumbled, though I heard a hint of respect in her tone.

"I don't give a shit," I told her. I truly didn't. All I wanted right now was to make Amore mine. I'd be damned if I'd sit back and watch her marry my brother. "I want updates on Amore's activities every day. Tell her I'm her security; I don't give a shit. But I want to know her schedule all day, every day."

I headed for the door when her question stopped me.

"Is that the only reason you want her?" I slowly turned to face her. If she was a man, I'd wring her neck. She was lucky she was Amore's relative and for some incomprehensible reason, Amore loved her grand-mother. "To take over the Perèz Cartel?"

"What makes you think I want her?"

"Don't fuck with me Russo," she sneered. "I've seen you two. You want her."

"What's your point, Regina?" I wouldn't be playing games with the dragon. I was under no illusion that she'd stab me in the back without a second thought.

She got behind her large, regal desk. The woman just loved her power status.

"It was the reason your father and Savio wanted her mother." She slowly sat down with a knowing smile. She didn't know crap.

I shrugged. "I don't give a shit about your cartel. However, since Savio created a marriage contract to keep her away from me and my world, I have no choice but to pull her knee deep into it." Regina's eyes widened. Oh, so she didn't know about the marriage contract either!

She survived running the Perèz Cartel all these years, had contacts and arrangements all over the world, yet she couldn't come to terms with Savio Bennetti.

"Who?" she asked.

"My brother. Does Savio know you took over the cartel upon your husband's death?"

Her jaw tightened. "No."

"Isn't the Perèz Cartel his main drug supplier?" It was a known fact.

"Yes, and as such, I charge him extra," she retorted with a self-satis-fied grin.

She loved having the last word.

I left without a backward glance, the door shutting behind me.

CHAPTER 52

Amore

I had been back a week and couldn't get away from Santino Russo no matter how hard I tried. Everytime I turned around, he was there. At Regalè Enterprise, at a fashion show, after parties, at my father's house. You'd think the man lived here. I kept running into him.

I teetered on the edge. He was invading all my thoughts and fucking dreams too. Adriano has been avoiding me, and I have no fucking clue what that was about. I had yet to see him since I got back. And his messages were short and evasive.

Men were just idiots. There was nothing else to say about that.

And my grandmother... I just had no words. She assigned Santi as my bodyguard. A fucking don was my bodyguard. Those two were up to something. Otherwise, why would Santi agree to that role? It wasn't like he needed money.

My eyes lowered to the picture of the note in my hand.

I read the note again.

Sins of the father are the daughter's to pay.
You crumbled my empire.
Now I'll crumble yours.
Blood for blood.
It's her turn to scream.

I found the picture of the message on my father's desk, drafted on a steel wall, surrounded by death. So many dead women, all with red hair. It was dated two years ago. Two fucking years and no words. No wonder Dad and Grandma agreed to send me to Italy. And now that I was back, everyone was on edge. Even my grandmother. And where in the fuck was Adriano?

Italy was so much better, I thought dryly to myself.

"Hey, sis." I started at my brother's voice. Luigi gently tugged on my ponytail. "Dad wants you in his office."

I quickly shut down my phone. It wasn't a subtle movement, so Luigi didn't miss it, but to his credit, he said nothing. I got to my feet and followed him. Dressed in my hot pink shorts and white tank top, I padded barefoot towards Dad's office. It was hot as Hades today; September in New York city was a sauna.

When I entered his office, my step faltered with surprise. Adriano was here. Dad sat behind his desk and Adriano in the chair across from him.

"Hey, didn't hear you come in." I greeted him with a kiss on the cheek. He gave me an odd look, almost like a warning. I raised my eyebrow, wondering what that was about but he just shook his head.

Pà smiled at both of us, like he was pleased about something. Though I couldn't quite figure out what that could be.

"Shut the door, Luigi," he told my brother.

I turned to see my brother close the door and take a stance in front of it, like he was standing guard, and it was only then that I saw him. My heart instantly plunged to my feet. Would this reaction ever ease up?

Santi Russo stood against the mantle of the fireplace, casually leaning. Standing like a statue in the middle of the office, I stared at him while my heart thundered under my chest. It only happened around him. While he watched me with indifference, his dark gaze almost angry, I struggled for breath. Like he sucked all the oxygen out of the room.

His hands casually in his pockets, he didn't seem to be suffering the same effect as I had.

"That's right, this is the first time you are seeing Santi since you've been back." My dad's voice sounded behind me. "You didn't forget Adriano's brother, right?"

Dad chuckled like there was a joke in there somewhere. I didn't bother correcting him. I've been seeing Santi every time I turned around but had yet to speak to him directly or alone. If it was up to me, I'd never be alone with him again.

I swallowed hard and my stomach dipped. There was no forgetting him. Ever! I dreamt about him every single night, touched myself thinking about him, hated him, and loved him. Though I wasn't sure why I bothered loving him. He didn't deserve it.

I swallowed hard. "No."

I tipped my head, praying my expression portrayed none of the turmoil currently brimming inside me.

"Good," Dad broke our staring silence. My fists clenched, my phone digging into my palm. I turned around and met my dad's gaze. He watched both Santi and I with a grim expression. "Because the news I'm about to share will bring you closer."

"What's this about?" I asked, as I let out a shaky breath.

"You are older now," he started, and I frowned. Twenty-one was hardly older. "I am very proud of you and both Mr. Russo"—my eyebrows scrunched as my eyes darted to Santi—"Santi's father," Dad corrected, and I returned my eyes to him. "We agreed to a contract arrangement to have you and Adriano married."

I blinked my eyes, watching my dad like he'd lost his mind.

"A contract arrangement?" I repeated, my voice sounding distant to my own eyes.

"A marriage contract," he explained. "You and Adriano are perfect for each other."

Slowly, I glanced at Adriano to see if this made any sense to him. His eyes met mine, a light shake of his head warning me.

"I don't get it," I muttered, then shook my head. "What are you saying, Dad?"

"You and Adriano will be married," he announced. "It is only fitting that our two families would be brought back together by your marriage. You brought peace to us, and this will protect you."

One heartbeat. Two heartbeats. Three heartbeats.

Then hot anger shot through my veins like a broken dam.

"No."

"Amore—" Surprise flashed in Dad's eyes at my firm refusal, but I ignored it and turned to my best friend.

I stood straighter, pushing my shoulders back. "No," I repeated.

The scent of cigars hung in the air. A clock ticked. Tension was building and would erupt at any moment. I have learned the cost of disobedience. It cost my mother her life. But this I couldn't do. I held my breath, waiting for the volcano to erupt. Though it remained to be seen whether it was mine or Dad's.

"You should at least hear Dad out." Luigi tried to mediate.

I didn't even spare him a glance. Instead, I met Adriano's gaze.

"You knew?" I rasped, the adrenaline pumping through my veins and feeding my fury.

"Yes." He was my best friend. He should have called me and given me fair warning. I would have done that for him. I slid a glance at Santi, but he still had the same indifferent look in his eyes. Oh my God, how could this be happening? How long has he known?

An eerie silence filled the room while a single word screamed in my head. *No!* I loved Adriano but not in that way. He was my best friend. Did he feel like that for me? This was wrong.

All wrong.

"No" I whispered, locking eyes with Dad. "I'll do anything, but I won't bend on this. I'm sorry, Dad."

Dad scratched his chin. Luigi watched me with concern in his eyes, Adriano seemed dumbfounded at my firm refusal while Santi seemed completely apathetic. Why would Santi allow this, knowing what happened between us?

"Amore, be reasonable." My eyes widened at Dad's unreasonable request. He was the one not being reasonable. "You and Adriano clicked. You have been close for a long time," Dad explained. "Friendship is a good basis for a marriage. It turns into more." I blew out a frustrated breath. This was ludicrous. "I want you protected and having a Russo for your husband will ensure you have your brothers' protection and Russo's."

Too bad it is the wrong Russo, I thought wryly. If I thought Santi dumping my ass was a bitter pill to swallow, it was nothing to this. It was clear Santi Russo didn't want me at all, if he threw me to his brother.

"I don't need protection," I muttered. "And from whom exactly are you protecting me?"

Maybe this would make Dad come clean. He didn't know I'd seen the message. I haven't told anyone except for DeAngelo.

"You never know what can happen," Dad reasoned with me. I wasn't surprised he refused to tell me anything. Disappointed, yes, but not surprised.

"But—"

"There is no but, Amore." Dad stopped me. "This has been arranged and breaking it would cause a war, a wedge between our families."

My heart sank. I didn't want to cause a wedge between our families. But marrying the brother of the man I loved was wrong too. On so many levels, especially since I slept with him.

I glanced back at my best friend. I loved him like my own brother, but I didn't want to marry him. Would I lose him if I said that out loud?

I had never thought my father would arrange a marriage for me. I heard it was how it was done in Cosa Nostra, but I wasn't actually fully integrated into that life. I'd told him on numerous occasions I wouldn't marry like that. Stuck in between my grandmother and dad, it had never occurred to me that I'd fall under the same rule as other women of Dad's world.

"What about Grandma?" I breathed out, grasping for straws.

"I'm your father," he bit out, his eyes a dark storm. I flinched at his harsh tone since he never used it on me. My grandmother was a sore subject. "I make decisions for you."

I swallowed hard and a cold sensation crawled down my spine while my lungs constricted. I wasn't willing to just accept my fate. Maybe if I grew up under my father's rule, I would have accepted his word and gone along with it. But I've spent too much time outside his world to agree and go along with it.

"I'm not underage," I replied, straightening my shoulders. "Grandma might not agree for my inheritance to be tied to the Cosa Nostra. Frankly, neither am I."

A spark flickered through Dad's eyes and his lip tugged up. I held my breath, unsure whether he was reacting positively or negatively to my comeback.

The phone felt slick with sweat in my palm, my grip hard.

"I'm glad you said that," Dad's reply was light. "Because Adriano won't be tied to the Cosa Nostra."

My head whipped to Adriano, our eyes meeting. He liked doing work for the Cosa Nostra and his brother. In fact, he hated leaving it to visit me in Italy. He lived and breathed the whole criminal world.

Usually, the two of us were always in sync, but right now it was hard for me to read him. I wasn't ready to accept my defeat though. If I married Adriano and he found out I slept with his brother, he'd never forgive me. Besides, Adriano slept around like it was a damn exercise.

"Has anyone asked if that is what Adriano wants?" I was running out of excuses to use.

"He's in agreement." Both Dad and Santi answered at the same time. I avoided Santi's gaze, but I felt his eyes on me the entire time. Adriano kept his gaze on me too. I felt stuck between two brothers, who I loved in very different ways.

Adriano's golden-brown eyes stared at me, and my heart sank recognizing the expression in them. Each spoken word by me pushed my best friend further away.

I shook my head. Maybe I was never meant to have a family, and this was the best way to break ties with the Cosa Nostra. It was a foolish, childish dream to have it all anyhow.

"I'm sorry," I finally said in a firm tone. "I won't do it."

I started for the door when my father's voice had me pausing. "Are you prepared to see men die for your refusal?"

He had cornered me. After all, it was what made him a don.

CHAPTER 53

Santino

Adriano and Amore left Bennetti's office without a backward glance, seemingly accepting their fate. It left me alone with Luigi and Savio. The former was worried I'd shoot his father. Not a bad assumption.

My blood ran hot at seeing Amore standing in front of me, that smell of strawberries invading my nostrils in the best possible way. Or the worst, depending how you thought of it. Every time I'd seen her this week, she'd shone, and I had to fight the urge not to beat down or kill any man she talked to. She saw me but avoided me like her life depended on it. She watched me with detest in her eyes.

Frustration clawed at my chest and my heart because she'd become everything to me. I wanted to drown in her, age with her, bask in her light and her smiles. I wanted to be the one to give her everything, to make her happy. I wanted her to run to me for comfort and happiness; just like the way she had in the past. In Italy.

Yet, that woman seemed to be gone.

Her eyes, the expression the moment she spotted me, seemed to burn through my skin and straight to my dick. The way her lips parted and her green eyes flashed made me want to taste her again. Each time she glanced my way, a wave of awareness ran down my spine and my dick responded. It was annoying as fuck. I'd had her, every way possible, yet it wasn't enough. I wanted more. My obsession with this woman only grew over time. A whole lifetime with this heiress would never be enough. Not until I owned every inch of her, as she owned every inch of me.

Leaning back, I rested my forearm on the mantel and let the anger burn through my veins and hopefully evaporate. I needed a clear mind to execute my plan.

"That went well," I announced sarcastically. Somehow I wasn't surprised that Amore stood up to her dad. And her final acceptance under the threat of dead men wouldn't last. Bennetti had no idea his daughter started fighting her own battles. "It seems you plan on dragging her down the aisle by her hair."

I'd never let him. I was the only man that could pull her hair. My fists clenched, the silkiness of her red mane a memory I'd never let go. Fuck, not something to think about right now!

Luigi's pensive gaze lingered at the door through which his sister had left. Maybe the idiot finally realized his sister had a backbone and could think for herself.

Savio's eyes darted between his eldest son and me. "If you two have something to say, spit it out."

Luigi shrugged. "I think she gave up too easily," he muttered. "Amore usually doesn't cave in. Ever. Even when cornered." He met Savio's gaze. "You know that, Pà."

Her dad shuffled paper over his desk seemingly unfazed, but he knew it too. I could read the man, but he was stubborn.

"She'll recognize it is for her own good," he claimed. "This will offer her protection of the Cosa Nostra while she lives the life her mother wanted for her."

"Might have been good to ask what Amore wanted," Luigi muttered under his breath, surprising me. I agreed. Despite her age, Amore knew what she wanted. She had known for a long time. She wasn't an insecure girl, unsure of her wants or dreams.

"Amore and Adriano have been joined at the hip from the moment they met," he spat agitated.

He really didn't know his daughter that well.

I ended the meeting by walking out of his office. Since he refused to amend the marriage contract, our relationship was tenuous at best. The only reason I didn't start a full-blown war was on Amore's account. He should count himself lucky.

Assuming Adriano and Amore headed to her bedroom, I walked down the hallway in its direction. I balled my hands into fists. Those two had hung out in her bedroom since they were kids. But now, the idea infuriated me.

Without knocking, I entered the bedroom. It was empty. Good fucking thing. It was my first time in her bedroom. Her private space.

The bedroom suited her. In the middle of it was a large, four poster bed, all the wood in rich mahogany but the bedding was a frilly white. The golden tones and white crown molding accented the entire room. A large part of her room was dedicated to her desk with drawings and a sewing machine along with a headless mannequin she obviously used for her fashion designs.

The large windows overlooked the back gardens, and it was where I spotted two figures. Reluctantly, I had to admit those two looked good together. They were closer in age and liked similar things, similar music.

It didn't matter. She was mine.

I left the room and headed back to the first floor and the terrace. Amore and my brother stood by the fig tree, seemingly in a serious discussion. Amore had her hands wrapped around herself, and I saw her lips softly move as she spoke.

My eyes ran over her white tank top that accentuated her breasts. She was still barefoot, her feet shifting restlessly. Most of her legs were bare in those tiny shorts, giving me a glimpse of her milky skin. It reminded me of her boyshort panties she liked to wear so much. *Fuck!* I still recalled how those thighs felt wrapped around my head as I ate her pussy. Those moaning sounds she made. Goddamnit!

Watching her with my brother caused my throat to tighten and jealousy to simmer. It didn't matter that she rejected him loud and clear in Savio's office. Animosity crawled through me, tainting my already black soul. Family was everything, yet for her... I was willing to break it. This obsession I had for her was like the sweetest poison I couldn't give up.

The question was whether she would forgive me for what I was about to do.

I watched her shake her head at whatever Adriano was saying, and then let out a frustrated breath. It almost seemed like they were arguing. In all the years those two had known each other, Amore never got mad at Adriano.

What were they arguing about now?

Amore's gaze flicked to mine, and instantly her expression closed off. She mouthed something that looked like '*Your brother is here*' and immediately their discussion ceased.

CHAPTER 54

Adriano

"How long have you known?" It was Amore's first question. I haven't seen her since our time in Ibiza and somehow everything had changed.

"About two months," I admitted reluctantly.

She stiffened and pressed her lips into a tight line. It was the only thing showing her displeasure. Sometimes I wished she'd argue like other girls, but not Amore. When she was pissed off, she got quiet.

The news of the marriage contract shocked her as much as it shocked me when I first found out about it. Unlike me, she was passionately and stubbornly opposed to it. I knew she'd be against it even before she openly opposed it. I wasn't sure how I felt about it. The rejection kind of hurt.

We'd been best friends for a very long time. I cared about her, loved her.

"Would marriage to me be so bad?" I questioned her. She was the only long-term woman in my life. Maybe there was a reason for it and this was it.

Marriage didn't seem like such a bad idea to me, though I wasn't thrilled about not working in the Cosa Nostra. I never thought of doing anything else. I was in it for life, but now I have been given a way out. I figured once we were married, we could discuss my position in the Cosa Nostra. I wanted to be Santi's underboss.

"Adriano, you don't love me," she murmured softly, her hands wrapping around her small body. Over the last few years, Amore has grown into a beautiful woman. A knockout. But somehow she slipped right through my fingers. Less and less she sought comfort from me.

"I do love you," I retorted stubbornly.

"Like a friend," she insisted. "And I love you like a friend. But marriage is a lot more."

"Then we make it more," I claimed with conviction. I could be just as hard-headed as her.

"Tell me one thing," she started, her expression serious. "All these years that we've been friends, have you ever thought of me as something more?"

Only once, but I was ashamed to admit it, so I remained silent. It would sound bad if I admitted I was jealous when she called out to Santi on her eighteenth birthday.

"Even when I posed as your girlfriend, it never occurred to you to actually *make* me your girlfriend."

Her gaze flickered over my shoulder, she tensed as a soft flush colored her cheeks.

"Your brother is here," Amore mumbled softly, and I turned my head to see Santi standing there. "You better go," she urged me.

The realization hit me like a thunderbolt. It was there all along in Amore's green eyes. All over her face. She was in love with my brother. Like pieces of a puzzle falling into place, things were finally making sense. It wasn't only my brother that wanted her; she wanted him too.

Santi went to Italy two months ago. When he came back, he was in an exceedingly good mood. Planned on going on *vacation* every weekend. Bullshit, we all called. He hadn't taken a vacation day away from the Cosa Nostra in his entire life. Yet now, he planned on going every weekend.

Then something happened and he got into it with Savio. It was all about Amore. He even shot Luigi.

Did Santi sleep with my best friend?

"I'm going to go," I told Amore.

Amore had changed in Italy. Or maybe it happened right before she left for Italy? The night at The Orchid suddenly flashed in my mind. The night I found her flushed in Santi's office, alone with him. It was the first time I had seen her pissed off at him.

I bent my head and pressed a fleeting kiss to her lips. I had done it many times before, but this was the first time she stiffened at the touch. Before the gesture was friendly, but now... I wasn't sure what it was now.

"I'll call you later," I said softly. "Trust me, everything will work out."

A dubious look flashed in her eyes, but she quickly masked it. It was another thing she had gotten good at, hiding her feelings.

"Okay." She didn't sound convinced. Although I couldn't blame her. Through the years, more often than not, I got her in trouble rather than out of trouble.

Santi always saved her, I thought bitterly. I got her into trouble, and he got her out. No wonder she fell for him.

I strode to Santi, throwing a backward glance over my shoulder. Amore was avoiding looking at my brother.

"Ready?" he asked me as I got closer.

My brother and I weren't exactly alike, but we were always close. Even when I fucked up shit, he'd give me shit fair and square and we'd move on. However, the last two months we couldn't see eye to eye on anything.

I understood now why Pà and Santi wanted to push me out of the Cosa Nostra, but just like Amore, I wished I was asked whether I wanted that.

"Yes. Are we stopping at your office?"

Santi was a workaholic. More so lately than ever before. Though it made sense now. He was fuming over Amore.

"I'll drop you off. I have some business to deal with." He was using his impassive voice on me, his expression cold and dark.

"Why?" I questioned him. It irked me that he kept me in the dark.

"Just some work stuff," he answered, his eyes on his phone, typing something out.

"I'm not out yet, Santi," I told him bitterly. "You could wait until

I'm married to push me out." Santi's cold expression met mine, and I knew I'd pissed him off. Lately, everything I did pissed him off. "Amore and I will expedite our wedding. I'm quite looking forward to my wedding night."

His jaw ticked and his teeth clenched. *Bingo!*

"This is private business," he said in a frigid voice. "And there will be no expedition of the wedding."

We strode through the Bennetti's place in silence, both of us in our own thoughts. If my brother refused to talk, then I'd draw it out of him.

We got into Santi's car and drove in silence.

"I was thinking," I started once we were almost in the city. "Once Amore and I are married, and her inheritance is settled, I want back in."

We both knew what 'back in' meant.

"Not smart." That was it. No explanation, nothing. My brother didn't even spare me a glance.

"Why not?" I argued. "She is running a billion-dollar business, and what am I supposed to do? Stay home and cook?"

He raised his eyebrow but remained silent, his jaw tightened.

"Santi, Cosa Nostra is all I know, and what I thought I'd do for the rest of my life," I muttered.

"There are other jobs," he gritted out. He was teetering on the edge, exactly where I wanted him.

The car came to a stop in front of my place. "You are right," I appeased him. "I will fuck her often and keep her pregnant."

That did it. Santi got in my face, his fist grabbing my collar and shoving me against the passenger window. As my body slammed against the door of his Range Rover, the car shook.

"Goddamnit, Santi." I lost my shit. Maybe Amore and Santi deserved each other; they were both stubborn as mules. "Let me help you."

CHAPTER 55

Amore

I haven't heard from Adriano for the past two days. Not since the news of our marriage contract was dumped on me and he said he'd call me. That he'd take care of everything. Nothing. Not a single damn text.

Until now. Fucking seven at night and he wanted to see me.

Meet me at our Long Island place. Urgent.

Damn it, what could be so urgent! I didn't want to go there. But what to say? I slept with your brother there, so things were awkward.

"Are you sure you are okay?" Uncle Vincent asked for the tenth time.

"Yes," I repeated, because *no* would require a whole lot of explaining. I literally just got home from work when Adriano's message came in. Uncle Vincent was on his way out the door and offered to drive me. "I should have driven myself over." It didn't even occur to me that the last time I was here Adriano disappeared, and I ended up sleeping with Santi.

"Text me, and I'll come get you."

"I should have brought DeAngelo," I muttered.

"Are the Russo boys threatening you?" Vincent's voice turned sharp.

"No, no," I quickly replied. "Just he would have stayed, you know. And you are busy." Lame excuses. "Anyhow, see you later."

Grabbing my purse, I pulled the door open and exited before another stupid comment left my lips.

The moment he pulled off, Adriano came through the door and pulled me into a hug.

"There you are."

"Hey," I greeted him. Somehow he felt familiar but foreign. I couldn't explain it. Our hug felt awkward. Before it was comforting, now it felt wrong, and I had a feeling he sensed it too. I still had no intention of marrying him. I just needed to figure out a way not to cause a war. I didn't want anyone hurt on my account.

"So, what's this about?" I asked him as we strode into the house. I found a nearby table and put my purse on it.

I padded down the foyer and hallway with Adriano while memories of my last visit to this house were a sweet torture. The Russo Long Island home seemed more grand than the last time, though only five months had passed. I couldn't help remembering all the fluttery feelings when I left this house last time after spending the night with Santi.

Hope. Love. Happiness.

Today, it was the opposite.

Dread. Still love. But also despair.

I really didn't want to be in this house. I'd rather be anywhere but here. It was reliving something beautiful that I have been trying to forget.

"I wanted your opinion," Adriano said as he took my hand and tugged me along.

"On what?" I asked him curiously.

"What if we got married here and lived here?"

My steps halted and I stared at him in shock. "Why?" Then I shook my head. "Actually, scratch that. I told you that I didn't think we were meant for each other in that way."

He grinned wide. "You thought. I disagreed." He bent his head and pressed a kiss on my cheek. I couldn't help stiffening. "We should get married," he continued as if he didn't notice me glaring at him annoyed.

"Anyhow, the house is plenty big, close to your folks, and Santi agreed he'd sign it over to me if we want to live here."

Fuck no! My mind screamed. I didn't want to live in a house where I lost my V-card to his big brother. Santi was a sick bastard to even agree to sign it over. Ugh, why was I even getting worked up over something that would never happen?

"What do you think?" Adriano seemed eager.

"Hmmm." I'd start having panic attacks if this shit didn't end.

"Is that yes or no?" *No.*

"Let's not rush it," I answered instead.

Adriano stilled, his eyes studying me. I held his gaze, but my heart drummed in agony. It would have been easier if I loved him instead of his brother. But no, my stupid heart needed a complication and now I was losing Adriano.

"Can you at least go check out upstairs and our bedroom?"

I swallowed. "Our bedroom?"

"Yes, the master bedroom," he retorted. "I think you might fall in love with it, and it will help make up your mind."

Not likely. "Okay."

Taking a step towards the grand marble staircase, I noticed Adriano remained glued to his spot.

"Are you coming?"

He smiled, a slightly smug look on his face. I swore he reminded me of Santi like this.

"You go ahead. I'll wait for you here. Large double door on the left. It's in its own private wing. You can't miss it."

I nodded.

Climbing up the stairs, my mind kept going through my options. I loved my dad and he'd always kept me safe, but I was positive this arrangement wasn't smart. Adriano and I could never be more than friends.

I followed the hallway to the left and opened the large double door to the master suite. I wasn't in a sightseeing mood. Instead, my mind worked, weighing options that would work for everyone's benefit and failing to find them.

I really didn't need all this shit right now. Ulrich Anderson was dead, but I needed to focus on finding where his father was. Not fumble through options on how to get out of this ridiculous arranged marriage.

I was so lost in my thoughts, that I didn't pay attention as I headed for the master bathroom. The sound of the shower didn't register until I walked in. My steps froze, spotting the outline of the man's body through the shower glass.

Santi is in the shower!

His muscular body was a sight to behold, muscles marking every inch of his body. Fuck, even his ass was gorgeous. His one palm leaning against the tile supported his weight as the shower cascaded down his mouth-watering body, his tan skin glistening. My insides clenched, and my body ignited into sparks.

Santi was just as beautiful as I remembered him to be, all hard muscle and beautiful golden olive skin. He was all rugged masculinity, exquisite and rough. The memory of the first time I tasted him in the back of the limo entered my mind. His salty taste became my need. His tortured groans when I'd take his cock into my mouth were my obsession. I loved seeing him lose control as I sucked on his smooth length, pleasuring him.

A guttural groan echoed through the bathroom and the realization shattered through me.

Get out! Get out now! my mind shouted.

But my body had a mind of its own and remained glued to the spot. Goosebumps covered my body and shivers ran down my spine. I needed him with a throbbing ache. Holding my breath, I took a step forward, and my eyes locked on his hand wrapped around his hard cock.

He was smooth and hard, his muscles tight, his inked hand pulling his shaft hard then slow. I glanced at his face, his eyes closed, neck corded with tension, and his mouth lax as he sought his release.

I bit into my lip to stop the whimper from escaping me. It was so damn erotic seeing him jerk off. His neck muscles strained, his rhythmic movements up and down making my thighs clench with a pulsing need.

I burned, the need to feel his hands on me again strong. I wanted to feel his heat under my fingertips as I explored his body. Yet, he was forbidden to me.

I was so aroused; the temptation and what I wanted most right here, within my grasp.

"Amore," he rasped on a moan, and my eyes snapped back to his face with a sharp gasp escaping my throat.

His eyes snapped open, his movement halted as our gazes locked, my heart drumming hard in my ears. The air stilled, the only thing between us an inferno of lust and desire. I held my breath in anticipation. A smart person would leave, but when it came to Santi, I wasn't smart.

Slowly, knowingly, Santi resumed moving his hand. Up and down. Our eyes locked on each other as he kept the rhythm steady. Up and down. Oh my God, I just wanted to lower myself down on my knees and taste him. My heart drummed harder, my breaths coming out in short pants.

God, I wanted him. More than anything else in my life.

His dark eyes never looked away from me, hunger in their depths. Awareness and desire burned in his darkness as his hand moved along his length. A soft moan whimpered through the air. It was mine, I realized astounded.

He continued watching me with his hooded gaze, my eyes lowering to his swollen shaft. His grip was tight, sure each time he passed over the crown. His movements became harder, and I bit into my lower lip to stop another moan from creeping up my throat. His strokes became faster, fucking into his fist with almost brutal movements.

Longing and desire pooled between my thighs. An unbearable pulsing ache. It was impossible not to imagine his salty taste on my lips, his cock inside my mouth. My wet arousal seeped into my panties, and I had to fight the urge to snake my own hand between my legs. It would be so easy. Oh so easy, and I'd get my release. Instead, I clenched my thighs, the throbbing desire almost intolerable.

My pants increased, and his movements almost synchronized with my short, throaty breaths. I should turn around and leave. This wasn't fair to Adriano. He was downstairs, waiting for me. And here I was gawking at his brother.

My breathing erratic and my heart pounding, I fantasized about Santi's cock inside my throbbing pussy, remembering how good he felt inside me.

His tempo went erratic, and I knew he was close. I've had him enough times to know his pleasure. I sucked in a sharp breath, my eyes glued to his cock as he pumped himself harder and faster.

"*Amore!*" he called out my name on a hiss right before he climaxed. His cock thrust one last time through his grip and cum shot onto the tile, so much seed sliding down the wall.

Jealousy ate at me watching the cum being washed off his fingers by the cascading water, washing away the evidence of his release. I'd never have him again, and I was jealous of all the nameless, faceless women that would get to taste this man. The sight of him was erotic, in the wrong way, but I couldn't lie to myself. The desire for this man would never diminish.

How could I ever marry anyone with that knowledge?

I swallowed thickly, my pulse buzzing in my ears. My heart beat so hard my ribs ached, but I was unable to move. Unable to leave.

The shower turned off; Santi stepped out and wrapped a towel around his waist. I jumped when he took a step towards me, the moment broken.

"What are you doing here?" I breathed out, voice hoarse like I'd spent hours screaming his name. "Adriano sent me to check the room. I thought this was our room." Then quickly added, "Adriano's and mine."

I'd never sleep in this house. And definitely not in this room. No fucking way. I'd imagine Santino thrusting into me, or him jerking off in the shower... No freaking way!

He walked by me and then paused at the doorway. "Not until you are married."

I blinked, confusion in my eyes. Why would Adriano send me up here knowing his brother was here? And in the shower for God's sake.

Santi disappeared into the bedroom, and I could hear him moving around. I wanted to shut myself in this bathroom, but Adriano waited for me downstairs. Yet if I followed Santi into the room, he might be naked.

My skin was tight and hot, my summer dress suddenly too heavy against my flesh. I could still remember how his hands felt on my skin and every fiber of me shook with need. This was how withdrawal felt, aching need for something you knew you couldn't have. Or shouldn't have. Another heartbeat, I steeled my spine and left the bathroom, rushing out of the bedroom without a glance at Santi.

Curse that man! There was no way I could ever come into this room and not picture him.

I rushed down the stairs in search of Adriano. Even if I married the wrong brother, I'd never live here. Ever! Even if my life depended on it. This place was Santi's... I'd see him everywhere. And that shower scene. Oh my freaking God! I could not unsee that. Would I even want to?

"Adriano?" I called out. The only voice I heard back was my own. "Adriano," I tried again, agitation lacing my voice and my nerves. If he left me without a word, I'd be majorly pissed.

I peeked into a large formal living room. Nothing. Large ballroom. Nothing. Dining room, kitchen.

He left, my instincts were practically shouting at me. *He fucking left.*

"Goddamn it," I muttered. "Fucking bullshit."

A familiar deep chuckle came from behind me and I whipped around, coming face-to-face with Santi. Again.

"What's the matter, Amore?" Santi's voice was a deep timbre soaking through my skin and into my bloodstream. He stood so close; I could smell his fresh, familiar scent. "I thought you enjoyed that little show in the bedroom. After all, you snuck in there."

Santino would be the death of me.

My cheeks burned hot. The audacity of this man! But he was right. I fucking enjoyed it. I loved sex with him. I went on dates with other men and just their kiss on my hand sent creepy sensations down my spine. Santi had ruined me.

My eyes traveled over his body. He wore dark jeans that hugged his strong, muscular legs just right and a white t-shirt along with black combat boots. He looked good in anything and nothing.

And that right arm, covered in ink, would forever be so fucking sexy in my eyes. I still remembered how our hands looked tangled together. His inked, olive tan skin against my pale one. How he'd bend me over the bed or couch, his forearms paralleled with mine, his hands clutching mine as he thrust hard into me.

The sweet spot between my thighs ached with need. It has been two months since I felt him inside me, since I had any man's hands on me, touching me. Yet it felt like two centuries without him.

His eyes burned, stirring the hunger for him in the pit of my belly.

"Where is Adriano?" I asked to break the unspoken lust sizzling between us.

He took a step closer. "I guess he left," he said.

My heart thundered so hard my ribs ached from the impact. There was only so much strength I had. If he touched me, I'd cave. I knew I would. He was already too close, his body an inch from mine. My skin tingled with recognition at his heat, demanding I lean into him and get my relief.

"What are you wearing, Amore?" Santi's question surprised me, and I looked down then instantly blushed crimson.

Stupid!

I wore the summer dress he bought me in Italy. It was vintage style with thick shoulder straps, snug against my upper body and flared down to my knees. It was his favorite color, green with large white polka dots. He joked that I reminded him of classic Hollywood movie stars.

"It's just a dress," I muttered. "Anyhow, I should go." Yet, I remained standing. I could blame it on his dark expression, the clear demand in his eyes. I was never very good with orders, but with Santi, it was a thrilling and exciting event.

"Don't," I breathed out.

He seemed to consider the word for a second. Just as I went to side-step him, he yanked me to his body, his mouth crushing against mine. There was nothing gentle about his kiss. It was rough, possessive and so... Santi. Nobody kissed like Santi.

My lips parted on their own, inviting his warm tongue into my mouth. His hand came to grip the base of my neck, holding me immobile.

I raised my palms with every intent to push him away, instead I pulled him closer as my fingers dug into his shoulders. He shifted forward, pressing my body hard against his. His rock-hard muscles felt good as I melted into his rough embrace.

A little moan sounded somewhere deep in my throat, and his kiss turned harder. He knew my body better than I did. He expertly thrust his tongue between my teeth, exploring every inch of my mouth. Every corner. Like it was our first kiss all over again.

A throbbing ache intensified between my thighs and another desperate moan escaped me when I felt the thick bulge of his erection nudging against my stomach.

More, please more. I wasn't sure if I uttered the words or not, but he understood my need. He trailed rough, hungry kisses down my face, across my jawline, his scruff rough against my soft skin.

"Look at me." His hand twisted around my ponytail, tilting my head up to look up at him. I forced my eyelids open. He was so close that I could see flecks of embers in his dark eyes. The need for him clawed at my chest. "How many?" I blinked in confusion at his question, frowning to get the meaning of it through my lust hazed brain.

"W-what?" I asked.

"How many fucking men have you had since I left Italy?"

A gasp tore from my lungs and something shattered inside me. Every dark, obsessive part of him lurked in his eyes, and the anger was the only thing I had left.

"Fuck you, Santi," I snapped. "It's none of your business."

He stared at me for the longest time, then released me.

"I'll find them," he stated matter-of-factly. "And I'll kill every single one of them."

My eyes widened at his proclamation. There was darkness around him, pulling me in, threatening to swallow me whole if I let him.

"And Adriano?" I whispered. The air instantly chilled a few more degrees. "Are you going to kill him too?"

He went deathly still and the silence around us screamed, threatening to swallow me whole.

"Has he fucked you?" he snarled, his fingers digging into my wrist painfully. "Amore," he growled in warning.

"Let me go!" I'd like to say my voice was firm but it was breathy. Raspy. Needy.

"Has. He. Touched. You?"

I stumbled backwards at his words. Did he think so little of me? I couldn't even think about Adriano inside me. Santi was tormenting me. I wouldn't let him.

"Tell me something, Santi." I refused to let him have the upper hand, to toy with me. The breeze swept through the open window of the kitchen, the air cool. A sad Italian tune carried from somewhere in the distance. It reminded me of Italy and our time together there. "When did you find out about my marriage contract?" I asked him, my voice oddly calm, despite my skin burning after our shared kiss.

His body tensed but he didn't move. "After Italy."

My heart skidded to a stop, realization that he had ended things the way he did because of that revelation. The hurt still lingered somewhere deep. He should have told me, maybe we could have found a way...

I stopped the train of thought. It led nowhere, only to a deeper heartache.

"Well, at least you aren't such a dirtbag to fuck a woman that has been promised to your brother." The words were harsh, but his actions were harsher. It bothered me that he didn't fight for me. From where I stood, it looked like he let go of me fairly easily. Which told me his feelings were never as strong as mine.

"Amore—"

"Don't." I shook my head. "Just... Don't."

"If I'd known, I would have—"

"What?" My voice rose a notch. "You would have what, Santi?"

"I wouldn't have touched you."

A sharp pain pierced through me, and a gasp escaped me. I was nothing but a piece of ass for this man while my heart bled in front of him, right onto the kitchen floor.

"That's good to know." I forced the pain deep down into a dark corner where the hurt of all my losses resided. "You know now though," I continued. "Why the kiss, touch, or words? You know now I am Adriano's."

His jaw ticked, anger clear on his face.

"Do us both a favor, Santi. Stay away from me. Make an excuse, be busy, go shoot someone. I don't give a shit, just don't come around."

I attempted to sidestep him, but his hand curled around my wrist, forcing me to stop.

"Let go of me," I hissed.

"Or what?"

"Or I'll scream so loud that my brothers will hear it all the way back at our house. And trust me, they will shoot before they ask questions."

His temper flared and he pressed me against the stone wall, the shadows hiding us from everyone in the house. Though why I had no idea because there was nobody around.

"Don't fucking push it, Amore," he whispered against my ear, his hot breath making my insides clench with need. That was all it took, his breath against my ear, and I melted like ice under the scorching sun.

This love for him was clawing at my chest, slowly destroying me, and I fucking hated it.

"Or what? You'll shoot me?"

"Don't you think I tried?" he growled. "Don't you think I tried to break the engagement?"

My eyes snapped to his, and I looked for the truth in his dark amber depths. Santi Russo might be a lot of things, but a liar wasn't one of them.

Maybe. I don't know. Fuck!

"Your father is flat out refusing to break the contract."

My ears rang. How long have I been hearing from Dad and my brothers what a Russo wants he takes? If he wanted me, he would have taken me from this unreasonable marriage contract and kept me for himself. There was a way; something Santi could have done to break the contract, but he didn't deem me worthy enough to meet my father's demands. If I thought my heart was hurting up until now, I was wrong.

Oh, how wrong I was!

Right now, his words tore at my heart, stabbing it a million times and ripping it to shreds. This pain felt like shattered glass against my skin, making me raw on the inside.

"Let go of me, Santi," I told him in a cold voice and my head held high.

When he didn't move, I jerked my arm out of his hold. I side stepped him, taking five steps, the buzzing in my ears drowning out pain.

"You want to know something funny?" I glanced over my shoulder to see him looking after me, his jaw pressed hard. "I would have given the entire Regalè Empire away if you would have asked me to." Something dark flickered in his eyes and his teeth clenched.

"Goodbye, Santi."

Without another word I strode away from him, my back stiff. I had to leave the room before I said something stupid. Grabbing my purse off the table on my way out, I opted to call Lorenzo rather than Uncle Vincent. My brother wouldn't grill me and threaten to rip the Russo men apart.

I left their home and started down their long driveway. I didn't get far. I was barely halfway down the driveway when a car pulled up next to me. It was Santi's Aston Martin. His passenger window slid down.

"Get in the car, Amore."

"No." I continued walking when I heard the car door slam. "Lorenzo will pick me up."

I couldn't bear to be around him. He couldn't even bother to fight for me, and I wanted to beg him to love me. It was sad and pathetic. *I* was pathetic.

"I will take you home." His big hand wrapped around my wrist and whipped me around.

"Get your hands off me," I hissed. I tugged on my wrist, but it was futile. He was much stronger.

"Don't be stupid."

I narrowed my eyes on him. "You are the stupid one," I gritted out. "I am sick and tired of being jerked around by you, Santi." His grip on my wrist tightened and his expression darkened. "You want me. You don't want me. You want me again, then you are done with me. Which one is it?"

"Amore—"

"Actually, don't answer that," I cut him off. "It no longer matters because I no longer want you."

"Liar."

I glared at him, hurt swelling in my chest. He could flip-flop from cold to hot and back again, dragging my heart through mud and leaving it to bleed. For him.

I squared my shoulders and jerked my hand out of his arm. "It was sex, Santi."

Another car approached and I recognized it as Lorenzo's. Right on time. Without another word, I rushed towards it. I couldn't wait to get out of here. Even his slight touch on my wrist burned through me and straight to my core. This lust for him would be the death of me. My heart I could hide, but not my body's reaction.

Once I got into Lorenzo's car, I slammed the door a bit too forcefully. My brother's eyes observed me, and my insides shook with agitation. The irritation danced over my skin, the itch to snap and relieve the frustration heavy.

Lorenzo's soft chuckle snapped me out of my fuming. "Lover's quarrel?" he teased.

My heart skidded to a halt and my breath stuck in my throat. "W-what?"

"You and Santi," he added, like we were talking about flavors of coffee. "You've had it in for him for a while."

"I-I..." I should deny it, but the words got stuck in my throat. The truth of the matter was that I had loved Santi for a very long time. It was hard to remember when I didn't love him. Innocent crush turning into an all-consuming love. Unfortunately, it was one-sided. For Santi, I was just another girl. Not even his type. He preferred blondes.

"You love him," Lorenzo finished for me. "If you try that 'it's that time of the month' bullshit with me, , I will pull over and give you an earful of ranting."

I sighed. There was no use denying it.

"I don't know how not to love him, Lorenzo," I whispered my admission, desperation lacing my voice.

"That's heavy," he replied, his eyes fleeting my way, observing me pensively. "I'll be the first to admit it, Amore. It surprised me when I first picked up on it. You and Santi just don't seem to have much in common."

"I know," I said. "But with him... I feel safe. Alive. Happy." I pressed my palm to my forehead. "I can't explain it. I thought it was just a crush. Except that the older I got, I felt more for him. The world just seems better with him."

He nodded in understanding. "I never realized you were such a romantic, sister."

"Me either," I retorted dryly. "I wish I could just turn it off."

"But then you wouldn't be you." Lorenzo had a way of making me feel better. Every time.

"Please don't tell anyone," I pleaded.

"Of course not," he promised. "I would never break your trust."

I reached over and placed my hand over his on the wheel. "Thank you!"

"The question is what to do about it," he muttered pensively. I pulled back my hand and placed them both on my lap.

"This whole mess with this stupid marriage arrangement..." I trailed off. Though I wasn't convinced that Santi would have kept me.

"To the wrong brother," he added.

Oh, was it ever the wrong brother!

"Either way, Lorenzo," I muttered. "I won't be marrying Adriano. I just have to figure out a way to stop this madness without causing war between the two families."

"Don't stress, Amore," he deadpanned. "If all else fails, I'll kidnap you. You won't be marrying Adriano."

My brows scrunched at the odd comment. He was never the one for drama.

CHAPTER 56

Regret tasted bitter.

I watched her walk away from me with her head held high. She didn't wear a crown, but she might as well have. The princess grew into a queen. Her words were clear; she would have given it all up for us to remain together.

Just the thought of giving her up killed pieces of me on the inside. But I refused to give her up. The heiress had become a permanent resident in my heart.

"What the fuck, Adriano?" I slammed my brother's body against the wall, rattling the bookshelves. He was still staying at Pà's place, so it was easy to swing by there. We were living close enough.

The fucker asked me to meet him at the house. I just came back from a visit to an underground drug club led by the Anderson Venezuelans. After Ulrich was killed, oddly enough, nobody disbursed. It was like he was still alive, guiding them. Or there was another goddamn Anderson brother that I had to find.

I had blood stains on my clothes when I arrived there and needed a shower. Imagine my surprise when Amore showed up in the middle of it all.

"What's your problem, brother?" Adriano smirked. "I thought you'd be thanking me."

I narrowed my eyes on him in annoyance. It has been too easy to annoy me lately. "You are my problem."

"Can you be more specific?" he drawled, grating on my nerves. "Does the idea of me fucking Amore bother you? Or the fact she will be my wife? Or that she would suck my dick?"

"What?" My voice was dangerously low. The anger burned my throat, right down to my chest, and marred my vision with a red haze. My blood iced over, trying to overcome the boiling rage. It wouldn't bode well for me to kill my own brother.

"I think she'll like getting on her knees for me," Adriano dead-panned. "She's always been so eager to please and—"

My fist connected with his mouth before he could finish the sentence. I hauled Adriano up by his collar and punched him with my other hand, straight on his nose. His eyes watered from the impact and blood instantly trickled down from his nose. I didn't stop. I landed another blow to his gut, then another to the jaw. The fire washed over me, all the tension of the last two months from denying myself what I wanted most of all in the world catching up.

A film of red tainted my vision, and my knuckles were bruised from the force of my blows, burning with each punch when his words pene-trated through the red mist.

"She loves you," Adriano said, spitting blood onto the floor.

He grinned, blood on his face and his teeth. He wasn't fighting back, and my fist paused midair. Maybe my brother had lost his damn mind. Would that warrant cancellation of the marriage contract?

Jesus! It was unreal how much that single thought consumed my mind. I wanted that woman with emerald eyes and red hair. Just her. It was driving me wild. Maybe I'd be the one to finally lose my damn mind.

"She loves *you*, Santi," he repeated.

Those words pierced a hole through my chest. "She told you?"

"She didn't need to. I've known her long enough to see it written all over her face. It was the reason I asked you both to be there. Thought you two could work it out. Apparently not, so you need my help."

I thought about his words. Neither Amore nor I mentioned the words. Didn't she tell me only a few hours earlier it was just sex?

I sat down on the ground next to my brother, both of us breathing hard. All this had become a clusterfuck.

"Do you love her, Adriano?" I didn't want to know the answer, but there had to be a small shred of decency still left in me to care about my brother and his feelings. Those two had been joined at the hip since she entered our lives. I owed him that much.

Though I still planned on blackmailing, kidnapping, and marrying her before she had a chance to marry my brother. Her father could make all the fucking plans he wanted, but she would be mine. I'd give him war if he wanted it. Fuck, I'd give him all my territory if it would appease him. But she would be my wife.

"I do love her." Adriano's answer shook something inside me. "But I'm thinking it is not as intense as this shit you have going on." Fuck, was it that obvious? "And more importantly, Amore has made it clear she only loves me as a friend."

Peace settled between us, and for the first time in a while, it felt like my brother and I finally saw eye to eye.

"Do you have a plan?" Adriano asked. I turned my face to him, then nodded. Pà would have pulled both of our ears if he saw the state of us right now. The Russo Don fighting his younger brother over a girl. He'd either kick us in the ribs or get a kick out of this situation. Bet he was laughing from up there or down there... wherever he was.

"Good," he muttered. "Because I have some information that could help you."

CHAPTER 57

Amore

Two days, one hour and thirty minutes since I ran into Santi and we shared that searing kiss. No, I wasn't counting hours and seconds. My stupid heart was.

I haven't heard from Adriano, and somehow it felt like I had lost both Russo men. Nothing seemed to be going my way lately. Dad was vigorously planning the wedding I didn't want. Lorenzo was constantly meeting with the Russo's, much to Dad's dismay. Uncle Vincent and Maria started dating. Even Grandma was constantly throwing curveballs my way.

Like today, she decided she would have a company party at Santi's nightclub. The Orchid. For Christ's sake! Of all the places in this city, this is the best one she could come up with. Unbelievable!

The only one that was acting the same was Luigi. It didn't bode well for this family at all. I loved my brother, but he could be so damn crazy and reckless.

DeAngelo and I arrived late by design. I wanted to spend as little time as possible there. I hadn't been to The Orchid since my first kiss with Santi. I really had to snap out of this Santi coma.

The driver pulled up at the entrance of the nightclub, letting DeAngelo and I out. There was a long line of people waiting to enter the club, but we went towards the guard and the private entrance. He must have recognized us and immediately opened the door.

We walked through the dark club, DeAngelo's keen eyes on our surroundings. Though considering the owner, I had a feeling this might be one of the safer places.

"This should be fun," I muttered, my mood sour. The dance floor was turned into a makeshift walkway. It wouldn't be a Regalè company party if a few models weren't strutting around, showing off some designs.

"We just have to make it an hour." DeAngelo didn't look too thrilled to be here either.

"Anything on George?" I asked him under my breath.

He shook his head. "I'd bet my life he is here in the city. We destroyed everything he owns in Venezuela. He has nowhere else to run."

My chest constricted at the thought of his betrayal. It made my stomach churn. He was the cause of Mom's suffering. I could forgive him for everything but that.

I wished Grandpa would have given the bloody cartel to Anderson. Maybe Mom would still be alive. That business wasn't worth her life. Nor my grandfather's.

My eyes roamed the room. Uncle Vincent was here along with Maria, and I couldn't help a big grin. I was happy for them. She was a good woman and Uncle Vincent seemed smitten. Though I did warn him if he hurt my business partner, I'd gut him. He chuckled like I uttered the funniest joke. I was rather serious. I liked her a lot and didn't want to see her hurt.

"My favorite sister!" A pair of hands wrapped around me and lifted me off the ground. I threw my head back and laughed.

"Lorenzo, how many times do I have to tell you," I said through a soft teasing smile. "I'm your only sister."

He rolled his eyes. "Minor, insignificant detail."

My gaze caught Luigi leaning against the wall, his hands in his black suit pockets. He was shooting intense glares across the room, and I followed his gaze to find Santi, Adriano, and Carrera standing together.

The three were talking and it seemed Adriano was on better terms with his brother.

How good for them! I thought bitterly but immediately regret hit me. Adriano and Santi loved each other and despite their disagreements, they stuck together. It was the way it should be.

"Why is Luigi mad at the Russos?" I asked Lorenzo.

He shrugged. "Santi shot him."

My head whipped around, searching my brother's face for signs of a joke. He was dead serious.

"When? Why?"

Lorenzo looked like he wouldn't answer me. Then a resigned breath left his lips. "Dad will shoot me if he knows I told you."

"I won't tell him," I promised.

"It was a few months ago," Lorenzo retorted. "Luigi owed Santi and surprise, surprise, our big brother didn't deliver."

I scrunched my eyebrows in confusion. "Like money?"

"No, not money. A favor."

Involuntarily my eyes darted across the room to Santi again to catch him already watching me. His heavy gaze sent a warm rush down my spine and heat rushed to my cheeks. I prayed it was dark enough that nobody would see it. This reaction to him had to go.

"How about a dance with your old man?" Dad's voice came from behind me, and I startled, spinning around.

"I don't recall ever seeing you dance," I told him. Truthfully, I wasn't in the mood to dance. I'd rather be anywhere but here. "And how come Grandma invited you and the Russos?"

Dad shrugged, then tilted his head towards the dance floor next to the makeshift runway. There were lanterns hung around the dance-floor, giving it a soft glow, and separating it from the rest of the room. The only people dancing were Uncle Vincent and his girlfriend.

"I love dancing," he claimed with a smile. Extending his hand, he added softly, "You can't avoid me forever, Amore."

With a heavy sigh, I reluctantly admitted he was right. I couldn't avoid him forever, but I couldn't help feeling angry that he'd commit me to something without talking to me or considering my wishes. That was the problem with the Cosa Nostra. Their notions were far too backwards for the current century.

I slid my hand into his and we made my way to the dance floor. The moment we stepped on the dance floor, a soft country tune came on.

I raised my eyebrow and smiled softly. "Country, really?"

"It was your mother's favorite." He pulled me closer in one swift move, and I chuckled, partly surprised.

"Wow, Dad," I muttered slightly impressed. "I never took you for a smooth dancer." We moved together to the George Strait song "Check Yes or No." I guess I shouldn't be surprised that he knew Mom loved country music.

"This was the first song that your mother and I danced to." His tone was wistful. I pulled away slightly, searching his face.

He rarely talked about his time with Mom. It was odd to think I came about due to his infidelity, and my mother's affair with a married man. I knew that being a bastard child in these traditional families was frowned upon. The only reason they tolerated me was because of who my father was.

I didn't give a shit. I knew my self-worth, and I had my grandmother to thank for that. It must have rubbed off. At least in all aspects of my life but my love life. All my insecurities revolved around a single, tall, dark-haired man with dark eyes and ink covering his right arm.

"She loved country music," I said in a soft voice. "A lot."

"You look so much like her," he rasped. "She would have been so proud of you."

I blinked, swallowing the lump in my throat. I often wondered whether Mom would approve of what I was doing. I didn't remember her ever raising her voice, never mind being violent. And here I was causing havoc. Though maybe I was more similar to her than my father since violence wasn't sitting well with me.

Mom and I shared a love for fashion and designs. We shared our physical appearance, other than my red hair. But other than that, I couldn't remember much of what her goals and dreams were.

"I- I-" I cleared my throat, thick emotions stuck in my throat. "I don't remember much of what she wanted me to do. Only her... last words."

Her last words calling for revenge.

Dad nodded, understanding in his eyes. I was thirteen when she died, but life was a series of constant adventures back then. She and George were always busy, and then in a blink, everything changed. We were taken, the cartel's thirst for vengeance against Mom for crimes she wasn't even aware of. And the worst betrayal was George's. He lured me into going after those orchids, and when we were taken, Mom came for me.

"Her last message to me was to keep you safe," he said. "And out of the criminal world. This marriage to Adriano will secure that."

My heart screamed in protest. I wholeheartedly disagreed with him, but I didn't want to ruin this moment.

"My only regret, Amore," he said, "... was that I didn't know about you until you were thirteen. Maybe I could have helped her and..."

And she'd still be here with us. Or would my father be dead too? I didn't know how it would have all worked out. Besides, my grandmother had a point. He was married and marriages in traditional Italian families were for life.

"Dad, how did you know to look for me in South America?" I asked.

A sigh slipped through his lips and his shoulders slumped. Suddenly, he looked tired. "She called me. First time in thirteen years." I held my breath waiting for him to continue. "It was before she went after you. She got a note from the cartel. Either she came willingly, or they'd start sending parts of you back in a box." I knew how the story ended but still dread shot through my spine. "I begged her to wait for me to get there. So we could go together."

My steps faltered, and suddenly I remembered. We stood in the middle of the floor, a few people dancing around us, but the two of us stood immobile. "She meant you," I whispered. "She kept saying, 'Your dad will save us. He's coming for us.'"

He nodded. "I flew out immediately, but she was gone before I got to Colombia. I knew she wouldn't wait. She said she would, but I knew better... Still, I'd hoped."

A shadow passed through his expression, and for the first time, it became clear that my dad was fighting his own demons when it came to my mom's death.

"I'm sorry," I whispered. My heart hurt for them. For me.

He nodded, sadness lurking in his dark eyes. "So am I."

"Did you love her or was it just a fling?" The question slipped out before I could hold it back. Grandmother had love for the duration of her marriage. She hadn't taken another man to her bed since. At least that was what she told me, not that I needed to know. She loved Grandfather, for all his ruthless ways. It didn't matter to her that he was a criminal. It didn't matter to me that Santi was a criminal.

Maybe it was something about the women of this family that craved darkness. I was starting to see a trend, though not in a good way.

We resumed the slow dance, the song fading in the background.

"I loved her, but my pride was too big back then." Our steps moved in sync while I hung onto every word, the glimpse of what had happened finally being offered. "The last time I saw your mother, she asked me where I saw the two of us. Future wise. I told her that I had purchased a penthouse for us. I should have known better than that. She wouldn't have accepted less than she deserved. Rightly so." I frowned that he would be so stupid to think that was good enough for her. He should have known that any daughter of Regina wouldn't be a side piece to any man. "She left me that day with the impression she was good with it. It was the last time I saw her."

I was convinced that Dad and Mom could have been good together. Despite their differences, they fit. Dad was dark, brooding, and ruthless. True mold of the Cosa Nostra. Mom was light, cheerful, creative, warm-hearted, and forgiving. Yet, they fit. The possibility of happiness was stolen from them.

We continued dancing in silence, both of us lost in our thoughts. I knew from my brothers that Dad's marriage was an arrangement, a marriage contract, and it was a normal occurrence in this world. It wasn't in my mother's world. Grandma married for love. I thought Mom loved George, but now, I wasn't so sure. Thinking back, it seemed like they were very good friends, but it was hard to rely on the fuzzy memory of a child. Grandma had said that George was Grandfather's acquaintance.

The song ended and I was surprised when it switched to another country song. Alan Jackson's "Big Green Eyes." Even more surprising was that Dad wanted another dance.

"Okay, Dad," I agreed. "You are full of surprises today." He chuckled but went along. One hand in his, I raised my other one, swinging it in the air, laughing. "Just follow the music. No steps."

"What kind of song doesn't have steps?" he muttered but he followed just fine.

"Bennetti, you've really got to keep up with the trends." Grandma showed up on my left. "Let's show them what we did during your sleepovers, Amore."

I threw my head back and laughed. "Do you know the words, Grandma?"

She waved her hand. "I'm a quick study." I recited the words and she followed them, and we broke into the same dance moves we used to do in the middle of her penthouse living room.

Seeing them like this, I relished in the fantasy of all of us getting along. All of us being happy. *I want it all*, the words I had once spoken echoed in my brain. It might have been selfish, considering so many people had nothing. Yet, the wanting wouldn't go away. I wanted my dad, brothers, uncle, grandma, best friend, and most of all, I wanted Santi.

Grandma must have not been too keen on moving her body the same way we used to, so instead, she and Dad resorted back to a two-step.

"I never thought I'd see you two dancing together," I remarked with a chuckle.

"We are practicing being civil for the wedding," Dad replied. The comment cast a shadow over my mood, but I refused to let it bother me. Grandma winked with a smile that reminded me of a cat that ate the mouse.

She had to be up to something.

The song switched again to Tate McRae's "That Way." Both Grandma and Dad gave up trying to dance freestyle. Lorenzo stepped up and danced with me while Grandma did an oldie dance with Dad.

The goosebumps broke through my skin listening to the words. I was addicted to Santi, all the while he was kissing me in the dark and away from everyone. I wanted him to lay claim, like he did when we were alone. I wanted to be his, yet just like with my own parents, it wasn't in my cards. It just hurt so damn bad.

My eyes flitted across the room and caught Santi's gaze burning into me, making me dizzy with the intensity of it. It would be so much easier if I didn't want him so much.

"Are you alright?" Lorenzo's voice was low and soft. "Adriano is watching you like he's mourning you."

I swallowed. Somehow when Santi looked at me, everyone else faded.

"I guess I should say hi to him, huh?" I muttered.

He shrugged. "I don't give a shit if you greet him. I just want to see you happy."

A loud whistle traveled through the nightclub and had us turning our heads. It was as if Adriano heard us talking about him. He strode towards us, with his powerful strides.

"What? No dance for me?" he asked with a wide grin.

My heart stopped and so did my legs. "Oh my gosh, Adriano, what happened to you?" I reached out and touched his face.

He shrugged, taking my hand away from his face but keeping it in his grip. "Got into a fight."

"With whom?" Lorenzo taunted. "A fucking boxer?"

Adriano laughed it off. "You should see the other guy," he retorted dryly.

My brother choked out a laugh. "I'm looking at him. The only thing that looks off on him are his knuckles."

My head swiveled Lorenzo's way, then followed his gaze. *Santi?*

Glancing at Santi's knuckles, they looked red and bruised, like always. Though it was hard to see in the dark of the nightclub.

"Your brother hit you?" I asked Adriano, frowning.

"Nah, we wrestled a bit." Adriano didn't seem worried about it at all.

"I don't know, Adriano," I snorted softly. "It looks like he mainly wrestled you."

As if pulling me with an invisible force, I met Santi's eyes again. If I was smart, I'd move to another city, so I'd never see him again. I was cursed with the memories of our time together. Yet, it was the happiest time of my life. I remembered every word, every kiss, every touch, and dancing together under the Italian sky.

Sometimes I wished I could just forget it all so every look his way didn't fluster me so much and make my heart ache with longing.

Adriano and I started dancing. Lorenzo grabbed a girl and started working his magic on her while every so often returning his watchful eye on me. Luigi remained in his corner, glaring towards Santi. The latter remained like a dark shadow glued to his spot, my body painfully aware of every single glance our way.

I had to stop keeping track of that man.

Grandma and Dad slowly made their exit as tunes turned more upbeat. I danced with Adriano to two songs. Just as I was ready to tell him I was done for the night, the music stopped for two heartbeats and re-started.

"Am I throwing you off?"

"Nope."

"I didn't think so."

My heart skipped, then memories flooded me. The song "Promiscuous" by Nelly Furtado came on and with it the painful memories of when I felt so happy. It was the last song we danced to in Italy before we left that little local restaurant turned dance floor. I thought we were both happy, and for a fraction of time, I dreamt of a bright future with the man I loved. How stupid was I?

My eyes shot to the DJ through the dark room, expecting foul play. But he was there alone, messing with his fancy equipment.

"You don't like this song?" Adriano asked innocently, and I forced a smile on my face.

"It's okay." If I never heard it play again, it would be too soon. "I'm kind of tired," I muttered, ready to head out.

"Oh, come on," he pulled me back to him. "Don't leave me hanging."

"Santi..." The wrong name slipped, and I could have bitten my tongue. *Goddamn it!*

Several heartbeats passed as Adriano studied me pensively. We stood motionless, staring at each other, his hand wrapped around my wrist, unwilling to let go.

"It's Adriano," he said softly. "Santi is my brother." I swallowed hard, my heart squeezing under my chest. "Remember?"

I nodded, feeling like shit. This marriage arrangement would cost me my best friend; I could see it coming at me like a freight train.

"Dance with me, Amore," he drawled. My feet remained glued to my spot, unwilling to move. "Please," he added softly. The look on his face hit me right in my chest. I couldn't refuse him again, unwilling to hurt him more than I already have. More than I would when I finally refused this marriage.

Our bodies moved in sync, but the sizzling attraction wasn't there - for neither one of us. He didn't have to say it; I just knew it. I'd seen Adriano stalk his prey and go into seduction mode. There was none of it here.

Our feet moved together, left and right. Back and forth. Then round and round. When he twirled me around and I twirled back to him, he caught me smoothly.

"You can tell me anything, you know." His words startled me. The statement came out of nowhere. "I'll always be here for you. The same way you were always there for me."

My eyes stung and the lump in my throat grew. I took a shuddering breath, my eyes welled up, and my skin got hot. I tried to clear my throat and swallow the lump choking me but instead, a tear trickled down my cheek.

His touch was feather light when brushing it off with his thumb. "You trust me that little?"

My eyes lifted to his, the dark gaze so similar to his brother's. Yet so very different.

"It's not that," I rasped. How could I tell him I loved his brother? Slept with him. That seeing him every day would be torture. All that man had to do was snap his fingers, and I feared I'd open my legs and let him do whatever he wanted to me. "I'm in love with someone else," I admitted softly. He didn't seem surprised. "I love you; I really do. But only as my best friend. It's not fair to either one of us to settle," I muttered.

An expression passed his face but then he smiled. "I know." I noted he didn't say he only loved me as a friend and something in my stomach knotted. "I want you to be happy."

It made me feel rotten to the core. Adriano was a much better person than I was.

The song ended and I sighed with relief. Too soon because Adriano kept dancing, keeping me close.

"Everything will change soon," he whispered. "Just let me enjoy a dance with you."

Our eyes met and I watched him in confusion. He was full of cryptic messages, and I didn't follow any of their meaning.

A slower song played, and a few other couples stepped onto the floor as Adriano and I slow-danced to the soft tunes of "Let Me Down Slowly." My thoughts traveled to two months ago. Santi didn't let me down slowly for sure. He just dropped me. Was I doing the same thing to Adriano? I guess there was no way to let someone down slowly if one person in the relationship was still in love.

My eyes flicked across the floor to Santi like a magnet. He was talking to Gabriel Carrera. Every time I saw him, the pain in my chest swelled, and it felt like someone stabbed a knife straight into my heart.

"Where are your thoughts?" Adriano asked, his mouth close to my ear.

With Santi. Always with him. I forced myself to look away, focusing on Adriano.

None of the fluttering feelings similar to when his brother whispered in my ear appeared. Was this how Mom felt being married to George after loving Dad? I didn't want the same fate. I wanted love, passion, everything. *I want it all.*

"Not sure," I answered.

"Remember the first time we snuck into Santi's strip club?"

Another sharp pain pierced through my chest, but I ignored it. I was growing accustomed to it. Raising my eyes and hiding my pain behind the smile, I nodded. It seemed so long ago.

Adriano bent his head and pressed his lips against mine. "It's okay to love him too." I gasped against his lips and stared at him wide eyed. "After all, he'll be your brother-in-law."

CHAPTER 58

Santino

I watched my younger brother kiss the woman that belonged to me, and I had to fight the urge not to pull out my gun and shoot him. What kind of bastard did that make me? Every cell demanded I take Amore and make her mine. Kill everyone, burn this motherfucking city to the ground. Nobody knew how soft her lips felt against mine, how she melted under my touch. That right was mine and mine alone.

Yet here I was, standing frozen while my blood boiled as I watched my brother make out with my woman. My fucking woman! No ring on her finger, no words, would take that away. She was mine!

The moment Amore entered the club the clock stopped. I sensed her before I saw her, like every heartbeat of hers connected with mine.

"Remember the plan," Gabriel groaned next to me. "It has to look convincing so her father is not suspicious."

"Fuck. Her. Father." I gritted out. Before I kicked my plan into motion, I'd talked to Savio one more time. It was his last chance.

Her father refused to amend the contract. Fucking again! All because she wasn't meant to be in the underworld. But that wasn't the only reason, and I knew it. He didn't want my blood-soiled, filthy hands on his daughter. Too fucking late! I'd touched her. I'd felt her soft flesh under my rough hands. Heard her moans. Felt her pussy clench. She was meant for me. Only for me.

Amore's brother joined Gabriel and me.

"You grip that glass any tighter, and you'll shatter it," Lorenzo muttered under his breath. I narrowed my eyes at him, daring him to say anything else. I wouldn't mind shooting someone tonight and maybe beat a few people too. It would be one way to relieve the tension. My anger burned hot, and not in a good way.

"Fuck, Santi! Get yourself together," Lorenzo growled. "No way in fucking hell I'll let you handle my sister in this state."

I downed the drink in one gulp, placed it on the tray and walked away without acknowledging him.

Lorenzo had offered to help me get Amore. He approached me yesterday. He said he was only doing it for his sister. Of course, I didn't reveal all my cards to him. I kept them close to ensure nothing went wrong.

CHAPTER 59

Amore

I stared at my best friend dumbfounded, trying to understand what exactly he meant by that comment.

I didn't want to cause a rift between the Russos and Bennettis, but his comment sounded dangerously close to agreement that we shouldn't get married. Didn't it?

Every cell in me objected to marrying my best friend, brother to the man I loved. Regardless of whether Santi wanted me or not.

The party at the club was in full swing, the music playing in the background while chattering and laughter filled the room, people danced, and models strutted on the runway. The place was full of men in suits and women in beautiful gowns, glittering under dim lights.

"How about we grab a drink?" Adriano offered.

"Great idea," I told him. It was getting slightly hot. I snuck a look at the clock on the wall. It still hadn't been an hour. Unfortunately.

We walked together towards the bar, every so often stopped by a familiar face.

"Were you always this popular?" Adriano asked as we left yet another couple. We still hadn't made it to the bar area. "Or did I not notice it because I always snuck away?"

I chuckled. He was right, usually he spent maybe thirty minutes with me once we arrived and then ditched me for a skirt. "No, I wasn't popular," I told him. "More like awkward."

He chuckled, gently pulling my ponytail. "You were never awkward."

"Amore," a voice called from behind me, and I turned around to see Maria catching up to us. A smile spread on my face. I saw her and Uncle Vincent dancing when I came in but didn't want to interrupt them on the dance floor.

I pulled my hand out of Adriano's and hugged her. "I'm sorry I haven't come around to see you yet."

"Not to worry, bella mia." She kissed both my cheeks. It reminded me so much of Italy. I often wondered why she didn't come to visit me there. She seemed like she would blend right in there.

"You look beautiful," I complimented her. She seemed to be glowing.

A wide grin lit up her face. "I know. This talented girl designed it."

"And this talented girl sewed it," I retorted back, and we both chuckled.

"Italy suits you. You flourished. I'm surprised some Italian boy didn't snatch you up." My smile faltered a bit, but I didn't comment. "And your dress, it is beautiful."

I glanced down at myself. It was a green dress with slits going up to my mid-thigh. There were tiny, clear beadings strategically placed, flashing a hint of sparkle when I moved, catching under the lights. I couldn't help it, but ever since Santi told me he loved seeing me in green best, I tended to lean towards wearing it. You'd think it would be the opposite but here I was. Though I had to wonder if subconsciously I did it on purpose.

I sighed. I could finally understand Mr. Russo's words. I wanted his eldest son but was given his youngest. And I didn't want to lose either one of them, yet they were both slipping out of my hands.

"You look drop dead gorgeous." Uncle Vincent joined us with DeAngelo right behind him.

"Amore is the best looking one in the family," DeAngelo said smiling.

Uncle Vincent slapped him on the back. "That's right, DeAngelo." Zio turned his eyes to Adriano. "No Russo deserves a Bennetti girl."

I shared a fleeting glance with Adriano and rolled my eyes. Though a warm smile played around my lips and my eyes softened.

"Thanks, Zio." My gaze roamed over his form. "You don't look too shabby yourself. Your girlfriend is treating you well. I like her very much."

He pulled me into an embrace. "I know, I know. I better not mess up with your business partner." He glanced sideways at Maria and his face instantly softened. Those two would be good together.

"Well, Adriano and I were on our way to the bar," I murmured, feeling happy and jealous at the same time for Uncle Vincent and Maria.

Before I moved off, he wrapped me in a tight hug. He was as tall as dad, so my face hit his chest.

"Didn't I tell you the Russos were bad for your heart?" he murmured softly against my hair. The words sent a pang of dread through my heart. I thought I hid all my feelings. Could Zio see right through me? Could others?

"Yes, Zio," I murmured against his chest. Except, I couldn't stop loving either one of them any more than I could stop breathing.

Adriano chuckled, humorously. "What are you two whispering about?"

I pulled back, pushing all my emotions away.

"Family secrets," I joked half-heartedly.

"And Amore Bennetti has plenty of those." My back tingled in awareness as Santi's voice washed over me like the waves of the warm seas. Turning around, I met his gaze and narrowed my eyes. Why was he here?

I kept my expression closed off as my eyes skimmed up to his face to meet his gaze. Bitterness swelled inside me that I should be subjected to his presence during a Regalè event. He looked too damn good. Too tempting.

Even wearing his gear in a Venezuelan rainforest during our encounter at the compound, he looked good, but in a suit... he had wistful gazes turning his way. Santi was born to wear a suit.

He wore a black three-piece with a crisp, white dress shirt and a black tie. I couldn't tear my eyes away from his strong, broad shoulders. His whole body was a muscular masterpiece. The way he stood there watching me, commanding me with just his gaze. Like he owned me.

The urge to lean into him was so strong, I dug my fingernails into the palm of my hands to keep still. My eyes lowered and locked on his tattooed hand at his side, holding his phone. I swallowed hard, and my heart fluttered so fast I had a hard time breathing. Those hands were mine; they belonged on my skin.

I had no right to him. He had no right to me.

His eyes dropped to my outfit, then lazily returned and lingered on my lips. A spark flickered to life in his eyes and his expression darkened.

From the corner of my eye, I spotted Grandmother approaching and groaned inwardly. It was getting too crowded.

As if Uncle Vincent and Maria heard my thoughts, they disbursed.

"Amore, darling." She hugged me and pressed a kiss on my cheek.

Adriano threw me a glance, rolled his eyes and left, pulling DeAngelo along. Adriano didn't care for my grandma. DeAngelo never let on either way.

She didn't even glance their way as they walked away.

Ignoring everyone else, she focused her attention on me. "I didn't have a chance to tell you earlier. You look so beautiful. I love the dress. Your design?"

I smoothed my hand down my waist. "Yes."

She took my hand in hers, and by the expression on her face, I knew I wouldn't like her next words.

"I want to make a speech today," she announced, her lips curved into a slightly sadistic smile. The one that she usually reserved to spite my father.

"Not today, Regina," my father's voice growled. Where did he come from?

"This is my party, Bennetti, and I'll do whatever I please." Her tone was full of venom. "Just because we shared a dance or two doesn't mean we are on the same side."

I shook my head. It wasn't like they were enemies but hearing them talk, you'd definitely think they were. There would never be any love lost between Grandmother and my father. And I was so tired of being stuck in the middle. My skin burned with the need to lash out, to scream, to tell everyone to go to hell, but I kept a tight lid on it.

"Cut your shit, Regina." Dad's jaw ticked; he was teetering on the edge.

I was an heiress to the Regalè Empire, the Perèz Cartel, started my own business, a daughter of an Italian Don, yet I was being pushed and jerked around as they saw fit. I was so fucking close to my limits.

Grandma's green eyes studied me, and I kept her gaze. A wave of agitation ran through me. She was waiting, looking for something... but I kept it together. Though in my head I screamed.

"It's getting late," I muttered, forcing a smile. My eyes skimmed over Dad, Grandma, and Santi. Others were smart and had left the battlefield. "I'm going to find DeAngelo and get going." *Before I lose my shit.*

Grandma just ignored me, her gaze shifting to the right of me where Santi now stood.

"Russo, thank you for allowing us to have this party here." Her eyes darted over Dad and rested on Santi for a few seconds before returning to me. "Amore's wedding will be the event of the century," she continued, and I swore she was taunting me. "It will be covered by papers around the globe."

"How do you know about it?" Dad hissed, and my eyes snapped to him, then to my grandmother. She wasn't supposed to know. I didn't tell her and just assumed Dad did. Then who would have told her?

"I have a right to know everything about my granddaughter, Bennetti." Her eyes flashed to me and then returned to my father, a storm lurking in her green gaze. "Have you noticed all the reporters and coverage Regalè Fashion is having tonight? It's all thanks to Amore's hard work."

Something was about to happen. I could feel it in the pit of my stomach. I stood still, my spine rigid, the tension around us so thick you could cut it with a knife. *I'm going to snap. Any second now.*

"I don't know why in the fuck you insisted we all come," he gritted out. "I already know Amore knows her stuff."

I hated these two bickering. I was tired and having Santi so close to me, set me on edge. My pulse thundered and my hand came to my chest.

Like I could calm my pulse or the agitation welling inside me. "Well, I'm going to—"

"Stay," Grandma ordered. I had to bite my tongue not to snap at her and tell her I wasn't a dog.

I glared at both of them, frustration crawling through my skin.

Dad's phone rang at that moment. "This is business," he muttered, looking at his phone. "I'll be right back." He pointed his finger at Grandma and gritted through his teeth, "You and I will talk later."

He strode away, leaving me in this clusterfuck.

Grandma's gaze shifted to Santi. "You ready, Russo?" Her gaze went cold. "I seem to recall you claiming you were more trouble than your father. It might be the only time that I agree with a Russo."

My eyes ping-ponged between the two.

What. The. Fuck. Is. Going. On. Here?

Santi eyed her coolly; he had that primal killer look about him and gave off warning signals in all directions. I noticed his fist clenched at his side and the edgy silence persisted. My nerves teetered, watching his dark gaze unwavering and threatening on Grandmother.

Grandma Regina usually evoked fear from people. Not from Santi.

Out of the blue, Grandma chuckled, glanced in the direction Dad disappeared then shook her head, dark amusement in her eyes.

"I'll happily watch as Bennettis and Russos kill each other off," she announced randomly.

I stared in confusion at Santi, but I couldn't read a single emotion in his eyes. This was the Russo Don, no soft edges. I had no idea what was going on between the two, but I knew it was nothing good. My blood went cold as I held my breath.

"Okay, let the show begin," she cackled. "Bennetti was always slightly blind. He couldn't see things right in front of his eyes."

"I don't give a shit what Bennetti sees or doesn't, Regina." His words were a dark warning as he watched her with a clear threat.

There were too many loaded looks happening between the two. I was clueless on the hidden meanings these two had going on. My pulse rate climbed to an all-time high, the anxiety replacing my earlier anger.

A shiver of uneasiness coursed through me, my eyes darting between the two of them.

"Grandma?" I whispered, dread pooling in the pit of my belly.

She looked away from Santi, and our eyes connected. Taking my hand, she patted it gently. "Not to worry, granddaughter. I have an announcement to make."

She strode off like the queen she was, and suddenly my temple throbbed like a fucking bitch. And I blamed Santi for it.

Glaring at him, I spat out bitterly. "What the hell was that?"

Santi smirked and did things to my insides. I bit into my lower lip, trying to replace this hot desire with pain. His eyes fell to my lips, darkening around the edges. His gaze burned like dark coals, sending my pulse into hyperactive mode. A nervous shudder trickled down my spine. This response to him was downright unhealthy. An aching pulse exploded between my legs and my body quivered with a lust that I was desperate to kill.

I had to get a grip on all this shit.

I had to tear my eyes away from him. I had to... I had to stop this scorching heat whenever I was around him. Then why was I standing here like a statue, staring at him, while the whole room faded into a background.

"Ladies and gentlemen. Amore Bennetti." Grandma's voice boomed over the loudspeaker, prompting me to jump. My eyes flickered towards the exit. It wasn't that far. If I speed walk, I'd be out of here in no time. Then the night would be over, and we could leave the family drama for another day.

Grandma tapped on the microphone, clearly aware that I wasn't paying attention. With an exasperated sigh, I slowly turned towards the elevated runway where my grandmother stood. Everyone had their attention on her like she was a goddess up there, and she relished being the center of attention, unlike me. The flashing of cameras, chattering of the reporters, it all ceased with anticipation of what Regina Regalè had to say.

I felt her gaze on me, and something unsettling came over me. I knew that look. She always wore it when she had to make hard decisions, the ones she didn't like but knew were the best outcome for the company. Or her family.

"You all know how proud I have been of my granddaughter."

Grandma's voice spread through every corner of the room. Even on Russo territory, she dominated. "And today, I have two major announcements to make."

Her eyes shifted to Santino right next to me and I wondered why. With a side glance, I pondered what was going on between the two of them.

Without a shred of doubt, I knew I hadn't fooled her in Italy. She knew I fell for Santino Russo. She called him the wrong man. Then why did it feel so right? My damn, stupid body wanted him and nobody else. My heart rejected the idea of letting another man in. It didn't matter how much this love hurt or if it killed me because a life without Santi wasn't worth living. He was part of every heartbeat and every breath.

The spotlight shone on me and instinctively, I faked a smile while my back stiffened. Being the face for Regalè Fashion House, I'd learned to hide behind a smile. Though I wasn't as good as Grandma. It was the reason I liked hiding behind designing. It was easier for me. My petty revenge to ensure Santi saw me everywhere backfired... a little.

"Amore has been part of Regalè Fashion House even as a little girl. For almost a decade now, in one form or another, she has learned the ins and outs of the company," Grandma spoke in her boardroom voice. "Over the last few months, she's been the leader this company needed." She let the words hang in the air. For dramatic effect, I guessed. Then she continued. "As such, I am permanently stepping down. My grand-daughter is ready to take full responsibility for *her* empire."

The smile on my face froze. She had talked about it for so long, but I hadn't anticipated that she'd make the final decision and announcement without talking to me first. The flash of cameras went into turbo mode and the sound of shocked gasps filled the room. The legend of Regalè House would forever be remembered.

She raised her hands and immediately the whispered chatter ceased, the flash of cameras stopped.

Smile, Amore. Mother's voice echoed in my brain. *Smile.*

I knew she'd drop another bomb on me. Whatever she had to say, it would send reporters into a frenzy. Otherwise, they wouldn't be here. Everything Grandma did was methodical and with purpose.

"She loves her dramatics," I muttered under my breath.

"That she does," Lorenzo whispered in my ear and my head snapped his way. "It is probably why she is so *popular*."

I rolled my eyes. He was right, she did.

"Amore, please come join me up here," Grandma demanded.

"Oh, Jesus," I mumbled under my breath, then answered, barely holding my smile. "I'm okay, Grandma."

"I insist. Now come on up here, or I'll have to get all the king's horses to drag you up here."

She would too. Not sure where she would find the king's horses, but she'd find a way. There was a reason why most men were scared of her.

I pushed my shoulders back and braced for whatever the hell was coming.

"Good luck," Lorenzo whispered.

My eyes darted his way, noting pity in his eyes.

"We should have stayed in Italy," I whispered.

"Too late now," Gabriel Carrera mused. Why did I feel like Santi, Lorenzo, and Carrera were ganging up on me? It was a ridiculous notion, but I couldn't shake it off.

"Come, Amore," Grandma urged me forward. "I'm not getting any younger here."

"Neither am I, Grandma," I answered her, sending the crowd into a chuckle as I took each step with a heavy heart, painfully aware of Santi's eyes on the back of my neck. Every fine piece of hair stood up on my body, like a magnet attracted to its opposite.

The grin Grandmother gave me spoke of trouble.

Please don't announce the engagement. I'm not ready. Please. Please.

I took her offered hand and joined her on the runway, my heart slamming hard against my ribs, threatening to break them with its force.

CHAPTER 60

Santino

S hould I feel guilty for snatching my brother's fiancèe?

I didn't.

Should I feel bad for forcing Amore's grandmother into a corner and blackmailing her?

Not one fucking bit.

Adriano has been chasing pussy all over the city throughout his friendship with Amore. Ever since I told him about the marriage contract, he'd gone into overdrive. Like it was the last piece of ass he'd ever get. He practically fucked any woman that glanced his way.

Not that it would stop me if he was devoted to her.

I was done playing by the rules when it came to Amore. There was a reason the Russos were considered cheats with more blood on their hands than the entire Cosa Nostra. And if they tried to keep Amore from me, the streets of this city would run blood red.

If her father wanted war, he would get it. I was the don of the Russo family. I have never been soft or the giving type. The only softness I'd ever felt was when I was buried in Amore's tight pussy, listening to her soft moans calling out my name. That girl is fucking mine. She wasn't a fragile flower that needed sheltering. She was capable of holding her own in the boardroom, in a fight, and in the bedroom. She'd be my wife.

Carrera was behind me. I'd forced her grandmother behind me. Okay, maybe blackmailed was a better word, but fuck it... the end justified the means.

I watched Amore's bare, graceful back as she walked towards her grandmother in that green dress, looking every inch an heiress and prima donna. This was what she had been groomed for most of her life. She wasn't born in the world of the Cosa Nostra or among the cartel. She was born an heiress. But now, the underworld pulled... No, *I* pulled her knee deep into it.

But I wouldn't let it rip her apart. I'd keep her safe at all costs, even from her own family. She didn't trust anyone; it was the reason she found herself in the jungle fighting that battle alone. With DeAngelo. It bothered me that it wasn't me, but I was grateful the son of a bitch kept her safe. That man had watched her from a young age and was trustworthy.

Life was a fucking irony. The kiddo with sad green eyes that sat on the dirty pavement put a lock on me and threw away the key. I fought it and lost. I didn't give a fuck if she was an heiress, or a cartel princess, or the don's daughter. Because none of it mattered to me.

Amore has been mine from that first moment and I have been hers.

"There we go." Regina beamed, looking proudly at her granddaughter. At her legacy.

"And this next news—"

"Grandma, can we talk first?" Amore's voice echoed through the microphone, though not as strong as Regina's.

Amore stood next to her grandmother, face slightly pale. The smile was still on her lips, but she looked more like a deer in headlights.

Regina patted her hand, though Amore didn't look comforted at all.

"And now Santino Russo." Regina waved her hand, calling me over. "Please join Amore and me up here." I bet it shaved a few years of her life to say those words.

The spotlight flashed on me as drums rolled. Regina had a knack for dramatics, which I fucking hated.

I buttoned my suit jacket and pushed my hands into my pockets. I strode across the room. The path in front of me cleared, the world of Regalè's rich, snobby pricks steering clear of me. My reputation in New

York preceded me, reminding people never to double cross me. Right now, it only mattered that the dragon queen of a grandmother didn't fucking try it.

"Don't be shy, Santi Russo," Regina called out. The woman was a pain in my fucking ass. Old as dirt but handled herself with grace and a sharp mind. I was six foot three, her grandmother was even shorter than Amore, probably around five foot three, but the way the dragon eyed me, you'd think she was my equal. It was probably what helped her rule her empire and the cartel so successfully until she could hand the reins to her granddaughter. "Come join my granddaughter, your fiancée, up here."

Gasps traveled through the room like an echo.

She fucking loved to play. I should have known she wouldn't make it short and simple. Luigi pushed off the wall he'd been leaning against all evening and his father joined in, both walking towards me. Savio's face was blood red, rage clearly all over him. Lorenzo and Gabriel came behind him and Luigi, holding them back.

It left DeAngelo, Renzo, and I to do the rest.

I stepped up onto the podium, taking my spot in front of Amore, shielding her from the view of the audience with my towering body. She looked even paler up close. A frozen smile on her face that watched me warily, confusion in her green eyes. Amore didn't have the dragon personality like Regina, but she had a backbone, smarts, and stubbornness.

"After my daughter died in the middle of the South American jungle, Amore found herself in New York. She had her father, Savio Bennetti and the Russo family protecting her. There are no greater New Yorkers than those two. And I can assure you that my granddaughter would keep the headquarters of Regalè Enterprise in New York, honoring the two great men in her life."

The applause broke throughout. The clicking and flashing of the cameras went into overdrive, and I couldn't help but admire how smoothly she handled it.

"Grandma, what are you doing?" Amore hissed under her breath, her eyes darting frantically between me and Regina.

Regina ignored her question and turned to the audience and offered them a smile. "And now a dance by my granddaughter and her future husband."

"Fuck," Amore muttered under her breath. "What the fuck is going on?" she hissed, her eyes searching me out.

"Language, darling," Regina warned her. "Now you two get on the dance floor."

"No, I don't fucking think so," Amore hissed, her fair skin blotching red with anger. I loved her little telltales of emotions, though I knew firsthand Amore hated them. Except when I was fucking her, then she didn't mind it. She let it all out.

I'll be back inside you soon, Amore.

CHAPTER 61

Amore

Santi's hand came to my lower back, steering me down from the stage and onto the dance floor. A quick glance around the room and I spotted Dad. His gaze connected with mine and a storm brewed in his expression. I almost expected he'd pull out his gun at any moment and start shooting. Lorenzo held him by his arm, whispering in his ear.

Luigi was pissed off too. Gabriel Carrera held on to him. I just prayed that my hot-headed brother wouldn't cause a scandal in the midst of Regalè board members, models and reporters. My eyes darted to Lorenzo, and he winked his assurance it was all good. Things were going to hell in a handbasket.

The tunes of an old Italian song came on, the same one we danced to back in Italy and my feet tripped. Santi caught me as the entire room watched us dance and somehow it dawned on me. Ever since I moved to New York when I was that little girl, Santi somehow always caught me when I was falling. Whether it was when I cried on the sidewalk or got sick after my first alcohol consumption. He was always there.

"What is this?" I asked him.

"A dance."

Tall and elegant, he led the dance with a compelling swagger of power and ownership. If not for his constantly bruised knuckles and an outline of a gun holster pressing against me, he'd easily fool me into believing him to be a gentleman.

"You know what I'm talking about," I reprimanded in a low voice. "Stop playing games with me." He turned his scowl at me, but I refused to let it scare me. *He* didn't scare me. "Where is Adriano?"

His hand tensed on my back, pulling me closer against his hard body. "He's no longer your concern."

That was it! No explanation, nothing.

"Yes, he is," I said, annoyance flaring in my voice. "He'll always be my concern. You don't get to tell me what to do, Santi. Not anymore."

Regardless of whatever just happened. Really, what just happened?

His dark eyes were devoid of emotion, and his face was an unnerving mask of calm. This face right there made Santino Russo a fearful opponent.

"If I kill him, he won't be your concern," he said coldly.

I gasped out, then blinked my eyes. "Y-you wouldn't."

The smirk on his face was dark and cruel. "For you, Amore, I think I would. I'd burn down this whole motherfucking city." I stared at him in shock, unable to form a single thought. The music sounded far away, like the two of us were in our own little bubble. "You are marrying *me* now. I suggest you no longer concern yourself with other men."

His words sent liquid fire to my core. *This is wrong, so wrong.* Yet, naked lust and an inferno traveled through my veins like volcanic lava. His fingers on my back shot lust through my bloodstream, but it mixed with my anger at being manipulated. Despite how much I wanted him.

"Santi, please. You can't..." I whispered, unsure what I could possibly say. *I want you, but not like this.* I wanted him to fight for me and now... I was doubting his intention. For the first time ever, my trust in Santino Russo faltered. Though my desire didn't.

I was his. Yesterday. Today. Tomorrow. Fifty years from now.

But I wouldn't let him trample all over me and the people I loved.

Without a word, one hand went into his pocket while his other was still on my waist. His hand took my hand again and he slipped a ring onto my finger.

"You will wear this," he growled, his fingers interlocking with mine.

For a fleeting second, his eyes dropped to my neck, where the last piece of jewelry he bought me hung. The air sizzled between us, my skin tingled with it, and I cursed this addictive love for him.

"I am tired of everyone deciding what I should do," I whispered. "You could ask me, you know." Something flickered in his eyes, but he said nothing else. I swallowed. "You used to ask me what I wanted," I rasped.

Our eyes locked and I held my breath, sure he'd have something to say but the music ended, breaking the moment. The crowd surrounded us instantly, coming to congratulate us on our engagement. My eyes searched out my father, who stood in the back with my brother, their jaws pressed in a hard line.

"You alright?" Santi's voice pulled me back.

I blinked my eyes at him. The first boy that wiped my tears. And now he would cause so many more for my father, for my brothers, and my best friend.

With a silent nod and tight lump in my throat, my words were barely a whisper. "Excuse me."

I went in the opposite direction of the crowd, desperately needing solitude. The best place was in the back room where the models hung around. Yes, it was hectic, but those ladies were usually wrapped up in themselves. They wouldn't pay attention to me at all.

My heels clicked against the marble of the large room. Every so often I ran into a familiar face, nodded and smiled, then excused myself.

I didn't want the wedding to Adriano. I wanted Santi. It has always been Santi. But not like this. Never like this.

CHAPTER 62

Santino

S he walked away from me, down the makeshift runway where at the far end of it Lorenzo would be waiting for her.

Striding through the hallway of my nightclub, I couldn't help but recall the first time I saw Amore dancing here. The plan was in motion and there was no turning back. Not that I wanted to turn back. There was no room for regrets in this life. Those made you weak, piling up like a rack of bones onto your makeshift grave. And I had no plans of dying. Not until I had years with my little sex monster.

I found my way to my office. If things go according to plan, Lorenzo would ensure she got here.

I left the office in the darkness and leaning back against the mantel, I rolled a cigarette between my fingers. I hadn't had a cigarette in fucking years, but now I'd fucking kill for a shot of nicotine. Bennetti's rejection still burned through my veins. Bitterness tasted like acid on my tongue. Amore was mine, and I'd kill anyone who tried to keep me away from her.

I guessed Bennetti had suspicions about the reasons I wanted Amore's marriage contract. His exact words were that he would never allow Amore to be touched by someone like me.

The joke was on him after the announcement that was currently trending on social media, wasn't it? Then why wasn't I laughing.

The air conditioning blasted cold air, and I welcomed it because this flame inside me threatened to turn into something stupid. Like killing Amore's father for opposing me.

The door to my office opened softly and the swishing of an emerald, flowy dress fluttering was the first thing I saw before she walked in.

"I'll find DeAngelo and bring him here," Lorenzo's voice traveled over.

"Thank you." Her voice was soft as she offered him a small smile. The door softly clicked, leaving her alone with me. She still hadn't seen me.

She looked beautiful. The cut of her dress was low, revealing her smooth, milky skin, with only thin strings crisscrossing her back. The emerald fabric hugged her curves, leaving plenty to the imagination. Heat ran straight to my dick.

She rolled her thin shoulders and her neck, as if the tension was too much for her. She was barely twenty-one and already running an empire, the side gig with DeAngelo avenging her mother's death, and her own business. She'd put any don of the Cosa Nostra to shame.

"Clusterfuck," she muttered under her breath with a heavy sigh. "Everyone in this place is nuts."

She rolled her shoulders again, and I itched to ease her tension with my hands until she melted into me.

"Already talking to yourself?" I asked, never moving from my spot.

She spun around, her dress fluttering through the air. Her silky ponytail hid her red curls from me and I couldn't decide if I liked it or not. It made her look sophisticated heiress but I preferred my sex monster. Though when she whipped around, it hit the door behind her, and I had to tell myself not to think about grabbing it. I itched to wrap her silky hair around my fist, force her down to her knees, and then demand she suck me off with that pretty mouth of hers.

Stop fucking thinking about it! I was already rock hard, and the images of Amore on her knees in front of me wouldn't help to ease this pent-up need.

"What are you doing here?" she questioned me. "And what the hell was that out there?" Her hand pointed to the closed door.

"This is my office," I drawled, ignoring her other question. "Just like you ran into my bedroom." She glared at me, and her cheeks flushed. "Or were you hoping for another show?"

"I've seen better." She smiled sweetly, taunting me.

"Wrong thing to say, baby," I purred as I moved closer to her. She remained unmoving, glaring. She could have fooled another man but not me. The shade of her green eyes changed ever so slightly with every emotion - anger, lust, sadness.

I reached out and took a strand of her ponytail, rubbing the silken strands between my fingers. Her breathing was slightly labored and her chest flushed red. It was another one of her tells.

"Answer my question, Santi," she warned, though there was no threat in her voice. She was too soft for harsh threats. "What the hell happened out there? What is going on between you and my grandmother?"

"Regina does what Regina wants to do," I answered. It was true enough.

I suspected admitting to her that I blackmailed Regina wouldn't go over well.

CHAPTER 63

Amore

My heartbeat drummed, making my ribs hurt from the force of it. Being alone with this man that I desired so much was risky. Especially after what just happened out there.

My head still spun from my grandmother's announcement. An engagement to Santino Russo!

My gaze traveled up his black vest, black tie, and that deep, dark gaze that could burn like coal when he was buried deep inside me. Despite our current circumstance and all the history, his presence felt warm and safe.

Mental check needed! Santi's office.

The music and laughter drifted through the closed door, but it almost felt like we were alone in the world. In our own universe. Just like that night when he gave me my first kiss.

And called it a mistake, I reminded myself dryly.

"What are you doing here?" I asked him. "And don't give me another bullshit answer."

Santi didn't miss a beat. "I'm waiting for you."

My brows creased. "Why?"

He leaned against the wall, his palm flat against it. He looked so casual that you'd think we were best friends. Yet, his eyes told a different story. There was dark tension looming in them.

"You are smart, Amore," he drawled, his tone dangerously soft. "You tell me."

I took a step to leave, but his rough hand grabbed my wrist.

"Tell me." His voice was low, demanding. Our eyes locked, and I watched in dark delight as desire flared in his gaze.

When he ordered me around, it made me clench with need. It was so wrong, but I couldn't help it. The moment I entered the office, the scent of spice, cedarwood, and uniquely Santi blasted all my senses. Combine it with my memories of my first kiss and it was dooming.

His close proximity was shattering all my defenses. From the first kiss, Santino Russo has seeped into my bloodstream and there was no flushing him out.

"I'm waiting," he purred. His hot breath laced my neck, sending shivers down my body. His dark eyes were pulling me in, seducing me. It would be so easy to drown in it, lean closer to him to soothe this ache pulsing through my veins.

"You want to chitchat?" I suggested sarcastically. Dark amusement ghosted through his gaze.

"Wrong, baby." His hand came to my neck, trailing the vein that connected my brain and my heart. It should make me smarter, but it would seem my brain and heart wanted the same thing. *Santino.*

He knew I still wanted him. There wasn't an ounce of doubt in my mind that Santi knew exactly how much I desired him. And that irked me and fueled my bitter anger more than anything.

I opened my mouth to speak, but before any words came out, he grabbed my arm and slammed my body against his. His mouth crashed onto mine. The kiss was raw and hard, possessive. He forced his tongue between my lips and took what belonged to him.

My legs quivered and my sweet spot clenched, knowing how much pleasure this man could bring me. He devoured me, his hand on the nape of my neck. He yanked my hair, tilting my head as he continued to consume my mouth.

All my thoughts evaporated, and I returned his kiss with greed. He ripped his mouth from mine and sucked on my neck, trailing kisses up to my earlobe.

"You are mine," he whispered in my ear. He thrust his tongue into my ear canal, and I nearly melted. My body pressed against him, closing all the distance between us, I needed him inside me. "Mine, Amore."

A moan shattered the quiet night, and he clamped his mouth to mine; our tongues swirled together in that familiar way.

Without warning, he broke the kiss, and the sense of loss was instant. We stood there, staring at each other, his eyes blazing embers.

"Why would you kiss me?" I rasped.

God, he smelled so good. Like home. The sounds of my ragged breathing filled his empty office, and it felt like déjà vu from my last visit to his office. If he said it was a mistake, I might just lose my shit.

His stare was burning hot.

"To erase the taste of Adriano from your lips," he muttered against my lips. "Besides, we are engaged. I can kiss you whenever I like." A surge of languid heat leaked into my bloodstream and pooled between my thighs.

"Santi, this can't happen," I rasped. My lips might have protested but my body didn't. My hands braced against his stomach, my fingers unwillingly curling into his muscle. His heat seeped through my skin and into my bloodstream.

"This is happening," he said darkly, matter-of-factly. "There are no alternatives."

He didn't make sense. None of this made sense. With his dark gaze on mine, he gripped a fistful of my emerald dress near my thigh and tugged it up. I should be protesting it, pushing him away. Yet my hands gripped his shirt, holding on to my rock, as soft whimpers slipped through my lips.

It was okay to kiss him now, right? The news of the engagement spread like wildfire. It wasn't how I envisioned it, but I wanted *him*. Loved him for so long. I'd take him. Made men took whatever they wanted. I'd take what I wanted too.

He fisted the fabric of my dress, skimming up my legs, his rough knuckles brushing against my skin and it sizzled. An empty ache formed low in my stomach, and I had to bite my lip to hold back a plea. I wanted him to touch me, overwhelm me.

One hand braced on the wall beside my head, his other touched the bare skin of my inner thigh. The ache between my legs pulsed with intensity. I parted my thighs, my body begging him for release.

"You want my cock in your pussy?" His words ignited fire through my veins.

His hand slipped between my thighs, cupping me over my panties and a moan vibrated through the room.

My palms lay flat on the wall, my back arching off it. My body was betraying me in the worst way possible. I didn't care.

I pulled at his lower lip, hungrily. His taste was addictive, like whiskey and sin. My eternal sin. Our tongues tangled, stroke for stroke. Finally losing the battle, my hands reached around his neck while he ran his hands down the back of my thighs, hoisting my legs up. I wrapped them around his waist and my back pressed against the wall.

Just like before, the thought came through. My first kiss was in The Orchid, with him. The man I loved forever.

CHAPTER 64

Amore

I loved him. I had always loved him. I tried to stop, but I couldn't. It was like trying to stop breathing.

But did he love me? Yes, he'd laid claim, but mafia men were possessive. It was in their DNA.

I gently pushed against him, breaking the kiss and gaining an inch of space. I opened my mouth but before I could say anything, the door flew open and slammed against the black tiled wall. My father, my brothers, Adriano, Grandma, and Uncle Vincent stepped in.

"Someone better explain to me what the fuck's going on," Dad shouted. "Right. The. Fuck. Now!"

Luigi and Dad pointed their guns at Santi's head and my heart froze with fear. Instead of applying some of the skills DeAngelo taught me, I stood paralyzed. I didn't want to lose another person I loved.

Santi immediately lowered me, using his body as a shield and pulled out his gun.

I was painfully aware of everyone's eyes. In particular, Adriano's. His gaze flicked to me and took in the situation. There was no misunderstanding what just happened. My hair was a tumbled mess, my lips were swollen.

I tried to sidestep Santi, but he refused to let me come around him.

Instead, he pulled me to his left side, his arm wrapping tightly around my waist. My eyes darted frantically between my family and the Russos. Adriano's eyes were focused on Santi, his jaw clenched tight.

"Well, Bennetti, if you need it spelled out," my grandmother answered. "It seems Amore and Santi got frisky with each other. And by the looks of it, she liked it."

"Grandma," I exclaimed at her crudeness while my cheeks grew hot. Why did she have to do that?

Ignoring her, I turned my eyes to my father. A girl never wanted to be caught in her lover's embrace by her family. This was humiliating, to say the least. Even worse was the fear of what Dad would do. I was under no illusion of who and what he was.

"Dad," I whispered, pleading clear in my voice.

Dad's disappointment washed over me like a cold shower. He didn't even bother glancing my way and a cold sweat trickled down my back. Dad and Santi stared at each other, both of their expressions grim.

I swallowed hard. "Luigi, please put your gun down," I begged. It was futile. He was more than happy to get Santi for shooting him. I looked at Lorenzo and was surprised to find him calm. He winked... again, while I was perspiring here. Lorenzo wasn't the winking brother type. Maybe his eye was twitching from all the stress.

My eyes traveled to Adriano. "Adriano," I rasped. It wasn't how I wanted him to find out about his brother and me. I tried desperately to communicate with my eyes, telling him I was sorry. "Please let me—"

"Congratulations on your engagement, Amore," Adriano deadpanned, his voice cold as ice. We stared at each other, all the years of friendship burning like a wicker house. "Sins of The Orchid finally coming to light, huh?" My throat squeezed tight. "I'm guessing something similar happened the night before you went to Italy, three years ago too."

"What?" Dad snapped, his expression turning dark.

"I-It wasn't like that," I rasped.

Dad's gaze snapped to me, and his expression darkened. "Luigi take your sister home." His voice was firm and cold. He refused to look my way.

"Don't you fucking move, Luigi." Santi's voice was commanding with a deep timbre of control that would unleash a ruthless man at any second. He held his gun by his side, finger on the trigger while Dad kept his aimed at Santi. "Amore stays with me."

There were no soft edges to Santi right now. There never were, except that I thrived in his control. I loved it. He gave me exactly what I needed.

My eyes flashed to Adriano. He didn't have his gun pointed at Santi and something stupid inside me warmed up. He still had his brother's back, just as my brothers would always have mine.

"Savio. Put. The. Gun. Down." Santi's words carried a calmness with a hint of animosity. It was his calm before the storm.

Dad and Santi stared at each other, no words spoken, but some meaning passing between them. Hell if I knew what. I just wanted it all over and done with.

"She was meant to marry Adriano, not you." Dad's dark eyes full of rage focused on Santi. "You are breaking the contract," Dad spit, his jaw tightened.

Santi's lips curved with sardonic amusement, his expression dark and unreadable. He took a step towards my dad.

"If that's what it takes," Santi growled. "Amore Regina Perèz Bennetti"—I flinched at the name and barely a flicker passed Dad's eyes. How did Santi know?—"... is mine. And if you try to take her, you will start a war. I will burn this fucking city to the ground, but she will be my wife."

Luigi and Lorenzo remained still, though Luigi's gun was still trained on Santi.

"She's not yours," Dad repeated stubbornly.

"I wasn't asking," Santi retorted in a hard voice..

"Santino, I told you before, and I will tell you again." Dad was reaching his limits. "Amore will never be yours. I will never agree to her marriage with you. The contract is non-negotiable."

Dad's gun was still aimed at Santi's head, and I held my breath in fear that he'd pull the trigger. Just one small pull and it would cost me so much.

"Fuck. Your. Contract," Santi snarled. "I'm the head of the Russo family, and I didn't agree to that contract."

Lorenzo cursed under his breath. It wasn't looking good. These men could kill each other, and it would take a few short minutes. I wouldn't let them; I refused to lose people I loved.

"I'm pregnant," I blurted out, my heart threatening to beat a hole in my chest.

Everyone's eyes snapped to me, except for Santi's. Though I felt his body tense. I had no idea where it came from. It was a bold face lie. Dad shot me a narrowed look, studying me. I wasn't a good liar. The fear twisted inside me, and I thought I'd get sick at any moment. Maybe that wouldn't be so bad. It'd convince them I was pregnant.

"How long?" Dad gritted out. His anger tasted like ash, burning my lungs with smoke.

"Two months." Jesus, I was digging myself deep. But I remembered years ago, Maria told me about a girl that got pregnant by a man, and her family would have killed him if she hadn't been pregnant. So instead of killing him, they forced him to marry her immediately.

Adriano scoffed. "Brother gets it all, doesn't he?"

I sucked in a shallow breath. The tension hung in the room like a dark, stormy cloud threatening to strike with deadly lightning at any moment.

"Please, Adriano." My voice came out scratchy, caused by raw emotions. I was slowly but surely losing my best friend. "Please let me explain," I tried.

"Don't look at me like that." His voice broke something inside me. It was indifferent, cold, and angry. "You are getting what you wanted. So is my dear brother. Aren't you, Santi?"

Glancing to my side, Santi's eyes were cold and narrowed on his brother.

"You've been fucking him for what... months, years?" Adriano's accusation had me flinching. "And not a word. Not a fucking word, Amore."

Santi got into Adriano's face before I could even hear the last syllable of my name. I watched frozen as Santi grabbed his brother by the collar, his face inches from Adriano. The tension was thick as I watched Santi shove his brother against the wall, rattling the door.

"You'll speak to my woman with respect," Santi growled, pressing harder against Adriano's windpipe.

"Stop." I pushed on both of them, but neither one of them bulged. "Please, stop it!"

They didn't even spare me a glance.

"You are such a hypocrite, Santi." Adriano pushed against his older brother, then went for a punch but Santi was too fast and too strong. He blocked his fist, then sent Adriano flying through the room. Adriano stumbled backwards, falling against the desk in the office with such force, it sent the vase flying off the desk with a loud crash echoing against the hardwood floor of the office.

"You better think twice about what you are going to say," Santi threatened darkly.

Adriano laughed bitterly. "Or what? You'll push me out of the Cosa Nostra. You already did, you fucking asshole. Funny how rules change now that you are marrying her."

"Adriano, please," I begged in a whisper. "We can talk about it and fix it."

Of all the people in this world, I had a handful I'd always count on. Adriano was one of them. He had never, *ever* hurt me. I spent more time with him than I did with my brothers and my father. And now, he was the one hurting.

"Like you talked to me about fucking my brother all along?" A gasp escaped me. Touché. He got me there. Though I didn't do it all along. It was before we learned about the marriage contract.

"Like you kept it in your pants," Santi hissed. "There isn't a skirt in this city you haven't lifted. Even after you knew about the marriage contract."

I wasn't surprised to hear about the latter. It didn't hurt either. It never hurt when he got involved with other women. It would destroy me if Santi had other women though.

"Didn't I tell you the Russo boys are no good for you, Amore?" Uncle Vincent growled. "You deserve so much better."

Dad's eyes narrowed on Adriano. "You cheated on my daughter?" He got into his face. "I should kill you right now."

My gaze lingered on Adriano. It looked like he was ready to beat him too. Adriano stood there tense, ready to be thrown out or beaten down. It was written all over his face. The years of standing by him kicked in.

"But you are not, Dad," I snapped, anger clear in my voice. "You will leave Adriano alone!"

All this was ludicrous. Adriano and I were never an item. You couldn't cheat on a partner that never agreed to marry you,

"Grandma, please," I begged. Would nobody come to their senses?

Ignoring me, she turned to Santi. "You better marry my grand-daughter, Russo," she demanded with a smirk. "Before the baby is born!"

"You have no say in this, you senile witch," Dad shouted.

"And why in the hell do you all care?" I shouted, losing my shit. Grandma's and Dad's eyes flashed in surprise. "Did it ever occur to either of you to ask me what I want?" I glared at my two family members that I have loved and who have been bickering for as long as I've known them. "Stop fucking deciding for me." I turned my eyes to Dad. "Both of you. Just fucking stop it!"

"Oh, shit." Lorenzo whistled. "My little sister finally put everyone in their place."

"Amore, I'm trying to do what your mother wanted," Dad said, ignoring Lorenzo and glaring at Santi. He turned his eyes to Grandma. "I told you Margaret told me to keep Amore safe and then you do this shit. Shoving her knee deep into the Cosa Nostra. And I told you to keep out of my business when it comes to my daughter's well-being, goddamnit! She is marrying Adriano, not Santino."

She shrugged. "Ooops, my bad." She smiled her sweet, conniving smile. "Russo said she was marrying him. Santino Russo."

My dad and grandma were hopeless. It wouldn't matter if I screamed at the top of my lungs from Mt. Rushmore, they'd still not hear what I had to say. It was like they couldn't see eye-to-eye.

"Didn't I say I host the best parties in New York City?" Grandma's chipper voice fueled the flames. She was talking to the only stranger in the group.

"And who in the fuck are you?" Dad spat angrily.

"He's a Venezuelan friend," Grandma purred. "Or maybe a foe," she added jokingly.

"Why in the fuck would you bring a stranger to this?" Adriano questioned her like she was batshit crazy.

None of this was getting us anywhere. I should tell them all to go to hell.

"I'm sorry, Dad," I whispered at last, the decision settling over me. "I want to go with Santi."

I didn't like disappointing Dad nor upsetting him, but I wanted Santi. Like the desert thrived under the scorching heat of the sun, so did my heart and body. I told him I'd give up my empire for him, and I would. From where I stood, it looked like he was fighting for me now. Or was it some power pull. I took a step towards Santi, and his strong arm wrapped around my waist as though he worried I might change my mind and leave him.

He watched me with a soft expression. "It's okay, Amore," Santi soothed, then returned to fix his stare at my father. "Your dad and I will come to terms. One way or another."

I closed my eyes for a brief second, inhaling and then exhaling slowly. His scent was my comfort and safety from the moment he brushed my tears away. I just hoped it remained that way.

Somewhere along the way, Santino became my home. My everything.

CHAPTER 65

Amore

We left The Orchid behind without a single person getting shot. An accomplishment! DeAngelo stayed with Grandma, Adriano with Carrera, Lorenzo with Dad and Luigi.

Santi drove smoothly down the streets, shifting gears. The Maserati's engine purred softly and memories of our last time in this car came to the forefront of my mind. It was the same Maserati he drove for our first date. The very same car he drove when he fucked me on the hood.

His heat practically warmed the car, and yet, I wanted to scoot over until his body was brushing against mine.

My hands curled into fists, forcing myself to remain still, the throbbing ache pulsing at the memory. My heart thundered; the need for him made my skin itch. Our earlier kiss had heightened the craving for him.

The silence in the car was tense. Not uncomfortable, but full of words I wanted to say, questions I wanted to ask, things I wanted to understand. And emotions I was scared to feel. Santi had hurt me twice already. When he told me the first kiss we shared was a mistake and when he dumped me after Italy... without an explanation. As if I meant nothing to him while he meant the world to me.

A cold void and emptiness hit me each time I thought about it. I loved him so fiercely, yet he ended it so quickly. It didn't seem to impact him much. Was I just sex to him? Yes, the lust and attraction was strong between us, but I also wanted his love. His devotion and faithfulness. His everything.

"I don't want to marry you, Santi." The words left my lips and they were a lie. Except my pride demanded them. "And I'd like to know how you know about the Perèz connection?"

"You are pregnant," he drawled. "Of course, we are going to get married."

I shook my head. He knew damn well I wasn't pregnant. "I only said that so Dad wouldn't shoot you."

He shifted gears, throwing me a flickering glance. There was no surprise in his expression at my statement. "Too bad. I was looking forward to having you barefoot and pregnant."

I rolled my eyes. So barbaric! "Yeah... barefoot and pregnant will never happen. I'm Amore motherfucking Bennetti. Even when I'm pregnant, I'll be working. If you are looking for the stay-at-home wife type, keep looking."

"Looking down on stay-at-home mothers and homemakers?" he taunted.

"No, I'm not. It takes an amazing person to be a good stay-at-home mother or homemaker. But it's not me." Amusement flickered in his eyes, and I realized he was teasing me. "How do you know about the Perèz connection?"

"I've always known," he drawled. "It was what caused a rift between our fathers. Don't you remember what my father said?"

"It was for drug connections?" I questioned. "I thought it was because they both wanted Mom."

He shook his head. "Pà loved Mamma. He wanted your mother for her connection to the Perèz Cartel. Your pàpa initially had the same motive but he fell for her."

"Seriously?" I gasped.

Santi nodded. Gosh, I'd got it wrong. So damn wrong. Were these men all about power and connection?

"Is that what you want, Santi?" I asked in a low voice. "Connection to the cartel?" I wanted to hear the words. The admission. Apology. Everything. "You are crazy if you think you'll force me into marrying you for it."

"Don't fuck with me, Amore," he purred. Jesus, the way he said my name had me melting on the inside. It was the curse and benefit of my name. I never knew whether people used it as my name or an endearment. "I don't give a shit about your connections or wealth."

He didn't? *Then what?* I wanted to ask.

"I wouldn't dream of fucking with you, Santi," I muttered tightly, though the word *fucking* had me blushing. But it was one thing I wouldn't budge on. I wouldn't settle in this life. It was the only one I had, and I wanted it *all.* I wanted him to tell me what I meant to him. "But I won't let you use me, then discard me. You've done that enough."

He stilled, and holding my breath, I waited. For him to dispute my words. To tell me I was his everything, like he was my everything. And with each heartbeat, my heart sank.

Bu-bum. Bu-bum. Bu-bum.

Realizing, he wouldn't answer, I turned to gaze out the window. The landscape we passed was a blur as the silence squeezed the breath out of my lungs and hope out of my heart.

Before my brain could process what was going on, he swiftly drove across two lanes and pulled over to the side. Woods stretched for miles out of my window, and I turned my head to question why he'd stopped. Before I could open my mouth, his right hand wrapped around my nape, his fingers threaded through my hair then turned my face to his. He was so close to me, if I leaned in just an inch, our lips would meet.

"Tell me you don't want me," he demanded. "Tell me you don't want my mouth on your pussy, my cock buried in your tight cunt, my hands on your soft skin, my tongue in your mouth." His grip in my hair tightened. I could almost feel his lips against mine and my whole body hummed in anticipation. Goddamnit, I did want him, craved him. "Tell me you don't want me, Amore Bennetti, and I'll let you go."

He'd got it all wrong. It was the assurance of his love I needed. He'd always have my body and heart, but I wanted his in return. I wouldn't settle for simple lust. Eventually that would fade, and in its wake, only my broken heart would remain. I wanted his heart forever. So that when we are gray, frail and wrinkled, we'd still have our love. Our hearts intermingled forever.

I opened my mouth, the words demanding his love, not just his desire, on the tip of my tongue when from the corner of my eye I noticed a black SUV. The vehicle approached fast, then suddenly slammed on its brakes.

Santi's curses filled the car. "Fuck!" The alarm in his voice scared me more than anything else in a very long time.

In the next second, he pushed me down, my face slamming against his thigh and a lungful of air escaped me at the impact.

"Fuck," he shouted, as he pressed a button and his body cocooned mine.

Before I took the next breath, machine guns started blazing, the sound around us deafening. Glass shattered all around us, the car alarm blasting through the air and piercing my ears. Santi's body covered mine, his arms around me as glass shattered and gunfire sparked around us.

Santi grunted in pain, but he never moved, his hard body a shield over mine. I grabbed his hand pressed over my ears and felt a sticky, hot liquid. Fear gripped my heart that thundered with terror. I could taste it on my tongue, unpleasant and thick.

Chaos played all around us, reminding me of the battlefield in Venezuela, and I wondered if finally George had caught up to me. He'd already cost me my mother. Would he cost me the man I loved too?

Suddenly, the importance of telling Santi how much I loved him seemed like a life and death situation now.

I love you, Santi. I have always loved you.

My lips moved. I felt them move, but I couldn't hear my own voice though the words screamed in my head. Maybe the gunshots drowned it all out.

I didn't want to die without telling him that I loved him. I had loved him for so long; I wasn't even sure when the crush changed into love. Maybe that night he held my head as I threw up a bottle of tequila in his strip club. Or when he saved me at the college party while I hid in the bathroom stall. A kid's hero turned into a major crush then a hard-core love.

I squeezed his hand, praying to God, anyone that would hear me.

Let us live. Don't let us die here.

The seatbelt dug into me, but the pain didn't register. My heartbeat drummed in my ears, and my breathing was heavy. Santi enveloped me in safety, but my mind screamed in worry for him. Without him, my life meant nothing.

I pressed myself further into his thigh, pulling him closer down on me. The gunshots went on forever, at least that's how it felt, before stillness fell over the night. I turned my head sideways, scared to lift it and get Santi killed. I was startled by the little I saw. The car windshield was completely shattered, there wasn't a single surface in my sight of vision that didn't have a bullet hole.

"Stai bene?" Are you okay? Santi's words were a soft whisper in my ear. The same words he asked the thirteen-year-old me. Even if Santi didn't love me, I knew he'd always keep me safe. *Always!*

I felt his hands run down my body, checking for injuries. "I'm good," I rasped, squeezing his hand that stayed on my head. "You?"

"Yes." He ran a thumb across my cheek. "I need you to be brave. Okay?"

"God, Santi," I murmured. "Those were the same words Mamma told me before she died. You better not fucking die on me."

I felt his lips on the crown of my head. "I won't."

I wasn't sure if he had any business making that promise, but I took it anyhow. We were sitting ducks if we remained, but if Santi attempted to drive off, he could get shot. Assuming the car would even drive in this shot up state.

Santi must have been thinking the same thing because he produced a knife out of somewhere and cut my seatbelt, then leaned over my lap and pulled the handle of the door on my side. It would make sense since it faced woods rather than the highway where the gunmen were.

"We've got to run, baby," he muttered. "I pressed the alarm button, but my men won't get here fast enough."

"Oh shit," I mumbled. "I didn't bring my running shoes nor my own gun."

I felt his mouth against my temple curve into a smile, despite our situation. This must be a walk in the park for him. I kicked off my shoes and climbed out of the car, Santi right behind me. He crawled over the console, to the passenger seat and then joined me in the dirt.

Voices traveled through the night air. Words in Spanish and my heart thundered. These men were after me.

Santi took my hand, stickiness soaking my fingers. I lowered my gaze and noted through the darkness Santi's hand covered in blood. I could barely see the ink on his skin. I raised my eyes to him, but he just shook his head, pressing a finger against his lips.

Tugging me along, we followed the shadow of the tree line and the coverage it afforded us. Once we reached a certain spot, we started running. Gunshots fired after us as we ran into the woods but we never stopped. To stop running was to die.

It was too dark to see where I stepped to avoid spiky holly leaves or sticks. Being barefoot, pain shot through the sole of my feet with each step, but I ignored it.

The voices of men, words in Spanish, were within earshot. The danger too close. Yet, despite the peril at our heels, I felt safe with Santi at my side. I wished he wasn't in danger because of me, but I couldn't regret the protection he offered. While DeAngelo did an amazing job at training me and helped me pursue revenge against my mother's killers, it didn't make me competent and ruthless like Santi. It wasn't something I could ever thrive in.

Maybe that was the reason I loved him. He provided that which I lacked.

My foot gave out, and I stumbled but Santi caught me before I fell to my knees. Sounds of screeching tires in the distance had me turning my head back in the direction we came from. It was too dark to see. The sounds of open fire started, and it sounded like a warzone.

"Those must be my men," he rasped. "We have to hurry and run in case there are some enemy stragglers. Let me carry you," he said in a hushed tone, as he went to pick me up.

My gaze zeroed on his arm covered in blood. It covered his usually red, rough knuckles. There was no pain on his face, but I hated adding more to his injury. I wanted to check his wound and stitch him up. Heal him, the way he has been saving me over the years.

Another round of gunfire traveled through the warm night.

"No," I whispered, shaking my head. "We are faster this way."

He knew I was right; it was written on his face. He struggled with doing what was best for us and best for me. He has always been the boy that saved me. Maybe he saw me more as a girl that constantly needed saving.

"I can do it, Santi," I claimed with conviction, squeezing his hand. "Just get us out of here." I forced a smile on my face, despite this life and death situation. If Santi was running, we were in deep shit. Usually he was a stand up and fight type of guy. "And then, I want boots like yours."

His uninjured hand brushed across my cheek. I thought he muttered "That's my girl," under his breath, but I wasn't sure.

I glanced around us, and deep forest was as far as my eye could see. It would seem that somewhere between New York City and Long Island, there was a wide acreage of forest.

"Are we heading back to the city or away from it?" I asked him, running my fingers across his palm. The night was cool, and my dress wasn't doing a good job of keeping me warm. Just a touch of him felt good, his body was a furnace. The contrast between his heat and the chilled night air sent a shiver through my spine and goosebumps broke over my skin.

Noticing it, he immediately slid his jacket off his shoulders. Of course, Santi noticed everything.

"I'm taking you somewhere safe," he murmured. "Open your arms," he ordered softly, and I immediately obeyed. It was how my body operated around him. It reacted, eager to please him. I slid one hand through the sleeve of his jacket and then the other, his warmth and smell immediately enveloping me. "The jacket is a mess, but it's better than freezing to death."

I could see his white crisp shirt sleeve soaked in blood. His right arm didn't look good at all.

"We need to check your wound." I lifted his arm gently. "I don't want you in pain." And I was worried about him bleeding out if there was a bullet wound.

"It's just a cut from the glass," he assured. "It has already stopped bleeding. Let's keep moving."

CHAPTER 66

Santino

I swear to God, I'd kill every single one of those motherfuckers. Once Amore was safe, I'd hunt and kill every single idiot that dared to shoot in her direction. Amore ran beside me without a single complaint; strength and determination etched on her beautiful young face. She was too young to deal with this shit. Just thinking about Amore hurt sent ice through my veins. I never wanted to let her out of my sight.

Truthfully, I expected retaliation but not this fast.

Amore announcing she was pregnant played into it perfectly. Though it was unexpected. I glanced at her finger with my ring. My chest swelled with warmth. I'd marry her as soon as we got to our destination. The initial plan I came up with was to take her to my city home and tomorrow to the city courthouse.

But this attack required a change of plans. I was flexible. As long as she said I do.

After cornering Regina into agreement, this party was a disguise for her to announce Amore's engagement to me. *The wrong Russo,* according to her father. And the Venezuelan stranger the dragon had dragged to witness the incident in my office back at The Orchid, he was connected to George Anderson. Cards started to fall into place.

When Amore's grandfather was murdered, the Perèz Cartel passed to his wife. Not because she was entitled to it. Upon her death, it would have passed to her daughter, Amore's mother. Since Margaret flat out refused, Regina took over earning herself a few enemies. She has been fighting for the power of the Perèz Cartel from the moment her husband died. Not because she wanted it, but to protect her daughter and granddaughter.

Until one day it would have passed on to Amore or her husband. Except she didn't know Amore's mother made Savio promise to keep their daughter out of it.

If Amore was murdered before she got married, the cartel would have gone to the Andersons. It was the reason the old woman kept herself surrounded with bodyguards from the Carrera Cartel. It was the reason DeAngelo, ex-special ops and a member of the Carrera Cartel, had been assigned to watch over Amore. The Carrera Cartel didn't want the Anderson's as their rivals.

Savio Bennetti wasn't aware of this. I suspected Margaret's request to keep Amore out of this world was a bit more involved than just marrying her daughter to someone outside the underworld. She was born into it, and not only through her father but her mother too.

Amore Bennetti wasn't just a pretty face. Strong, beautiful, smart, loyal.

She was everything. I wanted her and starting a war to have her was worth it. Every single member of the Bennetti family today knew how much Amore meant to me. She was mine. I never made empty threats and burning the city down to keep her with me was the least people should fear.

I wanted to make sure she never had to worry about anything, just doing what she loved. Fashion, design... fuck, whatever she wanted. As long as she was safe and loved me.

When I heard her whisper those three little words attached to my name as gunfire blazed and glass shattered all around us, a strange kind of peace came over me. In the midst of gunfire. *How appropriate.*

I was her darkness and she was my light.

Eight years ago, a red-haired girl with wide, shimmering emeralds met my gaze. I still remembered the intense feeling that shook through me... the urge to protect her at all costs. Make her smile, see her eyes shine with happiness, not with tears. And she trusted me! Blindly. Completely.

Even as she got a glimpse of my ruthlessness, she never shied away. As she grew up, she became stronger despite her softness. Ambitious and fair. Protective of the people she loved. So much that she would burn down the world to protect the ones she loves. She was my match in every way.

I had never known this kind of peace. And to know that my kind of love and obsession didn't terrify her left me speechless. *She* brought me back to life.

Maybe my black, selfish heart recognized her all those years ago and waited for her to become a woman. I had been hers from that moment on.

My chest grew all warm. For fuck's sake, I thought it might actually glow like a damn lightning bug. I wanted to give her everything she deserved and more. Make her happy so she'd always laugh, and I could hear those soft sounds every day. Have babies with her, little girls with her emerald eyes and smile that could light up the city.

Though not sure how well that would bode for my heart and sanity. My possessiveness and obsession was already in turbo mode. It would go into insanity if we had little girls. We'd make sure we had lots of boys too. *I'll need a lot of help to keep everyone away from them,* I thought wryly.

"How much longer?" Amore asked in a soft voice. We had been running and walking for an hour. I was fairly sure we'd lost the men coming after us and she had to be exhausted.

Now, I just had to get us to the spot where Renzo and I kept an emergency escape vehicle and get us to my cabin.

"You good?" I questioned Amore. She hadn't complained once.

"Yes." Her hand was still in mine. I had no intention of letting it go. Ever! "One thing's for sure," she remarked in a dry tone.

"What's that?" I asked her curiously.

"We'll sleep well tonight after this hiking adventure." She glanced my way, her green eyes shimmering, and my lips tugged up into a smile. Her dress was stained with my blood, her feet probably bruised, and yet, she still found humor.

"You might be right," I retorted, smiling. "Though next time, we'll do a better job being prepared."

"Ah, Santi," she fanned herself with her other hand. "So many promises. I can't wait."

I gently tugged her hair, just the way I used to do it before the marriage contract came about. She took her lip between her teeth and nervously chewed on it, making my cock stir to life.

"I'm thinking you know who those men are." I changed the topic to something more serious. It was time we started to come clean about some things.

She rolled her eyes. "Well, duh. It is either someone that wants you dead or someone that wants me dead."

"Smarty pants." I tugged on her hair again. "Now, tell me," I ordered. When her head snapped to me, I added with a smile, "Please, baby. It's about time we compare notes; don't you think?"

Amore might be young, but she was strong and smart. It was time we joined forces and worked against this threat together.

She took a deep breath. "I guess you should know since you were shot at because of me," she muttered. She tilted her head up to the sky. "You are going to think I'm crazy."

"I don't think you are crazy," I murmured. "After all, you are going to marry me."

"We haven't settled that yet," she retorted dryly. "But now is not the time for that."

"We'll see about that," I told her. "Now tell me what is so crazy."

"I think my stepfather, George Anderson, is alive."

"Did you see something in Venezuela?" I asked her and her head whipped my way. Before she could ask anything, I added, "Yes, I know you went to Venezuela with DeAngelo. And you tried to slice my throat."

Her lips parted. "H-how did you know? Did DeAngelo—"

I shook my head. "No, that man will never betray your trust. I'd recognize your ass anywhere, Amore. I know how every inch of you feels." She chewed on her bottom lip in that way that drove me nuts. "I could never mistake you for someone else, my sex monster. And you called Gabriel, Ink. Nobody else calls him that."

She rolled her eyes trying to play it off, but she knew she had made a mistake.

I twirled a silky piece of her red strands around my index finger. "Your red hair is something," I murmured softly.

She frowned. "You realize there are a lot of redheads out there."

There were no other redheads for me, no other women but this one. She checked all the boxes for me and then some.

I stopped and took her face between my palms, lowering my head so we were inches apart.

"I held your hair wrapped around my fist as you sucked my cock, as I fucked you from every position imaginable, buried my face into it, and you think I'd ever want any other redhead?" I shook my head and even in the dark, I could see her blushing. "Or any woman, for that matter."

I pressed a kiss to the tip of her nose, then let go of her and we resumed walking. "Now tell me what makes you believe George is alive."

Her brow furrowed at my abrupt subject change. I wanted her to think about those words. For now, we'd focus on the immediate threat.

"A tree. Remember I told you George and I went to search for the orchids." I nodded. "There was a tree where we found them, and George carved my initials on it. We hiked by that tree on our last trip to Venezuela. My initials were still there."

I frowned. "So?"

"They were A.R.B." I watched her and the meaning slowly sunk in. "I didn't know that I was a Bennetti then. All my legal documents showed me as Anderson back then." She chewed on her bottom lip again. "The man in Venezuela," her lip quivered lightly. "The one I killed, Ulrich Anderson." I had never regretted killing anyone. They all deserved it. But it bothered Amore. Despite what the Andersons did to her, killing wasn't in her.

"He told me the Andersons wanted me dead because Grandfather promised to hand over the Perèz empire and then reneged on it." I waited for her to continue, her internal struggle evident. "I asked him about George and whether he was alive. He denied it but.... I don't know. Maybe it's all crazy."

She didn't finish it. It didn't sound so crazy, nor farfetched. With the death of Ulrich Anderson, all threats should have ceased, yet the Perèz Cartel didn't retreat. It meant someone was still leading them. George Anderson wasn't such a far-fetched concept.

"Maybe it's not so crazy."

"Remember I told you Mom ordered me not to go into the jungle," she asked in a soft, quivering voice. I nodded. I could never forget anything Amore told me. She was never a chatty girl, but I always listened to everything that came out of her mouth.

"Yeah, I remember."

"George knew," she rasped, her voice full of anguish and emotions. She blamed herself. "He knew Mom forbade it. But he encouraged me, said we should go, the two of us. She left for her business trip to the city, and he said she'd never know. We'd see the orchids and be back before her."

"George had a lot to gain," I added. "He led you into a trap."

"I think so too," she murmured. It was heart wrenching to see the pain on her face. She had loved him, believed him to be her father, and then he betrayed her in the worst way possible.

"What made you believe he was dead in the first place?" I questioned her.

"It was only recently I started to question it," she admitted. "Maybe I'm stupid or naive."

"You're not," I protested. "He's just a conniving, greedy bastard that targets innocent kids."

She sighed deeply. "They tortured Mom in front of me." Her voice was full of anguish at the memories, and I squeezed her hand. "Asking her about Grandpa's cartel business. Where did it go, who got it? Mom didn't know. I had no idea what they were talking about." A tiny hiccup escaped through her lips.

"Amore, if it hurts to talk—"

She shook her head. "No, I think it's better if I get it all out." It clawed at my chest to see her pain. "They hurt Mom in front of my eyes, but George... they took him somewhere, and I never saw him again. In the first days, I could hear his screams, but I never saw him. Why would they torture Mom in front of me but not the man I believed to be my dad?"

My eyes snapped her way. "You didn't see him tortured? Are you sure?"

She swallowed. "Positive. Only his screams. Ulrich said he and his brother wanted me dead to pay for what George did to their mother, but she was dead way before Mom met George."

"Does your grandmother know that the Perèz Cartel were the ones to kill your mom?"

"It wasn't really Perèz. It was the Anderson Cartel that kept working with the Perèz Cartel members who refused to work for Grandma. Both she and Dad knew," she admitted. It fit Regina's explanation. "But Dad didn't know that Grandma was blackmailed. To name the Andersons, a rival Venezuelan cartel, owners of the Perèz empire. She refused because it would have meant instant death for Mom and me. When we were held captive in the jungle, she reached out to the Carrera Cartel and made a deal. To save us in exchange for the drug business."

Regina Regalè might have gotten one over on me, I thought wryly. She led me to believe her granddaughter didn't know she was leading the Perèz Cartel. Yet, Amore has known it all along. My lips tugged up. Maybe that was the reason the dragon woman survived running a cartel for so long!

"The Carrera Cartel found you," I told her. Suddenly, it made sense. The Carrera's interest in her, how they came to save her, why they guarded her so fiercely. They hated the Anderson Cartel, and it was in their best interest to keep Amore and her grandmother alive.

"Yeah, the man, Raguel Carrera, stayed with me until Dad came to Colombia. DeAngelo was there too."

I shook my head in disbelief. She must have been worth quite a bit to the Carrera Cartel for the head of their cartel to stay with her. "That's Gabriel's father."

She tilted her head, her eyes pensive. "You know, somehow I'm not surprised."

"DeAngelo is Gabriel's cousin," I told her.

"I've known all along that DeAngelo was related to the Carreras," she admitted. "It's why he helped me search for the Andersons."

Despite the tiny slither of jealousy that DeAngelo got to be my woman's protector, he'd kept her safe while she was on her mission to avenge her mother. My little creative fashion designer in the jungle of Venezuela, full of fucking men that wouldn't think twice about hurting her.

My hand came to the nape of her neck and pulled her close to me. "There will be none of that anymore," I growled. "I'll keep you safe. You want someone killed; you tell me. I'll do the deed and deliver their heads to you."

Her eyes fluttered to my lips, her smile making my heart hum in satisfaction. "That's all a girl could ever ask for, huh?"

"What else?" I asked her, my mouth brushing against hers, our breaths mixing together. "Whatever you want, it's yours, Amore." Fuck, I wanted to hear her say that four letter word. Five letter word in Italian. Over and over again. "You know, all of me has always been yours," I told her.

Her soft gasp steamed the air between us. It wasn't the most romantic setting, but I didn't give a fuck. There was no better time than now.

"Your heart," she sighed against my lips, placing her small hands on my chest. "I want your heart, Santi."

Then she wrapped her arms around me, pressing her face into my chest and satisfaction purred in my chest. This felt so fucking right.

"You have my heart," I admitted against the crown of her fiery red hair. "It took me a while to realize it, but you've had it all along. I love you, Amore Bennetti. For as long as Russo blood flows through my veins, I will love you. You are my heartbeat, the blood pulsing through my veins, my oxygen. You are my life."

A tiny hiccup and sniffle sounded in the dark of the moonlit night, and I pulled away to search her face. Something sharp pierced through my chest, worried I'd blown it and lost her before we had a chance to start our life together.

Her shimmering eyes of cool moss met my dark gaze, and her hands came around my neck, pulling me down to her.

"I love you too, Santi." Her soft voice matched the expression in her eyes. "I have loved you for so long, I'm not sure I know how not to love you."

CHAPTER 67

Santino

T he rush of relief was instant. Jesus, I was so fucking whipped for this girl, I didn't know if I was coming or going. We were running through the woods, her barefoot and me with a bleeding arm. Yet, the world felt right.

"Good," I half-joked. "Otherwise, I'd tie you to me and you'd still be mine. I'm never letting you go."

She chuckled softly, her right palm against my cheek. "Well, that's comforting. And so damn romantic, I can't help but be impressed."

Taking her hand off my cheek, I pressed a kiss to her fingers, my ring shining, even under the dim moonlight. "Do you like the ring?"

She glanced at it. It was a band with emeralds and diamonds; the stones matched the stones in her necklace. "I love it," she purred. "I wouldn't have cared if you gave me a ring from a bubble gum machine. I'd love anything from you."

I chuckled. "My heiress with a plastic ring? How would that look?" I asked jokingly.

"I don't care because you are worth more to me than all the money in the world."

God, I couldn't wait to get to our destination. We resumed walking.

Adrenaline still pumped through my veins, and I didn't feel tired at all, but Amore was probably reaching her limit.

"I should probably tell you, I forced your grandmother to announce your engagement to me tonight. Behind your father's back."

"You don't say," she remarked mischievously. "And here I thought you and Dad played well together."

I grumbled my response. Ever since he'd denied me Amore, I avoided him more for his own health than mine. I couldn't risk shooting the guy.

"Why did you shoot Luigi?" The question from Amore came out of nowhere.

"Who said that I shot him?"

"Lorenzo."

There was no point in lying about it. "Luigi failed to tell me who you were promised to. It seemed a better option to shoot him than your father."

"Santi!" Her voice held a note of reprimand. I was head of the Cosa Nostra, but Amore could easily bring me to my knees. "I want a big, happy family if we are to get married. No shooting each other."

"What do you mean *if*?" I growled. "We *are* getting married."

"No asking, huh?" Her voice was light. "No getting down on one knee and the whole shebang?"

I chuckled. "You will marry me, baby. If you want me to get down on one knee, I will, but we'll get married regardless."

"God, you make me hot when you are so demanding."

I slapped her butt lightly. "Save it for when we are safe."

"And cleaned up," she added, giggling softly. "Ohhh, I can't wait, Russo."

"You'll soon be a Russo too, baby." Fuck, I'd never felt this happy before.

Continuing our walk in silence, both of us lost in our thoughts, the future looked bright. My arm throbbed but the cut had stopped bleeding a while back. I mulled over the information Amore had given me. We had to get rid of George Anderson.

"Santi?" Amore's voice was tentative.

"Yeah."

"You should think about letting Adriano work for you," she said in a soft voice. "That's all he's ever wanted. Even after catching us earlier, he stood by you."

"How do you figure?" I questioned her, interested in how she would know whose side Adriano was on.

"Just the way he positioned himself," she muttered. "He'd never hurt you."

CHAPTER 68

Amore

S anti's jaw pressed tightly, but he didn't comment. I couldn't understand this man. Maybe it was the don in him. I couldn't understand my grandmother either, nor my father. There seemed to be a trend here.

My muscles were sore, and my feet ached. We'd been walking for hours, and the terrain wasn't easy on my feet. This was a good lesson to have a pair of sneakers in every damn car I entered. Exhaustion was slowly creeping in.

"We're here," he finally announced, and I glanced around. We were in a field with a red barn ahead of us and a line of trees behind us. It was dark, the bright full moon throwing shadows over the entire area. "My car is in the barn."

I scanned the area warily. "There won't be farmers coming out, shooting at us, I hope."

"We are safe," he said. "I own this property."

I raised my eyebrow. I guess I shouldn't be surprised. But for some reason, I assumed he only owned the building in New York and the only property he owned outside the city was his parents' Long Island house.

Once we came to the barn door, there was a fancy digital lock on it. I watched Santi put in a code and it popped open. He pulled his gun out of the holster and entered first with me right behind him. He switched hands so he could hold his gun in his right hand. We could hear a cooing noise, a low and sweet sound through the barn.

The moment the door creaked, the cooing noise ceased, and birds flew through the air and out of the barn or to the far corners where they felt safe.

"We're good," Santi said.

"Because of the birds?" I asked him.

He nodded. "If someone was here, the birds wouldn't have been here."

He reached to the side and flipped a switch, dim lights flickering as the inside of the barn lit up.

"Such high-tech security," I mused. "We need more of it."

He chuckled, pulling me along as we strode to the black Jeep Rubicon. Just being out of the woods felt better on my feet. Opening the door, he helped me climb into it. The relief was instant. I have never been so happy to sit.

"Let me check your feet," he murmured, taking them into his hands.

"They are filthy," I protested.

"I want to make sure there are no injuries."

I rolled my eyes slightly annoyed but couldn't help the fluttering feelings in my chest for his caring. His arm was injured, soaked in blood, yet he worried about my feet.

"Just cuts," I muttered, extending my leg for his inspection.

"We'll have to make sure to clean out your cuts when we get to our place," he told me.

"I'm more worried about your wound, Santi."

"We'll patch each other up." A smirk played on his face. "Maybe a steamy shower together."

I rolled my eyes again, but my lips tugged up. At this rate, my eyeballs will be stuck in the back of my head and my lips in a permanent smile around this man. Only Santi succeeded in having me go from one extreme to another, from pain to pleasure, angry to laughing, sad to happy.

He got in, reached underneath the wheel, pulled out the key then started the ignition.

"You've got to love a Jeep," he muttered. "Never fails me."

"How long has this car been sitting here?" I questioned him. I was sure the battery would be dead.

"I try to make it here once a month to check on everything. I haven't been in two months."

"Lucky," I muttered.

"About time," he retorted back.

As he sped down the highway, he reached across and opened the glovebox. Nervous he would crash, I took his hand.

"Tell me what you are looking for."

"Nervous, baby?" His smirk was doing all kinds of wrong... or right things to me.

I chuckled, despite my exhaustion. "I'd rather we don't crash. I want a lot more sex before I die," I insisted, smirking.

He laughed, deep and hearty. The sound made my heart swell with warmth and my pulse skipped a beat. God, I wanted to make him happy. No rhyme or reason, I just wanted to make him happy.

"There is a burner phone in there," he said, his voice warm.

I dug through the glove compartment. It took me a few seconds before I got it and handed it to him.

"Thank you," he said.

He turned it on and as he waited, I asked curiously. "Who are you calling?"

"Your father."

It wasn't what I expected. "Why?"

"I might be pissed off at him," he deadpanned, "but he loves you, and if he hears about the attack, he'll lose his mind. No sense in giving him a heart attack."

I reached out to Santi, placing my hand on his thigh and squeezing it gently. "Thank you," I murmured. He was a good man.

He dialed the number, ringing coming through the phone. The next second, I heard my father's voice answer.

"Santino here. Amore is safe."

A loud exhale. "Jesus fucking Christ. I was worried sick." Silence followed, and I was sure my father thought back to the way we parted. "Thank you, Russo."

My dad might be a lot of things, a criminal, a hardass, and who knows what else, but he had a good heart. And he knew when he owed someone. I loved him despite not knowing him for the first thirteen years of my life. George was a fraud. It had never been more evident than now when I could clearly see all that my dad had done for my safety.

"No problem," Santi answered. "I'm not taking her to my city house. I'll keep her safe."

I expected my father to protest, but he surprised me when I heard his answer.

"Good," he agreed. "Keep her safe, Russo. Don't make me regret letting her go with you."

Santi growled, but I gently squeezed his thigh again, leaned over and pressed my mouth on the stubble of his cheek.

"She will be," was all Santi ended up saying.

"I want to talk to my daughter."

Santi handed me the phone and continued driving, speeding as far away from the city as possible.

"Hey, Dad," I greeted him. I could hear him clear his throat, but no words came over the phone, so I continued, "Don't worry about me. I'm sorry to stress you out."

"Don't worry about that." Dad's voice sounded strained. "Be safe. I just want you safe."

"We are." I cleared my throat, uncomfortable with the next words. "I'm sorry about what happened earlier tonight," I continued in a soft voice. "I don't want you to think—"

"Amore, no matter what you did or do, I am still proud of you." I swallowed hard. Those words meant so much. "I love you." My dad rarely spoke words of affection and emotion was thick in his voice. "Even though sometimes it seems I'm too controlling, I want you to be happy. Your safety is my priority."

"I love you too," I said softly. "Santi will keep me safe."

"He better if he wants to live," Dad grunted, and I couldn't help but let out a soft chuckle. "But I know he will. After all, he went through a lot of trouble to make sure you marry him. And as long as you want that too, I'll support it. But if he makes you cry, I'll kill him."

"Don't worry, Dad," I retorted jokingly. "If he makes me cry, I'll make him cry too."

Dad's deep chuckle sounded through the phone, making me swell with happiness.

"Okay, my little warrior, give the phone to Russo," he said, a trace of laughter still in his voice.

I handed the phone back to Santi with a wide grin. Maybe I could have it all. The two men exchanged words. I didn't follow, my head practically in the clouds.

Santi hung up, then took my hand into his, brushing his lips against my knuckles. "My Amore," he drawled, his lips curved in amusement. "Seems I'm getting a father-in-law that will kill me unless his daughter is smiling every time he sees you."

"I'll be sure to smile." I grinned. "Unless I want to get rid of you," I teased.

He grimaced. "When did my fiancée become so bloodthirsty?"

"Since she fell in love," I shot back.

He let out a breath of amusement. I loved how relaxed the air between us felt. A simple evening and everything has changed. To distract myself, I checked on his right arm to make sure it hadn't started bleeding again. Satisfied I only saw dried blood, I leaned my head back against the seat.

Silence fell in the car. Pulling his jacket tighter over me, I inhaled deeply. His scent lingered around me and comforted me.

I suspected Santi kept quiet because he wanted me to get some rest. I tried to remain awake, but it didn't take long for my eyelids to grow heavier with each mile behind us. The freeway was empty, and Santi drove smoothly and steadily, the sound of the engine soothing me to sleep.

"Get some sleep," Santi recommended in a low voice.

I murmured something unintelligible then sleep took over.

CHAPTER 69

Amore

I woke up with a foggy brain and hazy memory. My body ached and exhaustion was heavy. Sunlight streamed through the windows, and I blinked against it. Reaching behind me, I felt a big body and scooted closer to it, pressing in further, needing the warmth. I needed a little more sleep, just a bit more rest.

A hard chest pressed tight against my back and the tattooed arm over my hip pulled me closer. The chirping of birds traveled through the air, the waves crashing against the shoreline. *Italy. I'm in Italy with Santi.*

I didn't want to wake up. Italy was our happy time. Just us and the sea. But that couldn't be. My thoughts distorted; I blinked a few times against the brightness of the room, trying to gauge where we were. The fog in my brain slowly started clearing up. The guns, tracking through the woods with Santi, driving for a long time. We must be at our destination.

Shifting my head, I glanced out the window. The view of the open seas stretched in front of me. That explained the sound of waves crashing against the shoreline. I turned around to find Santi behind me, both of us still in dirty clothes from last night's party, his hand on my hip bloodied.

"Santi?" I whispered and his eyes immediately opened.

"You okay?" His voice was hoarse.

"Yes. But your hand," I told him. "It's bloody."

"Shit." He removed it from me. "Sorry, babe."

On a groan, I sat up, my head pounding hard.

"How are you feeling?" he asked.

"Like I got run over," I mumbled, pushing my hand through my hair, then taking his hand in mine. "You?"

"Something like that," he muttered, closing his eyes. I was so glad to be here with him despite the danger lurking.

"We have to clean you up," I told him. "I'm worried about infection. I should have checked it last night."

He never opened his eyes. "I pulled the glass out and disinfected the cut."

God, this man! "All by yourself?"

"Hmmm."

"You should have woken me up," I reprimanded him. "What kind of wife will I be if I'm not helping you with that kind of stuff?"

"Next time, I promise," he said. I went to rise only to be pulled back. "Sleep a bit longer," he muttered sleepily.

"Let me get a wet cloth and at least wash your arm," I told him. It was hard to tell if his arm was fine underneath all that blood.

"How about a shower together?" he questioned, peering at me under his eyelids.

My body instantly warmed up, totally onboard for it but worry outweighed the lust. A lazy smile spread over his lips. He read me so well. Before I even answered, he was out of the bed, lifting me up, despite his injury, and continued straight into the en-suite bathroom.

"Santi, your arm," I protested, giggling.

"It feels great now."

He sat me on the bathroom counter, then turned around and started the shower. He started stripping his clothes off, and I shamelessly watched him. Watching Santino Russo strip was addictive, hot, and the best view a girl could possibly wish for. I was captivated and under Santi's spell. It was like drowning and not bothering to come up for air. He became my air.

Once he was completely naked, my hands lifted of their own will, skimming lightly over his hot body. Opening my legs with each of his hands taking the back of my knees, he situated himself between my welcoming thighs.

CHAPTER 70

Santino

A more's dainty hands wrapped around my shaft and a groan echoed through the bathroom. Her gaze was glistening like shimmering lakes, her lips parted like touching me gave her pleasure. My cock thickened and hardened effortlessly under her touch. It didn't matter that I'd only had a couple of hours of sleep. It was all it took. One touch by her, and I could slide into her tight pussy and be in my own personal heaven.

I slept better the last few hours than I had since Italy. And it was because she was in my arms. When we got to my cabin yesterday, I carried her into the house and placed her in bed. She was out like a light. I left her to sleep in her clothes, cleaned my cut, and then did the same. It was a long drive up and almost three in the morning by the time I slipped into bed, next to her.

Pulling the dress over her head, she sat there naked. All for my viewing. I couldn't resist, I reached out and rubbed her nipple between my thumb and index, squeezing it. She moaned loud, her head tilting back, watching me through her half-lidded, hazy gaze.

She was the hottest woman I had ever seen, my siren. Everything about her pulled at me. Her pale skin, her perky nipples, her parted mouth. She was my perfect contrast.

"I need you, Santi," she rasped.

She wrapped both her arms around my neck, the heels of her feet digging into my ass as she rubbed herself against me.

My fingers dug into the flesh of her hips roughly, holding her in place. No protest left her lips, just those little noises that drove me nuts. Her fingers scraped against my scalp, running them through my hair.

I lowered my head and sucked her nipple into my mouth, nibbling on it until shudders passed over her body. God, she was amazing. She was trembling, incoherent noises escaping her lips. The only thing I picked up was my name on her lips, and it made me want to pound my chest.

Releasing her nipple, I placed both hands under her butt and lifted her up, then walked us under the shower stream. I backed her up against the tiled wall in the shower, her legs still wrapped around my waist. She gasped against my lips at the cool sensation of the tile against her back.

She gently pushed against me, breaking our kiss.

Her eyes had changed to deep, dark green, her cheeks flushed crimson, and her mouth parted. Seeing her like this was such a turn on, I could watch her and jerk off. "Santi?"

"Yeah?"

"Can I suck you off?"

Jesus! Like I was doing her a favor.

"I'll fuck your mouth until tears stream down your face." I wasn't sure if I was trying to warn her off or give her a way out.

She gave me a beautiful smile. "Promise?"

Good God, it would be fucked up if I came right now before we even got started.

She wiggled out of my arms and slid down my body. Amore stole my breath away each time I gazed upon her. Her milky skin glistened under the waterfall of the shower. She was a work of art, like a classical Venus painting by Botticelli.

I had never wanted anything so much as her permanently attached to me. It scared me how vulnerable it made me feel, but it was even scarier to think I could lose her. I'd tattoo a ring on her finger, like her name became permanently etched on my heart.

She slowly lowered herself onto her knees, her eyes never leaving my face. The shower water stream behind me, keeping it from hitting her face. I wanted to see her cry as she gagged full of my cock; fuck her until I spilled inside her warm mouth and filled her belly with my cum.

My hand twisted through her mane with a fist and gently tugged; while with my other hand, I traced my thumb over her bottom lip. Her pretty mouth immediately parted, her tongue wickedly brushing against the tip of my finger.

"If it's too much, tap my thigh."

I eased my cock into her mouth and her little *mmmm* sound almost had me blowing my load. *Jesus Christ!* She eagerly sucked me down as I slowly pumped into her mouth, her eyes locked on mine. As if she was relishing in luxury and having the best time of her life.

My dark desires crept up my spine and I picked up my pace, thrusting deeper into her mouth. And harder. Until I was hitting the back of her throat. Her eyes fluttered shut, her hands on my thighs and fingers curling into my skin. But the look on her face... it was one of bliss. Euphoria.

"Open your eyes," I rasped. "Look at me while I fuck your mouth and see what you do to me."

Her eyes opened, a soft jade shimmering with lust. Her full submission to me was the highest aphrodisiac, the sweetest surrender. Pleasure built up in my spine with each thrust deep into her throat, threatening to break me.

I should ease up but seeing her like this... it did something to me. Tears slid from the corner of her eyes, her gaze locked on me, but I didn't offer reprieve. This was the selfish Russo. I'd take it all from her. I cupped her face, wiping away her tears with my thumb.

For a fraction of a second, I debated pulling out. Some women found it degrading. While I didn't care much for others, Amore... I never wanted to hurt her. As if she sensed my internal debate, her hands ran up my thighs and squeezed in encouragement.

It was all I needed. Her consent. Her approval.

"My cum will fill your belly," I grunted, savoring every moment.

Another thrust deep into her throat and my head fell back, my eyes closing as I drove into her again and orgasmed like never before. Every time was better with her, more addictive. Maybe it was her willingness, the look on her face telling me she loved this as much as I did. Or maybe it was her love for me. Fuck if I knew, but I was certain it would be like this with her for the rest of our lives.

Amore swallowed all my cum, her little noises ready to get me hard again, and my fist still gripping her hair. I slowly let go of her. She slowly eased back, my cock sliding out of her pretty, smart mouth. She leaned back, licking her lips. It didn't matter that she was on her knees; she owned *me.* Amore was permanently inked into my heart and soul.

Her lips curved into a soft smile, like she knew she owned me and would keep me. She fucking better.

I yanked her to her feet and sat her on the shower bench, pushing her legs apart with my hands, her glistening, pink pussy on full view. Fuck, I was getting hard again.

I kneeled between her parted legs. "My turn," I growled.

Sweet fucking Jesus Christ! She was soaking wet. I leaned my face between her thighs, parting her with my fingers and taking a long lick. She tasted like the best dessert. Strawberry, desire, and her... just her.

A visible shudder passed over her body, her hips lifting, grinding against my mouth.

"Please, Santi," she breathed out. "Oh, God. Please."

This was how I wanted her all the time. Greedy and demanding. Just as I was with her. Just the two of us, getting lost in our oblivion.

Our gazes held as I circled her clit with the tip of my tongue, her body vibrating with need and shudders rolling through her soft body. Her tongue swept over her bottom lip, her pants getting louder, her eyes hazed with desire.

I kept eating her out, the need to see her fall apart driving me. I wanted to ensure she knew who she belonged to, who owned her. She rocked against my mouth, chasing her orgasm and it didn't take long. She came with a cry, her body shuddering against my tongue and my name on her lips.

I was hard as a rock, ready to bury myself inside of her tight little cunt. Not giving her time to come down from her high, I slid my hands under her butt cheeks, I lifted her up, her legs wrapped around me.

My cock at her hot entrance, I brought her down roughly until I was deep inside her, filling her to the hilt. Pushing her against the shower wall, I thrust brutally inside her again. Soft whimpers left her mouth and her back arched off the wall. God, she was perfect! Writhing against me, her hips rocking, grinding, and demanding her pleasure. Amore owned her pleasure, as well as mine.

"Santi," she whispered. "God, I love you."

I felt her nails sinking into my shoulder blades, a look of pure bliss on her face. Losing my control, I picked up my pace, thrusting rough and deep into her tight cunt. My own personal heaven.

"I love you." My voice was rough, grunting. I craved her. She was the only human on this planet that could tear me apart. "I'm yours."

Grabbing a fistful of her hair, I pulled back her head, exposing her pale, fragile neck. My lips found her pulse point and I sucked on it, nipped it, leaving red marks for all to see. I wanted to mark her for the whole world to see. For the whole world to know that she fucking belonged to me.

My ring on her finger.

My red marks on her skin.

My last name attached to hers.

I grazed my teeth against her pulse, thrusting crazily into her pussy. "I love how good you take my cock," I praised and felt a shudder pass her body.

She was panting, rolling her hips to meet each one of my thrusts. She was the best drug, my only drug.

"P-please..." Her eyes hazed, and our gazes locked. Everything faded but this woman that would soon become my wife.

I drove into her hard and fast. She writhed, and I was too far gone as I relentlessly pounded into her. Her pussy clenched around my cock, strangling it in the most delicious way. I could feel she was close. With one hand still firmly holding her, I raised my right hand and wrapped my fingers round her fragile neck. She leaned into my big hand and that trust did something to me every time. I could snuff the light out of her, but she trusted me. Her pulse thundered under my fingers. I lightly squeezed her neck, my thrusts deep and fast while her cunt choked my cock.

"Come for me, baby," I ordered with a squeeze on her neck, and she came undone. Her green eyes shone as she orgasmed, her skin flushed red and her body shuddering. I fucked her rough and hard through her orgasm, my mouth on her, smothering her, drinking in her moans. Her heat and the strangling hold of her pussy took me over the edge, and I came hard.

CHAPTER 71

Amore

The orgasm I just had left me limp in Santi's arms. I had died and gone to orgasm heaven. I couldn't even gather the energy to move, never mind get soaped up.

A soft chuckle had me lifting my head off Santi's shoulder. His dark eyes shone like black diamonds. "Don't tell me you are done for the day?"

I put my forehead back on his shoulder. "No, but let me catch my breath first," I muttered. "I'm slightly out of practice."

Another laugh rumbled through his chest. God, I loved hearing him laugh. It took him five minutes to wash my hair and body, then wash himself off before we both stepped out of the shower to dry off.

"I have nothing to wear," I told him, eyeing the dirty dress on the tiled floor.

"You can wear something of mine, and we'll go get some clothes for you."

"Where are we anyhow?" I questioned him.

"You'll find out soon enough."

Two hours later, both of us showered, we climbed back into the Jeep. The house we were staying at was beautiful, situated on a cliff and overlooking the ocean. We were somewhere along the coastline of the North Atlantic.

I eyed Santi. He looked good, though I wondered why he didn't dress down. He wore his dark three-piece suit and of course, a gun. I wore one of his dress shirts that came down to my knees and boxers underneath. I tied one of his ties around my waist as a makeshift belt.

"So how often do you come up here?" I questioned him as we drove through the deserted, back road.

"When I want to be alone."

"Sorry you had to drag me along then." I wasn't. I loved being with Santi. Anywhere. It wouldn't matter if we were in a shack, as long as we were together, I'd be happy.

"I'm not."

Watching him drive, I felt my lips curve into a soft smile. It was my reaction to him when I was happy. I could just burst from smiles and love.

The atmosphere in the car was comfortable, his hand on my thigh and my finger tracing over his ink. The move was familiar, intimate. Before I could get all mushy, because that was what his orgasms did to me, I changed the subject. "So where exactly are we, Santi?"

He glanced my way, his sunglasses hiding his eyes from me. It should be criminal to be so handsome. *Oh wait, he is a criminal!* He barely had any sleep, yet he looked rested and fresh. And oh so damn hot.

"Rockport, Massachusetts."

My head whipped his way. "You drove all that way?"

"Hmmm."

The question was whether we were safe here? Or maybe the danger was mainly in the city?

We drove for about thirty minutes until we were in the heart of the town. It was a beautiful little place and sort of romantic, a small seaside village like you would envision in the old days. He parked the car and scanned the area. You couldn't take the don out of Santino Russo.

"Okay, stores are that way." He tugged me along to the left.

"I'd much rather sightsee," I murmured, my eyes darting every-where. The town was busy, swarming with visitors, families on vacation.

His eyes roamed my body, his eyes burning my skin with his hot gaze. It spoke of dirty words and deliciously filthy things he could do to my body.

"Not dressed like that, you won't." His voice was a delicious mixture of gravel and sin, sending my heart into overdrive. He stood so close to me, his towering body brushing against mine. It felt like a warning to any other passerby to fuck off. He might as well have shouted to the world, *She is mine!*

"I forgot," I rasped breathlessly. God, what this man did to me!

Taking my hand in his, we headed down the street. We stopped at the first store, walking through the door hand in hand, a gentle *ding* announcing our entrance. My thoughts traveled back to two months ago when we did something similar in Genoa. Things felt so so different back then. It had only been two months, but so much had changed. But one thing remained the same, I had loved him then, and I still loved him now.

"Italy all over again, hmmm?" My head snapped his way. It was like he was reading my thoughts.

"I loved Italy," I admitted softly. His thumb came to my cheek, his rough pad gently rubbing against my soft skin.

"I know. We'll go back." I knew he'd keep his promise. "For our honeymoon and every summer."

Pressing my cheek into his touch, I breathed deeply, his scent seeping into my lungs. "And some holidays."

"Whatever you want."

Suddenly, I realized I couldn't wait to become his wife. Our admissions last night sealed the impending wedding, but we didn't set a date. Or place.

Mine.

Two hours later, the Jeep was packed with bags; we'd bought out the store. Santi went to the local grocery store where he talked to a man, reciting a list of things he wanted delivered to his place before we headed to grab a bite to eat at one of the delis.

I bit into my Mediterranean sandwich, moaning at the taste of it. "Oh my gosh, this is good." I must have been hungrier than I thought.

Santi's gaze darkened and warmed, full of every emotion, sending a shiver across my spine.

"Not as good as your pussy," he murmured, and my cheeks heated.

"Santi!" I scolded him, glancing around us to ensure nobody else heard him.

He let out a breath of amusement. "It's the truth. Now eat because you'll need all your energy tonight."

I eyed him suspiciously. "Why?"

Though I suspected the answer and liked the idea of it. Maybe I was a nymphomaniac? I just couldn't get enough of him. Though if I was honest, I loved feeling like that.

He smiled, wickedness dancing in his eyes. "You'll see."

"You know, we better find some other hobbies we both enjoy because eventually sex will get old," I said, bringing my sandwich to my mouth.

He laughed deep, his eyes shining with amusement, and I realized making Santi laugh was another aphrodisiac. Seeing him happy. It did things to my heart.

"Not very likely, my sex monster," he teased, shaking his head while a smile still played on his lips. "I'll never have enough of you, and I'll be sure you never get enough of me. But we can certainly work on other hobbies too. Now eat!"

There would be nothing else coming from his mouth; I knew it. So, I shrugged my shoulders and bit into my sandwich again. I devoured it like I hadn't eaten in days. He was eating too, and every so often he'd glance at his phone.

"Can you get me a phone too?" I asked. "I still have some work to check on and can't just disappear without lining up backups."

He met my eyes, his brow raised then shook his head in disbelief. "You must be the only twenty-one-year-old worried about work, my little heiress."

I scoffed. "I bet you were worried about your papà's business way before my age."

"You are right," he admitted, scratching his chin. "It is rare to see it in a woman."

I threw my head back and laughed. "First, that is sexist. And second, thanks for calling me a woman." I shook my head. "I swear, Santi. You can be such a man."

The smile he gave me was startlingly beautiful, and my breath hitched at how much younger he looked when he smiled like that.

"I'm glad to hear it," he muttered. His eyes traveled over my head, and I followed his gaze to find Lorenzo standing there.

"What are you doing here?" I exclaimed, jumping up to hug him and he wrapped his arm around me. "Is everybody okay?"

Blending in with local tourists, he was wearing white golf shorts and a black polo t-shirt. He didn't play golf.

He chuckled. "Everyone is fine." He pressed a kiss on my cheek. "I came to be your witness."

I glanced at Santi in his black three-piece suit with confusion in my eyes.

"Witness?"

"We are getting married."

Three heartbeats passed before I could think straight. Suddenly, his choice of wardrobe today made sense. He would dress formally for his own wedding, no matter how small or casual it was.

Yes, I wanted to marry him. I couldn't wait. But like this? My dad and grandma would be heartbroken. They wanted to see me married. It was every father's dream to walk his daughter down the aisle. I couldn't take that away from him.

"No, Santi," I mouthed, my voice somehow gone. Maybe because I really did want to marry him, be his wife today but there were a few critical people missing.

"Yes," Santi said, his eyes drilling into me.

"Santi…" I started but wasn't sure what to say. If I said I didn't want him, he'd know it was a lie. I have wanted him for such a long time, he was part of me. Just like the air I breathed. I loved him; I've told him as much.

"Dad won't be happy," I muttered, pleading with Lorenzo. "It will piss him off; might cause a war. And we just came to a mutual agreement."

Lorenzo put his hand in his pockets and leaned against the column next to our booth.

"Actually, if we wait and let everyone think about it, it will cause a war," Lorenzo reasoned, his voice calm. "Once we tell them you are married, it will be water under the bridge, and we can all focus on this threat looming over you."

I exhaled. "You are supposed to be on my side, brother."

"I am. Always."

"Dad just told me last night that if this was what I wanted, I have his support. We should just wait." I pushed my hand through my hair. "Grandma and Dad might not forgive doing this without them."

I swallowed hard. Have you ever wanted something so bad that when you finally got it, you were too scared to take it? That was how I felt right now. Scared of the consequences and hurting people I loved. I have finally got what I have desired for so long. I should seize the opportunity and take what I want. I have never been scared to take what I wanted before. Yet... I didn't want to do it at the expense of Dad and Grandma. I went after the orchids, and the repercussions were grave.

"What about Adriano?" I whispered my question and saw Santi's face harden into a cold mask.

"You won't be seeing him," he snapped. "Now, finish your lunch, and then you'll get dressed. You are taking my last name today."

"I don't have a dress."

"I picked one out while you were trying on clothes."

I stood still, watching him and trying to understand why the urgency. My gaze darted to my brother, but he just nodded his assurance. Yet, why did I feel dread pooling in my stomach?

"Santi, I want to marry you," I rasped. "I really do. And I will. But not at the expense of Dad, Adriano, and Grandma. I want to do it right. Last time I went for what I wanted without..." My voice trailed off and I swallowed hard, emotions choking me.

Santi took my hand and pulled me down next to him. "We will have a wedding, a big one. In the church with your father, brothers, Adriano, Regina. Everyone under the sun." I blinked hard, my eyes stinging, and I feared tears might start flowing. "I am not doing this because I want to jab your father or think you'll change your mind." He brought my hand to his lips, placing his mouth on the pulse of my wrist. "I won't deny it, a part of me wants to make you a Russo, tattoo my name on your finger so the entire world knows who owns you. Today! More than anything. But I'd never do it if it hurts you." A small exhale left me. "The reason we need to do it today is... to keep you safe. And your grandmother. Your grandfather had a clause that if something should happen to his descendants and wife, the Perèz Cartel went to the next spouse. It leaves George Anderson as that person."

A sharp exhale left me. How did I not know about that clause? I watched him with a guarded expression. Santi was head of the Cosa Nostra. He was powerful, but people always wanted more power.

"Do you want the cartel?" The question slipped out, a grip around my heart squeezing tighter and tighter. So many men wanted the power that the Perèz Cartel offered. Look at the Anderson men. And now...

"I don't give a fuck about it," Santi's voice was deep and full of conviction. "You, on the other hand, I love and want. For the rest of my life. That cartel business could come or go, I wouldn't miss a beat. But losing you... *you*, Amore, is what would end me. There is nothing, *nothing*, I wouldn't do for you."

A delightful shiver rolled down my spine at his possessive tone. Maybe I was stupid, but I believed him. Santi was ruthless, maybe a tiny bit psychotic, but he wasn't a liar.

"Okay," I whispered.

"It's the right thing to do, Amore," Lorenzo added. "After all, you two have been screwing for a while now."

And the moment was gone. "You are such an ass, Lorenzo," I snapped, narrowing my eyes, and watching my brother's eyes shine mischievously. Turning my back to him, I addressed Santi. "Where is this dress?"

We stood in the court, Lorenzo and Santi on each side of me. It almost felt like those two were my guards. I had to laugh though because if I didn't want to do this, I would have fought them. Screamed. But I did want it. More than anything else in this world.

We'd do a big wedding for Dad and Grandma. This was just for us then.

My heart raced and my hand squeezed Santi's hand holding mine. I was nervous. Since I got back to the States, my life had been a whirlwind. I never imagined it'd bring me here, to a little Rockport courthouse with Santi holding my hand.

The dress I wore was beautiful and simple. White, classic, timeless. The front square cut left my chest open, his necklace the only thing around my neck. The dress had thin straps, leaving my shoulders naked, and fit around my upper body like a glove, then flaring down my legs, stopping above my knees. Santi even thought of shoes. Sandals with small heels.

"You look beautiful," Lorenzo muttered, kissing my forehead.

I smiled nervously at him. "Thank you for being here." I wished I could have talked to Adriano, explained, but Santi refused the idea that we should tell him.

My pulse beat hard as we were guided into the room where the Justice of the Peace waited for us.

"Mr. Russo," the judge greeted him. "Thank you again for the generous donation to the city."

I narrowed my eyes at Santi. When in the hell did he have time to arrange all this and bribe the man? But then nothing surprised me with Santi. When he wanted something, he made it happen.

"Thank you for accommodating the same day license," Santi retorted.

And the ceremony started. I didn't hear a single word from start to finish. The words of the judge sounded far away and the only thing that registered was the familiar touch of Santi as he held my hands, the light scent of his cologne and the heat he ignited in me.

"I do." Santi's words were firm, claiming, and final. His eyes burned with intensity threatening to pull me into its flame. His promise of forever echoed through the small room and my heart sang with happiness. I believed he'd protect me, honor me, and cherish me. Most importantly, he loved me.

It was my turn, and my voice shook as I repeated the words. Emotion was thick on my tongue and in my heart.

The boy that brushed my tears away. Gave me my first kiss. My first orgasm. My first heartbreak. My first and last lover. My husband.

The exchange of the rings followed. He slid the same band back onto my finger. Lorenzo gave me a band for Santi. He said my mother gifted it to Dad before she left. It felt like his blessing. And Mom's. With a trembling hand, I slid the ring onto my husband's finger.

Then his lips pressed against mine, possessive and claiming, sweet and soft. And I was forever his.

"I proclaim you husband and wife." The judge's words were final.

"Amore Russo," he murmured against my lips. "I like that."

So did I. A lot.

CHAPTER 72

Amore

The sun shone bright, sounds of families and children laughing carried on the warm summer breeze. And the glow in my heart competed with the bright day.

His hand slipped into mine, and I followed his lead. Our fates were sealed, forever intertwined. Like our hearts, our souls, and fingers as we held hands.

"There is a dessert shop around the corner," Santi announced. "We'll have cake and ice cream."

Lorenzo walked right beside me, eyeing a group of women in their bathing suits. Some things would never change. I playfully bumped my shoulder against Lorenzo. "Stop staring."

A reminder of Adriano washed over me with that simple playful move. A pang of guilt hit me in the chest. For the first time, for as long as we'd been friends, there was a probable threat of losing him. He probably hated me.

I should be panicked, worried, what Dad would say when he found out we got married behind his back. But somehow, I wasn't. Santi's reasoning made sense, and another don, like my father, would find the logic in it. But Adriano worried me.

Despite it all, I couldn't say that I was sad. A peaceful, happy feeling settled in my chest. Kind of like it did when we were alone in Italy. The whole world faded, leaving me with the man I loved.

Santi was always the one for me. He was my protector, love and home all wrapped in one.

"I thought you didn't like sweets?" I bit my lip to hold a smile. I knew what he was thinking, but he wouldn't say it in front of Lorenzo.

"There is only one dessert I like," Santi retorted, his gaze flickering with amusement. "But you get married only once. So, I'll share cake and ice cream, or anything you'd like. With my wife."

His wife. It felt like I was dreaming, and the moment I woke up, reality would slap me in the face.

"You two wait until you get home to start the dirty talk," Lorenzo complained, with a shake of his head. "After all, you are my baby sister."

I really did love Lorenzo. Our age difference didn't matter, we always got along. "And you are my big brother," I teased him. "I might have to protect you from gold digging ladies that keep eyeing you like candy."

With a feigned expression of interest, his eyes darted left and right. "Where are they? Are they cute?"

All three of us burst into carefree laughter. There was still another threat looming, but right now, we'd enjoy the moment. Lorenzo pulled out his phone. "Okay, a few pictures. For evidence and memories."

The cake sat in front of us, and Santi cut a small piece. He had the baker make a cake specially for us, with ice cream as the topping. *Pink cake for my goddess,* he said.

He picked up a piece with his hands.

"Open," he ordered, and I immediately parted my mouth. His gaze burned like a lit match, igniting an inferno that threatened to turn me to ash before we even consummated our marriage. It was probably a moot point, since we couldn't keep our hands to ourselves from the moment we got a taste of each other.

He put a small piece of cake into my mouth, and I closed it, trapping his finger. Our eyes locked, his full of promises. A hot shudder ran down my back, tingling between my thighs pulsing with need.

This love and desire we shared... it was all-consuming, soul-shattering. The kind that you happily let consume you.

He slowly pulled his finger from between my lips. My heartbeat drummed in my ears, in sync with the throbbing ache at my core.

"Jesus you two," Lorenzo muttered. "I have pictures. Lots, though I think they might belong on an X-rated site."

Santi gave him a dark, warning look. "Okay, okay," Lorenzo muttered, raising his hands in surrender. "Not on the X-rated site. I'll text you the pictures and delete them." He grinned his *'up to no good'* smile. "Thank you for the invite. I'm going to go."

He stood up and my gaze flickered to him. "Thanks for coming," I said, offering him the cheek as he leaned over.

He pressed a light kiss on it. "I'm happy for you, sister," he whispered low against my cheek. "If he ever makes you cry, come to me, and I'll make him pay."

"I will," I promised softly. There would never be the need for it, I knew it in my heart. Santi must have heard Lorenzo because there was dark amusement in his eyes. Probably his *'you can try but you'll never succeed'* look.

Lorenzo left and I returned my attention to my husband. *My husband!* I'd never tire of that.

"My turn," I told him and lifted a smaller piece of cake, knowing he didn't like sweets. He opened his mouth, sending a rush of languid heat through my veins. I watched him swallow, licking the remains of the cake from his lips.

He lifted another piece of cake into my mouth, and I took it. Though right now, it was the last thing I wanted or needed. I slowly chewed on it, wishing his lips were on mine. The unique taste of sin that tasted amazing, but only when Santi kissed me.

"I'm done. I want to go home." My blush burned my skin, but it didn't match the pulsing heat between my thighs.

"Yeah?"

With a light nod, I stood up and extended my hand. He was home. It didn't matter where in the world I was as long as I was with him. His warm, big hand grabbed mine and we rushed towards the Jeep. The moment we climbed in the seats, Santi's hand reached beneath my skirt and dragged his knuckles over my clit through my panties.

A moan escaped me. He put the car in drive and drove through the main street full of people, keeping his hand up my dress and rubbing my pussy as my insides clenched. His finger slid inside my panties, dipping into me and my hips bucked.

"Don't come until your husband allows it," he growled with heat.

My eyes flared open, meeting his hot gaze. His finger lazily pumped in and out of me. I hadn't been touched by anyone since Italy, but over the last day the greed for him increased tenfold. The withdrawal kicked in shortly after each fix.

"Please," I panted, his thrusts harder as I threw my head back against the seat. "Oh God... please."

My body quivered and shook with need. I needed this release. He removed his finger and pulled my panties back into place. My eyes snapped open, and I watched him suck his finger clean.

"Why did you stop?" I breathed hard.

"Your first orgasm as a married woman will be with my cock in your pussy," he said. His hard bulge didn't escape me. "So you will wait."

"I can't wait," I whimpered, shoving my hand down my panties, fingering myself. "I-I need it now."

I stroked my clit, almost anticipating Santi stopping me. But he never did. Instead, his gaze burned. I watched through heavy lids, my finger mindlessly rubbing on my clit. *I'm so close.*

"Santi," I moaned. His hand came around my wrist and stilled my movements.

"Stop," he ordered, and a whimper left my lips.

He swerved to the side of the road, then his hands dug into my hips and lifted me onto his lap.

"Fuck it," he rasped. "I can't wait till we get home."

Yes! I thought victoriously.

My fingers fumbled with his pants, then reached for his cock. He was smooth and hard. Our mouths collided in messy, sloppy kisses, both of us grunting. My heart thundered.

He ripped my panties, the shredding sound echoed through the car.

"Some things never change, husband?" I breathed out, my mouth against his.

His hand pulled my dress straps down, and he cupped my breasts through my bra. Then as if that wasn't good enough, he pulled the cups and bent his head, latching his mouth to my nipple. He sucked on my breasts as his hand lowered and gripped my ass.

"Fuck," I panted, my whole body on fire.

"You're so wet," he groaned. His fingers dug into my ass. "So pretty when you pant for my cock."

I slid down his length, and we both shuddered the moment he filled me to the hilt. He was so big and hard, his length felt better than ever.

"Santi," I moaned and started rocking my hips.

His hand came up and grasped my throat. My eyes locked on his whiskey gaze and like so many times before, I pushed my neck into his strong grip, knowing he could snap my neck with one move and trusting he wouldn't.

"Do you like this, wife?" he demanded, his voice hoarse with that hand banded around my throat. His other hand tugged my head back with my hair fisted in his grip; my neck was exposed to him.

"Yes," I cried out. "Harder. Give it to me harder."

Self-control around my husband was non-existent. *He* was my vice.

He slammed into me, his hips working like pistons underneath me, pulling my head so I could see where our bodies connected.

"Mine." His claim was harsh and needy. "Watch me fuck you, wife."

Lowering my eyes to where our bodies connected, my forehead against his, I watched his cock slide in and out of me. The sight was erotic, making my muscles clench with need as his thrusts became harder. Faster. Deeper. My body welcomed it, craving the man that owned me.

"Yes," I moaned out. Each thrust into me, ripped another throaty moan from me. "Yes, please."

His lips smashed into mine, his tongue fucked my mouth at the same time his cock fucked my pussy. White-hot pleasure burst through me, my veins on fire with need as my inner muscles squeezed around him.

"Come for me!" he roared, tearing his mouth away. As if under his command, my body tensed and the orgasm shot through me, spiraling me into a blissful void where nothing existed but us. His thrusts shallowed, his body tensed, and then he spilled into me with a loud groan, calling out my name.

Bum-bum. Bum-bum. My heart beat for him.

We stayed locked together, our breathing the only noise in the Jeep. His big hand roamed my back, his mouth showering my neck with kisses and my heart swelled. This felt like the love that songs were written about. That kept people going. He loved me.

CHAPTER 73

Santino

Amore fell asleep in my arms, exhausted and naked. We'd stopped twice and fucked hard before we made it home. Then we did it in the kitchen. Hallway. The living room. On the balcony.

I took her hard in every possible way and every imaginable position. I was like a starved man after years of fasting. Her long legs were wrapped around me, her inner thighs wet with my cum. Her hair was sprawled across my chest, sweat still lingered on her pale skin.

Mine, I thought possessively.

If I was honest with myself, there was never an ounce of possibility that I would have let her walk down the aisle and marry my brother. I had never been the giving type. But the knowledge that she was now forever tied to me settled me. Soothed me. Putting me at peace.

Amore Russo. It sounded so fucking right.

My phone beeped, and I reached for it, careful not to wake her up. She needed rest, and I was selfish taking her body even after she begged for reprieve. Sex monster. It would seem she turned me into one too.

I read the message and my heart sank. I hoped I was wrong. I prayed I was wrong. More for Amore than myself. She didn't deserve that kind of betrayal, not after everything else. I hadn't connected the dots until last night when she admitted her suspicions about her stepfather.

It was time I ended it all.

Five days of bliss. This week competed for the top place with our week in Italy. Happiness and obsession were a five-letter word. Started with A and ended with E... Amore. Just like her name. Her love was my light.

We spent five days in my Rockport home. And just like in Italy, we got into a simple routine. She'd wake up to coffee already made. With her on my lap, both of us checked our work emails and handled business. Unlike other women, Amore didn't obsess over the wedding. She told her grandma and dad we got married; the former demanded the wedding of the century. The latter grunted about walking her down the aisle. And Amore promised both, letting her grandmother plan the wedding but run everything by her.

Bennetti wasn't happy when I told him Amore's new last name. Not that I gave a fuck. He couldn't take her from me anymore. Though he insisted on a formal church wedding.

Fine.

Once I eliminated the fucking threat of the man that should have stood by her, rather than turned on her.

Amore focused on running Regalè Fashion and her Orchid business. Sometimes she'd lay out paper all over the floor to draw, take pictures and text back and forth with Maria. I'd asked her not to share that we got married. Regina and Savio would keep it to themselves too.

Amore usually fixed lunch, then we'd go into town for ice cream, or walk down to the beach. Then we'd end the day preparing dinner together or just call in delivery, curl up on the couch and watch Marvel movies. We have yet to make it through a whole movie without getting *sidetracked*.

If it was up to me, I'd stay here forever, but first there were things that needed handling.

CHAPTER 74
Amore

T had only been twenty-four hours since Santi and I got back, and I already missed the cabin. It turned out my firsts with Santi continued. Our first argument. He wanted me sitting at home, waiting for him to eliminate the threat. I had to work. I couldn't miss the first board meeting as the head of Regalè Fashion house. After hours of back and forth, we finally met in the middle. It must have been a first for Santi because he acted like I had attempted to murder him.

"Santi, you knew who I was when you married me," I said, agitated and annoyed. "Just as I knew who you were!"

"I'm not saying you cannot work," he growled. "Just to wait."

"It is a board meeting," I gritted out. "They can't hold it without me, and the date has been set for months. I'm not asking you to put your role in the Cosa Nostra on hold. Don't ask me to put my role as head of Regalè Fashion on hold."

He stalked towards me, his palms cupping my face. "I'll fuck you straight through the board meeting and you'll forget all about it."

His hand cupped the back of my head, his mouth brushing against my lips so lightly, but it was all it took. My body shivered, eager for a rougher touch, harder kiss. His fingers fisted in my hair as he scraped his teeth against my bottom lip and my hands instinctively locked around his neck.

"I want to feel your pretty pussy around my cock, wife," he purred, his voice smooth, like the most delicious sin. "Slide my cock inside it, so you can feel me every time you move. Every goddamn time."

A shiver ran down my spine and a whimper left my lips in response to his filthy words.

"Will you let me?" His voice was guttural, his breath hot against my ear.

I panted, the throbbing between my thighs unbearable. "Y-yes."

His free hand fisted on my Chanel skirt, pulling it up as I rubbed myself against him. I lowered my eyes, watching his tattooed hand against my white Chanel business skirt. Through my lust hazed brain, I realized he was seducing me in order to distract me.

Clenching my teeth and my thighs, I brought my palms to his chest and gently pushed against him.

"No," I breathed out. God, it didn't sound convincing to my own ears, never mind his. To prove to him that I meant it, I pushed harder.

"Santi, stop."

He stopped, an exasperated look on his face. "What happened to my obedient, submissive wife?" he mused.

"You never had an obedient wife," I pointed out. I decided not to comment on the submissive. My desire to please only came out in the bedroom, and only for him. Inhaling deeply, I ignored the temptation to spread my legs wide and forget about the world. "Santi, I have to go to this meeting," I told him in a firm tone. "Theoretically, they could vote me out. Grandma worked really hard for this company. I can't destroy it my first week."

"Second week?" he suggested.

I narrowed my eyes on him, pressing my lips together. He couldn't demand I sit at home and wait for him like a good Italian girl?

"Damn it, wife. Where did this stubborn streak come from?" he grunted.

"If I don't stand my ground, husband," I retorted dryly, "... you'd walk all over me."

He shook his head and pulled the phone out of his pocket, then dialed. Twenty minutes later, Carrera and Renzo were my bodyguards. DeAngelo went with Santi, much to both of our dismay.

So on my first day back to work, I was married and heavily guarded. I sat through the board meeting with Gabriel Carrera and Renzo breathing down my neck as we went through our quarterly reports and next year's projections. Thankfully, that was the peak of excitement.

So far my second day was just as uneventful, and I had DeAngelo back as my guard. He was in his office, right next to mine, and I had designs spread all over the floor of my own office, narrowing down selections when the sound of my phone beeping brought me back to earth.

Standing up, I grabbed my phone and saw five missed messages from Santi.

You have five minutes to answer. Or I'm coming for you and punishment won't be pleasurable for you. Only me.

My lips curved up. Jesus! I had it bad for my husband. A threatening text message and my response was a throbbing ache between my thighs.

Without delay, I typed up a response, my fingers flying across the screen.

Leaving now. You can punish me.

I pressed the send button and a naughty idea snuck up on me. Smirking, I immediately started typing.

I'll get on my knees, tie my hands behind my back, and you can fuck my mouth. And my ummm... back hole.

Feeling smug, I pressed send again and shoved the phone into my purse. I couldn't wait to get home. I had no doubt Santi wouldn't let me off the hook for that one.

Five minutes later, my heels clicked against the hallway floors of Regalè Enterprise as I hurried across the quiet building over to the elevators. I hit the button several times, an eerie feeling tingling down my neck, which I couldn't shake off. The building was empty, and we were among the last to leave.

DeAngelo was waiting for me in the garage. I sent him ahead while I cleaned up the last bit of the paperwork. I was happy, deliriously so. The only thing missing was Adriano. I had to make things right with him.

He had been MIA, and it started to agitate me. We used to talk and text every day. And lately, nothing. Admittedly, we didn't have much to say since this whole engagement was kind of awkward. But we had been best friends and, as such, we should work things out. How many times had he left me alone at the party while he chased a skirt? I never gave him a hard time.

The elevator door slid open, and as I stepped into it, my thoughts were lost on the items I had to finish for the new design. It was easier to focus on design and business among all the chaos. Somehow, everything had gone quiet on the cartel front. I started to think maybe my theory of George Anderson was wrong after all.

It's not like I'm a criminal mastermind, I thought wryly.

I hit the button for the garage as someone else stepped into the elevator and hit the lobby floor button. The door closed as I lifted my gaze and met Adriano's eyes.

"Adriano!" I exclaimed, surprised to find him here. "What are you doing here?" I asked hesitantly.

Something flickered in his eyes, though I couldn't home in on it. Before I could think further about it, he responded, "Santi sent me."

My brows scrunched, confusion flooding all my senses. He literally just sent me a text. Why wouldn't he have mentioned it? "Why?"

"He wanted to make sure you were safe," he replied, a smile spreading across his face. Good, maybe they hashed out their disagreements. "He's in the lobby."

Adriano was dressed in a black three-piece suit. I didn't usually see him in a suit and his appearance threw me a bit. He looked even more like Santi like this. I studied his face and noted he wore his usual carefree expression.

"Wonderful," I retorted. I'd see Santi even sooner. "Maybe we could all go grab dinner or something?" I suggested hopeful. I wanted us all to talk through what happened. I had some apologizing and explaining to do. My actions hurt my best friend, and I wanted to make it up to him.

The elevator made its way down, floor by floor. My eyes traveled to Adriano, noting traces of perspiration across his forehead.

Hmmm, maybe it's hot in here. My black Chanel dress was light, made out of silk. I imagine it would be hotter in a suit.

Ding. The elevator slid open to the empty lobby. A wide-open space, the marble floors and panoramic door to ceiling windows on the opposite side of it, looking out to 5th Avenue.

Stepping out of the elevator, I glanced around, searching for Santi.

"I don't see him," I said, looking over my shoulder at Adriano.

He frowned, his eyes searching out the lobby. "He was just here," he muttered.

"Why didn't he just come upstairs with you?" I questioned him, my eyes roaming around as if Santi would appear out of thin air.

"You know how he is." He shook his head. "Hates anything to do with your grandmother. He didn't want to run into her."

True. Santi didn't like her, but he usually didn't avoid anyone.

"Hmmm." I continued my way towards the lobby exit door. I went through the roundabout circle door and found myself on the concrete, the sounds of the city and cars honking filling the air.

New Yorkers never even paused to throw me a glance. Men and women in suits rushed to their destinations, whether to homes where their families awaited, dinner dates, or parties.

I went to turn around when something pressed hard against my back.

"Don't move or I'll end you right here." Disbelief washed over me.

"Adriano?" I whispered, my mind struggling to understand what was going on.

A black SUV pulled up in front of us, and a tall man I had never seen before stepped out. I watched in horror as he came around and opened the back door to the car.

Stupid! So stupid!

I should have kept DeAngelo with me. The entire time.

"Miss," the guy holding the door called out. "Please get in."

My eyes traveled over him. He wore a Dolce & Gabbana black suit with matching shoes. He seemed young, though apparently old enough to be kidnapping people.

I should have known only a man wearing Dolce & Gabbana would be a criminal and traitor. Gangsters seemed to like Dolce. They had to kill in style and die in style.

"Get in, Amore." The barrel of the gun at my back pressed harder. Adriano's voice was rough. Jesus, what has happened?

Frantically, my eyes searched for anyone familiar. But nobody even paid attention to us, no one wanted eye contact in this city.

"Now," he rumbled. "Or I'll have you bleeding on the concrete."

Getting into that car was the worst thing I could possibly do. Before I could say another thing, he shoved me into the car. I stumbled, my knees hitting the floor of the car while my purse landed on the street. I went to scream, to make some noise, anything when Adriano's hand covered my mouth.

Fuck, where is the security when you need them!

I struggled against him, kicking out, sinking my teeth into his hand, but it was for naught. He was much stronger than I was and held me at an angle that prevented me from elbowing him in the ribs the way DeAngelo taught me.

Jesus Christ! It almost looked like he was humping me. Only in New York would nobody even blink at a scene like that.

He slammed the door behind me. I started screaming, banging on the glass but it was useless. It appeared the damn SUV had bullet-proofed glass. The driver and Adriano climbed in.

"Stop screaming, or I'll just shoot you," he growled, never turning back. "He'll be pissed off he doesn't get to finish you off himself, but he'll get over it. He wants you dead anyhow."

My eyes widened.

Who? I wanted to ask. George Anderson?

Was he really still alive? Or was it someone else? I didn't know. Ever since our last trip to Venezuela, I've become too lax. So stupid! Probably the reason why I'd never succeed in running a cartel business. I'd get killed the first week on the job. And by none other than my best friend. How did things between us go so wrong?

Damn it! That was a stupid and careless decision to send DeAngelo ahead of me. I prayed that DeAngelo would get impatient and come looking for me. Unfortunately, he was an incredibly patient man.

Shit! Shit! Shit!

"Don't try anything," Adriano growled. "I can have your family find your brains splattered against this floor." He chuckled menacingly. "Assuming they even find this car or you."

I went deathly still at his words, watching him warily while my heart hurt. It fucking bled. My best friend wanted me dead. Our years of friendship and all the moments we shared since the day he entered my life sped through my mind. I would have never dreamt it would lead us here.

He pulled out his phone and dialed a number. I watched his every move. I wasn't ready to die, not by his hand or anyone else's. Though in my mind, I already tried to come up with something to get through to Adriano. To reason with him.

"I got her," he spoke into the phone, his gun trained on me.

My eyes darted between the driver and Adriano. I could try and clock the driver over the head, but we'd risk a crash. Besides, Adriano threatened to shoot me. Could he follow through? In my heart, I refused to believe it, but I wasn't sure if I could trust my heart right now.

Maybe I should make him talk? So I could figure out if there were any windows for me to escape.

"What are you doing?" I asked him. "Where are you taking me?"

He ignored me. Frustration clawed at my insides as anger boiled in my veins. I couldn't understand how a man who had been my best friend for years could do this. The betrayal was devastating.

"Why, Adriano?" My voice choked. I thought I had a family, a best friend, and a brother-in-law. And yet again, I was being betrayed. "Why?" I asked again in a raspy voice. "I should at least know why you betrayed me before I die."

I noticed the driver 's eyes flicker to me in the rearview mirror, but they immediately returned to the road.

Adriano sneered. "You betrayed *me* with Santi." I couldn't argue with that, but it wasn't as if I could control who I loved. In truth, I loved them both. Very much, only in very different ways. I blinked hard, desperate to keep tears at bay. "We were friends first. You were supposed to be my wife, not Santi's. Our parents arranged it."

I swallowed hard. I hurt him and now he was hurting me back. "What is your plan? To kill me?"

"You started this, Amore." God, was this really my best friend? I couldn't recognize him. "I'm going to finish it. No more errand boy for Santi. No more being second best."

How was it possible that I never picked up on his resentment? Was I really such a bad judge of character?

"You are not second best," I rasped, my voice shuddering. "Please, Adriano. We can fix this," I pleaded. We are supposed to be family. Take care of each other. Not kill each other. This was lunacy.

"I *am* fixing it," he drawled. "I will take over the Cosa Nostra. And your little cartel empire will finally be led by someone other than your bitchy grandmother." Fear shot through my veins, turning my blood ice cold. "That dragon lady will be next."

"Adriano, are you nuts?" I hissed. I wanted to grab him and shake some sense into him. I'd always stood by him, even when he was reckless. But this was way beyond reckless. He'd get us *all* killed. "Please be reasonable. The Andersons will betray you. They killed my mother, and she had nothing to do with the cartel. They'll kill you too when they get what they want."

Couldn't he see that? It was so damn obvious.

He blew out frustrated breath, like he thought I was a brat and his patience was running out.

"I've got it all worked out," he said matter-of-factly.

Frustration clawed at my chest, the need to smack some sense into him so strong that my fingers itched to connect with his cheek.

"Santino will never allow you to be part of the Cosa Nostra," I gritted out, annoyed.

He laughed. "Then I'll kill him too. He has a little surprise coming his way."

What?

"You won't succeed. My father, brothers, and Santi will come for you." I shook my head whether in denial or disbelief, I wasn't sure. "Adriano, please," I attempted again. Despite everything, it physically hurt my chest to think of Adriano getting injured or killed in the crossfire. "You are going to get yourself killed. Please don't do this. I am sorry I didn't tell you about your brother. I meant to but—"

"Shut up!" he cut me off, his voice bitter. "I know exactly what I am doing."

The car came to a stop and Adriano practically jumped out. The back door swung open, and his hand reached out. I scooted away but unsuccessfully. He grabbed a handful of my hair and yanked it so hard, I winced as the sharp pain exploded on my scalp.

His features turned deadly and savage. "We'll see how much you've got to say with my gun against your temple."

The barrel of his gun pressed against my skin felt cold. It didn't matter that DeAngelo had trained me to fight and keep a cool head. It all evaporated into thin air, replaced by frozen fear.

I don't want to die.

CHAPTER 75

Santino

My lips curved into a smile reading Amore's message. I couldn't wait to fuck my wife. I'd order her to strip the second she walked through the door. And then, I'd ensure she followed through with her promise.

Tension and the need to feel her again rushed through my bloodstream. She was my heroine. I'd never get enough of her. I didn't like her going to work, not until we'd eliminated this threat with George Anderson. But Amore was a stubborn heiress, determined to do what she had been raised to do. To lead her empire.

I admired her for it. I loved her for it. Though it clashed with my need to protect her.

In all honesty, I wanted to take her away, keep our honeymoon going. Just the two of us, in our own bubble, where nobody could get to her. Where nobody could hurt her.

It was the worst possible feeling, this vulnerability for someone, the fear of losing what you loved. I swore a long time ago, I wouldn't allow a weakness into my life. No women that could touch my heart. I saw firsthand what it did to my father. But how was I to know she would have been a kid that would attach herself to me, need my protection, and then grow up to be a gorgeous woman that would take my heart.

My cell phone rang, and I picked it up, expecting it to be Amore. "Yeah?"

"Santi, they got her." DeAngelo's voice shattered my world.

A deathly stillness came over me. My gaze locked on the front door, expecting Amore to walk through it any moment, despite the news I just got.

Lead and cold settled in my stomach, unlike any other I had ever felt before.

"Santi, you there?" Anger crept beneath my skin, fueling the rage... and fear. Fucking fear for a red-haired woman that was mine. "Goddamnit, Santi."

I had to swallow down the burning rage, the cold fear. Swallow it all so I could focus. Bring her home.

"What do you know?"

"I was waiting for her in the garage. When she didn't show, I went to search for her. She is nowhere to be found."

Amore tended to get sidetracked when working. It could be that she just found her way back to her work lab and lost track of time.

"I'll call her," I told him.

"Don't bother. Her bag and her stuff was sprawled all over the pavement in front of the building."

Fuck. I didn't get a heads up. Why? The worry for her rattled me to my bones. There wasn't much that I was scared of in this life.

Losing Amore was a bone chilling fear clawing at me. "I have to make a call," I told him and hung up.

I scrolled through my phone book and stopped at the name that could break me if he didn't come through. I pressed the call number, each ring costing me years of my life.

"Yeah."

"Does he have her?" My voice was cold and hard.

"Yeah." Heartbeat. "Location share."

Beep. Beep. Beep. The call ended.

I glanced at the screen and the location sharing acceptance button flashed.

It was a no brainer. Accept.

CHAPTER 76

Amore

To say the situation wasn't good was a gross understatement. The house sat on the edge of the city. A red brick three-story building rose in front of me, surrounded by a low iron fence and a charming iron gate. Wild orchids swarmed the gardens, vines snaked up the brick siding. It looked like a damn jungle. The gardens and the house were in need of a major clean up.

Something struck me as familiar about the house, but I couldn't quite place it. My nerves were shot. To think clearly was impossible right now.

Any other time over the past eight years, I always had someone close by to save me. Now, it was just me. I'd have to be resourceful and figure out how to get out of this situation.

Adriano nudged me forward with his gun pressed against my spine, a cold reminder that he was no longer on my side.

As they shuffled me down the little stone path and into the house, I frantically searched for any way out. There were four men around me. More outside the gate patrolling back and forth. If they thought they were inconspicuous, they were idiots.

I walked through the entrance of the house and spotted more guards. All for me. It would be comical and flattering if it wasn't so tragic. They needed so many men just to guard me... seriously, they gave me too much credit.

Once inside, they shoved me into a living room and pushed me onto a couch. Only Adriano and one other guard followed me in.

"Stay here," Adriano ordered in a cold tone that sent shivers down my spine. He had *never* used that tone on me. I didn't even know he had it in him. "One move, and the men have permission to shoot."

"What a beautiful welcome," I muttered.

"I could offer a better one," he snarled. "Now behave."

A guard eyed Adriano and me suspiciously. Then a string of Spanish followed. I caught every third word, and I wished my language skills were better.

Adding it to my bucket list if I get out of this alive, I thought wryly.

One second we were eying each other, the next he fisted my hair with one hand while with his other grabbed my shoulder, his fingers digging into the muscle. Pain shot through my shoulder blade, causing my eyes to tear up.

The other guy kept talking and I got a sense whatever he was saying agitated Adriano.

I opened my mouth to snap at my ex-best friend when Adriano glared at me. "Keep your mouth shut," he bellowed.

My eyes darted to the other guy, and I spat out angrily. Sometimes when hurt feelings and anger mixed, stupid words poured out of my mouth.

"You might want to rethink the way you treat your prisoners," I hissed at both of them. "Santi will have your goddamn head for this."

Okay, I should have their head for this, but I knew my limitations. I wasn't my grandmother. I admired and loved her strength. While I knew there were certain aspects of me that were similar to her; I was damn well aware that in other ways, I was nothing like her.

"Who knows, Santino might be dead right now," Adriano drawled, his lips curved in a cruel way. He chuckled at my expression of horror, though there was no humor in his eyes.

I dug my nails into my palms. There was nothing I'd rather do than claw his face and wipe that grin off it. I loved Adriano, but he needed some sense beaten into him. Unfortunately, he held a gun aimed at me. I'd never make it off the couch, never mind clawing his face.

We stared at each other. The animosity in his eyes plunged a hole in my chest. It hurt badly. Last time I'd felt such pain was when I lost my mother. I wanted to beg him to stop, to remember all our years together, to remember his family. His father. Yet, none of the words came. My throat constricted with emotions and each shuddering inhale made it harder to breathe.

"Santino Russo will meet his death at the same time as you, *princesa*," the guard taunted in a hard voice.

I held my breath, the meaning of the words clear. Yet, I struggled to understand them. Adriano would never hurt anyone. He wasn't like that. Yet, the man that stood in front of me was a stranger.

"Adriano betrayed you and Santi," the guard continued after realizing I wasn't going to say anything. "So he could take over. Greed wins every time," he added, a victorious look in his eyes, mocking me. My brain refused to believe his words. He was just messing with my head.

"No," I mouthed in shock, shaking my head in denial. The word escaped before I could hold it back and satisfaction gleamed in his eyes. His statement pierced through my heart like a knife that would forever be wedged into it. The images of mine and Adriano's years together flashed through my mind like iPhone memories. The only thing missing was a soundtrack.

Besties Forever. We were supposed to be best friends forever.

He knew how badly I hurt after Venezuela, the panic attacks. He helped me heal, protected me from the boys and girls in school.

Unaware of my internal turmoil, the guard started circling around me and Adriano, then back to me while his eyes darted around at each sound. He was edgy, checking windows and doors, then checking in with every guard outside. I thought Adriano was with them, but he seemed to be suspicious of him as much as me.

I sat unmoving, trying to calm my nerves, pain swelling inside me. This betrayal hurt. Really bad. Maybe even more than George's that I only learned about as an adult. With each tick of the clock, my heart beat with another painful thud.

Fuck!

Sometimes it seemed better not to feel anything. It was so much easier than feeling so much. I flicked a gaze at Adriano. He stood unmoving, no emotions on his face.

My best friend.

My ride or die.

Or so I thought.

Three hours of his constant circling, his muttering and I was ready to lose my cool. He was harping on my nerves. His constant movement irked me. It rattled my nerves. I was certain he was getting on Adriano's nerves as well. He might not be my best friend now, but I knew Adriano well. Besides, I caught him rolling his eyes behind his back a few times.

My eyes kept ping-ponging back and forth between the other guard and Adriano. At this point, I was getting on my own nerves too. I had no phone to call 911. No drawing paper. Nothing to distract me. Just me sitting on the couch. Doing nothing drove me bananas.

Just as the guard was getting ready to make another circle around the living room and finally wear a hole into the rug, an explosion blasted.

The entire house shook. The guard lost his balance and stumbled against the coffee table, rattling it. Gunshots echoed outside and to my surprise, Adriano pulled me off the couch and onto the ground.

"Cover your head," he hissed. "Stay down."

Nodding, I followed his instruction.

"What the—" Someone else spat out curses in Spanish.

"Get the girl," the guard shouted in Spanish. Amazingly, my language skills understood that one. "Take her to the bunkers."

Jesus, that didn't sound good at all.

Adriano's fingers curled around my upper arm, pulling me onto my feet. "Let's go, brat."

My head snapped his way and I glared at him. I wasn't a brat. This fucker... of all the bullshit. He had to screw around with my worst enemy.

"I'm guessing these are not your guys?" I mocked though it was probably stupid and proved his point of me being a brat.

The roar of another explosion sounded too close for comfort. Angry shouts and gunfire broke the silent aftermath, you'd think we were in a warzone. It was too close for comfort. Or maybe help was coming?

A man burst through the door, and every single man aimed the gun in his direction. He put his hands up in the air, a stream of Spanish curses slipping through his lips. Yes, I understood those too. What could I say? Priorities when learning a language.

"We have to go," he urged in a hushed tone and heavily accented English. "Now!"

"Where are we going?" I asked with wide eyes. These guys would get me killed even before I came up with an attempted escape plan. "It sounds like a damn war out there. We should stay here."

The crazy guard that was circling for the past few hours like a caged animal came up to me and stopped. A heartbeat of nothing. Then his hand flew through the air and connected with my cheek, sending pain and a burning sensation through me. It felt like my cheek exploded.

"There is an underground bunker here," Adriano said, stopping the guard from another assault.

"How do you know?" the guard asked him suspiciously, his eyes ping-ponging between Adriano and the guard that just barged in on us.

"Anderson showed us," the guard answered. "To me and Adriano."

I still struggled to process all this. My best friend working with Anderson made my stomach churn. The betrayal hit me right in my chest, with each heartbeat. It hurt badly. I would never have dreamt of Adriano doing this. He did some dumb stuff. *We* did some dumb stuff. But this was surpassing it all. And it would cost lives.

"Show me," the guard demanded. His eyes darted my way, and dread pooled in the pit of my stomach.

"Let's go," Adriano answered, grabbing my wrist hard and tugging me along. The other two guards followed close behind, scared I'd take off at any moment.

We exited into the hallway and the worst images played in my mind as sounds of bullets traveled through the air. Who was killing who? I hope Dad, Santi, and my brothers weren't here. I didn't want them killed. But then on the other hand, I wanted them here. To kill all these men so we could finally end it all and live our lives.

"Stop stalling," one of the guards spat out, hate coloring his voice.

Adriano nudged me roughly forward and I continued on. I didn't know what to expect in this bunker. Would they torture me? Like they did Mom. Maybe they'd just shoot me and end it all.

We made our way from the main floor to the basement through the side staircase, keeping our bodies low, slithering against the wall. The sun had set, and the glow of orange still lingered in the distance.

Another set of stairs, and we were in the basement. The guard surveyed the area before peeling himself off the wall and rushed across it and through the door. I waited, debating whether to fight them or run. I went to shift away when the other, antsy guard pointed a gun at me. Jesus, where did he keep that shit?

I held my breath, waiting, not sure for what.

"You try to run, *princesa*," he hissed. The word *princess* sounded like the worst insult. "And I'll shoot you without warning. Don't test me," he added with a threat.

Adriano shoved me in front of him, keeping his gun at my back. How was it possible to know someone so little? First George, now Adriano. Jesus, who was next?

Adriano pushed me roughly across the hallway. Stumbling, I tried to gain my footing but couldn't reach anything to hold on to. My hands flew through the air, my knees connected with the concrete floor and my palms landed face down. The roughness of the floor scuffed my knees and the palms of my hands, burning almost instantly. A whimper formed in my throat, but I quickly swallowed it. I wouldn't give them the satisfaction. I wasn't that little girl in the jungle of South America anymore.

I steeled my spine and stood up, straightening to my full size. They might think I was an easy target but Santi, Dad, and my brothers wouldn't be. They'd shred them all to pieces. If I knew Santi well, he'd hunt them down and make them all pay.

Santi, I thought with a heavy sigh. I fought him to go to work and for what... to get killed. *Please God, just let me get out of this one. I'll listen to my husband better*, I added wryly. Maybe there was some obedient, Italian girl in me after all.

Adriano's phone beeped, a trendy, different beeping sound. Not like his normal ringtone for messages. He didn't bother retrieving his phone. "That's Anderson. I have to meet him."

He threw me a fleeting glance and left without another word. Just like that. No parting words. *Nothing.*

I watched his back disappear from my view and my life. The profound loss shattered me right to my bones, making my knees weak.

"Move it," the guard barked.

I narrowed my eyes with agitation but kept my mouth shut.

"Where?" I rasped in a low voice. God, I hope I got out of this alive. "There is no door here."

Without another word, the other guard started running his fingers through the wall, his movements frantic.

"What are we looking for?" I asked in a hushed voice.

"Secret mechanism, a lever," he explained.

"Don't fucking talk to her," the other guard hissed. "She'll be dead before today is over."

A breath caught in my throat; my heart raced against my chest, and adrenaline rushed through my veins. I swallowed hard, breathing becoming impossible. Panic slowly rose, the buzzing intensified. DeAngelo would definitely be disappointed if I just stood here and waited for this asshole to dish out his revenge. I had to figure out something, fight them. If they planned to kill me, I might as well go down fighting.

More shouting and more bullets echoed throughout the house.

"I found it," the guard exclaimed. He pressed down on something, and a hum sounded from behind a wall. I stood immobile, the drumming in my ears drowning out everything.

I stilled for a moment, letting the calm wash over me. One guard was at my back, the other was at my left. If I wanted to get out, left was the way out, but I needed to eliminate the bigger threat, which was the asshole guard that seemed to have anger issues. So I decided to attack him first. At least, slow him enough so I could get a head start.

And run towards the bullets, I thought wryly. But if the attackers were their enemies, maybe they were my friends. It was the only plan I had.

Shifting my body ever so slightly, I swung my elbow hard and fast into the guard's gut. I didn't bother glancing behind me, I shifted to the left. The other guard stood there, and I stiffened my shoulder, shoving him with it just like DeAngelo taught me.

Just like football, he said. Except, he kept forgetting I wasn't the sporty type.

I barely made it two steps before a gunshot sounded. As if in slow motion, I heard it, felt it pass right by me and hit one guard in the chest. I had no idea where it came from. My ears rang, drowning out the noises of glass crashing and gunshots upstairs. As if in slow motion, I watched his body fall to the ground.

Another shot. A body slumped behind me.

My throat closed as I watched blood pooling on the ground. The look of shock on his face, blood seeping down the side of his mouth. The way his eyes widened, fear in them before his light went out. It reminded me of another sight.

Drip. Drip. Drip.

Mom's sliced throat, blood pooling out of her mouth. So much blood. Devastating fear in her eyes right before her throat was sliced. Before the light extinguished in her eyes. Forever. I blinked my eyes, forcing the images out of my mind. The betrayal must have triggered bad memories.

My eyes darted around, searching.

"Hey, you okay?" Familiar voice. But I couldn't see him. "Amore, are you okay?"

I blinked my eyes and that's when I saw the shadow on the steps to the bunker. It was my brother.

"Lorenzo," I whispered, unsure whether I was hallucinating.

He took my hand and squeezed gently. "Yeah, your favorite brother."

A strangled laugh escaped me, though there was nothing funny right now.

"I'm so glad to see you," I murmured. "What are you doing here? In their bunker?"

Oh. My. God.

If he was on the enemy's side, I'd lose my shit.

"Waiting to rescue you," he retorted dryly. "You have no idea how much I hate waiting." He tugged me along, gently nudging me into the bunker. "We have to go in there."

I was terrified to trust him. To have another betrayal to taste. Lorenzo wouldn't do that to me. Right? But then I never dreamed Adriano would betray me either.

The moment we hit the bottom step, the metal door closed in behind us with a loud metal clunk, concealing us in darkness. The locking mechanism of the door sounded loud and hard, the wall closing in on us. It was hard to see in the dark, the only light coming from the end of the narrowed hallway.

Blood rushed in my ears, making me dizzy. I desperately tried to focus on the wild beating of my heart and force myself to calm down.

Breathe, Amore. Breathe!

The words from so long ago. Different day. Different panic attack. Santi's voice pulling me from the fog.

I was stronger. Maybe, just a little bit. But still stronger. I focused on my breathing. Breathe in. Breathe out. Repeat.

It was working. I could get through this. We *would* get through this. Life wouldn't be so cruel to give Santi to me, a family, just to tear them all away. My family was my heart, without them, I was nothing.

At the bottom of the stairs, a small room waited for us. No windows. One chair. One bed. Nothing else.

"Sit down, Amore." Lorenzo's voice was a command. He was no longer an easygoing, flirtatious brother. He was a made man of the Cosa Nostra. He led me towards the bed. I sat down on the edge and placed my hands in my lap. Lowering my eyes, I realized with shock, there was blood on my hands. Just drops. Maybe some of it splashed on me. I turned them over slowly. *Blood on my hands.*

It started with an orchid and a man that trapped me. Mom's death bloodied my hands. I was guilty for following George. If I hadn't, she might have been alive.

This felt like an end. The question was whether it would be mine. Despite Adriano's betrayal, I didn't want him dead.

"He's here," I rasped to Lorenzo in a breathless whisper. "Adriano is working with them." My voice broke with the last word, and suddenly, I felt like crying. Like that girl that Santi found on the pavement in front of his father's restaurant.

I clenched my hands together, my nails digging into my skin. I didn't want to act like an overly sensitive, soft girl. But it was hard. This was my best friend we were talking about. I loved him. I thought he loved me. Except that it wasn't the romantic kind of love.

The bunker shook and a yelp escaped me. A humming noise followed, signaling the opening of the door. *Click.* The door opened.

"I know you are here, Orchid." A taunt in a familiar voice, sent cold shivers down my spine. "Time to end what we started eight years ago. I'll make you squeal like your bitch of a mother."

Suddenly, I felt like that little thirteen-year-old girl, caged like an animal. Left to watch her mother tortured. Cold sweat trickled down my spine, each breath brought on a feeling of nausea.

Death! The man coming for me meant death to me. And his name was *George!*

"Where is my little orchid?" The voice shot ice through my heart. He'd tainted Mom's love for orchids. He'd ruined my childhood.

Frantically my eyes shot to Lorenzo who came to stand by my side. I tried to get to my feet, but my knees shook so bad. I was no good to anyone in this state. Still, I steeled my spine, still in a seated position, and inhaled a deep breath. Or at least I tried.

"Fire one bullet, and I'm throwing a grenade into the bunker." My chest constricted at hearing the familiar voice. "And throw your weapons onto the ground."

My eyes searched frantically. This was like my worst nightmare.

"I'm waiting," he taunted. "Tick, tock. Tick, tock."

My brother threw his gun to the ground.

Holding my breath, I watched as a man descended the stairs with five men behind him and two at each side, protecting him. It hardly seemed like a fair fight. So many of them against just the two of us, weaponless.

"Hello, Orchid," he drawled, his voice toneless. His cold, unflinching dark stare met mine and images from the last time I saw him flashed in my mind. Blood, screams, betrayal, death.

I never knew this man, I realized. His thin lips curved into a grimace, a taunting smile. He despised me, his hate gleaming in his eyes. It couldn't be more evident.

This was like my worst nightmare. He was supposed to love me, cherish me. Protect me. Yet, he lurked in the shadows of my life for years hunting me, waiting to kill me.

He betrayed *us*. Hurt *us*. Left *us* to die.

"You've given me a run for my money," he said with menace in his voice, then flicked his gaze behind him. "Hasn't she? Come here so she can see you."

I watched as a pair of black combat boots descended the stairs, revealing more and more of a man's body. My mind revolted against recognition, and my stomach churned.

No, no, no, no.

My heart shattered and a piercing pain followed deep in my chest.

The worst betrayal.

Were the men in my life always destined to betray me?

Each second, each step felt like a bullet to my heart. Up until this moment, even with Adriano kidnapping me, I hoped, wished, believed, he'd come to his senses. Betrayal tasted bitter. My best friend.

"Adriano," I whispered, the pain at seeing his dark cold eyes piercing my heart. I knew of his betrayal. Yet, it still hurt like a bitch. Nothing screamed of a confirmed betrayal like standing behind the man who wanted you dead. Yet I refused to admit defeat. I refused to give up on him and my mind revolted at losing my best friend. "What have you done?"

My eyes shifted to the man I called my father for the first thirteen years of my life. Yet, a true father would never do something like this. He tortured my mother. He caused his own son's death by sending them after me.

George Anderson was twisted. Selfish. Evil.

With renewed strength, I stood up off the dingy, little spring bed, noises of protest with my every movement. Keeping emotion off my face and my feet planted firmly on the ground, just in case I get an open window.

My brother's eyes came to me, a jerky nod, hard determination in his eyes. I hoped I mirrored some of his courage.

Lorenzo and I would fight them. Together.

I watched the man that was never my father... not really! And not just by blood.

The past eight years weren't kind to him. He stood tall, thin, his hair disheveled and white. Not silver white, but dull, gray. His thin lips curved into a grimace, a taunting smile.

Somewhere deep down I hoped it was all just a set up. Yet, there he was, standing proud and tall in front of me. The familiar features I had cared about for so long. The resemblance to Santi at this very moment struck me as more evident than ever.

The ruthless mobster.

But Santi had a heart. He loved me. He was ruthless but fair. And Adriano... I always thought he was softer and kinder than his brother. Yet the coldness in his eyes right now... it froze my heart.

George's betrayal seemed mild compared to Adriano's. Today hasn't been a good day.

Adriano's lips pressed into a thin, grim line, a blank expression on his face. He avoided looking at me, his whole posture rigid. How could he stray so far away? I was blind, too wrapped up to see he needed me. It was all my fault.

I tried to sidestep Lorenzo, reaching my hand out to my best friend. "Adriano, please," I pleaded. "You're my best friend." My voice cracked with emotion.

I had to save him. Santi could get through to his brother, make him see reason. Adriano was pushed too far by my betrayal and Santi cutting his connection to the Cosa Nostra. If only Santi was here; we had to save Adriano.

"He's no longer yours." George's tight smile and cold eyes gave me the creeps.

"Adriano," I whispered, ignoring George. That man was beyond redemption, but Adriano... I had to save Adriano. "Why?" I choked out, my throat squeezing with emotion.

"You chose him," he responded, his voice emotionless. *Him.* I chose Santi, except that I hadn't. Not really. I had been Santi's before I even understood what that meant. With the first tear he dried.

"He had enough of being a sidekick," George snarled. "Just as I had enough of being used by your mother, being her sidekick."

I stared at him, wide-eyed, my heart pounding against my chest.

"What do you mean?"

He laughed. "That whore made me believe you were mine. She dared to play me for a fool. That was the second mistake by the Perèz-Regalè family."

He stepped forward, the hate in his eyes could burn hell, making me stagger backwards.

"Y-you had her tortured," I gasped out, choking down the frantic beat of my heart. "All because you couldn't handle her relationship before she married you?" I took a deep breath. "You know there is divorce for that."

He snarled. "But what's the fun in that! And I'm not an idiot. I knew of your grandfather's marriage clause." He made me sick to my stomach. Shooting him in the head was too nice of a treatment for him. "Do you know what the first mistake was?" he mocked.

I knew what it was, but I kept trying to buy time. Not sure why since everyone in this room seemed to hate me. My eyes shot to Adriano, pleading with him without words. I wanted him to see how sorry I was. That I loved him. He was family, just as my brothers were.

My gaze flicked back to George. His face was almost distorted with hate when he looked at me.

It's a thin line between love and hate.

There would be no mercy from him, I knew it without a doubt. Even if I died today; he would die. Santi would hunt him down to the edge of this earth and kill him.

"What was the first one?" I rasped in a strained voice.

"Your grandfather fucked me over. I was supposed to own all of the Perèz Cartel. Imagine my surprise when it all went to your grandmother upon his death," he snarled.

There would be no reasoning with George. I could offer him the cartel, but he wouldn't believe me. Besides, it wasn't mine to offer. Grandma still ran it.

"Once you are dead and that bitch of a grandmother of yours is too, it will all be mine. I will rule the most dangerous cartel in the world."

Lunatic! He reminded me of the ridiculous villain from the *Austin Powers* movie. All he had to do was start laughing like a maniac. Except, George left a trail of actual dead bodies behind him.

I choked out a laugh. "You'll get nothing. Because it will all go to my husband."

He brought his fingers up to his chin and tapped pensively. "But you are not married yet! Good try though."

"But you see," I started, taunting. My fucking turn to mock. "I *am* married. Blissfully so. In fact, today marks a week of wedded bliss."

The tension in the silence that followed was heavy. Adriano broke it. "No matter. Because Santino is going to die too. I'm taking over the Russo family. I share the sandbox, unlike my brother."

"You are insane," I spat. I couldn't see the man that cared for me for the first thirteen years of my life. "You are seriously screwed in your head." I turned to look at Adriano. "Please, Adriano. Don't do this, come with us."

I tried to convey with my eyes that I'd save him. I'd fight for him. I wouldn't let anyone hurt him.

"Shoot her, Adriano," George issued the command.

I held my breath as I watched with terror my best friend raise his gun and point it at me. In all my life, I never thought I'd be staring into the barrel of my best friend's gun.

CHAPTER 77

Santino

I stood at the top of the stairs, hidden in the shadows with Renzo by my side. It fucking killed me to hear the hurt in Amore's voice. I wished I could have spared her, told her the truth, but it would have been a risk. It was important for this plan to work, or we would have had the threat of the Anderson Cartel looming over our heads for the rest of our lives.

Lorenzo waited in the bunker, expecting Amore to be brought in by George's men. It was to ensure George's men didn't try something with Amore. I'd burn this world just to ensure she was safe. I never wanted to see pain shimmering in her eyes, only happiness.

Rage filled me at George's betrayal. My clothes and hands were soaked in blood, the fight outside got intense. It turned into a warzone. My shoulder was burning, and I had a nasty cut down my shoulder blade. But the pain didn't register because rage consumed me, ate at me with his betrayal. Fucking Anderson was so stupid, he hadn't noticed that his men stationed on the top of the stairs were gone. We'd killed every single one of them, and he was trapped. There was no running away this time.

He was cornered. In the house that was gifted to him and Margaret on their wedding day. No wonder we couldn't find George's hiding place. It was still under the maiden name of Amore's mother. She never lived in this place because she didn't want to be in the same city as Savio Bennetti.

"Shoot her, Adriano." George's voice traveled up.

Renzo, DeAngelo, and I shared a glance. DeAngelo at our back. There was no way he'd accept being left behind. He considered Amore his little sister. I watched my brother raise his weapon, aiming at Amore, and DeAngelo's faint hiss sounded behind me. I gave him a warning look.

"Adriano, please," Amore begged, tearing my heart open with her soft pleas. "Please don't do this."

I glanced at Renzo and DeAngelo. There were five guards surrounding George and Adriano. Two right behind them, one on each side and one in front of George. The fucking guy was paranoid. He used them as human shields for protection.

I pointed to the two guys in front of us, who stood behind George and Adriano. In a silent hand movement, I mimicked slicing their throats before pointing to the one man standing on each side of George and gesturing to the gun at my side.

With a quick nod, Renzo and I took a silent step down, and I let the ruthless killer inside me loose. Nothing mattered right now but my woman. Savio and Luigi with their men were right outside, ensuring nobody crept up on us.

Without hesitation, Renzo and I snuck up on the men watching George's back. My hand came around, covering his mouth, and in one swift move, I sliced his throat. His blood gurgled out of his mouth and his neck, but I kept my hand firm on it. Not a sound.

Glancing at Renzo, I noted he'd done the same. Silently, we lowered the bodies onto the step. It was amazing how a soundless gurgling of blood was too loud to my ears when it was about life and death for my wife. It would have been easier to shoot them all, but the steps were too narrow, and we'd risk one of them shooting Amore. Or Lorenzo. She wouldn't forgive herself if her brother was hurt because of her.

Another nod and shared glance with Renzo. Two more steps. Raising my gun, I aimed at his head and pulled the trigger, edging the bullet in the back of his skull. Not sparing a glance to his slumping body, I went after the next nearest man. One last man, and then George.

Saving Amore was the priority now.

Commotion happened all around us. They knew we were here; there was no avoiding that. But they were outnumbered.

DeAngelo shot through the man next to George's left side. George ran to the corner, pulling Adriano along. I slipped up behind the last guard and slashed his throat. He clutched onto it, his blood spraying all over me as he gasped for air.

"Santi, your right!" Amore's scream had me glancing to the right. I grabbed his shoulder and did the same to him. Fuck, where did these two guys come from?

Another man charged at me, and I grinned savagely.

"You won't save him," I told him. "So you might want to consider running."

He refused. My ammo was gone, but I had my knife. I moved quickly and charged against him, plunging the blade into the man's heart, then pushing him to the floor. I felt nothing but satisfaction as I watched him gurgle and choke on his own blood.

Wiping the blade against my pants, I scanned around.

All the guards were dead.

"It is your turn to die," George's voice came from my left. "I'll unload the whole magazine into your body. I'll turn you into lead."

"Fucking coward," I spat, my voice rough. Adrenaline pumped through my body but slowly exhaustion crept in. The last three hours were hell, the worry for Amore piercing me through my chest.

I promised myself George was the deadest fucking man to ever exist. He'd pay for their betrayal. His greed for the Perèz Cartel was his downfall.

"Say goodbye to your wife," George drawled. "She'll be right behind you."

I kept my expression unmoving. "I wouldn't be so sure."

He followed my eyes to find Adriano's gun pointed at his skull. My little brother who wasn't so little anymore.

Adriano's savage grin matched my own. "You didn't really think I'd pick you over family," he mocked. "Over my best friend."

A soft gasp traveled through the small room, and I turned to my wife. Her lower lip trembled, so many emotions in her emerald gaze. It fucking hurt that she had to believe Adriano betrayed her. But we couldn't risk one slip. I had to keep her in the dark. There was only one thing that didn't go according to plan. George moved up the kidnapping by two days.

Before any of us knew what was happening, Amore elbowed George into his stomach, his grip around her loosening enough that she freed herself from him and ran into my arms.

"There you are," I rasped against her hair, inhaling deeply. I'd survive anything, except losing her. I needed her by my side to live.

She smiled softly, pressing a fleeting kiss onto my lips. Then she turned around to look at her best friend, her hands clenched at her chest and her eyes on Adriano.

"I-I thought—" she stammered. Her voice shook badly.

"We can take care of this," I murmured against her forehead. "Or you can. It is up to you."

Her eyes darted to Lorenzo who nodded his agreement. Then back to Adriano.

"Revenge is yours, Amore," Adriano told her. "Either way, he's dead and out of our lives forever."

She sniffed, reminding me of the day way back when I first saw her. A girl with shattering pain in her eyes and a runny nose who still showed so much courage.

A short nod. Amore took two steps and kneeled to pick up Lorenzo's gun, resolve in her eyes. Atta girl. My woman! We all wanted her to have closure, whether it was her pulling the trigger or one of us. But George Anderson would no longer be a threat.

She aimed the gun at his skull, determination in every ounce of her fiber. Sharing a short glance with Adriano, they both nodded at the same time. They were good at sharing thoughts without words. After all, they had been joined at the hip since Amore entered our life.

George's eyes flashed with surprise, but he didn't seem too concerned. Stupid fool.

"You don't have it in you to shoot me," he deadpanned.

A lone tear trickled down her face, but she stood her ground. "I'd rather torture you, but I'll settle for killing you."

Flicking off the safety, she fired five rounds into his body. "Now, you're full of lead. Bastard."

He fell to his knees, the light extinguished in his eyes.

She slowly lowered her arm to her side, turning to me. I knew that look. I saw it in Adriano's eyes. She wasn't a killer; neither was my little brother. He was a hustler, but he hated taking a life. I suddenly saw more similarities between my brother and my wife than ever before.

Their light way about them. Both of them had a heart.

Dropping the gun, she threw herself into my arms. The smell of strawberries enveloped me, soothing me. After hours of rage, worry clawing at me, it had all finally subsided. Calmness replaced it all.

It didn't matter that I was a bloody mess. Just that she was safe.

"I think you should work from home," I mumbled into the crown of her head. The relief swam through my bloodstream, washing over me like a high dose relaxant.

She choked out a laugh. "I won't argue about it for a few days."

I pressed a kiss against her temple, holding her and sending a silent prayer to whoever was listening. Life without her wouldn't be worth living. She made *me* feel alive.

Nuzzling my head into her hair, I knew with her by my side, I'd endure it all.

"Is she hurt?" Savio's voice came from behind me. I knew he wouldn't be able to resist coming inside. After all, it was his daughter. DeAngelo and Renzo watched too, all of us exhausted, breathing heavy.

"She'll heal," I told him. She hurt; I knew she did. George's body lay not five feet from us, a reminder of the betrayal.

She turned to her father, hugging him tightly. The old man's hand shook as he placed it on her hair. She went to move to Lorenzo, but Savio pulled her back. "Jesus, Amore. Let me hold you a bit longer. I almost lost you."

"It all ended well," she murmured against his chest. "Don't think about it. Let me hug my brothers and then I want to talk to Adriano."

"No," I told her firmly. "Not here."

There was death and blood everywhere.

I took us out of there, through the front door, her eyes darting everywhere. There were dead bodies lying around, and I knew it bothered her. I wished I could have spared her all this, but there wasn't another way to get rid of George. The fucker refused to show his face until Amore was captured.

She chewed on her bottom lip, her hand squeezing mine with such force, I thought she'd break my bones. She didn't even realize she was doing it. My chest squeezed with worse pain than the beating and stabbing I endured over the last two days. My SUV was waiting with the driver, and I opened the door for Amore to slide into the back of it.

Sending a quick note to Regina, letting her know she was safe, I got rid of my phone and turned to face the open car. She sat with her back straight, her feet dangling off the side and a pensive look in her eyes. It was a lot to process.

She leaned over, her head placed against my chest, and her arms came around my waist. After what had happened, she just needed comfort. I tangled my fingers through her flame-colored hair, the scent of strawberries drifting in the air as the warm breeze swept through. The sound of the city in the distance was drowned out by our heartbeats beating as one.

"I thought you..." she whispered against me. She lifted her head to meet my eyes. "I'd never see you again. And Adriano..." Tears stained her pretty face, freckles on her nose more pronounced when she was upset. "I thought I'd lost him." Her voice broke, a hiccup escaping her lips.

I cupped her face with my hands. "Adriano would *never* betray you." Emotions flickered across her face. "He'd sooner betray me than you."

She sniffled. "No, he wouldn't."

"Let's agree to disagree," I teased, kissing her forehead because I had to feel her skin against me. It was the only thing keeping me sane.

"He helped us capture George. He came up with the idea to get George out of hiding," I murmured against her forehead, then pulled back. Her shimmering greens stared at me. "Adriano figured that the two of us had something going on. Even before you got back from Italy.

The night at the Orchid... it was so the word could spread. That way when Adriano wanted revenge, it seemed sincere."

Her throat bobbed, emotions flickering in her expression. "Don't cry, baby," I begged her. I could handle torture and crying from anyone but her. "I would have told you, but we had to make it convincing."

Her hands flew around me, her mouth showering kisses all over my face. "I love you," she whispered. "So damn much." Her lips slammed against mine. "And I love how criminally smart you are." Another kiss. "I love everything about you. How you love your brother, how you refuse to kill my father knowing how much he means to me. Your sneakiness to get what you want. Fucking everything."

My chest hurt in the best way possible at her admission. "Ah, Amore Bennetti Russo, my heiress. I love you too."

Her shimmering greens met my gaze. "Always?"

"Fucking always, baby."

Adriano approached from the house that at this point looked like a battlefield. My eyes flicked to him, then to Amore who still hadn't noticed him. I took her chin between my fingers and gently turned her head.

Her eyes softened, while her lower lip trembled with emotions. My little sex monster was emotional.

"Adriano." Her soft voice choked. We shared a glance. She had to work it out with him. The last few weeks were hard on both of them. They had been joined at the hip for so long, cutting the cord wasn't an option.

"Go ahead," I told her. "I'm going to talk to DeAngelo and your brothers. But after you talk to Adriano, you come back to me."

"Always."

In one swift move, she left me and ran to him.

Yes, a low grumble left my lips. And yes, I'd always be overly possessive of my wife. But she chose me, gave her heart and body only to me.

And I knew when Amore Bennetti gave something, she gave it her all.

CHAPTER 78

Amore

Adriano's arms were open as I threw myself into them.

My hands clutched his neck with a mixture of relief and *'I wanna kill you for giving me a heart attack'*.

I pulled away slightly and we watched each other in silence. So many words, so much had happened.

"I'm sorry," we both started at the same time and laughed.

"You first," he offered.

I was tempted to make him go first, but at the same time, I needed to get this guilt off my chest. Taking a deep breath, I met his eyes, almost as dark as my husband's.

"I'm sorry I didn't tell you about Santi," I said, keeping my voice mournful. "I...well, I always had a crush on him." He tilted his head, and I rolled my eyes. "Like a bad, crazy girl crush. But I thought I'd grow out of it... eventually." His lips tugged up slightly and hope fluttered in my eyes. "Then that night at The Orchid. I kissed him. Or he kissed me." Gosh, I was rambling. I pushed my hands through my hair, nervous tension flowing through me. "Anyhow, he called it a mistake. Said I was just a kid. I was pissed off and then went to Italy. I came to terms with the fact that he'd always see me as a kid."

He cocked his eyebrow. "Okay, so how did it get to sleeping with him?"

I winced. "Ummm, after your pà's funeral. You left to do something. One thing led to another... and here we are."

He remained silent, and for the first time, his eyes were unreadable of the thoughts that swarmed his mind.

"I don't want to lose you," I said. "I should have told you, but it wasn't that easy. How do you tell your best friend you are crushing on his big brother and that he rejected you?"

He shook his head. "Kind of like you just did."

"I love you," I told him, taking his right hand in mine. "I love how you stood by me in school, always listened and talked to me. How you took me for our ice cream runs. I just... well, I love Santi differently."

I hoped he understood what I was trying to say.

"I have to tell you, thinking about you and him..." He shoved his free hand through his thick, dark hair. "Yeah, I try not to think about you two together. You seem so innocent and he... well, I heard a few ladies comment that he likes it rough."

Heat singed my cheeks. There would be no elaboration on that comment. His dark eyes shone sardonically, and for a fraction of a second, I saw Santi in him. They were brothers after all.

"I love you, Amore." He pulled me into his arms. "Besties Forever. Remember?"

A strangled laugh escaped me and I wrapped him in a tight hug. "Forever."

Epilogue

AMORE - TEN MONTHS LATER

S unlight shone through the windows of the villa, the sounds of the waves crashing against the shoreline and guests chattering traveled on the mild breeze.

I stood in the bedroom, *our* bedroom, in Santi's villa in Italy. The scent of the orchids was everywhere, and it reminded me of Mom. The flower no longer represented guilt, but love and healing.

She had done for me what any parent would do for their child. It was what had led me here, to this amazing family. To my husband.

The ceremony was a moot point, but I wanted to make Grandma and Dad happy. So we were getting married. Again. By a priest. The only things I insisted on were the location, flowers, and my dress. Everything else, I let Grandma have free rein.

Much to Dad's dismay.

My eyes traveled over the vast, blue sea. This was where I felt most happy. Santi kept his promise, we came to visit any chance we had. We ended up moving to his Long Island home, and the master bedroom where I caught him touching himself in the shower became our bedroom. It became our home. I was closer to Dad and my brothers, and during the week Santi and I drove to work together.

Yes, I was back to work. I let my crazy, obsessive, loving husband take over the security of the Regalè Headquarters, and every other branch we owned.

Much to Grandmother's dismay.

But hey, we couldn't get everything we wanted in life, I told Grandma. Nobody had it all. Though some days, it really felt like I was damn close to having it all. I told him once I wanted it all, this felt like it.

The door swung open, and Adriano walked in with his suave stride and a wide grin.

"Are you nervous?" he greeted, smiling. His eyes traveled over me. "Want to run away? You'll be a runaway bride, and I'll be a runaway maid of honor."

I burst into laughter. That was another thing I insisted. For my best friend to be my man of honor. Not sure if it was a thing, but I made it a thing.

"I'm not nervous." I smiled back. "I can't wait for this circus to be over and everybody to be kicked out of here."

This place was Santi's and mine. And our family's.

He placed both hands over his ears. "Please don't tell me what you will be doing tonight."

I rolled my eyes at him.

"Yes, please don't talk about that." Dad walked in, followed by my brothers and uncle. Honestly, I was surprised Grandma wasn't swarming me. Instead, she ended up being the only one to give me space since we'd arrived.

Dad, on the other hand, was fretting over me like a mother hen. I didn't mind it, but I wasn't exactly crazy about it.

"Ah, my favorite sister," Lorenzo exclaimed, and I shook my head.

"Your only sister," I said.

He waved his hand in the air, like that little piece of information was irrelevant. "Are you ready to get this party started?" he asked.

With a firm nod, I lifted my long dress with both my hands and walked over to Dad. I met his gaze and caught his eyes, dark and glistening.

I leaned over and pressed a soft kiss on his cheek. "It's okay, Dad."

Inhaling deeply, he shook his head. "If only your mother could see you."

I lowered my eyes to my bouquet. Orchids of every color.

"She's watching, Dad," I told him softly.

Ten minutes later, my clammy hands gripped the bouquet with one hand and my father's arm with the other. I wasn't nervous. Yet, my heart fluttered fast and light as my eyes met the dark gaze of my husband.

He watched me walk toward him, darkness and sin in his eyes offering me pure bliss for the rest of my life. I couldn't wait.

As we walked down the aisle, my steps were just a bit too fast.

My heart too eager.

My love too endless.

Because Santino Russo was mine forever.

THE END

Acknowledgments

I want to thank my friends and family for their continued support. To my alpha and beta readers - you are all amazing.

To the best alpha reader a girl could wish for. **Susan C.H.** You always have my back. Thank you, **Beth H.** for having my back. And to my ladies, **Mia O. and Jill H.,** and a countless number of others - THANK YOU!

My books wouldn't be what they are without each one of you.

To my editor, Rachel at **MW Editing**. You are MY lady.

To my rockstar cover designer **Eve Graphics Designs, LLC**.

To the bloggers and reviewers who helped spread the word about this book. I appreciate you so much and hearing you love my work, makes it that much more enjoyable!

And last but not least, to all my readers! This wouldn't be possible without you. **THANK YOU!**

Thank you all! I couldn't have done any of this without you! It is a dream come true for me.

Eva Winners

Connect With Me

Want to be the first to know the latest news?
Visit www.evawinners.com and subscribe to my newsletter.
FOLLOW me on social media.
FB group: https://bit.ly/3gHEe0e
FB page: https://bit.ly/30DzP8Q
Insta: http://Instagram.com/evawinners
BookBub: https://www.bookbub.com/authors/eva-winners
Amazon: http://amazon.com/author/evawinners
Goodreads: http://goodreads.com/evawinners
Twitter: http://Twitter.com/@Evawinners
TikTok: https://vm.tiktok.com/ZMeETK7pq/

Made in United States
North Haven, CT
20 May 2022

19355056R00319